THE OATHBREAKER'S SHADOW

Amy McCulloch, a Canadian living in London, fits writing around work as an editorial director at one of the UK's leading children's publishers. She was bitten by the travel bug at an early age while accompanying her parents on buying trips for their oriental carpet business. It was this love of travel that inspired her to set a novel in a hot, desert location (moving to freezing Ottawa, where her first winter hit -40°C, might have had something to do with that too). She studied Medieval and Old English literature at the University of Toronto. *The Oathbreaker's Shadow* is her first book. *The Shadow's Curse*, available from Doubleday Canada, is its exhilarating sequel.

Connect with Amy on Twitter: @amymcculloch

THE
OATHBREAKER'S
SHADOW

AMY McCULLOCH

Doubleday
Canada

Doubleday Canada and colophon are registered trademarks of
Random House of Canada Limited

Library and Archives Canada Cataloguing in Publication

McCulloch, Amy, author
The oathbreaker's shadow / Amy McCulloch.

Illustration by Sophie McCulloc—Title page verso.
Issued in print and electronic formats.
ISBN 978-0-385-67826-1
eBook ISBN 978-0-385-67825-4

I. McCulloch, Sophie, illustrator II. Title.

PS8625.C86O27 2013   jC813'.6   C2012-906563-3
                                              C2012-907013-0

This book is a work of fiction. Names, characters, places and incidents are products
of the author's imagination or are used fictitiously. Any resemblance to actual events
or locales or persons, living or dead, is entirely coincidental.

Printed and bound in the USA

Published in Canada by Doubleday Canada,
a division of Random House of Canada Limited,
a Penguin Random House company

www.randomhouse.ca

10 9 8 7 6 5 4 3 2 1

This book is dedicated to my family.
No matter where we are, we are always together.

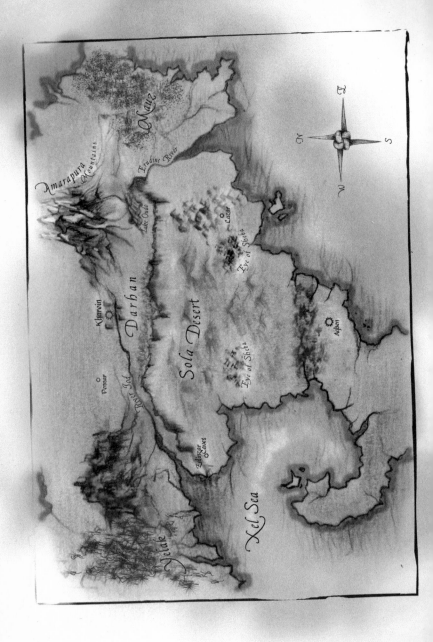

PART ONE

1

Raim sat in the crook of an old, cracked tree, one leg dangling in the breeze, his head leaning back against the trunk. Long, needle-like leaves shaded him from the oppressive heat and hid him from the view of his grandfather, in case he was looking to assign Raim yet another chore. He just wanted a moment to himself. From his vantage point he could see his clan's settlement of yurts, the dome-like tents that made up his home, and watched as smoke lifted lazily out of the circular holes in the centre of the roofs.

A rustling at the base of the tree distracted him. He looked down and spied two of the younger clan boys, Lousha and Nem, huddled around a small parcel wrapped in white paper.

'Do you swear you'll guard this for me?' Nem whispered to Lousha, while keeping one chubby brown hand on the goods.

'Yes!' said Lousha.

'Cross your heart?'

'Yup.'

'Suffer like a traitor in Lazar?'

The other boy shuddered, but nodded.

'Will you make a knot for it?'

'A knot?' There was a moment's hesitation as Lousha chewed on his lower lip. 'Fine, let's do it.'

They scrabbled around for something to tie it with. Lousha ripped a loose thread from his tunic while Nem plucked a long, dark hair from his head. Then, with solemn determination etched on their faces, they folded one thread on top of the other and held them in a loose loop.

'Do you promise me you'll guard this until I return, and will you seal your vow with this knot?' said Nem.

'I promise, and I seal it with this knot,' said Lousha, and then they both pulled until the two threads became one. Nem nodded before jumping up and disappearing into the village of yurts beyond.

A corner of the paper lifted in the breeze, and a hint of sticky sweet honey aroma wafted into the air. Honey cake. A Darhanian delicacy, it was baked only for special occasions, like this afternoon's ceremonies. The scent tantalized Raim's nostrils, as if he could taste the pastry already, sense the flakes crumbling and melting in the heat of his mouth – and he knew the boy below was feeling the same temptation. Lousha waited until he was sure his friend had gone. Then he inched forward for a closer sniff, putting his nose right down next to the ground and taking a deep breath. One finger, and then another hesitantly stretched in the pastry's direction.

Don't do it, thought Raim. Almost as if he had spoken the words aloud, something seemed to hold the boy back. He stared down at the tatty piece of knotted hair and thread in his hand. He bit his lip. Raim bit his lip too, and dropped to a lower branch, sending showers of needles to the ground.

Lousha snatched the parcel and held it protectively to his chest and craned his neck to look around, brow furrowed in suspicion. *Look up*, Raim silently pleaded. If Lousha knew he had an observer he wouldn't be so quick to break his promise. But with the cake now in his grasp, so tantalizingly close to his mouth . . . the boy flicked the thread as far as he could. Then he ripped the paper off as fast as his little fingers could manage and stuffed the cake into his mouth.

Raim sighed and began counting inside his head: *One, two . . .*

The discarded knot began to fizzle. A flame sparked to life, then quickly dissolved into a puff of black smoke.

. . . three.

Before the first of the honey cake crumbs had dissolved on his tongue, the smoke blew back over Lousha's hand and seared a bright red mark into his palm.

The boy screamed in pain and clamped his hand into a fist. Then he screamed in fear as the smoke refused to leave him alone. He tried to beat it away with his hands but it wouldn't budge. He got up and started running in circles from it, but the smoke followed him like a swarm of angry bees.

The noise attracted the attention of the nearest yurts' residents. A small crowd gathered around, laughing at the sight. Unable to help himself, Raim started laughing too. The boys were still at an age when a scar from a broken promise meant nothing except for an hour's nuisance.

Lousha spotted his grandmother in the crowd and tried to run to her, wishing to hide from the shadow by ducking behind the long folds of the woman's dress. But she backed away from him, unable to let him near, her nose wrinkled in disgust. She let her voice be heard, though, as she herded the boy back to their yurt with her angry shouts.

'What's going on here?' A familiar voice carried over the laughter of the crowd. It was Khareh, Raim's best friend – and the heir to the Khanate.

'Your pardon, Prince Khareh.' The boy's grandmother bowed low. 'My grandson here has broken a vow and must be punished.'

An amused smile played on Khareh's face. 'Is that so? Come here, little boy.' Lousha took a few sheepish steps forward. 'Who did you make this vow to?'

'To Nem.'

'And where is Nem?'

The boy shrugged.

'Nem?' said Khareh, louder. 'Are you here, Nem?'

The crowd parted, and the other little boy appeared. Tears streaked down his face. 'Lousha ate my cake! He promised he wouldn't!'

'Lousha, are you sorry for what you have done?'

Lousha nodded.

'And Nem, can you forgive him?'

'No!'

At that, the shadow swirled more violently around Lousha and he let out a cry of distress. The smile still didn't leave Khareh's face. 'I suppose you really wanted that cake, hmm?'

Nem nodded.

'But I'm afraid you can't let your friend endure this torture any longer. A cake is just a cake, and someday your vows will be worth more than that.'

Nem scowled a little, but as Khareh's smile slipped from his face, even the little boy understood the danger. He looked over at Lousha. 'I forgive you.'

At that, Lousha's shadow swirled into the air, and his scar faded to nothing. Lousha's grandmother ran up to Khareh, dragging Lousha with her, and fell to her knees. 'Thank you, Prince. You are most magnanimous.'

Raim could barely suppress a laugh. Khareh could hardly lecture on forgiveness. Just a few years ago, that little boy would've been Raim. He and Khareh used to constantly push each other to see who could endure the most scar torture. Khareh would force Raim to promise to

7

score a goal during a game of gutball and they would tie the knotted piece of string around his neck. If the other team saw the knot, they would hound him, doing whatever they could to prevent him from scoring. If he failed, if he 'broke' his promise, then the curse would descend upon him. He would scream in pain as the scar appeared and a dark shadow would haunt him, just as had happened to Lousha. For an hour or so he would be a repulsive figure, unable to make contact with anyone. Then, once the curse had subsided enough for his grandfather, Loni, to take him home, he would be scolded, and punished hard – first for accepting such a useless promise, and then again for breaking it. Khareh would also be punished for forcing a promise upon him and making him endure the torture that followed – but Khareh would never forgive. But then the elders would stop scolding and smile a little to themselves, for they knew it was important for young children to test the consequences of their actions, so that they knew what to do when they were ready to make real promises.

It wouldn't be until they reached the Honour Age – sixteen – that a true promise could be made. And a true promise had serious consequences. Breaking a knotted promise meant excommunication to the desert in Lazar, with the community of exiled oathbreakers known as the Chauk.

There was no escaping this fate. If it was just a scar you could hide it, as Raim had watched Lousha do, clenching his palm tight. But it was the shadow that you could not escape. It was the shadow that others saw, judged and sentenced the oathbreaker to exile. It was the shadow that followed you all the way to Lazar and made sure you stayed there. Just the thought of it made Raim shudder.

The tree shook violently, sending a shower of sharp needles onto Raim's head, and he grabbed hold of the trunk to stop himself from falling. He spun round to see a familiar set of mischievous dark eyes clamber up on the branch beside him. Khareh was wearing an ornate black tunic with a high collar, richly embroidered with gold silk dragons in mid-dance. It was probably worth more than most villagers' entire possessions, but Khareh didn't care if he ripped it climbing up trees. Khareh was the Prince of Darhan. He was allowed not only to own expensive things, but to ruin them as well. 'I've been searching every tree in the camp to find you,' he said.

'It's called a hiding place for a reason. Plus, there's a good view from up here. Especially of that little show – what was that about?'

Khareh shrugged. 'Can't have a shadow hanging about today, can we? It would be bad luck. Come on, I've got something to show you. You've got a few more hours before your brother's sacrifice, right?'

'One hour,' said Raim, unable to hide the massive grin on his face as Khareh referred to his brother's wedding as a sacrifice. He tried to stay serious. 'And I can't be late. My grandfather will kill me.'

'Oh, old Loni won't mind. That's plenty of time,' said Khareh, with the small half-smile and glint in his eyes that meant he had no concern for Raim's schedule.

There was no way Raim wouldn't go with Khareh, however, and Khareh knew it.

With a shrug, Khareh leaped off the branch and Raim followed awkwardly, landing with a thump on the dusty ground. Even he wasn't dressed for tree climbing today.

They were high up in the Northlands, in a tiny village where the plains of Darhan met the Amarapura mountain range. The only time any of the tribes came to the village was if one of their members was marrying into the Baril, the scholars of Darhan. To Raim and Khareh, being Baril was to live a life of interminable boredom. It was the only class that did not prepare in any way for warfare, despite danger lurking at almost all of Darhan's borders – and sometimes within.

As the brother of the Baril entrant, Raim was not only forced to sit through the entire hours-long ceremony, but also to do so wearing the most elaborate (and most uncomfortable) formal clothes he owned. His indigo tunic was as stiff as unboiled rice and reached down to the top of his ankles. It closed across his body, fastening with three clasps at the neck – too close to his face in the sweltering heat – three on his shoulder and three more under his right armpit. A wide belt, dyed in the deep green of the Moloti tribe, wrapped around his waist. He wished he could wear his normal clothes, loose-fitting trousers and a waist-length tunic made from wool instead of the heavy, poor-quality silk. Unlike Khareh, though, Raim had to take care of his clothing. Any caked-in mud meant an hour of scrubbing for Raim later; every tear meant pricking his fingers with his awkward, fumbling sewing. Not his idea of a fun evening in the yurt.

Worst of all were the shoes. Instead of his normal well-worn, fur-lined, thick-soled boots, he was in delicate slippers with pointed toes that curled backward. On the tip of the curl was a ball that jingled when he walked. By the time they had clambered over a rocky ridge to reach the edge of the glade, the annoying golden bells were crammed deep into his tunic pocket.

They broke into a run, feeling the short mountain grass crunch under their heels. They passed by a herd of goats, their bleating urging them on. Then Khareh stopped. 'Wait here,' he said, as he ran on a bit further. He was standing over what looked like a stick beaten into the ground.

'Ready?' Khareh yelled. Then he appeared to pull something with all his might. 'Get down, now!'

Raim fell to the ground and put his hands over his turban, just in time to feel the wind slice overhead. He flipped round and sat up, watching the object as it veered towards the goats, scattering them. It made a sharp U-turn in the air and came straight back at Raim.

'Vows alive!' He scrambled to his feet and rushed towards Khareh. By the time he reached his friend, the object had lost steam and skipped onto the ground, snipping the blades of grass. It was large and round, with tiny spikes that were sawed down almost to the edge.

'What in Sola was that?' Raim spluttered, catching his breath.

'Oh, I stole the disc from one of the workshops back in Kharein. Don't worry; they were going to throw it away anyway. But this' – Khareh gestured to the pole in the ground, his eyes sparkling – 'is my newest invention. Marvel, Raimanan, marvel!'

Khareh was the only person who called Raim by his full name, and only when he was feeling particularly proud of himself. Raim hated it, but was so used to hearing it from Khareh's mouth that he barely cringed. He only suffered Khareh's use of the name because, even though he was his best friend, he also had the power – as Crown Prince – to order Raim about as he pleased. Thankfully he didn't abuse it too often.

Khareh was Crown Prince despite not being the son of the current leader, Batar-Khan. But when the Seer-Queen had not produced an heir after the first five years of marriage, a prince had to be chosen. The council of Darhanian warlords had convened and chosen Khareh, the son of the Khan's brother, as the official heir. So now, whatever Khareh wanted to do, he did, no matter what the consequences. Raim admired Khareh's independence, but didn't covet it. Khareh was always experimenting, innovating, testing the boundaries of what he could get away with and questioning the rules if he was told they couldn't be broken. He had big dreams about how to improve Darhan, to make it a real force to be reckoned with.

Raim recognized the pole – it was identical to the ones used to build the frame of a yurt. He wondered whose yurt was tilted after Khareh had sawed off this piece. When Khareh was inventing, nothing could stop him. Once he had even cut up the Seer-Queen's prized headscarf in order to get material of the perfect tensile strength for his goat parachute – 'in case bandits attack and we have to drop the goats off a mountain,' he'd said. That was the other thing about Khareh's inventions. They rarely made any sense to Raim.

Khareh picked the disc up off the ground and placed it delicately on top of his contraption. In his hand he held a long, thin metal rod, which had little grooves on it all down the side.

'Not quite enough nicks,' Khareh said. 'Do you have your knife on you?'

'Here you go.' Raim lifted the hem of his trouser leg and pulled out a small dagger from the strap around his calf. The blade was pitch-black, matte, and made from ochir, a translucent metal that seared black during the forging process. Owning one marked him as an apprentice of the Yun, Darhan's elite guard, the sworn protectors of the land and all of its inhabitants. When he received his acceptance, he would be given his own sword, one made especially for the Yun. They had perfected a method of preserving ochir's translucent quality and it resulted in a sword that was harder and clearer than diamonds. It was near indestructible. When wielded properly, it dazzled the eyes of opponents, confusing them with tricks of the light. Battles between the Yun of Darhan and their enemies were magnificent to behold, the near-invisible blades striking against ordinary metal.

But before he could even hope to be accepted, he had to pass one final test: a duel against a fellow Yun apprentice. He was to face Lars, the second son of one of the eight noble Darhan warlords – and one of the most fearsome young warriors in Darhan.

Khareh took the blade and scratched more notches into his metal stick. When finished, he threaded the stick through the eye cut into the hollowed-out wood and pulled back with all his strength. For a second, the disc jumped and hovered above the invention as if surprised to be mobile. Then it spun off hastily over the field. This time, it didn't come back.

Khareh looked delighted. 'Don't have to be a sage to make things fly!' He flipped the blade back to Raim.

'No, you'd have to exist first. Sages are legend, make-believe.'

'Gods, your ignorance is really annoying sometimes. Don't the Yun teach their students anything? Anyone who says sages don't exist is a fool. I've read about them. There were magicians in the past who could command whole armies with their power, who could self-heal and levitate things, like swords – they could even make themselves fly!'

'Sounds to me like you're the fool, for believing in that goat's dung.'

'It's not goat's dung. Anyway, I wouldn't expect you to know anything about it. I hear the real sages are south. In Aqben.'

'Let them rot there, then. Aqben houses only devils,' Raim said, repeating the typical adage used whenever the south was mentioned.

Khareh raised an eyebrow, and shrugged. 'So, you're not worried about the whole first-chance-to-fight-to-be-Yun thing, are you?' he asked, changing the subject.

Raim bit his lip. 'If it was an ordinary fight, I wouldn't be. But this is *it*. I heard one of the other villagers saying they'd crossed with Lars's tribe not a month ago. His father was saying he's really bulked up this year, as big as an ox. And that he's going to have a Yun for a son, soon.'

Khareh grimaced. 'What would the warlord know about his son anyway? He's probably not seen him since we last did. Lars has been off training with his mentor.'

It was Raim's turn to grimace this time. 'While I've been stuck here herding goats.' Then he shrugged. 'But it's not like I could leave Dharma and my grandfather alone to go off to train, especially with Tarik wrapped up with his studies. And I'm lucky that my mentor has been here, so I have had plenty of practice.'

'True. Besides, that's not the real issue, is it? Isn't this

Lars's third and final try? It's not you who should be worried, it's him. With you as his opponent, it looks like we might be watching heads roll this tournament after all!'

'No, it's his second try. It's Jendo's final one though.' Raim frowned. Every Yun apprentice knew that if you didn't pass the third try, your life was forfeit. It was why he couldn't joke about it as Khareh did. It could be his reality in another two years, should he fail all three bouts.

Khareh seemed to read his mind and shrugged. 'You're the best fighter the Yun has trained in generations and you know it. Well—' He broke into a maniacal grin. 'Except they never had me, of course.'

'Is that a challenge?' Raim's eyes darted around and spied a metal pole Khareh had discarded while making his invention. He grabbed it and spun it around in his hands. Khareh was partially right. As a prince, Khareh couldn't join the Yun, since he needed to study and be trained in his royal duties. But he had studied sword fighting for as long as Raim, and he was the only sparring partner – other than Raim's own Yun mentor, Mhara – who always gave him a good run. And Mhara was Batar-Khan's official Protector, and chief of all the Yun.

Lars was older. No one really expected a Yun apprentice to win their first attempt – after all, Lars had a whole year of growth and experience on Raim. But still, he felt confident. His training had settled into his muscles like knots tying everything into its rightful place, joining all the movements together. If he couldn't trust his body's promise to execute the moves his mind asked it to, then what could he trust?

There was a dangerous twinkle in Khareh's eye, and he snatched up another pole, ready to scuffle. Khareh taunted Raim about his weaker left side. For the most part, Khareh was the aggressor, pushing Raim backward with quick, strong strokes. Raim remained on the defensive, absorbing his opponent's blows. He tried to focus on anticipating Khareh's next move, on his footwork or his sword strokes, but still he couldn't help imagining what it would be like to fight with a real Yun blade. *Soon I will be a great warrior, leading the Yun as the Khan's Protector. I'll lead the army that will finally unite all the tribes of Darhan and then maybe I'll . . .*

He blinked. Khareh swung at his pole with all his might and it popped out of Raim's hand and fell to the ground with a thud. For a second Raim stood in shock, his hands splayed palm out in front of him and his legs bent like a frog. Mhara called this the 'moving mountain' position. Winning now was as impossible as shifting a mountain with your bare hands.

The low, clear sound of a bone horn sounded out over the field and snapped Raim back to life.

'Gods, the wedding!'

Khareh spun the pole in his hand and speared it into the earth. 'Saved by the horn,' he said with a grin. He turned serious when he saw the devastation on Raim's face. 'Just keep your focus. You will win. You have to.'

2

The priest's voice was slow and monotonous as he led Tarik, Raim's brother, and his young soon-to-be wife, Solongal, through a series of complicated vows and sermons. Raim had never seen his brother's betrothed before. They were an odd pairing. His brother was tall and as thin as a stick of bamboo. Khareh used to joke that Tarik had too many bones as so many poked out of his skin at odd angles – especially his Adam's apple, which jutted out of his throat like a second chin. By contrast Solongal was several inches shorter, with a squashed round face and hooded eyes so small they seemed like little black peas in a sea of rice pudding. They both held long pieces of string in their hands, and at the end of each vow the priest signalled for them to tie a knot in the string to form an elaborate pattern. Slowly they were sealing their fate as Baril.

Tarik was tripping over his words, the letters in his mouth tumbling out as cumbersome as an elephant wading through mud. He wasn't handling himself well, but anyone would be nervous in the presence of Qatir-bar, the first of all the Baril priests. When Qatir-bar had appeared, Raim had been awed. The man was shaped like a spear, with a gaze that was just as sharp. Around his neck, lying on top of his pristine white robes, was an intricate necklace of knots that represented his Baril vows. But it was his forehead that drew the most attention. It was almost completely flat. Tarik had told him in the past that the Baril spent so much time deep in prayer with their heads on the ground that their foreheads flattened, but Raim hadn't believed him. He wondered how long it would take for Tarik's head to get like that. Tarik was so pious, he imagined it wouldn't be too long.

Raim sat cross-legged on the ground a few rows of people back from where the priest and the couple were standing. Baril marriages were the exception in Darhan. For a man and a woman to promise to remain together and raise a family until death was a foreign concept to most tribespeople. It was a luxury they could not afford. Life on the steppes was hard at the best of times and it was necessary for each person – man or woman – to continue to work for their clans in order for life to continue. When she came of age, a woman would promise herself to her chosen partner and his tribe, and her children would become the tribe's children, raised by the elders. After the birth, the parents would return to their clan roles – perhaps as soldiers in the army or as weavers or tenders to the animals. When they grew too old to perform their role, they would return to their old tribe as elders to raise the tribe's children, and so it would continue. On the steppes, idleness wasn't a sin; it simply wasn't an option.

Loni was one of the Moloti tribe elders, and he had taken in first Tarik, then Raim and then Raim's sister, Dharma, as his grandchildren. Tarik and Dharma were Raim's siblings by adoption, not blood. Raim knew almost nothing about his true parents, not even their clan profession. It didn't matter; he had his own path to follow. His father could be the lowliest dung collector in Darhan and Raim would still aspire to be Chief Yun.

Beside him, his grandfather was squinting forward to capture every moment of the ceremony. In fact, most of the other people around Raim were leaning forward, but they were falling asleep, not craning their necks in interest. Raim yearned to join the ranks of the dozing. He felt his eyelids droop, heavy with sweat and boredom. But Loni's hand, hard and bulbous, pressed down on his, snapping him back to attention. Raim scolded himself. He should try to stay awake. It was his brother's wedding after all.

To keep alert, he ran over his moves for the upcoming Yun trial. He put his recent tussle with Khareh out of his head. *It's only nerves*, he told himself. He had allowed himself to get distracted. He wouldn't let it happen again. Step left, parry, retreat. Forward, strike to the shoulder, swoop down to the knee, protect his chest with the shield. Knock the enemy's weapon out of his hand, finish with a fatal blow to the neck. Well, without the last move in the actual duel.

An involuntary shiver ran down his neck. Was Lars thinking the same thing? He tried to think back to what he could remember of Lars's first attempt. Raim had watched from the very front – all the Yun apprentices who had yet to reach their Honour Age stood side by side to form the ring in which the older apprentices fought, to keep the crowds back. Lars had done well – the duel had lasted a long time, with neither side backing down easily. Eventually, though, Lars had tired. That had been his mistake. If it had been Raim in his position, he would have spent all of the next year training to increase his stamina. To avoid the same problem, Raim would have to try to end the duel quickly, before *he* became the one that ran out of fuel.

The priest raised his hands and Raim scrambled to his feet with the rest of the crowd. As he stretched to shake the stiffness from his back and neck, Raim caught sight of Khareh surreptitiously making his way over to where the royal family was seated. Under a carefully erected shelter lay Batar-Khan, the Seer-Queen, the Khan's advisers and their entourage. The Seer-Queen was barely feigning interest as she was attended by servants clad in pristine white linen, trying to create a breeze in the still, stifling air by waving fans of woven reeds. She was supposed to be one of the most powerful women in the world, with the power to 'see' into the future. The Baril were charged with examining dozens of women to find the one who could pass the test and become the Khan's principal wife. Somehow, a remarkable number of ugly daughters of important warlords turned out to be 'seers'. When it was Khareh's turn he would have to marry whomever the Baril chose – and that was an obligation Raim didn't envy one bit. Heat pricked the back of his neck as he thought of the girl he would be seeing in only a few short days. No, he knew who he would choose if he could. Suddenly, he really envied the breeze Khareh was enjoying.

With the sun at its peak, the royal tent was the only source of shade on the flat ledge about halfway up Mount Dahl. The entire village had climbed the long, circuitous path carved into the mountain in the early morning, when the sun was low and hidden by the mist. But now the sun beat down on the weary audience with its powerful rays. Raim slipped his finger under the edge of his turban, trying to release some of the sweat that glued the cloth to his forehead. The villagers steamed around him, forced to sit on the hard ground outside and endure the entire ceremony with the sunshine reflecting off the smooth, flat rock.

Finally, the moment of the ceremony Raim had been waiting for arrived. The moment when the apprentice Tarik-en-bar was to become Tarik-bar: a Baril priest. Raim stood up on his tiptoes to see over the crowd. Tarik's length of promise string was tied in a complicated web of knots, each of which was an oath to the Baril to obey their laws.

Qatir-bar turned to Tarik. 'Tarik-en-bar, son of the Moloti tribe, this string is your word. And with this string do you vow to join your life with Solongal-en-barja, daughter of the Temu tribe, until death takes you?'

'I vow this,' said Tarik, all traces of nerves vanished and replaced with a calm solemnity. In one swift movement, he knotted one end of his string to Solongal's.

'Let this knot be your vow to Solongal-en-barja, and may you never witness the flames of your betrayal.'

The priest then turned to Solongal, who repeated the vows back to Tarik. She in turn knotted her string to Tarik's and pulled the knot tight. They were promised together, now and for always.

Qatir pulled a blade out of his robes and sliced through the piece of string joining the two circles of knots together. He placed one loop around Tarik's neck and pronounced him Tarik-bar.

Raim bristled and his shoulder blades tightened under his skin. The knotted necklace gave his brother an instant authority, making him seem stronger and wiser. Raim, despite being three years younger than Tarik, had always been the leader of their family. Tall and muscular, he towered over his eighteen-year-old scrawny sibling. While Raim spent nearly every hour training to join the Yun, Tarik learned to read and write, preparing for a life of quiet domesticity and study. But now it was different. Tarik-bar had purpose. Tarik-bar had a knot.

Instinctively, Raim clasped a hand to his left wrist.

Underneath the heavy cloth of his tunic, so small he couldn't feel it – although he knew it was there – was a tiny indigo bracelet he had worn on his wrist since before he could remember.

The bracelet had the tiniest knot in it, almost imperceptible unless you ran your fingers over the string and noticed the tiny bump along the way. It had grown with him as his muscles expanded from Yun training; the bracelet was a part of him. Sometimes he paid it as little mind as a birthmark. Other times – like now – it felt as heavy as an iron clamp. Raim swallowed hard and repeated his mantra back to himself: he hadn't reached his Honour Age yet, so whatever promise the knot held – if it did hold a promise – it couldn't mean anything. He let the moment of fear pass from his mind, then pushed his left sleeve up until the bracelet was visible. Just an insignificant thing. A tiny bit of string. It meant nothing.

He looked up. Tarik-bar and Solongal-barja turned their backs to the crowd and walked towards the gaping black hole that led deep into the mountain, following the Baril priest. Sound seemed to follow them into the cave, until all that was left outside was an unearthly silence. No one breathed. No one moved.

The silence was shattered by the clatter of a horse's hooves. A Darhan soldier thundered round the corner – a scout from the outlying borders. Normally scouts wore camouflaged clothing, but this one had changed into the sky-blue turban of a messenger. Raim's thoughts immediately turned to war, and he wondered who had invaded Darhan this time. What else could be important enough to interrupt the Khan during a solemn Baril wedding?

Men and women, caught in the soldier's path, yelled in protest as they were forced to leap out of the way of the charging stallion, heading straight for the royal tent.

Raim could see that Batar-Khan was fuming with anger that the ancient ceremony had been interrupted. The Khan snapped his fingers at his most senior adviser, Altan, who immediately stepped forward and barked at the man, 'What is the meaning of this?'

The soldier leaped off his horse and bowed low at the feet of the adviser, without lifting his eyes from the ground. 'Please, Altan-leder, I must speak with the Batar-Khan in private.'

The Great Khan sensed the urgency in the man's voice – the entire congregation could. He hesitated for a moment, then with a regal wave of his wrist, he ushered the man towards him as the servants dropped a curtain over the tent's entrance to separate the Khan from the congregation.

Raim watched Khareh closely throughout the commotion. Khareh signed a message to Raim in the language he had invented for them after learning in one of his lessons that the savage desert nomads, the Alashan, used sign language to communicate while hunting, so as not to spook their prey.

'If they can do it, you bet that we can,' Khareh had said as he tried to invent enough signs to keep their conversations interesting. There had to be signs for at least the most basic of words and phrases: *yes, no, you're on your own now.* 'And just think! That way we can talk to each other without any of these stone-heads knowing.' Khareh was always trying to think about ways to get around his bodyguards.

Back on the mountain ledge, Khareh repeated the message, and Raim decoded: 'Meet me in the glade in ten minutes.' He signed back that he understood and Khareh disappeared behind the curtain with his uncle.

Suddenly, Raim remembered his brother and swung back round to look at the mountain. But the entrance to the cave was empty; his brother now a sworn entrant into the Baril.

Raim swallowed down a lump in his throat, which threatened to escape as a tear. He felt like applauding Tarik's achievement. He felt like yelling a goodbye into the mouth of the cave. He felt like running after his brother and making him promise to visit. But he did none of those things, and simply lowered his head to the ground, allowing himself to be swept along with the rest of the tribe who were beginning to descend from the mountain ledge.

His brother had a knotted purpose now, a clan. And soon, Raim would have a purpose of his own. He was going to join the Yun, and leave his old life behind for ever.

Raim would never see his brother again.

3

Rumour and speculation buzzed in the air like a swarm of behrflies swept up from the desert. Clumps of nomads chatted noisily with one another as they began the slow descent down the mountain and all the while they wove their excitement into a tale they could pass on to the next village they visited. For a people who moved constantly, news was a valuable trading good, and stories were bartered as much as sheepskin. This story would be a juicy one to tell to anyone they met.

Raim didn't even make it halfway down towards the glade before Khareh caught up with him, the prince's face flushed with excitement. In fact, Raim couldn't remember seeing his friend so happy since he had been named a prince in the first place.

'You won't believe this,' he said, shifting from foot to foot, unable to stand still. 'They've found a *real* sage.'

'What?' Raim spluttered, pulling Khareh off to the

side so that the passing tribespeople wouldn't hear.

'You heard me. A real live sage! Apparently they found him on the outskirts of the Sola desert near Mauz and they're so scared of him, they've brought him here, to the village, to be dealt with straight away! You coming?'

Khareh didn't wait for an answer, but there was no way Raim was going to miss out on seeing a sage in action. He felt his heart catch in his throat at the thought, but he tried not to let himself get too excited. At least twice a year some crazy man or woman – most often clanless – would come forward claiming to be a sage. And each time, it was a disappointment. But Raim had almost never seen Khareh so excited. And Khareh was normally the most scathing and sceptical of all, despite his belief that real sages did exist.

As they darted in amongst the rough, dusty streets of the village, tribespeople and villagers alike stopped in their tracks to wonder just where the prince could be running off to this time.

They arrived at the royal caravan. It was stationed outside the village – there was nowhere for it to fit within the restrictive confines of the tiny settlement. Besides, even though the caravan was portable, it was infinitely more comfortable than any of the ramshackle village houses. Sometimes Raim forgot just how opulent it must appear to those unused to seeing it. It was built up off the ground on a platform of wooden planks. It had eight wheels so it could be transported easily and pulled from village to village by four oxen. The exterior was wrapped in the pelts of snow leopards and tied together by ropes that had been dipped in gold. But the most dazzling adornments were the seven rugs that represented the pledges of fealty from seven warlords of Darhan to Batar-Khan. Mhara reminded him constantly that this was the highest number of oaths any single Khan had managed to unite under his reign.

Highly skilled clans of weavers created the carpets – and the competition for a commission from the Khan was fierce. Weavers held a prestigious position in Darhan society and men and women with nimble fingers and an eye for colour would be quick to try and join one of the most highly regarded clans. Their skills were always in demand, which made an accomplished weaver extremely valuable. When a promise knot was formed, the most respected way of honouring that promise was to weave the story of how that vow came to be into the carpet.

The carpets then represented the source of the Khan's power: absolute loyalty.

Raim crept into the royal yurt behind Khareh. They had been friends for so long that no one took any notice of the fact that he was there. They zigzagged round members of the royal entourage lounging on pillows on the ground until they reached where Altan was standing.

Raim felt a sudden rush of cold, like an icy winter draught blowing under the felt of an unsealed yurt. It wrapped around him and made him shiver, a deep-seated shake that started in his neck and travelled all the way down his spine. But it was the height of summer, and he wasn't shivering from cold; he was shuddering in disgust.

Amidst the rich golden ornaments, the lush silks and the sweet-smelling incense, Raim's stomach was turning, boiling over with a nausea that caused sweat to drip down his spine and the bile in his stomach to rise.

He wasn't alone. All around him, people were looking pale and physically shying away from the far corner of the room. Not Khareh, though. If he was feeling any discomfort he wasn't going to be the one to show it. Raim tried to emulate his friend's iron-hard will, and attempted to compose his features.

There could only be one source: a shadow. And that shadow belonged to a frail, cowering old man in a tatty tunic that must have been white at some point, although now it was stained red with dust. He had a very long beard that was tied in a bizarre bow under his chin. The thick beard could not totally conceal the dark slash of a scar running from underneath his nose, across his lips to his jawline. It wasn't bright red, like the scar from a fresh betrayal, but paler, almost flesh tone. And behind him was the swirl of a grey shadow – not black and threatening as shadows normally were, but thick, bulbous and swirling grey as a storm cloud. Out of the corner of his eye, Raim saw Mhara take a protective stance, her hand moving to her Yun sword. Raim was confused. Were this man and his shadow dangerous? He wasn't behaving like any oathbreaker he had seen before.

Altan stepped forward from his position behind the Khan's seat and addressed the trembling man. 'Prisoner of Darhan. You requested an audience with the Khan and by some miracle you have been granted it. If it results that you have wasted His Royal Elegance's time, you will suffer punishment beyond the torments of your most horrific nightmare.'

The man didn't respond, at least not out loud. He continued to stare at the ground, not willing to make eye contact with anyone in the room, but he noticeably straightened a little, rolled back his shoulders and took a deep breath.

The cloud-shadow was in front of the man now, hovering over one of the Khan's intricately woven prayer rugs. Raim couldn't understand it. If it had been any normal shadow, they all would have been instantly repulsed. Instead, it had managed to approach the crowd while their attention was focused on Altan.

Khareh let out a sharp cry of astonishment and the eyes of the entire room snapped back to the old man. A collective gasp escaped the audience as the corners of the prayer rug in front of him began to lift in unison, each muddy yellow fibre along the fringe quivering, though there was no breeze inside the yurt. Raim and Khareh jostled for position but Khareh pushed in front. Raim craned his neck over his friend's shoulder, trying to get a better look. The old man was staring intently at the rug and stretched his hands out over it, the palms facing downwards. His beard trembled as he chanted an incantation.

The rest of the richly woven carpet rose up slowly until it tickled the underside of the man's nose. Then his eyes opened, and the rug flew over the heads of the guests. It did a circle, a loop and a turn in front of the Khan before landing gracefully in front of the man. With a flick of his hand, the rug rolled up into a tight cylinder. He picked it up and brought it over to the feet of Batar-Khan. He bowed low, but after a moment he lifted his hooded eyes to meet the Khan's. Raim was shocked by his brazenness.

What followed was a wall of silence. Sages were people of legend – at least, that was what Raim had been taught and he'd never had reason to doubt it. The old stories, passed down by the elders, told of a time when the strongest Khans were the ones with a sage at their right hand, performing magic that gave them the edge on the battlefield. But that was long before even the oldest elder had been born, and for as long as any memory could reach every trace of sage magic had disappeared, lost for ever – or so it had seemed. But now, here was a real sage, one who could make carpets fly. Now that caught Raim's attention, and Khareh's too, by the hungry look on his face.

But Batar-Khan didn't look impressed. No; from Raim's point of view he looked almost nervous, the tendons popping out of the back of his hands as he gripped the edge of his throne.

'Arrest him.' The Khan waved his guards over and they

grabbed the man brusquely under the arms. 'This man has a scar and he is haunted. He is clearly an oathbreaker. He was found heading away from Lazar, in clear violation of his exile.' He spat after the name, before settling his gaze back on the cowering man. 'His sentence now is death.'

'No . . . please, no!' The old sage struggled, but despite his magic, he was weak and frail and had no strength to rival that of the Khan's guards.

'Stop! What are you doing?' Khareh sprung forward and grabbed one of the guards. He turned to Batar-Khan, still gripping a fist full of the guard's tunic. 'Uncle, don't you understand what a gift this is? We could learn something from this sage.'

'Khareh, step away.'

'I will not. By arresting this man you are making a mistake.'

'Are you daring to question my judgement?' Batar-Khan stood up and pulled himself to his full height, well over six feet. His enormous bulk only added to the impression of power he made as he strode over to where Khareh stood; compared to the slender Khareh he seemed a giant. 'You may be the prince but be careful with your words.'

'I think you are a fool if you do this.'

Batar-Khan responded by hitting Khareh hard over the face. 'You would disrespect me so?' he roared. 'I told you to take him away!' he said to the guards.

Then he turned on the rest of the crowd. 'Everything

that has passed in this room today will remain secret. You will *all* knot for this. Now.'

They could not refuse the Khan. Raim watched as every person in the room, every guard and adviser, and even Khareh, removed long pieces of thread from their belts and chanted in unison after Batar-Khan: 'Our eyes today have seen nothing. Our lips will let pass no information of what has happened here. For this you have our solemn vow. This promise shall be fulfilled after three full circles of Naran.' Then each rushed forward and knotted their vow to the Khan's long cloak, joining the thousands of promises that already fringed his royal robe.

Raim was shaking. Although he too had been a witness, he was too young to make a vow of any kind. He had not yet reached Honour Age and so could not make a true promise to anyone. He was scared enough, though, not to let any knowledge of what he had seen slip from the room. He sneaked a glance at Batar-Khan, and saw an emotion on the Khan's face he didn't expect to see: fear.

But then he caught sight of Khareh's face: dark and glowering, black eyes narrowed in anger. Khareh was ready for revenge. Raim wouldn't exchange being in the Khan's boots for all the riches of Darhan.

Only Khareh would dare challenge the Khan like that. But no one would dare challenge Khareh without living to regret it.

4

Shell-shocked and still gaping, Raim stumbled out of the royal yurt only to be accosted by his grandfather.

'Raim,' Loni hissed. 'I told you to come straight back home after the ceremony. I've spent the past hour looking for you.'

'Why didn't you just send an errand boy? You could've saved yourself the trouble,' said Raim, desperate to have a moment to think over what he had just seen.

'Because' – Loni took a few more steps until they were well out of earshot of anyone else exiting the royal yurt – 'Yasmin has returned. With the aksha herb. Now, we can brew memory tea.'

The news stopped Raim in his tracks. They had been waiting for Yasmin the healer for over three months, so long had passed since her last visit.

They hurried to where they had camped, a temporary settlement for the twelve families that made up the Moloti tribe and the other, smaller group of five Temu yurts that had brought Solongal. Raim was unsure whether the chills running up and down his spine were from the early evening air or from excitement over the sage's visit . . . and now Yasmin's. Raim was surprised at how quickly the air cooled near the mountains. His ignorance of the weather cycles made him uncomfortable. This area was not like the rest of the steppes, where his tribe spent most of the year. In the steppes he knew everything, from when the sun would rise to when the rains would fall. Every Darhanian knew. They grew up learning about the land and their environment. Here, in this unfamiliar and rarely visited mountain place, the rocks sapped the heat from the air as soon as the sun disappeared behind the lowest peak and Raim was not prepared for the sudden cold.

Their yurt had been set up far apart from the rest of the village. It was a good thing too, Raim realized, as the stench that reached his nostrils sent his senses reeling. Drinking memory tea would not be a pleasant experience, he predicted.

Loose pebbles clattered over his thin shoes, sent flying down from above. He looked up at the mountainside, a sheer rock face that served as shade from the heat. His eyes traced the line of smoke that led up from his own yurt to a jagged ledge almost halfway up the cliff. There, almost completely concealed by the rock, were six or seven people. They stood rigid like statues, backs pressed stiff against the cliff, and had veils of grey cloth over their faces, leaving only slits for eyes.

Raim's eyes widened. It was Yasmin's clan of healers: the Otoshi. She really had come.

Smoke unfurled from the base of the yurt as his grandfather held open the curtain door. Raim pivoted round when the thick, wool cloth cascaded shut behind him. His grandfather was staying outside, keeping watch so they wouldn't be disturbed.

The strange, sickly sweet scent made his own home feel uncomfortable, like he didn't belong. It stung his eyes but through the smoke he made out the cross-legged silhouette of Yasmin. He picked up a cushion from the floor and moved it so he sat opposite the old, sun-ripened woman dressed in grey.

Yasmin was Loni's partner, and therefore Raim's adoptive grandmother. But she was a renowned shaman and the greatest healer in Darhan. Her immense skill with herbs and poultices, combined with her vast stores of knowledge, made her invaluable to the tribe of healers. She was not allowed to retire and look after Darhan's youth, like Loni had after he had grown too old to continue his job as a tracker in the army. But she had kept a closer eye on Raim than would normally be expected throughout the years, all because of the little indigo string bracelet Raim wore on his left wrist.

He had come to them as a baby, the string tied around his chubby wrist, and his grandfather had only noticed it when he'd first unwrapped him from the torn and dirty linen cloth he'd been bundled up in. It was traditional for elders to remove all traces of a baby's ancestry, so that the child's future did not have to be tied to their parents' past. Loni had tried to cut the string off with shears, but it refused to slice.

Loni had worried, then. He had worried so much he had tracked down his long-lost partner, Yasmin, to seek her advice. Even when Raim had only been a young child, he had noticed the whispered conversations and darkened looks exchanged between them where his little bracelet was concerned.

His life apart from that remained unchanged. He still trained to join his chosen clan – the Yun – and prepared for his Honour Age. But the bracelet was like a shadow over his achievements. Yasmin visited them at least three times a year, from wherever the Otoshi were in Darhan, no matter how far they had to travel. And always with the same purpose: to try to remove the knotted bracelet.

After Yasmin had left them the last time – after new meditation tricks designed to unlock his mind had failed – Raim had slipped his Yun training dagger beneath the string and tried to slice through it. It didn't break, or even fray. But in a way he was glad. Someone had given this to him, and he wanted to keep it for just a little bit longer. To everyone else – the other tribe members, Mhara, Khareh – he claimed the bracelet was a good luck charm from his sister Dharma that he would remove once he joined the Yun.

There was a small fire between them and on top of it sat a squat, round black pot. Yasmin did not look at him as he sat, but continued to stir the contents, occasionally sifting in more of a powdery green substance with her other hand. After a few moments, more thick white smoke appeared at the rim of the bowl. She blew it, hard, into his face.

Immediately he reeled back into a vision: a memory. It was ten years ago, and he was just a young boy of five, still years from his Yun apprenticeship. He was sitting on a rock, in the middle of nowhere, with Yasmin and her clan of healers. The air was different from that in the heart of the steppes, and yet it was not mountain air either. It was air parched of water. They were at the edge of the Sola desert.

The wind picked up Yasmin's shawl, lifting it from her face, so much smoother and softer in memory. She grabbed Raim's hand, held it firmly palm up, then curled his fingers shut. When he opened them again, there lay a bright white flower, its edges lined with silver.

'Eat,' she said.

'Drink,' she said. 'Drink,' more firmly, and Raim snapped back to the present as his fingers grasped the steaming-hot cup she was handing him. He looked nervously at the murky brown liquid.

'This is strong stuff, huh?' If just breathing the fumes

could trigger such vivid memories, he wondered what would happen when he drank it. He wrinkled his nose as he brought the cup to his lips. The rim scalded his lower lip, but as the liquid sloshed into his mouth he realized it was cold. The sensation shocked him; the cup fell to the ground and the spilled tea stained the carpet.

'Ach!' Yasmin righted the cup to preserve the remaining tea. 'We searched for months looking for that berry.' She put her hand on his forehead. 'Feel anything?'

Raim shook his head.

'You need some sort of stimuli. Try touching it.' Her nails, long and curly like pig's tails, drummed against the thread-bare carpet which covered the floor.

He ran his fingers over the string until he felt a slight abnormality. Then he took a deep breath and squeezed the tiny knot.

'Nothing,' he said after a few seconds, and slumped down onto the cushion. Raim thought he caught the smallest frown on Yasmin's face, but decided it was just a wrinkle fidgeting – every line on her face seemed to possess a life of its own.

'Think of something else,' she said. 'Think of the Yun.'

Instinctively his hand went to his apprentice blade, and memories of the Yun induction ceremony flooded in front of his eyes. Almost eight years ago he had been chosen to train to join the Yun, along with a host of other young boys and girls. They were all given an initial test. They were each given the chance to shoot with a Daga bow –

the second greatest weapon in the Yun arsenal after the signature sword. Raim had shot the target – an apple balanced on the tip of a post – straight through the middle.

It was the first time he had ever met Mhara. She was the Khan's Protector, and therefore the most powerful person in the Yun, someone to be feared and admired. He remembered the first words he ever heard her say: 'I will take him on.' And then it was settled. He was to be apprenticed to Mhara.

He distinctly remembered her coming up to him, and his hands trembling as he held them out and she placed the ochir blade in his palms. Next to him, solemn and rigid as a board, was a young girl with thick black hair braided in pigtails that reached down to her waist. Her name was Erdene, and she wasn't trembling – she was beautiful and serene. Her bravery had made Raim bite down on his lip and focus on showing the same courage. The memory faded.

'So it must work,' mused Yasmin. 'Try again, this time, focus your mind back. And' – Yasmin smirked – 'don't you dare start thinking about a girl.'

Raim grimaced, but he was already focusing on the vision he had seen during their last session. The last time they had tried to figure out the promise within the knot, they hadn't used memory tea, but rather a series of exhausting meditation sessions. Yasmin had posed Raim in a series of awkward body positions designed to open his mind to the universe. At the end of the sequence, cross-legged and with his eyes closed, he had only seen one image: a woman's hands gripping tightly around his own.

He pressed down hard on the knot while trying to create a clearer picture of the hands. Their colour could only be described as wet sand, until they opened and they were lighter, like dry sand. Around these two images of wet and dry, more of the picture came together. Wet – wet was important because the woman was sweating, she was shivering and afraid, no, terrified. Dry – he was dry, his mouth was dry and his eyes were dry and no wonder, as he gnashed his teeth together and tasted gritty sand. Were they near the desert? He heard shouts, felt shoves, started falling. A voice yelled his name and then spoke other words in a language he didn't understand.

He then said a word in this strange tongue, the only word that still made sense to him: 'Mother.'

He saw her eyes, dark as chewed grass, visible though the rest of her face was covered, and saw those eyes being dragged further and further away. Then he was wet again. Wet. Water.

Raim opened his eyes and saw Dharma, his adopted younger sister, splashing water on his face. He sat bolt upright and looked around but there was no fog, no tea, and no Yasmin.

Bright light momentarily blinded him. His grandfather stood in the doorway.

'Time for you to get up,' he said.

'Where's Yasmin?'

'Gone.' His grandfather looked at him and, for the first time, Raim saw pity in his eyes. 'We leave for Kharein in an hour. The time for you to join the Yun is now upon us.'

5

Raim spent the rest of the morning packing down his tribe's yurts: the duty of the young and strong. He started with the one he shared with Dharma and his grandfather, and – before yesterday – with Tarik. As he loaded the latticework frame of the yurt onto a cart and creased giant folds in the felt that served as the outer walls, he realized that when he, Sola willing, joined the Yun, his grandfather wouldn't be able to maintain such a large home. Loni would have to barter down for a smaller tent to share with Dharma until she grew old enough to choose a new clan. Then he would be too old to take care of any more young children. Once Dharma was gone, he would be forced to join a cheren – a community of elders with no more purpose in life. A cheren was where the old men and women of Darhan went to die.

But for the moment, they had this big yurt to transport. Dharma dashed around the thick felt, setting pots and pans and their other belongings down in their rightful place with practised precision, so that when Raim folded them together it would balance equally. Then it was time to get it all loaded onto the camel: a much more difficult task than Raim would have liked. Their camel was a surly beast that Dharma had named 'Batu', which implied 'loyal' in Darhanian, but Raim would've preferred to call him 'Berke' instead, which was closer to 'difficult'.

'Ready?' Raim called to Dharma. She had managed to get Batu to lie down and was standing in front of him with a distracting bright orange carrot in her hand, whispering comforting words into his ear. She looked up at Raim and nodded, her expression deadly serious. Without waiting for Batu to complain, Raim grabbed the sides of the felt and hauled them up onto the camel's back.

'Quick, Dharma!' As he had done many times before, Raim held the bundled yurt firmly between Batu's two humps so he couldn't topple the burden to the floor. Dharma leaped into action, dropping the carrot into Batu's waiting mouth and picking up the stray ends of rope they had left on the ground beneath Batu's belly. She scrambled onto the felt pile, rope in hand, and swiftly tied a knot, securing the bundle on his back. Once it was all done, she jumped back onto the ground.

'We did it!' Dharma said, smiling. Raim looked around. Everyone else was still trying to load up their camels. He and Dharma were the first to be finished.

'No!' piped up another voice from not too far away. It

was Lousha. 'You're not finished until your camel is up and in the line.'

'We are finished!' Dharma protested. With her hands on her hips she looked more like Lousha's old grandmother than a ten-year-old girl. 'The last knot has been tied!'

'Are not!' he shouted back, tongue out.

Raim picked up another carrot and placed it in Dharma's hand. 'You'll get Batu moving faster with another one of these.'

Dharma giggled. 'You're right – you'd be no help with this part anyway, it's clear you two don't like each other very much!' As if to confirm her statement, Batu launched a globby, orange-flecked ball of spit to the ground at Raim's feet, and stared at him haughtily.

Now Raim laughed. 'All right, all right, I'm leaving. I'll go see if Loni needs any help . . . don't let Lousha get the better of you now.'

'Never!' she said, already waving the carrot in front of Batu's face to try to get him to his feet. Eventually he deigned to regard the carrot worth the effort, and ambled up with no sense of grace whatsoever: haunches first, until he was stretched out almost like a cat, then dragging his front legs reluctantly up to standing. He took a few lumbering steps forward, more like a newborn calf than an old, disgruntled camel, and Dharma had to alternate between walking and skipping to keep up with the animal's long strides.

Raim started moving towards the back of the long line of people, where the goats were grazing. That was where Loni would be. When Tarik had been with them, he'd helped Dharma with the tent while Raim pulled the goats. Now Loni had to do it. Dust plumed in the air as carpets were shaken out, a week's worth of dirt returned to the soil. Raim covered his eyes and mouth with his arm and ran through the earthy clouds.

Their tribe was large and rich by Darhan standards, with the twelve families each owning at least one camel and one ox in addition to all the goats. They were goatherders by tradition, and the young children of the tribe were given the duty of encouraging the animals from pasture to pasture. Most tribes were lucky to have even one camel and some families were forced to share. His village was immensely fortunate. Raim's close friendship with Khareh meant the tribe often travelled with the royal caravan. Together with all their servants, the royal entourage was easily three times the size of Raim's tribe.

It was also the friendship between Khareh and Raim that had allowed Tarik the leisure time to study for the Baril, a privilege usually reserved for the particularly wealthy. Preparing for the Baril meant spending a few months of the year learning how to read and write under the watchful eye of a Baril monk, usually at Pennar, the only temple outside of the Amarapura mountains. Most of the time a tribe needed all of their young men to herd the goats, guard the yurts or hunt for food. It would have also meant that Raim would not have been able to join the Yun. While he had undeniable talent, his strong limbs would have been better suited to tending to the animals and the tribe would not have been able to lose him to Mhara twice a year for training. Like all the people of Darhan, he would have been trained for warfare anyway, but by the general army, who sent officers to each tribe to give every Darhanian a lesson in combat.

Invasion was a constant threat in Darhan, especially from the unallied tribes, who refused to be joined under Batar-Khan. If Raim's tribe travelled close to the borders of Mauz, they knew they could be called upon at any moment to fight. Raim had been only seven years old the first time his tribe had been called up to go to war. He remembered hiding behind a stack of dusty old rugs, watching Tarik struggling to put a boiled leather vest on over his tunic and to balance the heavy quiver of arrows on his back. Tarik had never been a fighter. All the younger kids, Raim included, had been rounded up with the elders, but they weren't free from helping out with the campaign. They ran along behind the army, scouring for dropped arrows that could be reused, scavenging weapons and armour from the fallen and bringing water to thirsty or injured troops. They faced the gore and the glory from an early age, and Raim knew his destiny was amongst the warriors.

But being part of the general army just wasn't the same as being Yun. No one, barring the Khan and the warlords, garnered more respect.

To find Loni, Raim followed the sound of bleating goats. Sure enough, as the dust began to clear, he saw his grandfather, heels dug firmly into the ground, trying to coax one of the beasts into motion.

'Where's . . . Dharma?' Loni spluttered between heaves.

'She's gone on ahead.' Raim moved behind the three oversized beasts and pushed their tails till they took small steps forward out of annoyance.

'What? You shouldn't have left her alone. I would've got them moving sooner or later.'

Raim looked into the surly yellow eyes of the goats and seriously doubted it. The people of the steppes treated their goats well – so well that they grew to the size of young horses. Raim had heard that goats were smaller and scrawnier than sheep in the South. It was no wonder. The Southerners, especially around the capital of Aqben, were well known to the Darhanians as a stagnant, lazy people, never moving, treating the land like a slave, working it relentlessly. When he thought of the South he was glad for the enormous, savage desert between them. No one except the savage Alashan and the destitute Chauk survived in the desert. And they survived only because they had no choice but to – they were not welcome anywhere else.

When the goats were all moving and the entire tribe had begun the long journey back towards the capital city of Kharein, Raim ran forward to find Dharma. The scene was organized chaos. The smell of fresh camel dung invaded Raim's nostrils and he held his nose as he passed by a particularly stinky beast. The neat single file line had degraded as families speeded up or slowed down in order to travel side by side and gossip about the messenger and the old man they had seen being driven off in a cart destined for the Garra prison.

Raim ran up behind Dharma, surprising her by hoisting her onto the back of their camel as he grabbed the reins. Her bright giggles in turn made him laugh, and he was glad that his grandfather had a lively young girl to raise after being stuck with two serious boys. Although he and Khareh never failed to make trouble and keep Loni – not to mention the prince's bodyguards – on his toes, Raim's dedication to becoming Yun meant he had always restrained himself, not daring to make a mistake that might ruin his chances. Khareh once bragged to Raim that he had run so far into the Sola desert he had thrown stones at the Chauk. While Raim strongly doubted whether anyone – even a prince – had that kind of courage or endurance, Khareh certainly had the freedom. He didn't have to worry about having Yun mentors to upset, or a grandfather to scold him. Batar-Khan rarely questioned Khareh – the scene in the royal tent had been one of the very few times Raim had ever seen the Khan confront his heir.

Raim didn't know what had happened to Dharma's parents, but it was well known that they were not of Moloti tribe origin, for she had arrived in the company of two soldiers. Loni knew. A new promise knot had appeared around his neck the same day she arrived. It wasn't hard to guess, though. Men and women who disappeared without word or warning were only destined for one place: Lazar.

'Pass me my loom, please, Raim,' she said, patting the top of his turban with her tiny hands as he walked. He threw the reins over his shoulder and fumbled through one of the saddlebags. He had taken special care to pack Dharma's travel loom close to the top of the pack; he knew she would ask for it. She was always weaving and the elders all complimented her on her skill. The loom was as wide as Raim's forearm and twice as long. Dharma used it to weave squares of carpet as they were wandering through Darhan, and later the squares would all be sewn together to create walls and floors for their yurts or blankets for cold nights. Even Raim, who was no expert in such things, could recognize the intricacy of her loom work, the woven figures so lively he could almost see them moving. With her skills, she could hope to join the Una tribe of weavers, who had won Batar Khan's royal warrant and were widely regarded as the most superior of all the weavers.

'Dharma, this is brilliant,' he said as he handed her the loom.

'Thanks! Loni taught me how to tassel properly. It's hard.'

'You're telling me.' Raim's own attempts at carpet weaving had failed miserably. His knots were uneven and the pattern never connected properly. He could wield a sword expertly with his hands but tiny strings befuddled his fingers.

The Amarapura mountains, their lofty snow-covered crags now Tarik's desolate home, disappeared into the northern horizon. The tribe marched on, working their way across the flat plains towards Kharein. The steppes – their territory – stretched for miles, flat and calm like water in a bucket. Although all around it spread extremes – mountains to the north, desert to the south, dense, thick forests further east and west – when Raim stood on the steppes nothing could be seen but land and sky. And if you did not know every inch of that land and sky intimately, getting lost was as simple as closing your eyes and spinning around in a circle. There were no landmarks beyond the blades of grass and no signposts except the stars. The universe opened for miles above them. Their land was like their history: eternal.

They travelled for three nights before reaching Kharein, not bothering to build their yurt every night but instead sleeping out under the clear night sky full of stars, until it was light enough to move again.

Every step they took closer to the city, their population grew. All tribes were on their way to the capital, some with a Yun hopeful, but most simply for the annual festival. The excitement that the festival created was a welcome change from the slow monotony of nomadic life. It was a time for all Darhan citizens to revitalize their skills and barter for supplies they would need for the rest of the year.

It was a chance for young people to decide which clan they might aspire to join and to what service they wanted to dedicate their lives. And for most Darhanians, it was the time to meet and choose a partner from outside their tribe.

But by far the most exciting event of the Festival was the Yun selection. Since every man and woman in Darhan was trained in basic fighting arts, watching the talented apprentices battle to join the best of the best was a great highlight. For the apprentices themselves, to win brought honour to the entire tribe, and this was Raim's chance to be the star.

Kharein itself was shaped like a pentagon and surrounded by a long, low wall. The wall served more as a way to section off the inner city from the masses of yurts that surrounded it than as any means of defence, as Kharein needed little defending. The flat, isolated land that surrounded the city meant that any attacking army could be seen from miles away, and would be met well before it reached the city. On every point of the pentagon stood a tall watchtower, guards keeping a vigilant eye for suspicious plumes of dust. During Festival season, the yurts were scattered around the outside of the city walls, clustered together by clan like white petals around a flower. This was the only time Kharein truly looked alive. Without the visiting population it was simply a dried-up bud – the centre of royal activity, perhaps, but not the home of people's hearts. The people of Darhan could not be settled. They moved constantly, shifting with the days of the year, the seasons, the animals. By the end of the month-long Festival even the merriest Darhan grew restless. They dispersed, seeds on the wind, and yet remained unified. It was the life of the Darhan, and had been for centuries.

When they finally stopped, Raim couldn't even see the outer wall for all the yurts and tents that had been set up. To an outsider it might have looked haphazard, but each tribe knew its place; each clan had their own position and style of yurt. Setting up their home again took about an hour, but Raim took pride over every rope, peg and inch of frame. If things went according to plan in Kharein, this would be the last time he ever set up his yurt with Loni and Dharma. After he took the knot to join the Yun, there would be no turning back to his old life.

He was finishing up positioning one of the woven tension bands that held the felt outer covering of the yurt in place when Loni stepped out of the door, Dharma holding his hand. 'We are heading over to visit the Una clan, to show off Dharma's weaving skill.'

Raim patted Dharma on the head as she went by. 'You'll blow them away. You're the best weaver I know.'

'Shall we meet you in Kharein? I know you have something important to choose.' Loni winked.

Raim swallowed down unexpected nerves and nodded, then waved them goodbye. He had to choose his promise string. The time had almost come.

When Raim was satisfied that their home was well built

and the frame wouldn't topple at the slightest breeze, he went inside. Hanging above a small shrine to the desert-goddess Sola, there was a small piece of jagged, silvered glass, which served as their only mirror. Raim stood in front of it and unwrapped the cloth turban from around his head. If he wanted to enter the city, he would have to do it not as a young tribemember of a lowly goatherder clan, but as a proud young apprentice, about to battle for his position in the Yun. Mhara had warned him that the battle could start at any time during the festival, and that he had to be ready to be called upon at any moment. For that, he needed to be dressed and ready to go, most importantly with his head bare and open to the sky.

He was ready. But was Kharein ready for him?

6

Raim walked out of the yurt dressed in the uniform of a Yun apprentice: a light, loose-fitting silk shirt under a knee-length brown robe tied at the waist with a strip of leather. Dark trousers made of coarse cotton billowed around his ankles. He kneeled down in the dust outside the yurt to tie up his boots, tucking the excess fabric from his trousers into the top before lacing them up. He felt more comfortable in these clothes than in any others – except, he imagined, when he would be able to change into the ebony-black robes of the Yun. When he was finally ready, Raim began to pick his way through the maze of yurts to reach Kharein.

He loved entering the city, and he let the excitement of the moment wash over him as he passed through the main gate. Although the surrounding wall was low, the main entrance was a tall gate with an intricate pagoda-style roof. All the largest and most important buildings in

Darhan were housed within the inner city: the Imperial Palace, the Rentai – Darhan's greatest temple – and the iron mill. The palace took up the entire northern corner, with a large open courtyard that served as a stadium for Yun tournaments and as a forum for the Khan's audiences and declarations.

Through the eastern corner of the city ran the River Iod, which transected the inner city walls. The iron mill was built over the top of the river, and a giant waterwheel turned the complicated mechanisms inside. This mill served many purposes and was the principal manufacturing workshop for all of Darhan. Although he had never been inside, Raim loved to gaze at the iron mill from the banks of the river. The Yun swords were forged there, in a secret room somewhere inside, and that made the place feel almost sacred to him.

He headed deeper into the city, following the throng. He spied people from every clan and tribe amongst the crowds: from the weavers, with their fingers dripping in yarns, to the soldiers, swords hanging from their belts, to ordinary goatherders staring wide-eyed at all the wares. Someone he would have been, if it wasn't for Khareh.

He owed Khareh so much because his life could have been so different. He felt as lucky as a raindrop that chanced to fall in a mighty river as opposed to on the dusty ground.

He had been only ten years old when they first met. He had been out on a hill in the middle of the steppes in the dead of night, forced into guard duty over the goats after one of the elders had spotted the menacing form of a lone wolf prowling the countryside not far away. The wolf was the most dangerous creature of the steppe. Its endurance surpassed any other, and even one that seemed far away could suddenly come and steal a prized kid in the dead of night.

Just not on Raim's watch. Even at ten years old, he hadn't been afraid.

He remembered he had almost willed the wolf to come, anything to alleviate the boredom that was fast settling into his bones. His eyelids had grown heavy, the burden of staying alert too much.

But that was when he heard the growl. Immediately, Raim's ears had pricked up, his heart rate speeded up and he willed himself to become deadly still. The growl came again, and this time Raim could place it – on the other side of the hill from where he and his goats were safely resting.

Slowly, Raim crept up to the crest of the hill, until he was at the highest viewpoint. The bottom of the hill on that side dropped away in a much steeper slope. That was when he saw it: the grey wolf, its fur matted and teeth bared. It was crouched down low, in a position to strike. A smattering of blood was scattered in front of it, and curiously there was a willow basket – ripped to shreds by the wolf's teeth – a few feet away.

Raim couldn't see the object of the wolf's ire, but he

couldn't hear any bleating either. He wondered if its prey was already half-dead, beyond saving.

He crept over the hillside, manoeuvring into a position where he could see the victim. But it wasn't a lamb at all. It was another little boy, standing with his back to the rock, cowering from the beast.

Even in the weak moonlight, Raim could see the boy's hands, red with blood. At first, Raim thought he must've been attacked already, but then there was another clue: a thick hunk of meat lay at the boy's feet.

There had been little time to ponder that mystery. Raim could see the boy had no weapons. He picked up a rock from the ground and drew himself up to his full height. Then he launched the rock at the wolf and ran down the hillside shouting as loud as he could. He leaped the last few feet as he reached the sheer rock face, and landed in front of the other boy.

He had thought the rock and the shouting might be enough to drive the wolf away, but not this one. This wolf was hungry; the scent of blood was in his nostrils, and a hungry wolf was also desperate. The creature eyed Raim like a soldier assessing a new foe, but Raim was only small then – and the threat was dismissed. The wolf advanced.

But Raim was prepared. He stared the wolf in the eye as his fingers fumbled behind his back for the whittling knife he carried at his belt. Fear was beginning to scratch at him now, threatening to pull his focus from the job at hand. Actually being face to face with a wolf was different from how he had imagined it. Being so close – the razor sharp points of its teeth, the terrible stench of its breath, the rabid look in its eye – made it seem all the more real and terrifying.

The wolf was advancing on them both now. Raim saw him bunch his muscles, prepare to lunge . . .

The other boy moved then. He scooped up the piece of meat and prepared to dash past the wolf.

Its attention diverted, Raim took the split second to leap for the wolf, even as it sprang for the other boy. He plunged the knife into the wolf's ribcage, trying his best to ignore the snarls and howls of pain from the creature. He gripped tightly onto the wolf's fur, not letting go as it thrashed from side to side, trying to stay out of reach of the gnashing teeth.

Then there was a thud, and then another, and the wolf slumped into his arms, two arrows buried into its side.

For the first time throughout the whole ordeal, the two boys looked at each other. The other boy's arm was shaking under the weight of the bow, but his aim had been true.

The moments after that had been a blur. The elders arrived – attracted by the shouting and commotion – to find Raim drenched in wolf's blood. That was when Raim found out the boy he saved was the son of a warlord. The warlord wouldn't let Raim go back to being a lowly goatherder, but told him that someone of his bravery and skill should be training with the elite warriors of

Darhan. That's how Raim had become a Yun apprentice.

Khareh had explained later that he had been trying to trap the wolf, so he could tame it and keep it as a pet. But instead of a wolf, he had gained a friend – and from that moment on, the two boys had been as inseparable as two humps on a camel.

Now, Raim was about to take his Yun test, and the only growl was from his stomach.

He found himself being drawn deeper towards the market stalls. The smell warmed him more than a freshly stoked fire and made his mouth fill with saliva. After months living on a diet of goat's milk, rice and the occasional piece of dried meat, the variety on Kharein's streets overwhelmed him. It seemed like everyone in Darhan – and beyond – felt the same way. The food market was filled to the brim. The Festival had well and truly begun.

But it wasn't just any food that Raim was after. If anything, it was the tyrfish from the River Erudine that was drawing him deeper into the market. The Festival was the only time of the year that the fishermen – the Erudees – brought their catch to the capital city. They transported it strapped to fragrant planks of wood cut from the forests on the border of Mauz. By the time they reached Kharein, the fish was rich with flavour – once seared on the giant wood-heated grills on the city streets it became Raim's favourite dish.

He followed his nose to the stall and handed over a few

bronze coins for a portion. It came wrapped in thin white paper, juicy and delicious.

Before he could take a bite, he felt a tug on the sleeve of his tunic. He looked down into the face of a young boy. 'Excuse me, are you a Yun apprentice?'

Raim smiled. 'Yes . . .'

'GRANDFATHER, I'VE FOUND ONE!' the boy shouted.

All of a sudden he was surrounded by people, jostling him between them like a gutball. In one instant he was being pulled at by a dozen young boys asking for advice, the next he was in amidst strong-armed merchants, like the young boy's grandfather, evaluating him for a good bet.

'How's your sword arm?'

'Not feeling a little weak in the shoulder?'

'Don't eat that Erudine crap, you'll feel sick for the bout.'

'I'll give you a hundred gold pieces if you let the other boy win.'

He knew apprentices often experienced a whirlwind of attention during the festival, but he never realized it was as bad as this. He felt trapped. Khareh was the one who normally got all the attention and Raim liked it that way. Khareh might embrace it, but Raim could currently think of nothing worse. He tried to push his way through the crowd to escape, but wherever he moved the hungry throng followed.

'Quick, follow me!' said a whispered female voice. A hand pressed on his back, then slid round to his elbow to lead him away. He whipped round just in time to see the girl's dark brown eyes urging him to follow her before she disappeared into the crowd.

Erdene.

A new kind of adrenaline fuelled him now, his heart speeding up to a thousand horse strides a minute in his chest. He caught sight of her again, and doubled, trebled his effort to get to her, finding a path through the crowd that had seemed so impenetrable before.

She ducked down an alley, and just as he entered it himself he saw her twist down into another. This part of Kharein, behind the market stalls, was a maze of cramped, darkened streets barely wide enough for a single person to move. He turned sideways to fit down the alley she had turned down, then stopped abruptly as a hand grabbed his belt and pulled him backward.

He tumbled into a small courtyard, a welcome square of space after the tight alley and hungry crowd. A line of freshly washed linens hung from a cord across two windows above them, motionless in the still air.

Or maybe the air only felt so still because he was suddenly aware of how close he was to Erdene. Close and alone.

He turned round to see her pulling the veil down off her head, strands of long black hair falling across her face. She pushed them off her forehead, threw her head back, and laughed. 'Gods, did you expect that? All those people clamouring for us. I guess the other apprentices have been through this before, so that's why we don't see them out and about so much before the duel.'

Raim struggled to form any suitable kind of reply, his mouth suddenly completely dry. She didn't wait for him to speak, though. 'Do you have any idea when they'll call us in for the fights? Last year it was at the beginning of the Festival, so maybe this year they'll make it the closing event . . . I hate to be kept waiting, don't you?'

His mouth tried to form words like, 'Yes, the wait is horrible,' but instead he ended up mumbling something vaguely affirmative.

Erdene didn't seem to notice. She leaned back against the wall, and when she looked Raim in the eyes, he was surprised to see them glistening. 'I'm so worried about the fight,' she said, biting her lower lip. 'I don't know if I'm ready for Jendo. It's his third try and . . . I want to be Yun. I want to be Yun more than anything.'

'Jendo is a good fighter, but he has his weaknesses,' Raim said, grateful she had finally picked a topic that would loosen his tongue. On this subject, he could talk for ever. 'He's steady, but he's not very creative. You can trick him – use feints, deflections. Come at me now.' He beckoned her over.

She blinked the moisture from her eyes, as if weighing up the decision. Then she pushed away from the wall and moved into a fighting stance. She bounced on the balls of her feet a couple of times, then snapped forward to strike at Raim.

He allowed himself to take the blow, absorbing the majority of the force on his left shoulder. Then, when she attacked again, he turned his body as if protecting his injured left side. He watched as Erdene's nostrils flared, as if she could almost smell his weakness. Then she went in again for the kill, but he used his uninjured right to deflect the force of her attack against her and almost flipped her onto the ground. Except he didn't let her complete the fall, catching her a few inches from the floor.

They remained in that position for a moment. It was only a moment, but it was long enough for Raim to notice he could feel the strong muscles of her back through her coarse tunic where he'd caught her, long enough to notice her hair trailing on the ground over his sandals, tickling the skin of his toes. He lifted her up to her feet quickly, before he noticed anything else.

Her face was hot and red with the exertion, but a wry smile crossed her face. 'I see what you did. Feinting. Got it.' She reached forward and Raim held his breath. She straightened his tunic by running her hands across his shoulders. 'There. Better.'

He smiled back, awkwardly.

'So, Raim, where's the Crown Prince? Aren't you two always together at the moment? That's what I heard . . . that you are close enough to be in line to be his Protector one day.' She raised an eyebrow.

Raim shrugged. 'Maybe. If he asks, of course I'd say yes. There are plenty of other worthy candidates, though . . .'

'Hmm.' She let her gaze run him up and down, and Raim felt shivers run down his spine. 'Well, you know, I've never met Prince Khareh . . . Even if I can't be his Protector, I might be able to do something . . . else for him.'

Raim shuffled his feet along the dusty ground. 'I'm sure I could introduce you to him soon.'

'At the party after the duels?'

Raim shrugged. 'Sure, why not?'

'Perfect. Thanks, Raim.' She stood up on her tiptoes and kissed his cheek. 'See you around.'

7

After he'd recovered from his encounter with Erdene enough to move again, Raim meandered his way back through the alleys in the vague direction he thought Dharma and Loni would come looking for him. He was of sound mind enough to check for any sign of the crowd he had lost in the markets first before leaving the alley. But instead, he saw an even more unexpected sight: Khareh.

'Ah, Raim, just the person I was looking for!'

'Oh, hey, Khareh. I'm supposed to be meeting Loni . . .'

'Whatever you need to do, it can wait; I have something far more exciting.'

'But Loni and Dharma are going to help me choose a promise string. I need it before the Yun battle begins, and that could be any time . . .'

'Think of it this way,' said Khareh, always the negotiator. 'You've already thwarted the gods of fate just by bumping into me. No going back now. You might as well give in and come with me.'

Raim shrugged and gave in, encouraged by Khareh's infectious excitement. 'So where are we going?'

'You remember that sage?'

'As if I could forget!'

'Well, I convinced Altan to give us a few minutes of alone time with the magician before he's formally shipped off to prison and executed. They're keeping him in a yurt outside the wall near the Rentai. We're going to make him teach me how to make a carpet fly.'

'My head.' Raim covered the top of his closely-shaven head with his hands. 'If I'm seen like this, I'll be recognized right away.' He thought back to the market square, the crowds.

'I came prepared,' said Khareh. He fumbled in the bag he was carrying and brought out a length of turban cloth and a small, dirty canvas sack. Raim wrapped the cloth around his head.

'What's that for?' He eyed the sack.

In response, Khareh dipped his hand into the bag and flung a handful of black ash from it into Raim's face. Raim found himself with a mouthful of dust.

Khareh started running.

'If you weren't the Prince, I'd kill you!' Raim sped after him.

'You could try!'

They ran, weaving through the tumultuous Darhanian

crowd, ducking under baskets and avoiding the rotting fruit that littered the ground.

'How can the sage teach you if he's sentenced to death?' Raim dropped his voice to a whisper as they got closer to the outer wall. 'Surely you can't learn magic just like that . . .'

'There has to be a way, I just know it. I will force it out of him if I have to.'

They exited the city through one of the smaller gates and Khareh singled out the prison yurt. They crept behind the back. The tent was specifically designed to hold prisoners and traitors. It looked ordinary on the outside, and blended with the sea of felted tents all around it. But inside there was a second room, the walls of which were made of thick black material, blocking out all light and sound.

Against the dirty beige of the yurt, Khareh's cloak sparkled. It was made from a bright blue weave covered with hundreds of tiny circular mirrors. Raim caught a quick glimpse of his reflection. His face was covered in ash, the black smeared all over his forehead, cheeks and nose. Contrasted with his dark eyes and the tanned skin visible around his hairline and neck, he looked a disaster. He prayed he wouldn't run into anyone who might know him.

'Khareh, you are a prince. You're destined to rule . . . not to be an apprentice to a sage.'

'I see no reason why I can't be both. A prince with magic. Think how good that sounds. And anyway, how can he refuse me? I'm the Khan. He's my subject, isn't he?'

69

He disappeared into the yurt with a grand flourish.

Raim stared in disbelief as the curtain fell. 'You're not the Khan yet,' he said, and slipped inside behind his friend.

Altan was waiting for them. Raim had always been wary of the Khan's adviser, with his crooked fingers and pointed beak of a nose. Khareh always said he was harmless, but Raim wasn't sure.

'You must be quick,' he said to Khareh. His breath caught as he spotted Raim. 'Prince, forgive me, I thought I said to come alone.'

Khareh just shrugged. 'And I decided to bring my friend with me.'

'But the prisoner will only speak to you.'

'So? Raim can hide inside. He won't be seen.'

Altan's eyes narrowed as he glanced over Raim's ash-covered face and hastily thrown together turban. He refused to say anything further, and simply pulled back the second layer of cloth separating the prisoner's room from the rest of the yurt.

Khareh strode in confidently, and Altan followed close behind. Raim slipped in last, creeping down low to the ground and staying close to the perimeter of the room. There was a stack of canvas sacks and fur pelts piled up along the far side. He squeezed behind it and kneeled down. From his vantage point, he could see the back of the prisoner. The sage's hands were tied behind his back around the centre post, angry black ropes coiled like snakes around his wrists.

'I wish to become a sage,' said Khareh. 'Will you be able to teach me?'

Raim shifted a coarse burlap sack. He could see Khareh's face but not the sage's. The sage was whispering and Raim struggled to hear a word.

'My prince . . . not worthy of your attention . . . humble servant.'

By contrast, Khareh's voice was strong and full of pride. Raim could sense his friend's excitement bubbling right under the surface. 'Prove your worth to me then, sage, and I will make sure you receive the respect you deserve in my court. The ancient books tell of a ruler so great, he united all of Darhan. He was a sage. Tell me how I can become him.'

There were more murmurings from the sage's limp form. Raim caught the word 'Batar'. Khareh grabbed one of the large urns near the sage and threw it to the ground, shattering it. Altan put his hand on the Prince's shoulder, trying to restrain him. Khareh shrugged him off. 'Sola take my uncle! Tell me what I need to do to become a sage!'

Tell him, Raim said in silent prayer under his breath. He had seen Khareh blow up at his uncle, his tutors and his servants. If things didn't go his way . . .

'Fine.' Khareh's voice was hard and cold, like iron. 'Have it your way. Tomorrow you will be sent to Garra prison, for a short stay in hell before you are executed. That death will come to you as a mercy, if my uncle has anything to do with it. We don't take kindly to oath-breakers who refuse their exile.'

71

Khareh turned on his heel, but there was a feeble 'Wait' from the sage. 'I can teach you,' the sage said, his voice ragged, then taking on a harder tone. 'But it will require the ultimate sacrifice from you.'

'Anything,' Khareh breathed.

Hands gripped Raim's ankles and pulled him under the curtained walls to the outer circle of the yurt. When he flipped over, he looked straight into the muddy green eyes of Mhara.

'I'm . . . uh, well . . .'

'Somewhere you definitely shouldn't be? Come on.'

Raim's stomach flipped with dread as she dragged him outside. But to his surprise, she said, 'Don't worry, I haven't come to punish you – although you were doing an incredibly dangerous thing just then. The situations the Prince gets you into.'

He followed her back towards the city, pausing at a water pump so he could wipe his face. They entered the city through the main gates, and into the jostling market.

'Mhara – how could the sage teach Khareh how to conjure?'

Mhara scoffed as if she hardly believed the magic to be real. But she had been in the royal yurt and seen it too, with her own eyes. 'I have no time for legends. No doubt he thinks he is a precious commodity. But to me, his magic is nothing.'

'So you don't believe he is a sage like in the old stories?'

'No, I am sure they died out long ago. He should have

stayed in Lazar, where oathbreakers like him belong.' Suddenly, she broke out into a rare smile. 'You know, Raim, you have been my best pupil. There is no doubt that you are the most promising apprentice the Yun has ever had. No need to blush, it is true. Your skills are far beyond your years.'

Raim beamed back, relieved that his antics hadn't got him kicked out of the Yun apprenticeship the day before his test. 'Khareh is already preparing all the celebrations for tomorrow. I tried to tell him that I hadn't actually won yet, but he wouldn't listen.'

Her smile slowly faded. 'You should be wary of Khareh,' she said, after a long silence.

'He's my best friend.'

'I know.' She seemed to stare straight into his skull. 'Has he made you his Protector?'

Raim shook his head and broke away from his mentor's uncomfortable scrutiny. 'But he will.' He paused, then added, 'And I would be honoured.'

'Do you remember when I told you about the Absolute Vow?'

Of course he remembered. How could he forget? It was the defining moment of his life, when he first realized that his greatest ambition – becoming the Khan's Protector and leader of the Yun – could actually come true. But it unnerved him to remember it now. Mhara obviously still held reservations about Khareh. Did she still not trust him to make the right decision about his own future?

The conversation had taken place three years ago, when he was long settled into his Yun apprenticeship. They had been riding together, Raim on Pouri, an old but experienced mare and Mhara on Crear, a magnificent black stallion. They were returning from archery practice. Raim was learning to synchronize the release of his arrow with Pouri's gallop, so that all her hooves were in the air at the time of the shot. It would improve his aim immensely. And he had succeeded that day, so Mhara was pleased with him. They would've continued to train long into the dark, but his ring had broken.

The ring was vital. He wore it on his thumb. The string on a Yun bow was too taut, the tension too strong, to be maintained by human fingers alone, let alone the fingers of a thirteen-year-old boy. To supplement their strength they used a ring with a curved hook protruding from it, like the talon of a bird of prey, which they wore on the strongest digit – the thumb to pull back the string. His was just made out of crudely sewn strips of leather – a hunter's ring really, not made for the challenge and rigour of warfare. He eyed Mhara's ring with envy and excitement. It was made of a precious white metal and richly engraved with symbols from her tribe and the khanate. One day, he would have a ring like that too. But for now, they had to return, so he could mend the leather talon, which had snapped off the circular part of the ring.

He thought she must have caught him staring at it, for she rotated her ring slowly as they meandered back to camp with their horses. 'Straighten your back more,' she said, commenting on his technique. 'And adjust your feet so your toes are just balancing on the stirrup. You need to be as nimble as a dancer when you shoot.'

He couldn't ask for a better teacher. While there may have been one or two Yun who could best Mhara in a sword fight, in archery she had no equal. What she lacked in arm muscle – and she didn't lack much – she made up for in accuracy and horsemanship. She could see impossibly long distances, finding targets across the miles. She never learned to read or write, and couldn't stand to look at maps, not even for strategizing. Instead, she would look out over the countryside and develop plans with her immense mental and actual vision. Anything close seemed to bother her.

Even people. She was the first Protector to be a woman in ten generations of Khans. If it had been any other woman, someone could have started slanderous rumours, accusing her of making the Khan unfaithful to the Seer-Queen or of seducing her way into power. But the Khan had been careful in his selection. Mhara had never been known to show affection to anyone. The closest she ever came were displays of pride and almost motherly tenderness towards her favourite apprentice, Raim. And even those moments were few and far between.

That day had been the first time she had shown him her promise knot to Batar-Khan. Mhara had drawn her curved scimitar out from its sheath and balanced it on top of her knees. The blade itself was deadly and beautiful – Raim had to shield his eyes from the glint. Sealed inside the translucent blade like an insect trapped in an amber tomb was a simple knot; simple, but it represented her Absolute Vow of unconditional fealty to Batar-Khan. The knot was preserved even though the process of being sealed in the mould with searing hot ochir would destroy ordinary thread. And – Sola forbid – if Mhara were to break her vow, the sword would shatter and the knot would burn, marking her like any other oathbreaker.

Mhara had been amused by his ogling eyes. 'Raim, even without your close friendship with Khareh, you would be asked by any Khan to be his Protector. Even Batar-Khan would ask you to replace me, should I die or lose my skills to age.'

'Naran forbid!' Raim wrinkled his nose. He didn't want to fight for Batar-Khan. Khareh was the only person he could imagine protecting.

'Raim, why is it that a Yun may make an Absolute Vow to the Khan, but a warlord may not?'

'Because it is not a warlord's duty to protect the Khan, but to protect the interests of his people. He can't give his life to the Khan because his life is given to his tribe.'

'That's right. So you understand an Absolute Vow, then? What it means?'

Raim remembered puffing out his chest at this, speaking with swollen pride. 'It means promising to defend your Khan at any cost. Being willing to lay down your life for him, without any hesitation! It means being able to die with honour and glory in the tradition of the Yun – just as you promised to Batar-Khan.'

But her stern expression was like a needle in his balloon of pride. 'Yes, I did. But do you know how many times I refused him?'

Raim shook his head, more out of disbelief than anything else. Mhara had refused the honour?

'Seven times.'

'No!' he cried out. He couldn't help himself.

'Yes. Over the course of an entire year, Batar-Khan – then just the Crown Prince himself – asked me seven times to be his Protector. I refused each time, because I wasn't certain of his character. Eventually, he proved himself to me, and the fact that he was willing to do that – to prove himself to someone of such a lower rank than himself – meant I accepted. Taking an Absolute Vow means giving your life to one person. In every way. There is no backing out. There is no changing your mind. Once the promise is made you are his Protector for life. You break this vow, you don't get exiled. You die. Is Khareh worth that?'

Raim swallowed. 'I know this. And he is. In every way.'

Mhara nodded but turned her head away. Raim felt a swirl in his stomach, knowing Mhara was trying to tell him something, but he didn't understand. 'You remind me too much of your mother,' she said. The remark was just an aside. Raim didn't even know if he had heard correctly, or if he remembered it right. Only that she had mentioned his mother. He had thought many times about asking Mhara more about her, but he dismissed it. Whoever his parents were, it didn't matter. If she had been important, Mhara would have said something. But Mhara never said another word.

She had never mentioned the Absolute Vow again either, but now, on the day before his final bout, she was asking about it again.

When he didn't answer her immediately, she obviously guessed what he was thinking. 'I did not bring it up again because I don't trust your ability to make your own judgements. I just want you to be fully aware of what you are doing when you make an Absolute Vow. Khareh is a very clever, very strong young prince. Yet you know as well as I do that he has another side – a thirst for power and an anger that could overwhelm him. These are different parts of his soul and it is up to you to make sure which parts become the most dominant. That will also be part of your duty as Protector, Raim – to protect Khareh from himself. Are you ready for that? I care for you, Raim.'

This time, it was Raim who nodded and turned away. She patted him on the back. 'Your grandfather has been asking for you. Find him, but make sure you are back in time to get a good rest. Soon, you will experience the most difficult day of your life.'

8

Raim wasn't completely sure where Loni and Dharma were in Kharein, so he jogged quickly back to the main gate, sticking to the alleyways as much as possible, and avoiding big crowds of people. He relaxed as soon as Loni and Dharma were in sight.

'Thought we would find you here!' Loni said with a grin. 'Didn't Mhara tell you to come find us?'

'She did, but . . .'

'Hiding out from the wolves baying for your blood, hmm? Well, let's get moving then – we need to get you your promise string. Then we can hide you away in the yurt, like the other apprentices.'

There was a merchant class in Darhan that dealt brisk trade in promise string. While in reality a promise could be knotted out of anything – a loose thread on a tunic or a snip of hair, as the young of Darhan were forced to do – it was considered extremely base and disrespectful to do so for anything important. More accepted was to buy two lengths of ready-prepared string from a merchant, which were then folded many times and worn around the waist like a belt.

The stringmongers' stalls were located on the bank of the Iod, close to the mill. Raim, Loni and Dharma picked their way out of the food stalls and through the rest of the market where merchants were selling coats and boots lined with rabbit-fur for winter, iron pots, tiny greenstone carvings of Sola – the desert goddess – and Naran – the sun goddess – and weapons of all shapes and sizes. Everything was displayed on hastily built stalls that collapsed against the walls at night. Nothing was very secure, or permanent, in Kharein. It was the capital city of nomads – if the need arose, it could be packed up and moved. The few solid structures – the Rentai, the palace, the mill – could be rebuilt somewhere else, if the land required it. The Darhan listened to the land. Respected it. They had moved before.

They reached the first stringmonger's stall. Bundles of rope dripped from the ceiling, every colour of the rainbow covering the stall's surface. Raim could barely make out the face of the merchant, as he too was covered in a brightly covered garment with geometric patterns all over. The merchant spotted him and cried out:

'Honour boy, I have just the string for you!'

Loni grabbed his arm before he could look. 'No, no, we will go and see Borum.'

'Yeah, I know,' said Raim. Tarik had bought his strings from Borum two years prior. 'His stall was further down the river, right?'

Borum was out in front of his stall, finishing up a deal with a girl and her grandmother. His mouth spread into a wide grin as he saw them approach and gold winked from every other tooth.

'Loni! Raim! I wondered when I would be seeing you. And delightful Dharma – I pray you have been putting your threads to good use.'

'Of course, Uncle Borum,' said Dharma, with an enthusiastic nod that made her black curls bounce against her shoulder. She had purchased ordinary thread – not promise string – from him in order to continue her weaving. 'I have just been to visit with the Una – they feel I might be ready to join them one day, if I keep on practising.'

'I don't doubt it, little star of Sola. And when you do, I will commission many rugs from you to decorate my home.' He turned to Raim. 'It's your turn at last! It must feel like an age to you – and just in time.'

'You have no idea!' Raim had never been more grateful to be born just before the start of the Festival season. If he had been born a day later, he would have had to wait another year before being able to take his Yun test.

'You must be very proud of your boy, Loni. Do you know, he will be my first ever Yun string-bearer, Sola willing?' He ushered them all closer to the stall and he disappeared round the back. Raim ran his hands over the different strings, each made of a different material. There were emerald-coloured strings of silk and maroon cotton threads. Some were so coarse they pricked his fingers and others were so delicate he was afraid they would disintegrate with a touch from his calloused hands.

'Perhaps, since you will hold such an important post in the future, you might be interested in something to reflect the stature of Yun.' Borum reached beneath his stall and produced a large rectangular box about the length of Raim's arm and as shallow as his palm. It was made of soft black leather, and he laid it out carefully in front of the trio. He clicked the lock and opened it. Raim's breath caught in the back of his throat.

Inside were a hundred strings of the finest quality, laid out side by side. Even to his untrained eye, Raim knew someone had laboured for many years to find them – and also that they would cost vast amounts of money. They were expensive because of the risk involved in procuring them. The stringmongers would pay special gatherers huge sums of money to track down supplies from the most difficult of places: the finest kork wool from under the chin of a goat that only thrived on the frozen caps of the Amarapura mountains, or strands of silk from glow-worms hidden in the deepest caves of Zalinzar.

They were all dazzlingly beautiful. One thread in particular caught his eye; a rich indigo with flecks of gold interwoven in the thread. It looked ablaze with fire.

'You have good taste,' said Borum, following Raim's eyes. 'You won't find anything finer. Would you like to try—'

But Loni interrupted before Raim had the chance to touch the beautiful thread. 'Borum, this is all wonderful but I'm afraid we will have to set our sights on something more modest.'

The old merchant's eyebrows rose, creating deep lines in his brow. He looked about to protest, but seeing the determination on Loni's face, he snapped the case shut. 'All right then. Tell me what you are looking for and we will go from there. Something similar to your brother, perhaps?' Borum perked up as he remembered Tarik had purchased promise string that was of much better quality than average. He motioned towards the fine silk strands spread over the left side of his stall.

'Hmm, well . . .' Loni pulled a small pouch out of his tunic pocket and emptied the contents out onto the stall. A few bronze coins and a smattering of silver spilled out. 'This is all I have.'

It was barely enough to buy threads of the most common variety, let alone anything interesting. Raim reached into his pockets and added whatever else he had to the pile. The total was still insignificant. Suddenly, spending money on the tyrfish didn't seem that wise at all and made him feel sick to his stomach. He didn't understand. How could Loni have neglected to save for his promise string? He had saved for Tarik, and Raim had seen the pile of money that Loni added to every month for Dharma. Where was his?

Borum's nostrils flared as he stared down at the pile of rust on his stall. 'I . . . see. Well, I'm afraid I'll have to go to my caravan to find something suitable. Nothing on display here is in that range. Forgive me.'

Once Borum's heavy form had lumbered away, Loni answered Raim's unasked question.

'I'm sorry, Raim, but I had to give your money to Yasmin for the memory tea. You know her services are very much in demand . . .'

'But she's my GRANDMOTHER. She took all the money saved for my promise string for what? So that I could have ten seconds of a fuzzy dream? I'm going to be the laughing stock of the Yun with some tatty bit of string to represent me!'

'She came to you as a healer, not your grandmother. If you want to use the skills of a healer, you must pay.'

'That's just it! I didn't want to use her skill for something so unimportant. She came to us, remember? So why do I have to pay for it?'

Before Loni could respond, Borum returned. 'You have two choices, Raim. Brown or brown?' He chuckled. 'I can't face giving my first Yun the worst of my stock. So take this – it is good quality wool from a yak that I haven't had a chance to dye yet. It's not luxury but it is not a disgrace either.'

Raim took the two pieces of rope in his hands and held up the ends. Immediately a warmth spread through his palms. These ropes would tie together the pieces of his soul. And suddenly it didn't matter that it was coarse and undyed; it was his to own. The next day, he would reach Honour Age and be able to pledge himself to the Yun. These would be the threads to do it. He opened his mouth to say thank you, but the words wouldn't come out.

Borum chuckled. 'You are welcome, Raim-en-Yun! And good luck in your duel tomorrow. Although rumour has it that you won't need it.' He winked.

Raim blushed a deep crimson.

Raim was still admiring the length of promise string when they were back at home. Loni had left him with his sister, so he could join in a tournament of a complex tile game with the other elders. He gave them strict instructions not to stay up too long after darkness fell.

There was a steady hum of noise from the thousands of people who were camped around them, but sitting next to Dharma inside their yurt, the low fire warming their hands, Raim felt comfortably alone.

Dharma was weaving again, and the flickering light from the flames illuminated the delicacy of her work in more detail, making it come alive. Dharma was a life-weaver. Instead of using geometric patterns to represent events, she wove people and the scenery itself into her designs. There was no doubt with this kind of work that she would one day be part of the Una tribe of weavers. Raim traced his fingers over the stitches of the mountains. Intricate weavings of Tarik and his bride stood stiffly beneath them.

'Do you miss him?' she asked, continuing her work.

He shrugged. 'We all have our duties. We all have to leave sometime.'

'I'll miss you,' she said. 'When you're Yun.' She bit her lip. 'Look.' She pulled out another loom Raim had never seen before. Somehow she had managed to conceal it from him within her own little saddlebag. She peeled away the thin cotton she had wrapped around it as carefully as if it were made of glass. There were four squares, each a scene that could be added to a carpet. The detail was vivid and lifelike.

'It's a bit early,' she said, eyes sparkling with accomplishment. 'But I wanted to be able to add the squares right away to the present I'm making you, so you can take it with you when you become Yun and you can always remember us. Look, this is you before the fight, in your apprentice clothes. Then here is you defeating Lars.' Sure enough there he was, knee bent and sword lifted in victory stance. The next square was the crowd waiting with baited breath outside the Rentai, while the final, secret test took place inside. It was the one part of the process that Raim didn't understand. No one was allowed to prepare for this test in any way, but also no one in the history of the Yun had ever failed. Still, he didn't want to be the first. The final square depicted the induction ceremony. His new Yun sword leaped off the fabric, Dharma had woven it so beautifully. Somehow she had managed to capture its translucent quality exactly.

'How did you . . . ?'

Dharma reached back inside her leather pouch and pulled out a headscarf made of glittering silver material. Raim recognized it as the only object left to Dharma of her old family. Loni hadn't had the heart to take it from her. There was a tiny ridge running through the otherwise perfectly smoothe fabric, where a thread had been removed. Raim felt the blood rush to his face when he realized what the young girl had done.

'Dharma, this is incredible.'

She cast her eyes down, embarrassed by his flattery.

'You are going to be Yun,' she said, packing the woven story back up. 'It deserved to be special.'

He didn't have time to say thank you. He had been so caught up in Dharma's weaving that he barely even noticed the dull thuds that had drawn closer to the entrance of their yurt with every passing moment, or the shadow that descended on their doorway. Translucent swords massacred the woven entrance and three soldiers, their faces obscured by elaborate masks, clambered into the tent. Dharma let out a scream and Raim leaped to his feet to protect her. But they seized Raim and pinned his arms behind his back, binding his wrists with thick coils of rope, and stuffing a rag in his mouth.

'You should know better than to sit with your back to an entrance,' hissed one of his abductors through the mask.

The last thing he saw before the opaque rattan sack descended over his head were Dharma's wide, brown eyes, filled with fear and hope.

It had begun.

9

When Raim awoke, his body struggled against the ropes while his mind fought to remember how he came to be bound in the first place. The Yun must have drugged the sack they used to carry him from the yurt. He could see nothing, the sack was still covering his head, and the surface he was lying on was hard beneath his spine. He let his muscles relax.

He had only a few moments to collect his thoughts before the sack was brusquely removed. He was lying on a short, low bench, staring directly into the face of Lars, his future opponent. The bonds were cut and Raim sat up, rubbing his wrists to encourage the circulation. Three other boys were recovering from their bondage in much the same manner. Their attention snapped to the three Yun soldiers standing in the centre of the room as one of them spoke: 'Fetch the others.'

It was impossible to tell who was speaking; the Yun still

89

wore their masks of bronzed metal. Yun masks were said to be cast from the face of Malog, the first Yun. The cowardly southern Khan, so the legend went, had mutilated Malog's features but left him alive. After fighting his way back to Darhan, he had commissioned a fierce mask to prove to the world he could never be broken. Whenever he greeted the Khan or attended special functions, he wore the mask. Modern Yun continued this long-standing tradition.

The door opened, and three girls walked into the room, followed by two more Yun. Raim sat up a little straighter as he saw Erdene amongst them.

The Yun removed their masks. All had long hair that fell out of the masks in greasy clumps. The leader's hair was braided, and she was instantly recognizable to Raim as Mhara, his personal mentor, and to the others as the Khan's sworn Protector.

'Apprentices,' she began. 'You are inside the Rentai, where you will spend your last night before the duels begin.' Raim felt her eyes wash over him as she assessed each apprentice in turn. The next Yun stepped forward, a tall, broad man called Silas.

'At this time tomorrow, only four of you will be Yun. And Jendo' – the boy opposite Raim quivered as his name was mentioned – 'this is your third attempt.'

Nothing more needed to be said. Raim glanced over at Erdene. He knew even before yesterday how much she wanted to be Yun; they all did. Her mouth was set in a small, firm line. Jendo's life was Jendo's problem. No mercy would be granted. Still, Raim couldn't help but feel disturbed by Jendo's rapidly paling features. But there was no turning back now.

'Your individual rooms are through the door ahead. Take this time to meditate, compose yourselves, prepare,' Mhara said. 'Just know it will do you no good. If your training is incomplete, or if your opponent has prepared more than you, your fate has already been sealed.'

When the Yun left, Raim thought he could almost open his mouth and taste the tension left behind.

'I'm not staying in here, I'm going to sleep,' said Grinda, the girl Raim knew the least about. She lived on the border of Yelak, the western forest. It was completely opposite to Raim's home terrain, and she had done most of her training away from the main Yun camp. Her decision, however, inspired them all to move. The girls, sticking together in a pack, quickly disappeared out of the room. Raim watched to see if Erdene would glance back, but she didn't. Disappointment slumped his shoulders, but he scolded himself: they all had bigger things to worry about.

Lars stood up and stretched. He was easily the biggest apprentice – the rumours had been right in that aspect, he had definitely bulked up since Raim had last seen him – and he paced the room, full of nervous energy. He kept throwing sideways glances Raim's way, and he knew the assessment was going on in both their heads.

'Cooped up the night before the fight,' Lars said, as if

this were the first time he had gone through this. Raim tried to catch his eye, but Lars avoided him. 'Could be your last night ever, right, Jendo?'

'Shut it, Lars.' Raim jumped to his feet.

'Don't get your tunic in a twist, Raim. I hope you've been practising. We wouldn't want to see Mhara's prodigy get the beating of his life in front of all of Darhan.' He gestured to the two other boys and they followed him out of the door. He paused for a moment. 'Besides, what do you care about old Jendo? Everyone knows you love Erdene.' He rolled his eyes as he said it and disappeared out of the door.

'I don't need your pity,' Jendo said when they were alone. 'Especially not from someone who has no chance of losing. You could smell Lars's fear; he's going to be me next year. But not you. You'll probably be Chief Yun one day. Heck, you're probably already Prince Khareh's Protector and you're not even in the Yun yet.'

'I was just trying to help.'

'Whatever.' He stormed out.

Raim was alone. He debated heading to his room but couldn't bear the thought of being cooped up in one of the cell-like private rooms of the Rentai. So instead, he lay back down on the hard wooden bench and waited for sleep to take him.

It wouldn't that night.

The roar deafened. It reminded Raim of when the wind

picked up over the steppes, churning and spinning into a fearsome tornado. But this was worse. He had never been close to one on the steppes and now his mind was a piece of debris, spinning and shaking, trapped in the centre of the whirlwind.

Raim paced the small room where the apprentices were being kept. He couldn't keep his feet still; excitement, fear, anxiety all coursed through his veins with an icy chill. One moment, he could barely feel his heartbeat, as if his heart had exited his body completely and was waiting to rejoin him after the duel . . . The next moment, his heart was all he could hear, the sound of it hammering in his ears, not allowing him to sit immobile and relaxed, as Mhara had told him to do.

There was an enormous cheer and Raim swung round towards the door, trying to envisage the scene outside. Thirty minutes before, Jendo had sat in the room beside Raim. Now he was out there, battling his fate. Was the cheer for Jendo, or Erdene? Who had won? Was it over? Even more importantly . . . after all this waiting, was it finally Raim's time?

A lid was placed on the sound, shutting it out. Suddenly, the silence terrified him more than the noise. He exchanged glances with the two other apprentices who were confined with him.

A masked Yun entered with a flourish. With two quick snaps, the Yun sent the other apprentices from the room, so only Raim was left. The Yun then stepped back, holding open the heavy curtain. Another strode in, cradling a bundle wrapped in coarse linen and tied at both ends.

'Mhara?' Raim couldn't contain his surprise when his mentor removed her mask.

'I couldn't very well let your Honour Age pass without giving you your gift. Come here.'

Raim quickly moved over to Mhara as she placed the bundle down on a wooden table.

'Give me your shield arm.'

Puzzled, he reached out and leaned his arm against the table. Mhara began to untie the bindings that fastened a thick slab of knife-dented leather to his arm. The band was supposed to serve as a kind of shield. 'This arm band will do you no good in your bout,' she said after she had removed it. He rubbed his forearm, clammy from sweat trapped beneath the band. Uncomfortable as it had been, he felt naked. He had never fought without it.

'This is more appropriate,' she said.

Raim gasped as she revealed his new shield. It was leather again, but of a much finer quality – thicker, tougher; it would sustain more blows. It covered all the way up to his shoulder and was jointed to allow complete freedom of movement. But most impressive were curved hooks of metal that protruded like eagle talons from the forearm piece. The metal claws allowed for more tactics in close combat – blows glanced off and the hooks ensnared skin.

Mhara began to lash the shield to his shoulder. He felt his body warm to it, the leather moulding to his muscle. It felt good. And now he was on a level playing field with Lars, who had also received one on reaching his Honour Age the year before.

When she was finished, she clapped him on his newly leather-bound shoulder and left without saying a word.

He was alone again.

He ran his fingers through his cropped black hair. He would grow it long once he became Yun. He caught sight of the only splash of colour on him: the indigo thread he wore around his wrist. Suddenly unease gripped him and he clasped his hand over the knot. It felt warm to him – too warm, almost burning. He snapped his hand back. It looked normal. He chastised himself for being so foolish. How could it mean anything?

In fact, it was time he lost the bracelet. He had reached his Honour Age now, and whatever the knot's promise had been, it wouldn't matter. His slate was wiped clean. Only now would vows have consequences.

He picked up his sword from the table and slipped the point underneath the thin piece of thread.

But before he could attempt to slice it away, a voice thundered from outside. 'Raim versus Lars.'

Raim swept away the curtain. 'What happened in the Erdene-Jendo match?'

'Erdene will take the final test.'

Raim's heart lifted and dropped at the same time.

He forced himself to remember: Jendo knew the risks.

Within a matter of moments, he was led into the arena. He felt his training take over his mind and body. He clenched and unclenched his fingers in rhythm, loosening the muscles in his arms. There was no more practice, no room for thoughts other than this fight.

As he stepped out into the ring, Naran shining brightly in the sky, all the rabid cheers seemed for him alone. The crowd was twenty-deep all around, kept out of the ring by an enormous circle of young Yun apprentices standing solemnly, hand on hip. Men, women and children hung out over every balcony, every window of the five-storeys-high Palace. He briefly scanned the crowd looking for Loni or Dharma, but it was impossible to make out a single face. The only thing he could identify was the royal box, where he spotted Khareh taking in all the action. The rest was simply a sea of people spread before him, masses of fists pumped in the air. He drank it in; responded with a fist pump of his own.

Lars came out from the opposite end, taller than Raim with features that seemed carved with a sword. His style echoed Khareh's: aggressive and quick. But Raim was ready.

There was no bow or approach. When they entered the match circle, it was time, mimicking real battle. No hand-shake, just charge.

From behind him, a gong resounded, signalling the start.

Lars charged with his sword low to the ground, holding it with both hands. Both their left arms hung heavily under the weight of their Yun shields, but although Raim hadn't had any practice with it, movement came naturally to him.

Adrenaline surged through Raim's muscles and all his senses were heightened. He could feel the tension in his arms, as taut as the string on his bow, ready to spring into action in an instant. This was what he was made to do. He was born a warrior. In that moment, he was intensely focused on his opponent and every second seemed extended in startling clarity. The roar of the crowd, the ringing of the gong, all unnecessary sound died away. He was left with the beating of his heart and the crunch of gravel underfoot as they ran towards each other. The outline of Lars's sword became more defined in his eyes, and Raim noticed a slight tremor in his grip. There was a bead of sweat rolling off his opponent's brow, and the salty tang of fear grew stronger in Raim's nostrils as Lars drew closer. Confidence swelled through Raim's veins to replace the adrenaline. It wasn't arrogance; it was a kind of certainty. A line from one of Mhara's lectures wafted through his mind. 'Duels are won before the first blow is struck,' she had said to him once. He had never understood until now: he knew he was going to win.

Lars swiped upwards, aiming for Raim's stomach. Raim knew the move; it was an attempt at disarmament. He dropped down his shield-arm as Lars's sword lifted and the blade jarred against two of the talons. They held against the force. Raim brought his own sword up against his shield, trapping Lars's blade and then shifted his arm so the sword was locked and Lars's shoulder was twisted awkwardly. Now, it was a battle of strength. Raim bent his knees and anchored into the ground. He had the upper hand.

Lars's face belied the exertion, turning bright red. But it was too much. Raim felt Lars's grip slacken. It was the moment he was waiting for. He immediately dropped his hand, snatching the hilt of Lars's sword as it fell. Now he had both.

Lars fell to his knees and placed his forehead to the ground, arms outstretched, the sign for surrender. Raim stood motionless, swords limp in his hands. He looked down at Lars, his mind racing to catch up with the events that had just unfolded. He raised his eyes skyward, to thank the gods, and in doing so he caught sight of Khareh in the royal balcony, his arms outstretched like he could reach down and hug Raim. Khareh's face lit up into a huge smile and he raised a fist in exultation. Finally joy and relief hit Raim like a tidal wave of emotion, and he found himself grinning back, as wide a grin as he had ever smiled. Then he lifted both swords to the crowd, crossing them like an X above his head, and let the cheers wash over him. Just like that, he had won. He was going to be Yun.

In the upper reaches of the stadium, the echoes from the starting gong were still ringing in the crowd's ears. The duel was over, scarcely before it had even begun.

The party vibrated. Drums and dancers, flutes and flags, chaotic mayhem surrounded the victorious apprentices. Young boys scurried up the long tall poles that lined the streets, the market stalls normally attached to them folded back for the celebration. They used leather straps to tie large bowls to the posts, filled them with dried and tarred grasses and set them alight. Their faces flickered in the fire-light, delighting in the warmth, before they jumped back down into the crowd.

Raim picked Dharma up and twirled her around. She beamed, her smile so infectious Raim felt his own smile stretch from ear to ear. She lightly slapped his shoulder.

'Now I have to take more thread from the scarf to make two swords!' she shouted over the noise. She had the scarf wrapped around her long brown hair. She untied it and threw it around Raim's neck. 'There! You look pretty!'

'Pretty?' Raim scrunched his nose in mock-disgust. 'I'm supposed to be a warrior, not look pretty!' He tickled Dharma's stomach until they both descended into fits of giggles.

'May I take over?'

Raim looked over Dharma's shoulder to see Loni. 'Of course,' he said, and passed her across to him.

As they leaned towards each other, Loni dropped his voice and spoke in a rushed whisper. 'Raim, I have to talk to you about the bracelet. It's urgent.'

Raim felt like rolling his eyes – was it really necessary to discuss the bracelet now, in the middle of a party being thrown in his honour? But the look on his grandfather's face stopped him. Worry – and something deeper than that, something terrifyingly close to fear – was etched all over his features. 'Really?' Raim's voice came out as a whisper too. 'Now?'

'Yes. Come quickly. Yasmin is at the yurt and . . .' Suddenly Loni raised his voice. 'Ah, Prince Khareh, looking for Raim, are you?'

Raim followed the direction of Loni's eyes and whipped round to see Khareh, who stood out from the crowd in his striking red and gold tunic.

'Sacred vow!' Khareh thumped him on the back. 'That must be the fastest Yun win in history!'

Raim forced a smile. 'Well, maybe . . .'

'Of course it was! Everyone is talking about it.' Khareh took his arm and began to lead him away.

Loni interjected, daring even so far as to place a hand on the Prince's sleeve. 'Prince, I beg your indulgence, I must speak to Raim before he goes anywhere.'

Without turning back, Khareh replied, 'No.'

'But—'

Khareh swung round now, his eyes flashing dangerously. He kept one hand on Raim's arm so Raim couldn't do anything but shake his head vigorously in warning. 'I said no! Nothing can be more important than my time with Raimanan, so be gone!'

Khareh was already leading him away from his grand-father, towards the palace. Raim looked over his shoulder, but Loni and Dharma had disappeared. Back to the yurt, Raim knew. He had to get back there; the anxiety in his grandfather's voice only added to the urgency. But for now, Khareh demanded his attention.

'You completely destroyed Lars. Didn't even give him a chance! I must have taught you that move.' The crowd parted for them as they meandered up the gold-edged staircase. 'Don't give me that look, you know I did.'

A goblet of bright-red liquid was pressed into his hands as he entered the palace, and Raim took a deep swig. The atmosphere was calmer inside than out, but it was just as crowded. They mingled with the nobility who con-gratulated Raim as he passed them by. Even Xal, Lars's father and warlord of Zalinzar, offered his congratulations. 'It seems my son still has a lot to learn.'

Raim just nodded.

'I knew he hadn't trained hard enough. It was a most embarrassing show on his part. Rest assured he will be punished. Still, your display was most impressive,' he finished, before bowing his head to Khareh and moving on.

Khareh beamed like a proud father.

Raim wasn't sure whether it was the excitement, the drink, or both, but when a group of girls waved him over, he felt himself gravitate towards them. Khareh grabbed his arm.

'Not yet, battle spear. You'll have plenty of time for that later.'

When they stepped out onto the balcony, they had a complete view of the revellers. Khareh swept his arm out over the crowd dramatically.

'That's all for you, you know.'

Raim rolled his eyes, drained his glass. His head buzzed. He looked into the bottom of the empty goblet, wondering what had been in it. He turned his back on the city. 'It's for all four of us. And it's the only day we all get to enjoy ourselves for a long time. And you're keeping me in here, away from all the fun.'

'No.' Khareh's voice was firm. 'It's for you. There hasn't been a Yun like you in living memory, that's why.' He paused once again, for added drama. 'I need you to swear to be my Protector.'

'You want me to make an Absolute Vow *now*?'

Khareh had never looked more serious. 'Yes, why not? I'm going to be Khan, and I want you there with me.' There was a hard edge to his voice. 'You will do it, right? I will have no one but you. I want the best.' He held out his own thread of blood-red wool.

'Of course.' Raim inserted as much confidence into his voice as possible. He fumbled with the string-belt around his waist and removed it. It felt odd to no longer be wearing it, especially as he had only chosen it the day previously. It would take the entire length of one thread for them to complete the knot that would seal his Absolute

Vow. It was the kind of promise that made you forgo all others.

Raim unravelled the rope to create one long line and handed it to Khareh. Raim watched as Khareh slowly wound the two threads together and Khareh's blood-red thread intertwined with his own. Even though Khareh's was made of the most expensive, finely spun wool from a rare mountain goat and his was spun from the backside of a yak, when they were bound together they became equally magnificent and important. Once Khareh had come to the end of the threads' length, he held one end loosely in his hand, and offered the other end to Raim. Raim gripped his hand as if they were about to start an arm wrestle. Instead, Khareh began the vows.

'Raim, do you promise to protect me, Khareh, future Khan of Darhan, against all threats, dedicating your life to my service above all, even your love for your family, until your death?'

It was a ritual they had both prepared for. Despite his mind's cloudiness, it performed as it was trained.

'No. You have that with my entrance into the Yun. That does not deserve an Absolute Vow.'

'Ah, but you must serve me above your Yun obligations, following my directions over theirs.'

'No, you have this as my Khan. I will not make an Absolute Vow over something so self evident.'

As they drew closer to the conclusion, Raim felt Khareh's nails draw blood on the back of his hand.

'Then you will promise me that should you fail and I die, you must pursue my murderers with single-minded intensity. Once that is accomplished, or should I die of natural causes, then you will kill yourself as your life shall serve no purpose without me in it.'

'I promise. My word and my life are yours. This is my Absolute Vow.' They completed the vow and pulled the knot tight.

A bolt of energy quaked through them, dragging them both to their knees.

Somewhere, a woman screamed. It was the worst noise Raim had ever heard, a high-pitched screech that rang in his ears and made him shudder with fear. His hand jumped to his blade, ready to fight. It sounded like a woman being tortured, being burned alive or flayed. And just as abruptly, it stopped. Raim spun round and looked down from the balcony ledge into the crowd below, his eyes scanning for evidence of a woman in distress. But everyone mingled as normal, as if no woman had been screaming her lungs out. He glanced up at the other balconies, to see if she was inside the palace, but he could see no one. He turned back and stared wide-eyed at Khareh.

'Did you not just hear that? We should call the guards . . .'

'Hear what, Raimanan?'

'That woman screaming!'

But Khareh wasn't really listening – his focus was on the

knot in Raim's right hand, and as he stared a huge grin spread across his face. Raim looked down too. The two strings, Khareh's red and his brown, were knotted together, a knot and a promise he would carry with him for the rest of his life. Khareh then caught his eye, and the smile shifted to his wry grin of amusement.

'I didn't hear anyone scream. Maybe you've had a bit too much Rago wine. Wait here. I have a surprise for you,' Khareh said. 'I think you'll like it.' He winked and then disappeared through the curtain.

The fabric parted again, but it wasn't Khareh this time; it was Erdene.

Wafts of her perfume reached him first, spice and flowery sweetness sending the blood racing through his veins. She was wearing her dress clothes, silky folds of white winking beneath a soft brown dress as she moved. Raim's eyes barely flickered over her outfit before she lifted her veil and he was stunned by her eyes.

'Oh,' she said, and he was startled by the acidity in her voice, the disappointment in her eyes. 'I thought you were the Prince . . . never mind.'

'Not this time, Erdene.' But he was too happy to see her to be upset. 'Well done with your duel, by the way.'

To his relief, she smiled. 'You too. I hate all this garb,' she said, irritated as her veil blew back into her thick eyelashes.

While she was distracted, he tried to stow the Absolute Vow knot away in his tunic until he had time to make it into something wearable. She noticed, and darted forward, grabbing his right hand and opening his palm so the whole newly formed knot, with the shock of royal colour twisting through it, was visible in all its glory. Raim blushed a deep crimson, a mixture of pride and apprehension as the magnitude of his promise became more and more apparent.

Erdene gasped. 'Khareh chose you already? I knew you two were close, I knew you were the most likely candidate but . . .'

'But I'm not even officially Yun yet? But he's not even the Khan?' he finished. 'I know. Keep it quiet until tomorrow, please?' He attempted once again to cover it, but she held his arm firm. He shivered as her fingers traced the knot in his palm.

'It's beautiful,' she whispered. 'And it suits you.'

Raim suddenly felt dizzy. The places where she was touching him burned like fire, his mouth went dry and his eyes refused to blink.

For a moment, Erdene's eyes opened wide, and her pupils grew to islands in a milky white sea.

'You will be Chief Yun.'

He nodded. She caught him in the upward motion, pressing her lips against his. Her mouth was full, wet and salty, tasting of olives and cinnamon.

He felt like he was suspended, like the only things stopping him from tumbling over the edge of a precipice were her lips. When she reached her hands around his neck, he put his own on her waist, struggling to get a grip on the silky material.

Her fingers fumbled with the ties that held together his tunic. She kissed the corner of his mouth, continued down the side of his neck. He was out of himself, out of his body, ecstatic.

There was a hesitation, then a sharp intake of breath that expelled itself as a scream. Raim came crashing down to earth. He looked down.

The sleeve of his left arm was on fire and the flames had caught hold of the hem of Erdene's tunic. She jumped back and slapped at the flames and they went out quickly.

Raim fell with his arm against the wall, trying to quench the fire. But it wouldn't go out. It wouldn't go out and soon his whole arm was consumed with flames. And yet he could feel no pain. The flames travelled up his arm to his shoulder before fizzling out in a curved wisp of grey smoke.

But the fire had left its mark. There, seared into his left wrist, was the mark of a broken promise, blood-red and hideous. Staring at Erdene's appalled face, her mouth twisted in disgust, he could see the horror of the taboo as clearly as if it were inked on her forehead.

But there was no shadow. They both stood in paralysed silence, waiting for the shadow to appear. But it did not come. He was not fully Chauk yet. Maybe there was still time. His sleeve was ash on the ground so he grabbed Dharma's scarf from his neck and threw it over his wrist.

Erdene didn't know, couldn't know, that he was ignorant of the promise's origin. She only saw the evidence of the greatest Darhanian taboo. She stared at his wrist as if the mark was still right in front of her eyes instead of hidden beneath the scarf.

He stepped forward, but she recoiled.

'Erdene . . .'

'What . . . what was that?' She was backing away.

He grabbed her wrist. 'Please, tell no one! There's no shadow, that means . . .'

She wasn't listening to him. 'It was red . . . a scar . . . I saw it.' She looked up at him, 'What does that mean? I must . . . I have to go.' She tried to wrench away from his grip.

Raim was desperate now. He could tell Erdene was going to straight to the Yun and all would be ruined. But he just needed time! Time to get to his grandfather. What was it his grandfather had said? *Raim, I have to talk to you about your bracelet.* His bracelet. This was what Loni had wanted to warn him about. Yasmin must've known that he couldn't make another promise – that he was already bound. *But to what? To whom?*

He had to discover the promise behind the scar and try to keep it, or else seek the person who forced the promise on him and get them to forgive the burden. He had just become of Honour Age today. His promise to Khareh was to be his first and his last. None of this was supposed to happen. Maybe Loni knew how to solve it? He had to find out before Erdene told the Yun.

His fingers still clutching her wrist, he brought his right hand up so that his new promise-knot to Khareh was in her line of sight. 'You see this?' he said, shaking the knot in front of her. She bit down on her lip. 'You know what this means. It means I will be Chief Yun.'

Understanding flashed through Erdene's eyes. When the time came, Raim would have great influence over where Erdene was placed in Darhan. He could keep her close to her homeland. He could elevate her to a position of immense power. Her hesitation inspired him. Seeing that she understood, he pressed on. 'Please, tell me you won't say anything.'

Her eyes narrowed, but she nodded.

He tried his luck. 'Promise me.'

This time she did wrench away. 'What right do you have to speak of promises?' She spun round, her hair whipping his cheek.

Bile rose in Raim's throat as he realized what she thought of him – of what everyone would soon think of him. He choked it back. 'Erdene, wait!' But she was gone. Raim sped out of the room after her, frantically looking down each end of the hallway, trying to catch up with her, or – failing that – to get to Loni.

Khareh's knot hung heavily in his hand, hidden inside the sleeve of his tunic. The knot he would have sealed visible in his Yun sword, like Mhara. He had waited his whole life for this moment and he wasn't going to let some meaningless vow wreck his initiation into the Yun. He had to get rid of the scar before it truly came back to haunt him.

He swept out of the doors, trying to retrace the path Khareh had taken him down, and then he hurtled at almost full speed down the stairs into the crowd. He almost cried out in relief when he saw Loni waiting for him at the bottom of the stairs. He caught Loni's eye and saw his grandfather turn from stern to worried to frightened – and Raim knew he must look a panicked mess.

'Grandfather, I—'

'Don't explain now. Quick, come with me.'

But it was already too late. Raim's sharp eyes spotted figures moving at the outer edge of the crowd – figures moving with purpose. Yun. They were coming for him. Erdene had sounded the alarm.

'Over here!' Loni pulled him sideways, towards another exit that was as yet free of guards.

'Halt!' A plain-clothed reveller swept his cloak back to reveal a translucent sword pointed directly at Raim. 'You are under arrest as a suspected oathbreaker.'

Raim sank to his knees in shame, unable to stop the tremors from racking his body.

10

Regular soldiers had dragged him from the party – none of the Yun would touch him and taint themselves by their interaction with an oathbreaker. They paraded him in front of the entire party, through the streets from the palace, and then threw him in a dark, damp cell beneath the Rentai. From hero to traitor, in one fell swoop.

All for a promise he didn't even know he had made.

Someone had to understand. He just needed a moment to explain. He knew his pleas would fall on deaf ears to the soldiers, but if he could speak to Mhara . . . he could tell her the truth. Panic rose in his chest, causing him to choke down air, as his mind considered the alternatives. What if Mhara wouldn't listen? What if they sent him into exile? He wasn't an oathbreaker. The panic threatened to engulf him – he felt his vision close, his heart pounding in his chest, his palms slick with sweat. *He wasn't an oathbreaker.* He clung to that thought like the reins of a runaway horse, desperate to bring the situation back under his control.

Some of Yasmin's meditation tricks came back to him as he tried to keep himself from panic. He needed to be sound of mind in case they came to question him. He closed his eyes and concentrated on feeling every muscle from his toes to his forehead. He focused on his breathing, trying to slow it down as much as possible. When he finished he felt better, calmer, ready to defend himself against the unjust accusations. His Absolute Vow knot to Khareh was still hidden in his tunic. He tied it in a loop and hung it around his neck. That would show them he still had oaths to keep.

The bolt on his door opened with a clank and an imposing hooded figure entered the room, features obscured by shadow. The figure lowered her hood. It was Mhara.

Her face and neck were drenched in sweat; Raim could see the outline of moisture on her tunic. He had been relieved to see her; now he was afraid. Her eyes were narrow; there was none of the kindred affection he was used to receiving from her. Now there was just anger – anger and something else, something unreadable.

'Tell me it isn't true, Raim.' But she didn't wait for him to reply. She strode across the room, dragged him to his feet by grabbing his sleeve and threw him out of the door. When they were in the hallway, she spun a knife out from under her uniform and sliced through Dharma's scarf so that the silvery fabric fluttered to the ground in two pieces. The crimson scar lay beneath.

She screamed in anguish at the sight of the hidden mark, the sounds from her lips foreign, feverish and incomprehensible. Her knife clattered against the ground; the metallic jolt seemed to right her senses. Raim scooped the pieces of scarf up from the ground. Holding them comforted him.

'You have to run.'

'But—'

'No buts, Raim! You don't understand what you have done! How could you? You were the Yun's hope, the future . . . I've distracted the guards, but not for long. You must go.' She shoved him down the hallway.

Out of sheer instinct and frustration, he shoved her back. 'I can't leave, Mhara. That would mean I couldn't join the Yun! I've dreamed about it my whole life! Not to mention the Absolute Vow I made to Khareh.' He grabbed at the knot around his neck. 'Don't you get it? I'm his Protector. I'm the Khan's Protector.'

'No.'

'No? What do you mean, "no"? Can't you see this knot?'

'I see the knot, but you will not be the Khan's Protector. Khareh will not be the Khan.'

'What?' The question came spitting out of Raim's mouth. It was the most venomous thing Mhara had ever said to him.

But Mhara just looked exasperated. 'They were going to make the announcement today, when all the new Yun had been initiated. The Khan's wife, the Seer-Queen, is pregnant! The child will be the Khan. Not Khareh.'

Raim stared at her in disbelief. 'It . . . it doesn't matter!' he said, more brazenly than he felt. 'I am still Khareh's Protector for life. I have made the vow. Whatever this stupid scar on my wrist means, I don't care. I don't even know what it's for! This is not supposed to happen! I'm not going back on my word to Khareh.'

Mhara just shook her head. 'They'll kill you. Look at the scar. Whatever promise you made then, was so you could have no other duty in life, not Yun, not Khareh's Protector, not even a lowly soldier, not anything. If you stay here, you die. Your only chance is to run.'

'But where?' Raim spluttered, the magnitude of her suggestion overwhelming him. 'And why would they kill me?'

'Don't you see? Your final test is to see whether you are free to promise yourself to the service of the Yun. How can you promise us anything when you have this scar?' She held up his wrist. 'And surely no one is stupid enough to make a promise without knowing exactly what it is and what the obligations are. They see that scar? They will kill you. You are unfit.'

'But I still have time to work out what the promise is! I don't have a shadow yet. If I leave now, without word to Khareh, I will be breaking my vow to him. Then there will be no chance for redemption. I will be cursed. I will be as good as—'

'Chauk,' she finished for him. 'You must go to Lazar. It is the only place left for you.'

'No! I would rather die. I will go back in the cell right now, give myself up.' He tried to storm past her.

She slapped him across the face. 'Don't be so stupid! If you truly do not know the promise you broke to form that scar, then Lazar is the only place where you might find answers to fix it. Don't you see that? Go now. Don't stop. Don't talk to anyone. Don't trust anyone. Run to the desert. Find the Chauk. It is your only chance.'

Raim pounded the stone wall with his fist in anguish, his cheek stinging. 'Fine.' He took a breath, and then bolted with her down the hallway. She stopped at the end of the corridor, her shoulders drooping out of what he hoped was relief.

'Go. I must return and face my own fate for helping you.'

Raim's eyes widened. 'Why did you help me? I know you have been my mentor, but you are Yun first – you are even the Khan's Protector. I am not worth losing that to you, am I?'

'No, you are not. I have fulfilled my own burden. I wish never to see you again Raim. This revelation hurts me more than you shall ever know. You are not dead, but you are not welcome here. You are as good as Chauk. And that, as you well know, is nothing.'

She spun on her heel and took off back down the corridor, her hard-toed boots clattering against the stone.

Raim ran. There was nothing else he could do.

11

Raim hurtled out of the Rentai, out into a city teeming with festival revellers. He stuck to the shadows, the darkness concealing his far-too-recognizable silhouette. He took refuge behind a cloth banner, which hung from a tall window, the knotted symbol on the flag of Batar-Khan looking down on him like an eye judging his escape. He said a quick prayer of forgiveness to Sola, then gave the banner a sharp tug, sending it tumbling to his feet. He threw it around his shoulders and over his head, using it to pass through the throng of people undetected.

He heard his name several times, and resisted the urge to look the speakers in the eye – despite the spurious gossip being tossed around. 'I heard from my uncle, who was inside the palace, that Raim promised himself to two warlords other than the Prince – can you believe it? That's why he has been exiled.'

'So greedy for power.'

'I hear he's been an oathbreaker all along, and only pretended to be eligible to join the Yun.'

'They say he's jealous of the Prince, and tried to kill him! Thank the gods he'll be in Sola's hands soon, the traitor.'

Raim gritted his teeth, put his head down and surged through the crowd, refusing to halt until he came to a hole in the dust-and-stone walls of the city's perimeter. He imagined the eyes of the Yun on his back, and the Rentai's tiered rooftops looming ominously behind him like a monstrous multi-winged bird. He pushed himself through the crack and darted through the maze of tents.

He ran, his feet pounding against the ground, past old men smoking pipes, past boys stoking the fires and girls drawing pictures in the ground with long twigs. One of the girls recognized him; he was surprised more people didn't after all the attention that had been showered on him over the past twenty-four hours. She shouted his name, but he ignored her and ducked and swerved between the yurts until he reached the edge of the camp, almost completely out of breath. He pressed down on his knees, unable to move. He had to decide where to go. No matter how insistent Mhara was, he couldn't go to the desert. He had to go somewhere he could solve his puzzle, his mystery. He needed to get back to Loni, but their yurt was on the other side of the city and that would be the first place the Yun would look. He had to keep moving forward.

He thought of the corrals, where the horses were fenced in. He was very close to them; already the stench of dried grass and manure grew stronger. If he could steal a horse, he could move a lot faster. Of course, if – when – they pursued him, most of the Yun would be on horseback.

When he reached the corrals, there was someone already there waiting for him.

'Where is your shadow? Where is it?' Khareh had madness in his eyes, and he launched himself off the fence and onto Raim, his fists flying. One caught Raim on the cheek, and sent him hurtling to the ground, too shocked to try and block the blow. Khareh fell on top of him, pinning him down.

'Khareh, no! I haven't betrayed you!' Raim said. He couldn't let his friend think that. He struggled to free himself from Khareh's grip, but he only held on tighter.

'But the scar!'

Raim could feel Khareh's gaze burning through the material on his arm. 'Yes, yes, there's a scar. But it's not from my vow to you! Look. Look around my neck. That's my promise to you – it is still intact.'

There was a long moment of hesitation, then Khareh sat back, freeing Raim's arms. Raim quickly reached into his tunic and pulled out his promise vow to Khareh. 'See?'

Khareh rolled off Raim and sat on the floor. Then he burst out laughing.

'I thought you had betrayed me, Raim. Gods, I was so angry.' He jumped up to his feet and extended a hand to

Raim. Full of relief that his friend believed him, Raim clasped it eagerly, and allowed himself to be pulled upright. 'You are the only person I trust – you're still my Protector, right?'

'Always,' said Raim, deadly serious.

'Good, because I need your help. The sage from the desert has revealed to me the first step to becoming a sage myself, but it's . . . unpleasant. First though, tell me everything. How can we fix this?'

Raim slumped against the fence, and ran a hand over his closely shaven head. 'Mhara said that the Yun want to kill me. The final test is making sure the apprentice is free to join the Yun, with no prior oaths that would make Yun induction impossible – becoming your Protector is obviously allowed, as that doesn't interfere with the Yun. But you know that bracelet . . . the one I used to say was a good luck charm from Dharma?'

Khareh nodded, his expression sombre now.

'It must have held another vow, a vow I made before I can remember.'

'But you have no shadow! That must mean something.'

'I know . . . but I have the scar. That is enough for the Yun. They believe the scar renders any vow I make after that invalid.'

His voice was barely a whisper. 'So does that make your vow to me invalid?'

'No, Khareh, no! I will always be your Protector – for life, like I promised. Look, surely the fact that I have no shadow means I'm not fully Chauk yet. I just need to find my grandfather. Help me get to him. He will know what to do. I just need time – time to find the person who I made this promise to and have them forgive it.' Raim looked into Khareh's eyes and saw the conflict that was raging there – the doubt mixed with the desire to trust. He knew Khareh so well . . . so well that he knew he would have great difficulty in trusting someone branded as an oathbreaker. If the situation were reversed, Raim wasn't sure he could overcome it. But this was Khareh. This was his best friend. If his *best friend* couldn't believe him, who would? He waited, to see if the tide would change. Then, there it was: the shift.

There was a look in Khareh's eye, a small, unreadable sparkle. 'I will give you more than time. I will help you.'

Raim hesitated. 'No – you should stay out of this . . . you should stay away from me, for now.'

'Don't be stupid. You'll never be able to do this by yourself. Maybe the Protected has to save the Protector sometimes. I tell you what, make me promise you something.'

'Khareh, I would never make you do that. I am a wanted man, a dead man. You don't want to make a promise to me.'

'I really want to help you, Raim. And this will prove my loyalty to you, just like you have proved your loyalty to me.'

The emotions of the past hour caught up with Raim all at once. His face burning, he turned away, so Khareh wouldn't catch the tears of anguish that were rolling down his face. He wiped them away brusquely. 'How have I proved my loyalty? By as good as breaking my promise to you?'

'No!' Khareh's shout shocked Raim. 'Look at your promise knot. It's not broken. You are still my Protector. I believe you. You won't have to go to Lazar. I have a plan. First, let me promise something to you. Anything, but make it a big one, make it important.'

There was only one promise Raim could think of. 'Khareh, promise me that you will take care of Dharma. The Moloti will be shamed by my apparent betrayal. All they will know is that I was arrested by the Yun . . . they won't understand. Protect her.'

Without hesitation, Khareh slapped Raim on the shoulder. 'Done. I promise.'

Raim removed the second length of promise string from around his waist. It felt strange to have used up so much of the string already. And the one knot he had expected to make today – the one to join the Yun – he would never be able to. Khareh tied his string to Raim's and sealed his promise of protection within the knot. 'Now here's the plan,' Khareh said, brimming with excitement. 'Take my horse, Garna, and ride her west to the monastery at Pennar. I can hide you there and we can figure out how to contact your

121

grandfather. It will all be fine. You can trust me.'

A blast from a horn, devastatingly close, made them both jump. Khareh pushed Raim towards his horse. 'Wait, do you have your dagger?' Khareh asked. Raim nodded. 'Quick, slash me with it. Don't be a fool, they'll never believe me if I'm unharmed, they know we're best friends. I'll say you attacked me, and then they'll believe me. I'll send them in the other direction.' For the second time he said, 'Trust me.' Raim hesitated for an instant, then gave him a quick, shallow cut on his forehead, where the wound would bleed the most. Khareh instantly looked a mess.

Raim grimaced as the red wound opened. 'That's the second time I've hurt you today.'

He had ridden Garna many times before. She was a beautiful beast, and unusually fast for a Darhanian horse. Darhanians didn't need horses for speed, but for strength and stamina. Now Raim was glad that Khareh always pushed to be different, however impractical. He lowered his voice, muttering softly, but she was comfortable with him and let him approach her. There was no time to saddle or even bridle her. Grabbing hold of her mane, he whispered a few words in her ear and mounted with a leg-up from Khareh.

'Vows speed,' he heard Khareh say as he dug his heels into Garna's flank.

Looking back, he saw the city disappear before his

eyes, along with all the family he had ever known and the dream of joining the Yun that he had harboured his entire life.

All because of one hidden, seemingly unkeepable, promise.

12

The miles flew past beneath Garna's hooves as she thundered across the steppe. For the first time, Raim cursed the flat and interminable terrain of his homeland. He couldn't believe that the Yun would be fooled by Khareh's deception for long. He was sure they would see him, or the great clouds of dust Garna was leaving behind her. He imagined every gust of wind blowing them closer, but whenever he looked back, he could see nothing following him but the ever-growing darkness.

Though she was fast, Garna could not gallop for ever and even before the sun had set Raim realized he could push her no further, especially without any nourishment. They were still a long way from Pennar, at least a day's ride if Raim kept his course straight. But if the Yun were to come they would take the straightest course, to warn the people along the path of a fugitive – a vow-fugitive at that, and the first ever Yun apprentice to be outcast before the final test. He remembered when his tribe had come across a man hiding from his destiny with the Chauk. The man had been stoned to death without mercy.

No, Raim would need to take a different road and avoid the well-trodden routes.

His stomach grumbled. With the fear subsiding, he was suddenly reminded that he had left Kharein without any kind of provisions. The clothes on his back stank of sweat and dirt from the ride, and his legs ached from straddling Garna bareback. His first priority had to be finding water and food, and then they would both be ready to make the final push towards Pennar. Along their current path there was no water source, but Raim knew that a freshwater tributary from the River Iod ran to the south of them, and came up the underside of an ancient monastery. All along there grew the wild vines of Raga, where he was sure they would find berries to eat.

He hopped down off Garna's back and rubbed her muzzle. Her deep black coat was covered in foamy white sweat.

'C'mon girl, let's get you some water.'

He reached down and pulled up some brush from the ground, careful to preserve the roots. He dragged it along the ground behind the two of them, trying to obscure their prints, which ran deep in the soil. Now that they were moving slowly, they had to be extra careful.

They walked for an hour, and when the darkness finally caught up with them it swallowed them whole. As he waited for his eyes to adjust to the night, he followed the sound of water, which grew louder with every step. At the edge of the river he collapsed, his knees sinking into the mud. The water ran fresh and cool over his cupped hands and he took several long draughts to refresh himself. Garna took her cue and jumped in, sending water showering over Raim.

'Hey, you!' He jumped in after her and put his hand around her neck, swimming with her and edging her on gently until they reached the other riverbank. He knew he had to keep going, without pause, if he was to make it to the sanctuary in time to cover his tracks.

The air around him was thick and pungent with the aroma of fruit, and Raim's mouth watered. The vines of Rago grew some of the most delicious berries in Darhan. They were often pressed and fermented to create wine, but all the tribes who stopped here on their journeys took advantage of eating the fruit raw, a delicacy found nowhere else. The berry could not be transported; it rotted only hours after being released from the vine. The ground beneath his feet was ankle deep in the decaying fruit, and he sighed. He wished he had chosen a food source that lasted longer.

The sharp end of a twig nicked his face as he pushed his way through the thickly tangled vines, and to punish the branch he chose its berries to feast on. He passed the largest bunch to Garna, who devoured the rare treat. It was the least he could do, for putting the innocent mare in so much danger and for pushing her so hard for the past few hours. He coaxed her onwards with more berries, but suddenly she refused to go further.

'What is it, Garna?' Even in the dark, he could see the whites of her eyes. 'It's all right,' he whispered, trying to sound reassured. He couldn't allow her to bolt now; he still needed her. 'We'll go another way. Let me just check things out.' He wasn't sure whether horses could sense intention or not, but she seemed to understand that he wasn't pressuring her to go onwards. She took steps back, while Raim cautiously pressed on. The vines were sealed across his passage, so densely packed they were like a wall. He took his dagger out of his boot and sliced away the branches that were at eye level. All he could see beyond was darkness, but the way seemed clear of more vines. He pushed the blade down the rest of the way, thankful for the Yun workmanship that made the edge slide through the vines like butter. He took a step forward.

The ground crumbled beneath his feet. Instinctively he groped for the vines, catching onto them with both hands. They snapped and he slid, the vines shuddering in his arms until finally they caught and held above him. The dagger clattered down into the black abyss. He hung there, in shock. Blood trickled down his arms from where the branches slashed his palms. He took in two deep breaths and gently pulled on the vine he held in his right hand. It seemed to be holding. He put his foot out and felt rock. He realized he could balance on it, if he was careful.

He used the rock as a ledge to lift his left hand up above his right and pulled with all his might. When he crawled over the edge again, Garna was lying down, looking at him with sleepy eyes.

'Yeah,' he said. 'I guess you told me so.' He sat down next to her but immediately regretted it, as exhaustion overwhelmed his body. He manoeuvred so that his legs hung over the edge of the cliff he had just discovered, forced by his training to always face his fear. There was no discernable landscape. It was as if he sat on the edge of the world, looking out into a starless universe. Even the air was still, like it too was playing hide and seek with Raim's senses. He suddenly felt his heart and throat close, claustrophobic in the dark. He leaned back against Garna's flank, his head rising and falling in time with her deep, even breathing.

He sat bolt upright. The back of his head was wet and sticky and when he reached behind he pulled leaves and thick clumps of seed out of his hair. He wondered how long he had been asleep, for though the darkness didn't seem any lighter he felt uncomfortably refreshed, as if he had rested for a long time. Too long for a man on the run. Garna was nowhere to be seen. He whispered her name tentatively.

There was noise, but it wasn't from any horse or other animal. There were human voices amongst the rustling of the vines and the sound of running water. Raim froze, squatting frog-like facing the tangled vines, his back to the abyss. He listened.

'Where?' The voice, a man's, was to his left.

'Further.' The voice, a woman's, was closer and almost directly in front of him, along the line he and Garna had entered. Raim took two small steps backward and felt the vines press and release against his back, where hours before he had cut them. His muscles tightened, remembering the steep drop that he would encounter if he retreated further. The voices became clearer. It hadn't taken the Yun long to track him down after all.

'I came as soon as I got the message you had caught the horse.'

'She emerged out of these vines.'

'Have you found trace of him? What if he abandoned the horse? Let us move away from here, get closer to Pennar.'

There was silence for a few brief moments. The woman's last words resounded in his head. *Pennar. How did they know?*

'Here is a trace. Blood. He must have passed through here.'

They were so close. There was no time to ponder over what they knew about his plans, or how they knew it. The vines to the left of him shuddered, and he knew what force was moving them. He slipped further backward, under the edge of the vines, his toes creeping over the precipice first. He lowered his feet until they found footing on a ledge and his body reluctantly followed suit, stopping when only his fingertips gripped the cliff's edge. He prayed he had been quiet enough.

His nose was pressed tightly against the rock and he breathed in dust and soil. Pebbles bounced over his head as the Yun drew close to the edge.

'An apprentice blade worked on this vine. Look at the smooth edges. He must be around here somewhere.' The man spat, and Raim felt the moisture settle on his fingertips. 'Traitor.' He took a step forward, but the woman stopped him abruptly.

'The vines of Rago obscure the edge of the stone cliffs,' she said, and as she spoke her foot came down hard on Raim's fingers. He winced, and prepared for capture. But she continued to speak. 'It is impossible to go further. He did not pass this way.'

The man's voice was gruff and insistent. 'But what if he descended? Should we not pursue him?'

'At the base of these cliffs begins the Sola desert. If he went down, there is no way to get up again, and he will perish under Naran. Nevertheless, we will post guards all the way along these cliffs from here to Pennar. If the Prince has informed us correctly, we will be watching from every direction. The traitor betrayed and was betrayed. There is no place for him here, no Darhanian will harbour him, no city or monastery will be safe for him. We will find him. And if he is already running across the sands of Sola, then so much better that death will be for him than if he stayed.' And Raim suddenly recognized the woman's voice. It was Mhara. And Mhara was not speaking to her Yun companion, but directly to him. She took a step back; he felt her weight lift off his fingers.

He thought of the promise-knot to Khareh around his neck. His promise was to defend Khareh, and Khareh's honour, even against the head of the Yun. Even against his mentor. This was his first challenge.

How did the Yun know about Pennar? Had they tortured Khareh? The thought was impossible. He was still royalty. Maybe they coerced it out of him. Memory tea?

'Let's keep moving then,' said the deeper voice.

'You go on ahead,' said Mhara. 'I want to examine this path more.'

Heavy steps moved away and when he could hear the man no more, Raim gritted his teeth and pushed up over the edge.

Mhara was standing with her back to him, her bow curving across her spine like a snake. 'It's not true,' he said, his hands curled into tight fists.

'Don't be a fool, of course it is,' she said, turning to face him.

'Tell me how you found out about Pennar!' He tried to keep his voice steady, but it broke with his desperation.

Her eyes held no pity, only anger at his stubborn refusal to believe. 'Khareh told us. You mean nothing to him.'

Raim heard a voice in his head: *She insults me. Don't allow her.* He knew at once it was the promise. He wondered how anyone at all could break a vow, not with their voice, the person's voice, in their head all the time, a constant presence. Khareh's voice was saying: *This is part of your vow to me, to defend me against anything, even words.* Meanwhile, Mhara still spoke. 'Go to Lazar!' she hissed. 'Don't you understand? Khareh betrayed you!'

'You lie!' *Get to Pennar,* he told himself. *Get to Pennar, get to Khareh, he will put things right.* He charged forward into the vines. Lightning fast, she was at him then, preventing his movement, her talon-like fingernails digging into his biceps.

'You go there, you die. There is nothing I can do to stop that. Khareh cannot help you with this. You must go to Lazar.'

'There, you said it. There is nothing you can do. Leave me be.' He shrugged her off, but Mhara groped for him again, trying to shake some sense into him. 'Get away from me!' He shoved her away.

The vines deceived both of them. Neither fully realized how close they were to the edge, how nothing lay beyond the edge of Mhara's boot but open air and a fierce drop. The force of Raim's shove didn't send Mhara aside, as he had intended, but backward. Her shoulder pressed up against the vines, and for a moment it looked as if she would be caught there, in that safety net of green. But the vines gave way, sliced neatly hours before by Raim's blade. Her foot lost its hold. Her mouth gaped in horror.

Raim screamed her name and grabbed for her uniform.

But the heavy sword at her side and the bow on her back unbalanced her further. Gravity took hold and pulled her into the darkness. Mhara was an inch from his fingers before he could see her no more.

'MHARA!' he cried again. He stared into the void and could see nothing. Hear nothing.

Jaw set, his limbs trembling, he crawled backward over the cliff, his feet searching for a ledge. He needed to find her. He needed to find out if she was still alive, to help her. And then he would fulfil her request – he couldn't rely on Khareh being able to help him. He would exile himself into the desert. He would become Chauk: the most hated and vilified of people.

PART TWO

PART TWO

13

After he had dropped down from the last hold at the very bottom of the cliff, he touched the sand, and immediately started searching for Mhara.

He found his dagger first. The red gem embedded in the handle glinted in the light of the desert moon, revealing it lodged in a crevice between two rocks. Somehow, the blade hadn't shattered. He silently praised the Yun craftsmanship, and then quickly put it away beneath his robes before it reminded him too much of all he had lost. He dropped to the sand, his knees slowly sinking into the soft surface. 'Please,' he prayed to Sola harder than he ever had before. 'Let her be alive. I would do anything to find her alive.' The adrenaline that he had been carrying with him since his climb down was slowly ebbing away, his mind pushing hard against the creeping advances of despair. But the dagger sparked an ember of hope in his heart that he would find her.

He redoubled his efforts. The darkness made it almost impossible, but if he could find her now there might still be a chance . . .

Hours passed, and the first rays of sunlight spread rapidly across the sky. As the cliffs around him brightened, he could see just how huge they really were. There was no way for him to climb back up; the fact that he had come down without breaking his neck he attributed to adrenaline-fuelled luck. He retraced his steps to where he had landed and searched again in all the places he had looked the previous night, in case the dark had obscured any clues. But every rock he shifted seemed to add to the weight in the pit of his stomach. He knew now that he was searching for Mhara's body – there was no way anyone could survive a fall from that height. Still, he scoured the edge of the rock. He dug in mysterious mounds in the sand. He tried to search for a ledge where her body might have landed, but he could see nothing.

He clenched his fists hard, but still his eyes filled with tears that stung and blurred his vision. Mhara was gone. The greatest Yun, teacher, person he had ever known would not even be able to receive the proper burial rites she deserved. Raim raged against the gods. Why had they taken her in such a degrading manner? Mhara deserved to die on the battlefield, surrounded by glory. He picked up one of the rocks he had shifted and hurled it at the cliff wall. It bounced off without even leaving a chip, so hard and impenetrable was the stone. And as angry as he was with the gods, he was stricken with grief and guilt and fury with his own actions.

I killed her. And there is no way to make it right.

Had he just followed Mhara's instructions from the beginning, she would still be alive. But it was his pride. It was his knot. It was his promise to defend Khareh. Mhara had tried to convince him that Khareh was treacherous, but he was duty bound to defend Khareh's honour. Was that not justification enough? Well, he had done his job. He had protected Khareh, and at the ultimate cost. Now he would honour his mentor by obeying her final command.

You must go to Lazar.

He turned round to face the desert, and the immensity of it almost overwhelmed him. East and west, and as far into the horizon as he could see, dunes dominated the landscape, rolling and churning like a thunderous sky crashed onto the ground.

He took his first hesitant step forward.

A few minutes after he had made his decision, he regretted it, but by then he had already crossed over the first hill of sand and could see nothing else but the slippery, shifting golden ground. And going back would deny what he knew he deserved. He deserved this exile, now more than ever. He had no idea how to find the Chauk. All he knew was that he had to walk – and whether his feet led him to Lazar or to death, the gods would decide.

It shouldn't have felt as hard as it did. After all, Raim had spent his whole life walking. If he started counting from the time he first stumbled across a thick red and blue piled carpet and into Loni's arms, he must have walked the length of Darhan ten times over. It was the Darhanian way. Each tribe walked from one pasture to the next, following the turning of the seasons and the whims of the cattle and the goats. As goatherders, Raim's tribe were nomads who put the needs of their animals before their own. Other tribes, he knew, might follow the rivers, watching for the telltale flicker of silver and gold amidst the translucent ripples that would indicate a large flock of salmon or tyrfish fit for eating. Yet, as random and unsystematic as their wanderings might seem to the untrained observer, they were as predictable as the rising of the sun and the moon. The elders called Naran, the sun, the greatest nomad in the sky, constantly wandering, cycling and searching for the ripest pasture for her herd, the Darhanian people.

But the sand was unlike any surface he had ever walked on. It seemed to defy him at every step. Each grain slipped out from underneath his boots. He slid and stumbled, discovered muscles on the insides of his legs that he had never used before. The sun that had once been so predictable and friendly to him now beat down relentlessly on his back. Every ray was a searing knife.

Raim's life had been like one long march, with his feet as his principal companions. So when they finally gave out from under him it was in shock and in tears that he fell to the ground.

He felt so weak, with his knees buckled underneath him and his face in his hands. His head was bare and open to the sky. Summoning some strength, he took the left sleeve of his tunic in his teeth and pulled. The material ripped and he tied it over his head and down across his brow, to try to shield his head and eyes from the worst of the sun. At least now he could see without squinting. His legs had taken him down the path of least resistance, but he saw he had travelled halfway into a deep valley between two mountains of sand.

A few of the Rago berries from last night were stuffed deep into his pocket, and the deep-purple juices had dyed the bottom of his tunic and smelled foul. He took two out, held his nose and squeezed what was left of the juice into his parched mouth. The liquid stung his tongue and scratched the back of his throat, as if the droplets were covered in tiny spikes. Instinctively he spat the disgusting juice into the sand. He watched as the sand drank the moisture up greedily, and for a brief moment turned purple, then gold again, as if nothing had ever happened. He missed the saliva the moment it left his mouth and felt jealous of the sand. He popped the wrung out flesh of the berry into his mouth and savoured the coolness preserved within its skin, trying to ignore the taste. He had to press his hand over his mouth to keep his stomach from rejecting it.

Feeling slightly better nourished, he decided to work his way back up to the top of the dune. If there was any hope of finding the Chauk, he knew he would have to keep himself at the highest vantage point possible.

Last night, he believed the desert to be lifeless and still. He couldn't have been more wrong. While it was true that Raim hadn't seen a plant or animal since he left the cliff, the desert seemed to possess a life force of its own. It shifted before his eyes. Whenever he glanced behind him, the scenery looked different from how he remembered it; he could never find his way back. His footprints seemed deep and well-defined when he made them, but by the time he took five steps forward the first footprint had disappeared. He could feel the wind whipping low against his ankles, and sometimes the sand flew up into his face and eyes. Every orifice was filled with sand, even the gaps between his teeth and the tear ducts at the edge of his heavy eyelids.

There was another nagging feeling too, growing stronger by the moment. Thirst. He wondered how the Chauk found water in this desert.

He kept aiming higher, keeping himself motivated by thinking that the next sandbank would offer a better view than before. The next one loomed before him like a giant pyramid and the line he was following was as thin and sharp as a knife blade. He moved as if in a dream. Slow and languid, his feet dragged in the sand. He was grateful for the feeling of heaviness. If he had been any lighter, he was sure he would be unable to anchor himself against the sliding dune. Yet, as he neared the top, the weather turned against him. The wind, bored now of breezing around his ankles, howled about his ears and shook him from his heat-induced stupor. It attacked him like a wild animal, and he tried to beat back the air with his arms, but it kept coming even stronger. It pushed him to his knees. Slowly, he began to slide down the side of the sand-mountain he had struggled so hard to climb. He threw his arms up towards the summit and clawed at the peak, trying to find something to grab onto. But it was as futile as grasping at air. He continued to slide – and when his arms gave up he started to tumble – all the way to the bottom.

His head thundered against the ground and Raim felt like he'd been hit with the hilt of a sword. He had fallen so that he lay on his back, his eyes tightly shut to avoid looking at the sun. He clutched his left arm to his chest. It was raw and bleeding. His arm had been bare to the sun's rays since he ripped the sleeve to protect his head but now it blistered and oozed, the burn wounds ripped open by the fall and now full of sand, which stung like salt. It was then that he realized he was crying, and he cursed the salty tears for stinging his arm and for wasting the precious water inside his body, which he feared might be all the water he would ever have again.

Raim awoke feeling exhausted. The sun was no longer visible in the sky, hidden by the massive mounds of sand that rose up on either side of him. He knew the sun, now his newest and most oppressive enemy, was still there somewhere, for the sky was light above him. It was impossible to tell if it was rising or setting.

Sitting up, sand tumbled off his torso in thick streams. It blanketed his legs and feet so thoroughly that only the tips of his thick black boots were visible. If he hadn't been so deathly tired he would have been frightened by how little the sand seemed to care for his existence. It would have swallowed him up whole, burying him beneath millions of tiny granules, preserving his body in suffocating, everlasting sleep. Slowly he shook the desert from the rest of his body. For one more day, he would fight becoming a feast for the sand.

He set his hands behind his back to boost himself to his feet but he yelped out loud as if bitten by a snake. The shock was not from a bite, though, but from cold. Half-hidden in the sand, his hand had touched a warped black iron pot. As he lifted it out it was easy to see why it had been thrown away. Sand poured through the cracks in its base like a waterfall.

A spark, a flash of life pinched the base of his spine, sending tremors through his desert-weary limbs. He had no idea how long the pot had lain there, but it gave him hope that someone had passed this way recently. He leaped up, but his legs refused to cooperate and he resorted to scrambling on his hands and knees.

It became clear as he crawled further that the sky was darkening, the sun setting, and Raim would soon have to make a pivotal decision. Adrenaline was fuelling his move-ments now, every pace strengthened by this sign of human life. The darkness and relative cool of the night would make travelling easier, and he would be able to move faster and further. But he risked losing the potential trail to other humans that he had only discovered by the light of day.

There was an even more pressing problem. The back of his mind buzzed and he felt a dull thud of pain, beating like a ritual song behind his ears. His fingers trembled, half from total lack of control and half from the knowledge of the terrible pain still to come.

The last time he had experienced the paralysing effect of a soli, a heat-induced headache, he had been just a small boy, and his grandmother had been there to comfort him. It had been one of the rare times she had wrapped her arms around him, soft and firm – a touch of maternal comfort most Darhan children were denied. He yearned for that now.

'Open your eyes.' He heard her voice. His eyes had been squeezed tightly shut against the pain. And there she was in front of him, her robe shimmering in the heat. She reached up and massaged the creases out of his temple.

He relaxed into her embrace. 'Grandmother . . .'

She lowered her hands and used her fingertips to prise open his clenched fists. In the centre of his right palm lay a simple white flower; it seemed to have appeared by magic.

'Eat,' Yasmin said. The petals were soft and fleshy, and

edged with silver. Jarumba flower; the best cure for a soli. He put the flower in his mouth and bit down.

But his teeth clashed together and in a flash the illusion was gone, his grandmother nowhere to be found. A mirage.

Raim kicked into the sand, the tricks of the desert adding to his frustration. Why hadn't his grandmother warned him about this? She was a medicine woman, a herb gatherer, a healer, a shaman! Her skills were renowned in all of Darhan, and she had had his whole lifetime to solve the puzzle of his secret promise. She should have known the Yun would not accept him if he had made another vow. But she had not warned him, and because of it he was now wandering, alone, in the most terrible place on the planet. How could he be punished so hard for a promise he hadn't known that he'd made?

The memory – and the pain – prompted him to move. He resolved to crawl forward until either the sun or the sand or the monsters took him. Tales of the weird and unimaginable creatures that dwelled in the desert were rampant in Darhan. Most centred on the vicious biting flies that hovered like living rain clouds over the sand. He knew these were no fantasy, if only because he had seen the evidence himself after a small swarm of flies had attacked a tribe while they were travelling through the southeast region of Darhan. An entire herd of goats had perished as a result of the bites while the herdspeople fled to safety. Raim's tribe had visited the scene shortly after, with the royal family. It could have been a herd of elephants that had trampled through that place, not simply a swarm of flies. The Khan's advisers had been at a loss as to how the flies had travelled so far north. They eventually came to the consensus that the foul winds had brought them.

Other tales of the desert were more fanciful – just old men's stories, or so he thought, until passing over the next dune brought him face to face with the skeleton of a great snake, the bones bleached white by the sun. The enormous spine curved round and round in a massive spiral. He hoped he would only encounter a skeleton and not the living, breathing beast. Suddenly, he realized that if giant snakes were real, then all the old desert myths could be true: like the birds that buried themselves underground and attacked good men's promise-knots if they inadvertently wandered into the desert – although how anyone could accidentally find themselves in Sola was a mystery to Raim – or like the patches of sink sand that would swallow a man whole and drown him before he could think to cry for help.

More frightening than any reptile or bird was the sound that suddenly swept high above his head, as if it were leaping from sand peak to sand peak while Raim was down in the valley. It was a voice – a human voice – but instead of hope, the memory of a thousand ugly stories of the savage people of the desert surged through his mind. Suddenly he wasn't sure if he wanted to be found by men who might drink his blood to quench their thirst or use his skin as shelter from the sun – perhaps death was a better option after all. He shook his head violently, trying to shed the fears. He thought back to his Yun training. He could defend himself if the need arose.

Raim took a deep breath and remained as still as possible, trying to decipher the origin of the words. They weren't in a tongue he recognized, though that still didn't rule the speakers out as Yun warriors sent to find him. He felt a pang in his heart. He should have been experiencing his first few days as fully fledged Yun, alongside Erdene. They would have been together more now – he wondered if she would have accepted his request for them to be partners, as well as comrades-in-arms. But then he remembered the look on her face when she had seen that it was him on the balcony, not Khareh. The disappointment. Even before the disgust of the scar, she hadn't wanted him. The realization stung, but he pushed it to the back of his mind. It didn't matter now, anyway. He was alone, in exile, instead – able to think of nothing but how to survive.

Night falls quickly in the desert, and as he had lain there listening to the voices, the last vestiges of daylight had disappeared, as if absorbed by the shifting sands. He crawled sideways up the sandbank in the darkness to prevent himself sliding all the way back down again. When he reached the top he lay down flat on his stomach and peered over the other side.

The voices were even less distinct now that he had climbed the dune but, as he soon deduced, it was because the speakers were on the move. Raim would not have seen them at all as the moonless night made for pitch-black darkness, were it not for the tiny, bobbing specks of light suspended above them. Even then, there was no sign of the person holding the lantern, until the moment when the light dipped low enough to outline a grey, hooded figure.

There were two of them, and they were moving fast. They weren't Yun either – of that Raim was sure. They were Alashan, the nomadic desert people. His mind told him to wait, to evaluate. These were dangerous people: violent and wild, uncultivated and utterly divorced from civilization. Even the Chauk were said to have some kind of organization, some history, some kind of community, however repulsive. These people were feral, and every ounce of good sense in Raim's body screamed at him to avoid them at all costs.

But, as seasoned desert dwellers, they would have water, and other means of survival. For the Alashan not only survived, but thrived in the desert, and if Raim wanted to do the same he would have to learn from them. He swallowed hard, almost gagging halfway through the motion, controlling himself only by slapping his hands over his mouth. His tongue felt like sandpaper; every taste bud was a thorn scraping the back of his throat, the roof of his mouth. He was parched. If he wanted water, he would have to go and get it. Even if it was from the most dangerous men and women on the planet.

14

The moment he found the container of water, its inconspicuous brown leather spout poking through the sand, he pounced on it like a wildcat and bit open the seal with his back teeth. He had been tracking the Alashan pair for the better part of the night and his weak limbs were wracked with shivers. Approaching them seemed reckless, and he couldn't think of a way to make an appearance without getting himself killed. So he followed behind, picking up occasional scraps that they dropped as they moved along.

The first gulp of water was painful, but delicious, sending his impossibly weak body into ripples of shock that nearly left him unconscious. He momentarily lost control of his fingers and lips, so the water poured continuously into his mouth and dribbled out, running down his chin and soaking his shirt. When he regained control he forced himself to take it slow, to conserve more. Despite himself, he took another sip. The temptation was just too great.

The improbability of the Alashan abandoning an entire container full of water did not strike him until it was too late. He wondered if he was suffering from a second wave of heat exhaustion. The tips of his fingers began to droop of their own accord, like wax dripping down a candle. The feeling trickled along his arms, loosening the joints. But as his knees buckled and all the muscles in his face slackened, he knew it was much more than simple tiredness. He had been poisoned.

Only seconds later and he was flat on the ground, his temple throbbing from where he flopped sideways – paralysed. His tongue fought to prise a gap between his lips, but they were sealed shut. His eyes and eyelids were the only external parts of his body that could move. He could feel his body try to tremble, but nothing happened.

A shadow crossed over his forehead and he rolled his eyes to the back of his head. A gaunt face, thin and hollow as a skeleton, peered down at him.

'*Genar – aik be maudin, cliq cliq.*'

It was clear the man was speaking to him, but Raim didn't understand a word. The phrase was repeated, louder, by another voice. Raim couldn't see the other speaker.

They continued talking for several minutes in a clipped and confusing speech, the tone flat and repetitive. The vibrations from the low tones in their voices reverberated through his paralysed limbs. But he wasn't immobile for long. The two men grabbed him – one by the feet and the other by the head – and carried him brusquely down the dune. At the bottom they forced more liquid down his throat and he dropped with a thud into unconsciousness.

The little finger on his left hand spasmed, but he stilled the rest of his body before it could give away any sign he was waking up. He kept his breathing in the slow, shallow rhythm of sleep. That much Mhara had drilled into him until it became instinctive; the seconds between his waking up and the Alashan noticing were the only opportunity he might have to gain some sort of advantage over his captors. She had been gone only a day but already she was saving his life.

Feel. Listen. Wait. Her words. Mhara had never exactly been expansive in her instructions, never saying more than she needed to.

Feel. Rope. Well-worn by the sense of it, with plenty of scratchy fibres grating against the skin of his wrists. Behind him was a sturdy wooden stake, taller than his head, but misshapen slightly so that a twist of wood pressed against his spine between his shoulder blades. His wrists were bound around it, and his legs tied in front. He pressed his tongue against the gag in his mouth. That was the loosest bond, and he could feel the fabric give against the pressure. Not enough, though. Not nearly enough.

Listen. He heard nothing. Not the footsteps of a nearby guard or the anxious whisperings of his captors. Not a breath of wind or a bird cawing overhead.

Wait. This was the hardest part. The silence bothered

him the most. What if they had left him here, to waste away the night, attempting escape only to roast in the sun the next morning? *Mhara, help me! What should I do now?* But her voice would only ever be heard in his memory, and she would never teach him anything new again. He wasn't ready for this. His learning wouldn't have ended once he had become Yun. When training became action – that was when he was supposed to grow the most.

Wait. But he couldn't wait any more. *I'm so sorry Mhara, I have failed you again.* He opened his eyes.

The sun was low in the sky again; he didn't know how long he had been unconscious for. As his sight adjusted, it seemed as though rocks surrounded him. Dark grey mounds littered the area. It wasn't until one of them got up and slapped him in the face that he realized they were actually people.

Four of the grey mounds got up and joined the one in front of him. Then, one by one, they spoke to him in the same strange tongue. Every time they had all had a turn to say their piece, the first would start again, but louder and more insistent. Eventually one of them leaned forward and ripped the gag out of his mouth.

Raim glared, with all the intensity he could muster. The five men were equal to him, though. They sat staring for what seemed to him like hours. Finally, he gave in.

'I can't understand you.'

A man to the far right made the slightest nod and the man directly in front of him removed his dark grey hood.

Except, as long dark hair and delicate features soon made obvious to Raim, 'he' was a woman – a young one, at that. Raim had never heard a girl with so deep a voice. She spoke to him in his own tongue, and her voice seemed more normal – though it was still laced with the deeper reverberations of the original language.

'Darhanian, yes?'

He remained still.

She laughed. 'Of course you are, look at you, your fat little body so unused to the heat, your fair skin so red in the sun. You are not the runaway we were looking for – we should have known, no Alashan would allow himself to be so desperate as to drink water from an unknown source. You were desperate. That's why we caught you, silly Darhanian.'

Raim felt his mouth gape open, but he closed it quickly, the corners still stinging from the gag. 'Fat' and 'fair' were not two words he would normally use to describe himself, but he couldn't deny his origins.

'You are not Alashan,' she repeated, even more amused by Raim's reaction, 'but clearly you are not Chauk, either. There is no shadow around you.' For the first time, confusion showed in her face, in a delicate twitch of her forehead.

Another of the Alashan snapped a sharp word, and the confusion on the girl's face disappeared. 'There is no other reason to enter the desert. You must have a death wish. We can quite easily fulfil that for you.' She took her time in running her slender fingers over the edge of her hood and pulled it back over her head. As her face descended into darkness, like all the others, there was a flash of silver in her palm, the edge of a sharp blade, and Raim felt his heart almost stop in his chest.

'No, wait!' A knife was already at his throat by the time the words had left his mouth. He was sure that had one of the others not raised a finger by the tiniest of increments, he would already be dead. These people were impatient. 'I am looking for the city of exiles . . . for Lazar.'

She narrowed her eyes, studying him closely. 'We grant free passage to the Chauk to reach Lazar, but to no others . . .'

Maybe it would be easier if the Alashan just made his decision for him and ended it right now. But no, he owed Mhara more than that. He owed Khareh more than that. He wouldn't go down without a fight. He struggled with renewed ferocity against his bindings, the stake tilting forward through his exertion. He twisted the bindings around his wrists, pushed up against the sand with his feet, tried anything to gain some sort of purchase against the ground. It wasn't working, although the Alashan were strangely quiet despite his protest. Instead, they were pointing at him. He looked down, and saw that in his struggles, the ugly red scar on his wrist winked its presence between the gaps in the rope bindings.

'You see?' Raim said. 'I . . .' The next words stuck in his throat. 'I am an oathbreaker.' Even as he said the words, the revulsion shuddered through his body. *No, I'm not!* he wanted to shout, but what good would it do him? He only hoped that would be enough to convince them to bring him safely to Lazar, and out of this desert.

All eyes were on the scar for a brief moment before a high-pitched whistle disturbed them. Another grey-clad figure – Raim was unsure whether man or woman – sped towards the five in council around him. The person spoke hurriedly in their language, making blatant gestures to the sky behind Raim.

He craned his neck to try to see the cause of the commotion. At first he could see nothing but pitch-black sky and stars that seemed to melt into the sand at the horizon. But just inside the edge of his peripheral vision he saw a place where the stars were beginning to distort and blur, as if a heavenly veil covered them.

Raim could tell by the Alashan's reaction that they thought this no divine gift. There was immediate movement all around him; every previously stationary grey mound now alive. The knife-wielding girl slid the ominous blade neatly into a hidden sheath and abandoned him to join the fray. Anyone whose face was uncovered quickly hid it again beneath the impossibly long grey hoods. They didn't hide their faces fast enough, however, for Raim to miss the expression of extreme anxiety on every one.

A neat line was quick to form, and when all but the council members had joined it they began their move forward. Then the council started leaving.

'Wait!' Raim beat his bound feet against the ground and cried out, but the word wouldn't come, only a desperate croak, his voice run ragged over the dryness of his throat. He would rather face the edge of a sword than whatever in the desert that was making even the ferocious Alashan run. He seemed to have caught their attention, for two of them stopped and started arguing. One of them was the girl with the knife.

They spoke loudly, but since he couldn't understand them Raim tried to focus on the hand gestures. They each used their hands very expressively, manipulating and bending their wrists and fingers in smooth motions. He wondered if the hand signals helped to interpret the speech, just as Khareh had said. All the words that they were saying sounded so similar to each other; he was amazed they were making any conversation at all. It sounded like they were just repeating one word back at each other time and time again. The unknown figure seemed to want him to die in the desert. He kept pointing at him, and then running a forefinger menacingly across his throat. The girl put her hands together, as if in prayer, and then separated them over her head like she was drawing a huge cup with the sides of her hands. Raim hoped it was the symbol for water, like the girl was praying for the man to take him with them, and give him a drink – though unpoisoned this time.

His heart sank when they both began to walk towards him, anticipating the worst. As they approached, the torch that the unknown one carried dipped low and Raim saw it was one of the older men. When they got close enough, the girl put her hand around Raim's throat and pressed his head hard into the wooden stake.

'I wanted to leave you here,' she said, directly in his ear. Her breath was dusty and close up Raim could see her teeth were small and white. She applied pressure to his Adam's apple, coming close, but not completely closing his airway. He gasped for air. 'I wanted to see the desert swallow you up. But this man, Mesan, he knows something of the significance of this.' She lifted up his wrist, which Mesan had untied from around the post. 'He thinks you should be allowed to travel with us to Lazar, despite your lack of shadow. I hope this isn't some kind of trick, but trust me, if you cross us you will find that being buried alive by the sand is a much sweeter fate than what I will have in store for you.'

. The man undid the rest of his shackles and Raim rubbed his raw wrists – the one with the burn in utter agony. By the time he staggered to his feet, the two had hurried off to join the others, fast disappearing. He took a stumbling step forward. He was so weak.

The girl looked back, once. And over the flat expanse of the sand, her voice carried: 'Run or die, little fat one.'

Run or die.

Run and have water. Run and find the way to Lazar.

Raim forced the last of his energy to his legs . . . and he ran.

15

Once he had caught up with the Alashan, he had expected to be bound again, but instead the man called Mesan had given him a spare grey cloak to throw over his shoulders. Raim supposed that by now there was no chance of escape, and besides, he had lost the inclination to run away. Just being around people, savage or not, felt like a blessing, and they hadn't tried to drink his blood yet. Raim looked back over his shoulder at the changing horizon. The mist over the stars had grown and parts of the sky were completely dark, as if someone had blotted the tiny lights out with a thick rubbing of coal.

He turned to join the Alashan, but the knife-girl was in front of him, blocking his path. 'You cannot walk with us.'

Raim frowned. 'But Mesan . . .'

'Mesan allowed you to travel with us to Lazar. He did not permit you to walk with us. No.' She took Raim by the shoulders and pivoted him round. 'No, you must walk

with your kind. With the other disgusting oathbreakers.'
She gave him a shove and walked away.

At first, Raim thought the girl was crazy. There was no
one else there except the group he was walking with. But
then, as the lights carried by the Alashan faded away and
his eyes adjusted to the complete darkness, he saw movement. Ten figures were moving towards him, five wearing
the grey hoods of the Alashan, five who were bare-headed.
These must be the Chauk.

Raim prepared for the tidal wave of revulsion he would
feel at the sight of the shadows they must all bear, but to
his surprise he didn't see any shadows at all. He breathed a
sigh of relief – although that meant the oathbreakers were
still to come.

The first man to reach him spoke. 'Don't worry, they
won't lose us, although it may seem like they try. But they
won't take you to Lazar.'

'What do you mean? Why not?' He started to walk
beside the man, but stumbled, weak with hunger.

'Here,' said the man. 'Eat this. It will help with the
weakness.' He pressed a small piece of hard root into
Raim's hand.

One of the bare-headed men swooped down on them
and surprised Raim so much he dropped the root. The
man was shouting, raging at the other: 'Dirty, rotten
scoundrel! Good-for-nothing scum, don't seek to make
friends; you are the lowest of the low, the vilest creature in
the world . . .'

As the man's tirade raged on, the one receiving it seemed unfazed. He simply bent down, plucked the root from the sand, brushed it off and handed it back to Raim. 'There you go. A bit gritty, but then you had better get used to that. Everything you eat in Sola's fair country will come with a side dish of sand. Just keep chewing it slowly,' he instructed.

Desperate for any food, no matter how unappetizing, Raim popped the root in his mouth. The sand squeaked as it caught between his teeth but the overwhelming sensation was one of relief – the root's hard shell gave way to a wave of nourishment inside. Raim felt stronger immediately.

Still the offender's tirade went on. 'Foul man, you should wish you had never been born, hideous spawn of the devil.'

'My name is Ryopi,' the first man said, his hand on his chest.

'You don't deserve your name any more,' said the ranting man, 'you disgusting, worthless soul.'

'Um . . . I'm Raim,' he replied to Ryopi, nervously eyeing the other.

Ryopi looked from Raim to his taunter and his left eye twitched. 'You can see him ranting away at me? So you are one of us. I had my doubts for a second. Where's yours?'

'Where's my what?'

'Your haunt. This charming fellow is my father's haunt.'

'I don't know what you're talking about.' Raim was

about to ask why the man was so angry but thought better of it. 'Why doesn't your father wear a hood?'

Ryopi grinned with all his teeth, but it set Raim on edge rather than at ease. 'He's not my father. He's my father's *haunt*. When I broke my vow to my father, his spirit appeared to punish me. Now he is here, every day, to remind me of my transgression.'

The root in Raim's mouth suddenly tasted like a rotten Rago berry, and his stomach churned with fear. 'But you have no shadow?'

'Of course I do. My father's haunt is my shadow. What did you think a shadow was? Not the same thing you saw when you broke a promise before your Honour Age, oh no. When you break a true oath, the shadow is the spirit of the person you broke your vow to, haunting you every day for the rest of your life. And if you can see and hear him and not just a shadow, then that means you are an oathbreaker too.' He swept his arm around at the others in the group, and suddenly Raim could see that all those not wearing hoods were haunts, tormenting their charges with words and gestures. 'They promised us all they would take us to Lazar. And look at us. We are still here, wandering this gods-forsaken desert. Maybe for ever.'

Raim took one step back, horrified. 'I'm not like you.' And another step. 'I'm not anything like you. Do you see anyone haunting me? Berating me? I'm going back to the Alashan, they have to see that I'm different.'

Ryopi started laughing – a hideous, shrieking cackle

that only increased as Raim turned his back on the Chauk and half-ran, half-stumbled towards the Alashan.

'Different? All they see is that blood-red scar of yours, oh yes,' Ryopi cried after him. 'Where are you going? Don't you see? You're one of us now!'

16

The ground slowly changed beneath Raim's feet. The sand seemed to clump into little pebbles, as if each individual grain was growing larger. Just as he had become used to walking on a surface that absorbed his movements, now he had to be extra vigilant with his steps so as not to turn his ankle on the loose ground.

A sharp whistle sounded from the front of the group. The Alashan came to a halt, and began to set up camp for the night – or, Raim supposed, for the day, as respite from the boiling sun. Mesan waved him over and handed him a bundle of tightly woven dried grass, wrapped up in a cloth blanket. In small groups of five or six, the Alashan un-ravelled the strips into long rectangles, which they then curved into the walls of a mini-hut. They threw blankets over the top to create a makeshift roof. The huts were clustered together in a large semicircle against the wind.

His bundle was much smaller than the others, clearly meant for one person. He moved to set it up amongst the Alashan, but they turned their backs on him, and whenever he tried to make camp someone would come over and angrily gesture in his face. It didn't take long for him to get the hint.

The Chauk were building their shelters a few hundred feet away from the Alashan. Words of harassment carried over the sand towards him, and he shuddered despite himself. He did not want to camp there.

That was when he saw the girl again. She had dropped her bundle on the outer edge of the Alashan semicircle, slightly apart from the others. She lowered her hood and pulled a long pin out of her hair so that it came loose from a bun. It fell almost halfway down her back in a thick braid. She was striking. As she bent down to begin her work, he could see the strong lines of her profile, the smoothness of her rich, dark skin and the delicate slant of her eyes. For an instant he was reminded of Erdene, and he felt his cheeks burn. The girl was nothing like the hideous, sun-withered Alashan women of old Darhanian stories, though she certainly seemed as strong.

His curiosity piqued, he walked over and began to pitch up next to her. He followed the lead of the others around him, pressing the bottom of the grass mat into the stony ground and piling pebbles around the bottom to secure it.

'What do you think you are doing?' The girl was standing over him.

He quickly stood up and rubbed his hands on the edge of his cloak. 'I'm Raim. Do you mind?'

'Of course I mind. Oathbreakers cannot enter our camp, at the behest of our leader, Old-maa. Set up camp with the rest of the Chauk.'

Raim bristled. 'I am not Chauk. Do you see anything haunting me?'

Her eyes narrowed. 'I see no shadow, true. But you are still an oathbreaker.'

'But I am also an oathkeeper.' He fumbled inside his cloak and pulled Khareh's royal knot out from around his neck. He hoped that the girl would understand what it meant. 'This is an Absolute Vow I made to the Crown Prince of Darhan. It is still intact.'

The girl's eyes studied the knot. 'That means nothing.' She turned away from him.

Raim sighed, and pulled the mat until it was outside the Alashan circle, but not nearly so far away as the Chauk. No man's land. She didn't ask him to move any further, so he took that as a sign and continued to build his shelter. As he was adjusting the blanket over the grass mat, he scraped his uncovered arm against one of the hard stalks. He cried out in pain, the blisters from his sunburn raw and oozing. He made the mistake of touching it where the pain was sharpest, but it only made the agony worse. He ground his teeth together to avoid crying out again. Inside his mouth, the pulpy root released a fraction more nourishment, and allowed him the briefest respite from the pain.

'What are you eating?' The girl was staring at him from behind his shelter. She kept looking over her shoulder, as if nervous one of the Alashan would spot her talking to him.

'I'm not sure . . . one of the Chauk gave it to me.'

'Take it out of your mouth,' she said. In truth, the root had been close to spent for a while now, but he had been loath to take it out lest that be the only food he had for a while. But he wanted to earn the girl's trust. He removed it.

'Now spread the pulp over your blisters. It's medicinal as well as a source of food.'

He did as she bid, and almost immediately the pain from the blisters calmed. Raim watched with intense fascination as the redness faded soon after. 'This is almost as good as jarumba flower.'

The girl looked up at him sharply. 'How do you know about that?'

Raim shrugged. 'My grandmother is a healer . . . well, actually, she's chief of the Otoshi clan of healers, the most prestigious in Darhan. She gave me a jarumba petal once, when I was suffering from a soli. It helped.'

'I see,' said the girl. She seemed almost impressed. 'What you were chewing was the root of a jarumba flower. The roots spread very quickly; alas, the flowers are much rarer. Also, the root can be replanted in the hope that we can grow it again wherever we are.' She turned and pointed at the Alashan camp. 'See there? We use the shelters to

167

store our food and supplies to keep them out of the direct sunlight, rather than as tents. We sleep outside during the daylight hours . . . the cloak Mesan gave you acts as a barrier to the sun. It will be difficult at first, since you must be completely still. And you mustn't eat anything except jarumba root during the day. Eating uses up your water. We will eat now, while there are a few dark hours left.'

He took a piece of dried meat that she offered him, grateful for the small kindness. She smiled over at him for the first time without irony or malice, suddenly seeming very young. It warmed him to think that maybe he was winning her over.

He felt like he could try his luck, now, and keep her talking. 'Where are we?'

'The Western Eye of Sheba.'

Raim raised both his eyebrows and looked around him, suddenly expecting to see a lake and swaying palm trees, but there were just rocks and low-lying brush. 'But I thought that the Eyes of Sheba were supposed to be oases!'

She shrugged. 'Perhaps once. Now it is just a tale that only serves to lure those out into the desert foolish enough to think they can cross it if they pass through the Eyes. They do not realize that the Eyes are worse – just because the sand has changed to rock, doesn't make it less of a desert. You will find as little water here as anywhere in Sola. At least out in the sands you have no hope. If I were you, I would abandon yours.'

There was another sharp whistle from inside the Alashan half-circle, and all heads turned to look at the western horizon. Raim followed their gaze but still could see nothing at all. 'What have we been running from?' he asked.

'A storm. A sand storm.'

'But I've been watching it and it looks so far away. It is only barely visible on the horizon. Surely it's not going to reach us here.'

He expected her to laugh at him for his ignorance, but she remained serious in a quiet, hidden way. 'It is not the storm we are running from. It is what the storm will send our way. We are lucky we spotted it. Often when they come, it is too late. Now, though, it is time for water.' She started moving towards the Alashan, who were gathering together.

'What is your name?' he asked after her.

'Wadi,' she said, without turning round.

He followed her; the mention of water had reminded him of how truly thirsty he was. But as she entered the ring of Alashan shelters, she turned to him and said, 'Stop. Look, I'm sorry but you can't come any closer. You have to stay outside the ring of tents.'

Raim winced, but didn't press his luck. This was his life now: rejected by everyone he came across, unless they were just as degraded as he was. He watched Wadi move towards the far side of the ring where more Alashan were gathering. He walked slowly around the perimeter of the camp, being careful not to pass the designated threshold. Through gaps in the tents, he could see the remnants of more-permanent structures – crumbling stone walls that reached no higher than his knee to which were attached tattered bits of fabric. They seemed almost useless for shelter, more like markers for previous resting places than actual cover.

Strangely, Raim found himself admiring the Alashan and their nomadic lifestyle; it reminded him of home. He was dreading spending the rest of his days in Lazar, chained to a single place, which only added to the horror of being exiled there. The Chauk were too ashamed by their actions to continue living a nomadic lifestyle: nomads were proud, free people, and by breaking their oaths they became so full of guilt they were too heavy to move like free men, and had to spend the rest of their days imprisoned in Lazar. At least, that was what his grandfather had told him. But was that true? So many of the old, deeply ingrained myths and beliefs had been dispelled for him lately, he was no longer sure.

An old woman, her form crooked and bent with age, sat cross-legged, digging a narrow hole in the ground with her index finger. The entire tribe began to gather around her. A man stood next to her with what looked like an extremely long, flexible pole that was folded over in many places. Raim crept closer. The pole was actually a hollow tube of plant stem covered in a kind of glaze.

He desperately wanted to ask Wadi what they were

doing, but instead he relied on craning his neck and standing on his tiptoes for a better look.

'Thank the gods, I was getting thirsty.'

'You don't deserve your water, scum.'

Raim jumped at the sound of Ryopi and his haunt's voices – he hadn't realized the man had come so close. Several of the Alashan noticed, though, and they hissed at Ryopi to move away. He cowered and crept backward until the protests died down.

Curiosity got the better of Raim, and he knew the only way he would get an explanation was by swallowing his pride and standing with Ryopi. 'What do you mean?'

'Ever wondered how the Alashan find water in the desert? Well, you're about to find out. That's the Old-maa right there; she's the Alashan's leader. She might look like an old crone, but don't let appearances fool you.'

Raim couldn't believe it. The ground here was as dry as the sand dunes – Wadi had said as much when she told him to abandon all hope. Gods, Khareh would have done anything to be here, witnessing this. It was one of the greatest mysteries surrounding the Alashan and the great barrier to crossing the desert itself: how do you find water?

The Old-maa detached a brown bag from around her waist and placed it on the ground next to her. She reached inside and pulled out a worm about as long as Raim's hand and as thin as his little finger. The woman held the wriggling thing by the tail and dangled it over a tiny cup of water. Raim gasped as the worm opened its mouth to display rows upon rows of teeth, which it gnashed at the water, just out of its reach. All the Alashan, except the woman holding the worm, dropped their foreheads to the sand in a low bow. Raim quickly followed suit. In unison they spoke a brief prayer, which Ryopi translated for him:

Sita, find your way,
Sita bring us life,
Sita run thy course.

Then Old-maa whipped the cup away and dropped the worm into the tiny hole she had been digging, and plunged the long straw the other man had carried in behind it.

The tube disappeared into the hole, the straw unfolding and unfolding many times over, until there was only an inch of grass visible. The woman lowered her mouth over the opening and drew in a deep breath. The effort pulled the skin even tighter around her gaunt face so that her cheeks almost disappeared beneath the shadows from her brow. When she lifted her head up again she held the worm delicately between her teeth and the opening of the tube was pinched tightly shut between her fingers. The worm's shape had changed drastically. The first of its previously thin and wrinkled segments was now fat and bulbous and it seemed more energetic, thrashing its body around in an effort to break free of the woman's grasp. Deftly, she dropped the worm back into its bag.

Beside Raim, Ryopi let out a long, admiring whistle.

He wasn't the only one – the Alashan looked especially impressed, and Raim saw Wadi clasp her hands together in delight. 'Only one segment, she truly is one of the best,' Ryopi whispered. Raim didn't quite understand, but the action wasn't over around Old-maa.

The man who had previously held the tubing moved first. He unlatched his water skin from around his neck and held it just above the woman's pinched fingers. Old-maa let go and water spouted out of the tubing and into the bottle. Not a drop was lost. In turn all the other Alashan filled up their bottles, the water gushing as if it would never run out. No water ever touched the sand, though. They were far too careful. Raim felt a rush of relief and happiness overwhelm him. He thought he would never have the taste of fresh water again, especially not here, in the desert. The Alashan were miracle workers. He didn't know how the worm found the water, or how the tubing worked, but at that point he couldn't have cared any less. All he wanted was a drink and soon he was going to get it.

After the Alashan had each had some water, Old-maa's piercing gaze turned to the Chauk. Raim stared back at her openly, but Ryopi tugged on his arm and hissed, 'Keep your eyes down. You don't want to miss out on a drink, do you?'

Raim shook his head violently, and cast his eyes to the sand. He got in line behind Ryopi, but the other Chauk kept pushing him out of the way until he was the very last

173

in the line-up. He was the new exile, and even amongst this group that made him the lowest of the low.

And when he shuffled forward for his turn, Old-maa deftly tied the end of the straw and passed it back to her helper to pull out of the hole. She barked at Raim in their strange language, snapped her fingers twice right in his face and then turned to shout at the rest of the tribe. For a moment, Raim was speechless. But thirst drove him to action. 'Please, I need water.'

Wadi stepped forward, and Raim felt relieved. She had helped him with the jarumba root; she knew he needed water desperately. But his relief turned to fear when he looked into her eyes and they had lost all trace of their previous warmth. 'Our leader, Old-maa, has decreed that you have not yet earned your water. She is asking if any are willing to do battle with you. It works like this: you fight one of us and if you survive then you are worthy of help. Since there is debate among us as to your status, and you yourself insist that you are not fully Chauk, you must prove yourself.' Then, she said in both languages: 'I will do it.'

She unbuttoned the clasp at the nape of her neck and let her cloak drop to the ground. She wore loose indigo trousers and a similar-coloured top that wrapped around her torso and her neck, accentuating her broad shoulders. Also around her neck was a pale sand-coloured pendant, the size of Raim's palm. She tucked it beneath the folds of the cloth.

'Don't think because I speak your language that I am any less Alashan,' she said, the challenge in her tone increasing. She pointed to one of the men and signalled an order with her hands. He disappeared for a moment, and then brought back a case with two short daggers in it. Wadi picked them up and spun them in her palms. The moonlight reflected off the metal edges. She thumbed the edges of the blades, then turned and threw one of them at Raim's feet. 'We are seeking an honest fight.' She seemed to repeat the words in her language, as they all nodded slowly in response. 'I am expecting a good one, what with that other knot you showed me.'

Mesan stepped forward, and Raim understood that he was going to adjudicate the fight. He made a motion with his hands that was easy for Raim to interpret. He wanted Raim to remove his shirt and cloak, so that he could battle in proper Alashan style.

Raim hesitated for a moment, but there was more insistent sign language, so he dropped his cloak to the floor and tore off the remnants of his shirt. All of his clothes were ripped and filthy, the complete opposite of the neat Alashan garments.

The only thing left was his Absolute Vow, hanging around his neck, and Dharma's scarf, which was still wrapped tightly around his wrist, covering the scar.

'You can hide it, but we all know what you are.' Wadi's entire face was wrinkled in disgust.

And Raim's inner Yun warrior jumped at this moment

of weakness in his opponent and in a single swift movement he scooped up the blade and lunged for Wadi,
narrowly missing her chest with his swipe. Surprising the
enemy was always an asset. He could sense training in
Wadi too, as her reflexes threw her backward and she
quickly recovered her composure. She tried for intimida-
tion. 'You are exiled from Darhan, but you are not Chauk.
The Alashan will never accept you – you will never
become one of us. You belong nowhere, you are nothing.'

He was unfazed. Mhara had said much worse to him,
and he had been much more in awe of her than of Wadi.
'If I am nothing, then I have nothing to lose.'

Old-maa stopped the talk with an impatient snap, and
they began again. Raim began to sidestep in a circle in the
same counterclockwise direction as Wadi. As he sunk into
his training, his steps grew springy and agile. The circle
grew tighter. When they clashed, Raim knew he was in
his element.

She was strong. The combat was much more physical
than Raim was used to. There were no swords here, no
great stretches of distance between them. Their blades
were each neutralized by the body contact of the other: his
forearm obstructing hers, her wrist smashing against
his chest. She was more skilled in technique than he was,
but his instincts hadn't often failed him in battle.

They reached a stalemate and backed off. The crowd
was energized and Raim could sense the change in atmosphere. The Alashan were realizing that he was a force to be

reckoned with. He wasn't a useless, untrained reject. They must have heard of the Yun; Raim couldn't imagine a part of the world where someone might not know of them. He would show them what a Yun could do, and he would prove to himself what the Yun were missing without him fighting for them.

On the opposite side of the circle, Wadi was being refreshed with water. Sweat glued long strands of black hair to her face and neck, her neat braid a shambles. She took another slug of water and Raim could see the curve of her bicep, the strength beneath her dark skin. Her eyes glinted with fire and her chest rose and fell in quick, sharp movements. She looked wild, her movements unrestrained – it was so different from the Yun way of fighting, which was all about discipline and control. This was raw. Real. Behind him, Mesan took a sip from his own personal water skin and did not offer any to Raim. Now he was reminded again of his other motivation: thirst.

When Wadi approached a second time, she dropped her arms and brought her shoulders back, as if she were relying on her feet rather than her hands. Raim noticed the shift, and when Wadi was close enough he spun the knife blade low to try to nick at her ankles. She jumped back, ready for him. The balls of her feet caught his throat as he rose, sending him flying onto his back. She leaped down onto him, the blade held tightly in her fist. But Raim was also fast. He rolled out of the way, swinging his knife hand around. He felt the blade make contact with her garment.

Once he sensed the resistance he made the extra push and heard the fabric tear. When he hopped up to his feet again, he saw that she had her hand over her stomach. Her fingers were crimson. He had drawn the first blood.

She charged. Raim's nostrils flared as they filled with the strange, sweet smell of her blood and sweat. They were fighting so close together, he no longer had time to think. He just moved, flinging his arms out in every direction to meet hers, unable to make a strategic motion or think a strategic thought. He was so intent on her blade hand, he missed her other sliding up between the action. Then it happened. She shifted so that her foot came down hard on his instep, putting him immediately off balance. Her free hand grabbed his blade arm, twisting it abruptly until he was forced to release the knife. Using her body, she gave him the last push that sent him tumbling backward to the ground while his weapon fell onto the sand. Quick as fire, her foot was on his chest, pinning him to the ground, the tip of her blade against his neck.

The entire world was blotted out to Raim except for Wadi's face, their lips so close he swore they were touching. Then her mouth spread into a huge grin, her eyes glinting with accomplishment.

'You're dead, Raim the oàthbreaker.'

17

There was a scream.

Raim thought it might have been his own voice. He had never felt so doomed in his entire life.

But another scream followed the first, and Raim knew it wasn't him that time. It took him a couple of seconds to realize that the blade against his throat had disappeared. He sat up to the sight of Wadi sprinting back to her hut and clambering inside. The circle was completely abandoned, with Alashan everywhere tossing their possessions and food out of their huts and into the sand to make room for more people.

He felt someone grab his arm. It was Mesan.

Mesan shouted, pulled him again. More indecipherable language. Raim sensed the urgency and scrambled along the sand back to Mesan's hut. There were already five people inside when Mesan crammed himself in and Raim had no idea how they expected him to fit as well.

Mesan was pointing at the sky but Raim could see nothing.

Then he heard it. The droning, he realized, had been there all along, but he and the others had been so involved in the fight that they had missed the first telltale sign. Raim pushed inside, crouching against the edge of the makeshift door – just a length of fabric thrown against the open entrance. The others were huddled under their grey cloaks, pulling the thick material so it covered every inch of their bare skin. There was one young child in the hut with them and his guardian was anxiously tying a scarf around the boy's face and sealing the sleeves shut with a piece of string. Raim looked down at his own, uncovered body and started to panic.

'My cloak!' he said to Mesan, who only stared at him with wide eyes. Raim frantically pointed outside, miming wrapping a cloak around his shoulders. 'I need it.' Raim pulled back the fabric that surrounded the door and peeked outside. The droning was so much louder now. The air was thick with sound. He spied his cloak lying in a crumpled heap about ten feet away from them. Mesan put his hand on Raim's shoulder. But Raim didn't look back. Instead, he bolted forward.

The whole camp was deserted. Everybody was hiding inside the huts and all the entrances were closed off. He sped towards the cloak, picked it up and swung it over his shoulders. He pivoted round, trying to get back to the hut, so agonizingly close.

When the first one hit him in the small of his back, he

felt like a stone had struck him. He stumbled. Another collided with the back of his head. He covered his face with his hands and flopped to the ground as they rained down on him, thousands of furry black pebbles. Then the biting started. He felt the first one sure enough from one of the monsters that had landed on the bare skin on the back of his calf. The pain was immense and his flesh burned as if he was being branded with a hot poker. But after that he could feel no other individual bites. His body felt like it was immersed in fire, the flesh melting in thick strips. Some of the flies crept into his ears, biting at his face and seemingly at his mind. The buzzing consumed his thoughts; the flies were all around him, on every inch of skin. He could feel their legs and pincers prise his lips, trying to get at the soft, moist flesh inside his mouth.

Thought stopped as a bolt of pain cascaded through him, searing agony unlike anything he had ever endured before. There was a tearing, a ripping. It felt like part of his soul was being wrenched away from him and he would never get it back.

And then: a sudden relief around his head. He removed his hands from his eyes and rolled over so he was looking up at the sky. There was a thick swarm around his face. They dived towards him, ugly, angry flying devils, but they were repelled by an invisible force. They couldn't get through. From the neck up he was protected. He thought he saw someone; a face, a body, standing over him, slapping the bugs away. He wondered if he had passed out.

Maybe he was dreaming or hallucinating: he must be, as the person he saw above him was Khareh.

He opened his mouth, but the dream-Khareh spoke first.

'Don't try to speak, or you will die from the effort. Stay still, Raimanan. Your body is working hard enough already. Just think what you want to say, and I will understand.'

First of all, Raim thought, *Thank you.*

'You're welcome.'

Raim felt his mind start and stop as if he were drifting in and out of consciousness. He closed his eyes and when he opened them again, dream-Khareh was still there. He thought, *Are you a dream?*

A chuckle from above him. 'You'll have to figure that one out by yourself.'

The world slowed, the flies floating down and around him like black snowflakes in a buzzing blizzard. His eyes rolled into the back of his head and he saw colours dance before them: greens, blues, reds.

Khareh's voice drifted into the back of his mind and Raim both heard it and felt it, like the sound of his subconscious. 'Hang in there, Raimanan . . .'

Finally, darkness.

When he awoke he was inside a tent, lying flat on his back. The flickering light of a lantern burned his eyes and he quickly shut them again. He ached all over. There was no part of his body that wasn't in pain. He opened his eyes again to a squint, as someone placed a damp cloth on his forehead.

It was Wadi.

He groaned. It was the only sound he could make. His cheeks and tongue were so swollen they seemed to engulf his mouth.

'Don't try to speak,' Wadi said. Raim was instantly reminded of his strange dream. Why had he dreamed of Khareh as his saviour, of all people?

Wadi continued. 'You're even more stupid than I thought . . . stupid, but stubborn. I thought you were dead. We all did. The flies were all over you. The amount of poison that must be in your system . . . The tribe has decided you are Sola blessed, and if Sola wishes to keep you alive, who are we to argue?' She made a clucking sound in the back of her throat. 'Now, drink this.' She forced open his mouth and held his tongue down with her finger. Then she emptied the liquid into his mouth. It burned all the way down his throat, and the added pain caused him to descend once again into oblivion.

He awoke to silence. He raised his tongue gingerly up and down in his mouth and was relieved to find that he could actually move it this time. He sat up. The pain in his palms as he put pressure on them was intense. He looked down at his hands. The ends of his fingers were tied together with thick strips of cloth that were soaked red with blood.

His palms were covered in huge, pus-filled boils. The skin was raw and peeling. He tried to close his fingers into a fist, but the swollen bites prevented much movement. It was the same for the rest of his body.

'Sorry about the bandages.' Wadi entered the hut from the outside. 'We had to tie your fingers up to stop you from scratching. You will have a difficult night tonight. Now that you are conscious, your body will want to rid itself of the poison. You are lucky it did not get to your brain. If they had attacked your face more, you would be dead or mind-lost now. Sola protect you.' She unwrapped his fingers, then offered him a sip of water from her skin.

'So.' The word came out with great difficulty. His throat was so dry. He allowed her to give him more to drink before he continued. 'I guess I earned my water. But I thought I wasn't allowed in the Alashan camp?'

Wadi shrugged. 'As I said before, you are Sola-blessed. The tribe convened, and they agreed that despite your scar, you are not fully Chauk. So until we reach Lazar, you may stay within our camp.'

'What were those things?'

'Behrflies. You've heard of them?'

Raim nodded, and winced at the effort. 'I've never seen them before . . . only what was left of someone after an attack.' He paused, feeling lucky to be alive. He didn't want to think about those flies now. 'How did you learn to fight like that?' he asked as he tentatively leaned back against the bundle of rags that was acting as his pillow.

She smiled. 'You learn things when you have to survive.' She dipped a square of cloth into a shallow bowl of yellow-tinged water and began to dab it on his hands. 'You weren't too bad yourself. Although considering you made a promise to be the next Khan's Protector – and that's supposed to make you one of the best all-round fighters in the world – perhaps your hand-to-hand combat skills could use some work . . .'

'So you do know what my Absolute Vow means. I wasn't sure.'

Wadi pulled a face. 'Just because we live in the desert, doesn't mean we know nothing of the outside world.' Then she relented, letting down slightly more of her guard. 'My mother was Alashan and my father Darhanian. Don't look so shocked, it's a rare joining but it happens! I stayed with my father in Darhan until I was six, as he was too sick to ever join a clan, so I know more about Darhan than most here. And I speak Darhanian, so I supplement my knowledge with bits and pieces from the Chauk we take to Lazar. Of course, most oathbreakers aren't willing to speak of the home they're exiled from.'

She dropped the cloth in the bowl again, and absent-mindedly stroked the edge of the pendant around her neck. 'You're different, though,' she said, and if it hadn't hurt Raim so much he would've smiled at her reluctant admission. 'But not so different that you couldn't get your-self exiled.' Raim winced at that, and it wasn't from the pain. 'What happened?'

Raim stared at his bite-ridden hands. The only place clear of bites was on his scar. He almost laughed. Even the flies were repulsed. 'I genuinely don't know. Ever since I was a baby, I wore this stupid bracelet with a knot in it. I knew it was a promise-knot, but it was made before my Honour Age, so it shouldn't have meant anything, right?'

Wadi nodded.

'Well . . . turns out it did mean something. And when I made a promise to my best friend, the future Khan, whatever promise I'd made before, I broke. And for that, for my ignorance, I got this. Exile.'

Wadi swallowed hard, and a little crease formed in the centre of her brow.

'I know it's a lot to take in, but it's true. I'm not an oath-breaker. At least – not that I know of. And it's even worse that I don't have a shadow. Maybe if I had a shadow, I could at least figure out who the promise was made to. But no.'

'But why Lazar? Why go there if you think you're not an oathbreaker?'

'Mhara. She's no longer the Khan's Protector.' Raim took a deep breath, but he couldn't stop his voice from cracking. 'Her last wish was that I go to Lazar. Her final request . . . before I killed her.'

Wadi froze, her expression unreadable. A drop of water slid down the edge of Raim's nose and dropped onto his lip. But before he could lick it away, Wadi jumped forward and wiped the drop away with her sleeve. 'It begins,' she whispered.

18

In a matter of seconds, he was drenched with sweat.

Mesan picked Raim up and cradled him in his arms. Raim's skin was so slick Mesan had to hold onto his clothing to maintain a grip. Wadi led them away from the tent, picking her way through the maze of shelters to the edge of the Alashan camp, out past even where the Chauk's dwellings were set up. Ryopi was the only Chauk who stirred, standing with his arms folded across his chest and his mouth in a firm line. Wadi sped past him until they reached the edge of the Eye, where the stone turned back to sand. She pointed at a nearby sand dune and spoke a few quick words to Mesan. She repeated them for Raim's benefit.

'He's taking you to the sand, so it can absorb the poison in your sweat. Come back to the camp when your skin is dry and your legs can support your weight again.'

Mesan walked slowly onto the sand and placed him

down on the very top of a small dune, then backed away.

Raim rolled over so he faced away from them and he shivered, although the sand boiled beneath him. Tremors wracked his body; his spine kept stiffening and relaxing, his arms flailing out of control. He was slowly losing control of his body. While he still could, he lay down onto his back and dug his head and shoulders into the sand. He knew the sense of stability was false, but it made him feel better anyway.

Still, poisoned liquid poured off him, collecting in the crook of his elbow and in the palms of his hands. It felt thicker than water, more like honey, and he had to fight his tongue from reaching out and tasting it. He tried to focus on the sky. There were millions of stars and a bright round moon above him. As he stared they seemed to blur and blend into one, the poison swilling behind his eyes until he wasn't sure whether he was seeing reality or dreams. He saw Mhara, Dharma, his grandfather Loni – even a brief glimpse of his brother Tarik as he disappeared down the tunnel into the mountain.

But above all those faces, dominating them all, he saw Khareh.

Khareh, who would now be thinking of him as a traitor, and a murderer.

Khareh, who would now be without a Protector.

Khareh, who had promised to protect Dharma from danger.

It pained him so much to be away from his best friend.

He would have followed Khareh to the end – but after Mhara, what choice did he have? He had to find answers, and if the only place for that was Lazar then he owed it to Khareh too. And yet . . . he couldn't forget that Khareh had made a promise to him in those last moments together. They were bound to each other now. Still he wondered if he would ever gain his full forgiveness.

Ironically, Raim knew Khareh would have loved to be in his place. Well, perhaps not recovering from a behrfly attack, but to be in the desert, learning all the tricks of the desert people. It had been Khareh's ultimate dream to cross the desert.

'And they say no boats have ever crossed from the Xel Sea because it is so dangerous and would take years and years, and that's even before the impossibly long camel journey to Aqben!' Khareh had divulged this juicy tidbit to Raim a few months ago, as they skipped stones on Lake Oudo. He had been listening in on one of his uncle's meetings, and he was always keen to talk to Raim afterwards about how he would do things differently.

Raim had laughed. 'How could anyone live on a boat for that long? It takes two hours to cross Oudo, a lake that is never anything but completely flat, and still everyone except the Erudees just end up drowning!' He'd watched as one of the boats passed them by in the distance, just some logs tied together with braided rushes, and a narrow strip of cloth for a sail. They were the most primitive mode of transportation Raim had ever seen. He had never been on the water, and he had no desire to. He liked his feet placed firmly on the ground.

'I can't believe you don't know.' Khareh had put on his most authoritative voice. 'But in the south they have boats as big as houses. Bigger even. And they sail in them for months and months. They can explore wherever they want.'

'Right. And your elephant has three trunks.'

'Still,' Khareh had mused, 'the quickest way to get down there would be to go through the desert . . . if you could reach the oasis in the Western Eye of Sheba, then maybe it wouldn't be so bad.'

Raim had been horrified. He'd looked around quickly to make sure no one was close enough to hear them.

They were alone. 'The desert? You're crazy. Why would anyone willingly go to the land of the Alashan and the Chauk?'

'You're right,' Khareh had said, after a long pause.

'Anyway, I overheard some of the old timers saying that the south was all a myth. The desert just goes on for ever and ever.'

'I don't believe that. And the first person to get across there would be thought of as truly great.'

Khareh would have ordered them to breed a million worms, Raim thought.

With a start he realized that neither Batar-Khan nor Khareh had their Protectors. He wondered who Khareh would choose as his replacement. It was too painful to speculate. And now that Khareh was no longer going to be Khan, the person he chose would no longer be Chief Yun. Even that wouldn't have mattered to Raim. He would still have been Khareh's Protector, even if the only people Khareh commanded were lowly goatherders.

Raim stopped daydreaming once another tremor – the biggest one yet – shuddered through his limbs, forcing him to squeeze his eyes shut tight. When it was over, Raim gingerly opened his eyes and realized that his sight had cleared, and the pain in his body had left him. He gingerly lifted a finger, ran it across his forehead, and it was dry.

He sat up, but instead of moving towards the camp he remained facing away from it. He sat with his eyes closed and his legs crossed, his hands balancing on his knees in the same meditative position Yasmin had forced him into so many times. Something gnawed at his memory, like a behrfly in his brain. The bites around his head were fewer than anywhere else on his body, that couldn't be denied. As Wadi told him, there was no natural explanation for their absence. *What if . . .*

The promise-knot he made to Khareh had been hidden under the cloak. He ran his finger around the thread, feeling the knot and knowing what it meant. After learning from Ryopi that shadows were really the spirits of the person the promise was made to, he spoke to the knot as if through it he could communicate with Khareh: 'I did not betray you. I will come back and I will prove myself to you.'

Strangely, though, that did make him feel better. He lay back down in the sand, stretching his arms above him. As he felt the warmth beneath his head, he was amazed by how silent it was and by how much the desert had changed to him in such a short time. Maybe it was just having company that made it better.

Beneath him, the ground trembled. At least, he thought it did. By the time he realized it was shaking, the movement stopped. Something sharp stabbed his forearm. He grimaced in pain, sat up abruptly and clutched his arm to his stomach. A thin line of blood trickled from a wound gaping like a mouth.

He looked at the sand and ran his hand over the granules. Everything was smooth; there was no sign of anything jagged. Finally he decided he had spent enough time out on the dunes and that he should go back to the camp. Wadi had said he could join the Alashan now; he no longer had to be alone. He wondered whether he could live as Alashan for ever. Would it be better than living permanently in Lazar, with the oathbreakers? But Raim knew better than that. Mhara had said he might find answers there. And more than anything else, Raim needed answers.

He stood up with renewed determination, but as he did something burst out of the dune, sending plumes of sand into his face. He shielded his eyes with his arms and stumbled backward.

Immediately the creature started attacking his chest, ripping the tunic off his body and stabbing at his skin.

Raim yelled and tried to beat it back with his hands. The moment he felt the creature falter, he started running back towards the camp.

It chased him, and he could tell now that it was a bird. And not just any bird. It was trying to attack his promise to Khareh, which meant only one thing: it was a garfalcon – a mythical bird of the desert than hunted promise-knots. Raim had thought them only a story to stop honest people from entering the desert, but here was one in the flesh. Its wings pounded against his ears and his shoulders as it tried to dig its talons into his arm and its beak into his chest. Raim came to an abrupt halt, hoping to throw the bird off him with the momentum. It worked for a moment, and he reached out with his other hand and punched the bird hard on a wing. Out of the corner of his eye he saw Wadi running towards him.

The bird was startled momentarily, and flew up. For the first time Raim got a good look at it. It was ghastly in the moonlight. The beak was long and curved, with a thick streak of red that ran down the centre; though the gash in Raim's arm meant the beak could have been stained by his own blood. The bird itself was a magnificent blue-black, and its wingspan was huge, the wings seemingly too big for its body.

It swooped down, lightning fast, and latched onto Raim's wrist. It dug its beak deep into his chest and ripped at the promise-knot. Then, the unbreakable broke. It snapped from around his neck and he could do nothing but watch in horror. The bird's talons remained fastened to his arm, the knotted string dangling from its mouth like the tail of an unfortunate rodent.

Wind rushed past his ears. The bird screeched and was pulled off his arm. It remained suspended in the air, a few feet away from Raim. Holding the bird by the throat was Khareh. Or rather, dream-Khareh.

'I'm going to kill it!' dream-Khareh screamed. He meant it too. A vicious curved blade was at the bird's throat.

'No, don't,' said Raim. He wasn't even sure if dream-Khareh could kill the bird or if this strange hallucination only appeared when he suffered immense pain. He wondered if he was unconscious, like during the attack of the behrflies. Absurdly he felt protective of the bird, and despite the fact that it was about to swallow his Absolute Vow, he did not want any harm to come to it.

Dream-Khareh stared at him in that same, dumbfounded way the real Khareh used to, like Raim was too stupid for words. Raim felt disconcerted. 'Let it go,' he said, more forcefully.

'You let this garfalcon eat this knot,' dream-Khareh said, 'and not even I can release you from this vow.'

Raim couldn't take his eyes off the bird. 'I never wish to be released,' he said.

Dream-Khareh shrugged. He released the bird, one ghostly finger at a time. The bird threw its head back so the string fell into its throat, and swallowed.

To Raim's surprise, the bird did not fly away. Instead, it came towards him. Raim flinched. 'Go,' he said to it. 'Go or this time *I* will kill you!' It answered him with a high-pitched screech and jetted off almost vertically into the night sky.

Dream-Khareh floated down towards him. 'Close your eyes,' he said. And Raim did. There was another flash of pain on his chest and then nothing.

'Raim!' Wadi was still sprinting across the sand towards him. In her hand was a slingshot. 'Raim, are you hurt? Where is the bird? I tried to shoot it but I thought I saw something . . . a shadow . . .' She slowed as she neared him and then stared, wide-eyed in horror, at his chest.

He looked down. His skin was ripped to shreds and blood poured out of the wounds in thick streams over the hardened muscles of his stomach. But where once the knot from his Absolute Vow had hung like a pendant around his neck, now what was left was a scar. It was not the same as the one on his wrist; crimson, angry, threatening and hideous to look at. Instead, it was ink black, and intricate against his olive skin, tracing the design of the knot as if it was still there. Most of all, it was indelible. It was his knot to Khareh, sealed in a mark of permanence on his chest, over his heart. For ever.

A grin spread across his face despite the pain, and he knew he must look mad. But he was so happy. No one could deny he was an oathkeeper now.

Wadi's brow was furrowed in concern. She tentatively

reached out and took his arm. 'Come on, let's get you back to the Chauk camp.'

'To the Chauk?' Even that news couldn't wipe the smile from his face; he felt delirious. 'I thought you said I was Alashan now.'

'Raim . . .' She was looking over his shoulder now, up into the sky. Raim followed her gaze and saw nothing – nothing, of course, except for his pain-induced hallucination in the form of a floating Khareh. 'Raim, you do have a shadow now. You are fully Chauk.'

19

'Well, boy. What a surprise you are. You never told us the oath you'd broken was to the *Crown Prince*. You must be brave.' Ryopi sidled up behind him, the mutterings of his haunt following him like a bad smell. The whole tribe – Alashan on one side, Chauk on the other – were gathered around Raim and Wadi.

Raim shrugged him off in disgust. 'I *told* you, I didn't break an oath out there.'

Ryopi eyed dream-Khareh, who was hovering near. 'Looks like you did to me.'

'No!' Raim almost launched himself at the man, but Old-maa held up her hand, which was enough to stay him.

She spoke, and Wadi translated. 'As Alashan, we do not knot our promises. We make them in the name of Sola, and that is all. She knows our hearts and she is the sole judge of our intentions. But we recognize the shadow that accompanies the oathbreakers. And a shadow has

197

descended upon you. This we cannot ignore. You must keep away from the Alashan, and remain with the Chauk.'

Raim glared at Old-maa. 'But I'm not like them! I can show you,' Raim said, with more confidence than he felt. In reality, he had no idea how he was going to prove it. Then he remembered what dream-Khareh had said to him during the behrfly incident. He thought, *can you read my mind?*

Dream-Khareh spoke back in his head, 'Yes.'

Then tell me how I am different from Chauk. He was pleading silently.

'All they see around you is a shadow, and all the Chauk's haunts appear as shadows too: but the Alashan already know your shadow is different. It's not dark, it's not menacing. It's not repulsive. I can make the shadow disappear, if you want.'

Do it then, thought Raim. He watched as dream-Khareh started edging away from him. *Move so far back that they won't be repelled. But don't leave me for good*, he quickly added.

'Don't worry,' dream-Khareh said. 'I'm here to stay.'

Dream-Khareh floated backward until he was out of sight.

A huge murmur scurried through the crowd.

'See?' Raim said, out loud this time. 'I am not the same as they are. I am not bound to my "shadow" because I did not break my promise. So please . . . let me stay with you for now . . . until we reach Lazar.'

Old-maa's expression changed, then, after Wadi had translated his words. She almost looked as if she was smiling. But it wasn't a pleasant look. Wadi was still speaking, her hand gestures getting more and more expressive. Old-maa pursed her lips, so deep that they almost disappeared into the wrinkles of her face. Then she barked several sharp, violent words at Wadi. Raim didn't need a translation to know what the answer was. Wadi shook her head and mouthed, 'I'm so sorry.' She slowly turned on her heels and followed the other Alashan who were walking away, leaving Raim and the Chauk behind.

'Oh dear, looks like you're stuck with us,' said Ryopi, and he repeated his cackling.

'Only until we get to Lazar.'

'I told you, they're not going to take us to Lazar. I've been with them more moons than I care to count, and that old crone' – he gestured at Old-maa, shaking his fist and spitting on the ground – 'refuses to go. She'd rather see us die out here in the desert than do her duty and take us to our rightful place. All because she's so good with that godsforsaken worm.'

'What do you mean?'

'That girl you talk to, Wadi, she told me about those worms they have. Not at first, mind, she won't often come near me because of him.' He jerked his thumb in his haunt's direction. 'But eventually I got it out of her. Those worms are bred in Lazar and it takes the Alashan many, many years and much dedication to train them. I've watched them train the one they're using now. They give up lots of water to the worm in order to give it the scent. The worms smell the water, or at least sense it somehow, and then they burrow deep into the sand until they find it. Then the Alashan follow the worm down with a special tube to keep the way open. Once it finds water, the worm will then attempt to consume as much of it as possible – and if it is allowed to do that, it will drink until it bursts, stupid creature. I've seen that happen too – and you should see the Alashan's faces. They're stricken. They even hold a funeral for the damn thing.

'But that's why Old-maa is revered among the Alashan. She can suck the worm back up the tube after it has only consumed one segment of its body's worth of water.'

'But if there's water underground, why don't they build a well?' asked Raim. 'Then they could have water all the time.'

'Yeah, don't think Old-maa hasn't tried. Except do you know how deep those worms go? Out here, digging a well would be next to impossible: they don't have the tools or the skill to do it. The sand collapses around them before they come close to reaching the groundwater. The desert might seem tough, but it's more fragile than you could imagine. I'm sorry, boy. I know you want to go to Lazar, even more than the rest of us. But don't believe a word that old woman says. As long as they got that worm, we ain't going anywhere near that cursed city. Get used to life in the desert, boy.'

Raim clenched his fists together and thought to himself, *Not if I can help it.*

'That's the spirit,' said dream-Khareh, and then he laughed and laughed and laughed at his joke.

20

It was almost too much for Raim to bear to think Khareh
was really there with him in the desert. So he blended the
words 'dream-Khareh' into the name Draikh to dis-
associate spirit from person. In all other ways but name
now, though, they were the same. The same sarcastic
comments. The same withering looks. The same best
friend.

'Hey, watch out,' Draikh said. 'Pretty girl coming up.'

Raim looked up.

'Hi.' Wadi was standing over his shelter, wringing her
hands. 'I'm sorry about Old-maa . . . she's stubborn.'

'Stubborn? She's more stuck in her ways than a
constipated camel,' said Draikh.

*Are you going to talk in my head over every conversation
I have?* Raim thought to his annoying spirit.

'Yup, pretty much.'

Well stop it, will you?

Raim tried to compose himself for Wadi, and not look like a crazy person who was having conversations with an invisible being. He shrugged, trying to act nonchalant. 'Don't worry about it. Look, I have to ask you something. Ryopi says you will never take us to Lazar. Is that true?'

Wadi nodded. 'Old-maa refuses to go there. Trust me, I have tried hard to convince her we have to go. The Chauk are so . . . pitiful. Despite what they've done, I feel sorry for them. All they want is to reach the city. They were just unlucky to have been picked up by us and not another Alashan tribe.'

'But *why* is she so reluctant?'

'I honestly don't know.'

'So get Old-maa to point me in the right direction, and I'll start walking there!'

'It doesn't work like that.'

'Why not?'

'Only Old-maa knows the way. One day, she will pass that knowledge on to her successor, but for now . . . Why do you think the Chauk need us in the first place? It is impossible to find Lazar without knowing beforehand where you are going. It's hidden deep in a mountain range in the desert.'

'So then what can we do?'

'I can try to convince her to take us to another Alashan tribe. A tribe who will accompany you to Lazar. But it will take time. We haven't come across another tribe in many moons. It is a big desert.' She smiled wryly.

'Yeah, no kidding,' said Draikh.

'Another tribe could be just over this dune, and we would never know,' she continued.

A high-pitched whistle sounded from inside the camp. Wadi's eyes immediately leaped to the sky.

'What is it?' said Raim, following her gaze, suddenly fearful of more behrflies.

'Daylight.' Sure enough, in the sky behind him the first few streaks of colour were beginning to appear. 'Quick, we only have a few minutes. Pass me your cloak and sit cross-legged.' He did as she asked and she threw the cloak over his shoulders, arranging it around him so that every inch of skin was covered. She turned back to the Alashan camp, then looked up to the sky again, and cursed. 'It's too late for me to go back now; the sun is almost up. It's easier if we sit back to back. Pull your hood over your eyes so your face is covered.' Again he did as he was told, as Wadi sat down behind him. Raim felt her back press against his, her spine, shoulder blades, and neck adjusting until they were both comfortable.

Maybe a little bit of extra time with the Alashan wouldn't be so bad, after all.

They marched on for a week through the desert, into the stretch that divided the Western Eye of Sheba from the Eastern, and still there was no sign of another tribe.

The first day they'd spent out of the Eye, the baby garfalcon had swooped down out of the sky and landed on

Raim's non-scarred arm, scaring him half to death. But it squawked a greeting and Raim had warmed to the creature immediately. He stroked the oily feathers on its head and neck, before reaching into his cloak for his skin of water. He tipped a droplet into the bird's throat. From that moment, Oyu, named for the sound it made when it drank the water, had remained Raim's constant companion, almost like another shadow.

Oyu waited out the heat by burrowing into the sand. Raim often marvelled at the bird's curious anatomy. Its wings, which looked so slick and dazzling in the air, were covered in a strange oil that seemed to repel grains of sand, enabling it to bury so deep that no trace of its presence was visible on the surface. Sometimes Raim was jealous – it was a great way to stay cool.

Wadi he hardly ever saw. Not since the day they had spent back-to-back in the desert. Afterwards she had been berated by Old-maa for spending time with him, and so Raim's only source of human company came from Ryopi. None of the other Chauk seemed to be in the mood for conversation.

'Blood traitor. Fool. Cursed one. Good for nothing but Lazar.'

Ryopi's haunt was always close by. Whenever Ryopi spoke, his haunt-father would move in front of him and stare directly into his eyes. Ryopi tried to avoid the piercing eye contact, and as a result never looked in the same direction when he was talking, his eyes flicking from side to side, his neck twitching. When he walked, the haunt followed close behind, playing with the edge of his curved dagger. The tiniest movement out of place and Ryopi would cry out as the blade was waved in front of his face. This behaviour was pretty typical of all the Chauk. They were all jumpy and agitated. Even time didn't lessen the pain. The haunts were smart; they adapted. If the Chauk became too complacent, too used to the insults, their haunt would step up their game, trying a different, even more agonizing tactic – like dredging up old, painful memories and reenacting them in front of their victim. Anything to get a reaction out of the Chauk.

Most of the time Ryopi attempted to ignore his haunt. But sometimes, like now, he snapped: 'Leave me alone! Leave me be!'

That only made it worse.

Raim cringed as a barrage of insults was launched at Ryopi. The man's shoulders crumpled under the assault, and he winced and cowered like a dog being kicked by an angry master. 'Give him some peace,' Raim shouted at the haunt.

At once, Draikh flashed up by his side.

'Give us all some peace, for Sola's sake,' Raim repeated.

'Stay out of this, traitor-boy.' The haunt shifted menacingly towards Raim, curved dagger in hand.

Draikh moved out in front of Raim. 'Stay where you are, haunt. You know I am stronger than you. Absolute Vow, remember?'

The haunt spat and threw another curse in Ryopi's direction, but was blessedly silent for a short while.

Raim thought for an awful second that Ryopi was going to embrace him, but the man simply attempted a cracked smile, revealing a flash of what he was like before he became Chauk. Raim could no longer contain his curiosity: 'What oath did you break?'

'Back in Darhan, I was a fisherman on the River Erudine. All the men of the tribe were called up to fight by our warlord when a tribe from Mauz attacked another further down the river. But someone had to stay and guard our homes and protect the younger members of the tribe – including my young sister and brother. I volunteered, and I made a promise to my father to keep them safe.' Ryopi managed to keep his gaze steady as he spoke, the first time Raim could remember him not being so twitchy. At the mention of Ryopi's siblings, Raim felt a pang in his heart for Dharma. He gripped the scarf over his wrist and squeezed it tight.

'But there was a woman . . .' Ryopi continued, now dropping his stare to examine the veins in his hands, 'from a neighbouring tribe. We had planned to run away together while the others were at war. I . . . I loved her. I knew what I was risking, and I thought she did too and I ran, thinking she would join me . . . alas, I am here, with the treacherous and the exiled, and she is not . . .'

'Disgrace! Fool! Vagabond! You renounced your family for your earthly desires. Speak no more or I shall slice out your tongue.' Ryopi's haunt-father stomped again on that conversation. Raim opened his mouth to shout at the haunt, but stopped himself when Ryopi shook his head and shrugged.

'This is my lot. This is what I deserve. This is what we all deserve.'

Raim felt a surge of anger flow through his veins. Anger and despair. Ryopi had truly broken a vow, knowing the consequences, and was now facing up to his punishment. But Raim didn't break anything, and still he was being made to suffer. 'Ryopi, are you sure you see no other spirit around me?' Raim asked, his voice cracking on the word *other* under the pressure of his desperation.

Ryopi shook his head. 'Another haunt, you mean? Nay. Just the Prince.'

Raim curled his fingers into a fist. 'The haunt is out there. I can sense it.'

discovered it was delicious cooked over an open flame, the skin burned to a crisp while the inside was creamy white and chewy.

Oyu was growing quickly, and soon his wingspan was as great as Raim was tall. He took to the skies as they walked, his black form disappearing into the night sky. His vision in the darkness was clearly remarkable; he brought back tokens for Raim, mostly gruesome things like bits of bone and once even the shed skin of a snake.

One night, Oyu swooped down and landed on Raim's shoulder. In his beak was a leather tie, which looked like those used by the Alashan to secure the tops of their water casks. But it was marked with a strange knife-cut design that he hadn't seen in this tribe. Filled with excitement and hope, Raim ran up to the Alashan group, forgetting the taboo. He was quickly reminded of it, though, as the tribe members at the back of the group spun round, knives in hand. He held up his own hands, trying to show he meant no harm. 'Please, I need to see Wadi.'

Wadi pressed through the crowd. 'What is it?'

'Look!' He showed her what Oyu had brought. 'That's not from this tribe, is it? It must be from another! They could be close!'

'Where did you find this?' she asked, urgency filling her voice.

'Oyu brought it to me.'

'Do you think he can show us where he found it?'

'I could try.'

Raim held the piece of leather in front of Oyu's face and dangled it. Immediately the bird took off into the sky before they had a chance to follow.

'He's heading north, over that dune,' said Draikh. 'Let's follow him!'

Raim turned to Wadi. 'That way.'

'Give me one second.' She took the leather tag from Raim's hand and disappeared back into the Alashan tribe. A few moments later, she was back, a smile on her face. 'Old-maa has agreed to meet this other tribe. Let's go!'

Raim found himself at the front of the pack, Draikh next to him on one side, Wadi on the other. Another few feet back were the Alashan, and further still behind them, the Chauk. It felt good to Raim to be useful.

Raim directed the group up the side of a tall dune. He heard a sharp screech from Oyu, and anticipation filled him as he realized they must be close. But when he crested the top of the dune, his excitement died. There was no other tribe.

But there was a body.

Wadi stood stock still in horror, seeing the peeling, blackened, sunburned skin and sand-drowned mouth of the dead woman. Then suddenly dry heaves sent her body shuddering.

'I . . . I didn't realize,' Raim spluttered, the weight of failure on his shoulders. Wadi composed herself and kneeled down beside the girl's body, beginning to brush sand over it. The other Alashan soon caught up, dropping all their possessions and coming over to help Wadi cover the body. The Chauk could hardly bear to look at all. It was obvious she had been one of them – a new exile from Darhan who had died before she could find an Alashan tribe.

Wadi poured the last handful of sand over the girl, covering her eyes. She drew a symbol in the sand and said a quick prayer: '*Sola chaka.*' Sola protect.

'It is as good a ceremony as we can give her,' Wadi managed to choke out. 'We almost never come across the dead in the desert. She must have passed only a few hours ago. The sand devours bodies quickly – and if not the sand, then the behrflies do the job.'

Loud shouts came from deep inside the crowd of Alashan. Echoes of grief rippled through the bodies like a shockwave, men and women falling over like trees in a hurricane. Raim rushed forward and pressed his way through to the centre of the group.

Old-maa was standing, hands on her head, wailing. Her eyes flew open as he stepped into the circle and her look was like a dagger through his heart. 'You,' she said in his language, and her voice dripped with all the malice and anger he had ever known. Then she stepped aside.

Oyu was there, his wings spread wide in triumph, the shadow of his beak etched out against the moonlit sky. The last great and indispensable worm of the Alashan tribe dangled helplessly from his mouth.

'Oyu, no!' Raim yelled, and he dived forward to try and grab the bird by the neck. But Oyu had already swallowed the worm and took off into the sky the moment he felt the tips of Raim's fingers brush his body.

'I . . . I'm so sorry,' Raim said to Old-maa and to the crowd. 'I didn't know . . . I couldn't stop him.'

'Enough,' Old-maa said, and to Raim's surprise she spoke in fluent Darhanian. 'You are a plague on this tribe and have been from the moment you joined us. You and your animal have killed our only waterworm and now, your heinous wish has been granted. We must reach Lazar within five moon nights, or else you have just sentenced the entire tribe to death.'

22

No matter how much Raim tried to apologize, the Alashan would have none of it. The increased speed and purpose with which they moved scared him – but so did the sight of the four lonely waterskins they carried, which contained all the water they would have to divide between the entire tribe until they reached Lazar. They still didn't move during the daylight hours – the risk of dehydration was too great.

Raim didn't want to think about what might happen if they didn't reach Lazar in time. Maybe then he would see the Alashan savagery come out. But he couldn't find it in himself to fear for his blood.

The Chauk moved with renewed energy too, relieved to be finally travelling to Lazar. But the thought of finally getting his wish – at the cost of the worm – made Raim feel sick to his stomach. So he stayed far away from both groups, as far as he dared. Oyu still followed him, and he also couldn't find it in his heart to hate the silly creature. It hadn't known what it was doing. The only thing that comforted Raim was the fact that he knew soon he would be leaving the Alashan behind. He would no longer have to be a burden to them and they could live their lives in peace again. Wadi, especially. Each time she tried to reach out to him, offer him some small kindness – even friendship, maybe – he found a way to throw it back in her face. Soon he would be gone, swallowed up by Lazar, and she would never have to think of him again.

The faster they moved, the faster the landscape changed. As they entered the second Eye of Sheba, giant rocks jutted up from the ground, like a forest of stone. By sheltering in their long shadows, they could squeeze extra hours out of the night.

Raim took to wandering in the hours when the sun was low, jumping from long shadow to shadow, taking a lantern with him but preferring not to use it most of the time. He wanted to challenge himself, racing imaginary foes from stone to stone. He had been feeling so weak lately, so unfit and lacking in training. It felt good – he relished the feeling of his feet pounding against the sand, enjoyed the ache in his thighs as he pushed himself harder. He flew past the rock he had dared himself to reach and aimed for the next one further along, putting his head down and swinging his arms to match the frantic rhythm of his sprint. When he reached the rock he barely stopped himself from flying headfirst into it with his arms, and he collapsed, breathless but, for the first time in a long time, *happy*.

He lay there, sweat trickling down his neck, and let his breathing return to its normal rate.

Loud voices suddenly set him on edge. He thought he had run far enough from the tribe that he wouldn't come across anyone. He peered round the edge of the rock and saw Wadi arguing vehemently with Old-maa. He couldn't understand what they were saying, of course, but Wadi's clenched fists and Old-maa's inability to control the volume of her voice meant it must be something serious.

'What's got their tunics in a twist?' Draikh asked.

No idea, thought Raim. *Must be something big, though*. Definitely something he didn't want to get caught in the middle of. He sidled away from his rock, careful not to fall within their line of sight.

Draikh, two steps ahead as always, cried out, 'Over here! Look at this!'

Raim sped over to where Draikh was floating, and had to catch his breath in awe. They were at the edge of a large basin of blindingly white sand, glowing despite the darkness – as if it had captured the sun's rays and kept them there on the floor of the valley, only slightly dimmed. Raim felt a shiver run through his spine as he looked down on a forest of trees – the ghosts of trees really, black and hard as rock, indicative of a time, centuries before, when parts of the desert had running water. Now their skeletons stood scorched a rich ebony by the harshness of the sun.

Raim slid down the side of the basin, sand tumbling after him, but his footing remained sure – a sign he was becoming more accustomed to life in the desert. He picked up a dead branch and in that instant it felt like a sword. Suddenly the tree closest to him was Lars and the basin was the arena. He gripped the hilt of his branch in both hands and swung hard at the tree, an almost three-hundred-and-sixty degree launch with all his might.

There was an almighty crack like thunder and the dead tree burst to life in a sea of splinters and black dust. Remarkably the branch remained intact, but he swung again and again at the tree, slashing and chopping until the last tendril holding it together snapped and it tumbled to the ground.

'You do know that tree was probably a thousand years old.'

Raim spun round, breathless, and looked up to the top of the basin where Wadi was standing, hands on hips. She slid gracefully down the side of the dune and picked up a branch of her own, turned it over in her hands and took a couple of swipes at the air.

'Fancy a real opponent, instead of taking it out on some dead wood?'

Raim grinned and nodded as they began to spar together. Wadi was better than most opponents he had faced but her swordplay didn't even come close to her hand-to-hand skill. She was throwing all her effort into the bout, though, her face glowing red with effort. Raim felt the anger in her blows, but somehow knew it wasn't directed at him.

He waited for the right moment, then swung the branch and hit her upper arm. She winced and called for time, clutching at her triceps. 'Ow!' First annoyance, then curiosity showed on her face. 'How did you do that?'

'It's your footwork that's off. You need to stay balanced. Keep your stance tight, the target small. It means I won't be able to get round you like I just did.'

Wadi nodded, her mouth set in a firm line, and they started again. This time, her footwork was better, and they sparred until they both called for a pause.

'Thanks,' she said between breaths. She tossed the branch-sword to the ground and rubbed her hands clean against her loose trousers. 'I needed that.'

Raim shrugged. 'Me too. The tree was getting pretty boring anyway. Hey – are you all right? I heard you and Old-maa . . .'

Wadi kicked at the ground. 'She won't let me go to Lazar.' The horror on Raim's face must have registered because she quickly corrected herself: 'I don't mean to *stay* in Lazar – I just want to see it. And now that we are finally going, she's forbidding me to go with her on the last leg of the journey. It's not fair. Before, she used to tell me I was too young – and I accepted that. But ever since I've been "old enough", she's refused to bring any Chauk there. Except now, of course.' She looked sidelong at him. 'You must be the unluckiest person I know.'

Raim didn't really have an answer for that, but he agreed. 'So what's Old-maa's new excuse?'

'That's just it. She doesn't have one. She probably doesn't want me to come because I'm not a true Alashan. I don't know how many times I can prove myself to that woman – I've done *everything*. I can do everything a true-born Alashan can do. Some of it better than the others.' She slumped down onto a log on the ground, head in her hands.

Raim stayed standing, unsure what to do. Finally, he sat down next to her. 'You really idolize her, don't you?'

Wadi shrugged, but then nodded. 'She took care of me. When I was born, my mother abandoned me to go back to the desert, and my father was left with me. He didn't have any kind of clan or purpose because he was very ill . . . barely fit to raise me, let alone do anything else. I raised myself and took care of him too. Then one day, out of the blue, he decided to bring me out into the desert. I didn't want to go, but he made me. He was my father – who was I to disobey? We walked and walked, deeper into the desert, and he refused all food and water from me. When he couldn't take it any longer, we stopped. He took out this' – Wadi took the sand-coloured pendant out from beneath her tunic and showed it to Raim – 'and put it around my neck. He said it was the only thing left of my mother. And then he died.

'That's when Old-maa and her tribe found us. I was curled up by my father's body, using him . . .' Her voice cracked. She took a few deep breaths. 'Using him as shelter from the sun. Old-maa has taken care of me ever since.'

'So . . . maybe you should trust her on this not-entering-Lazar rule,' Raim said, gentle with his tone. 'From what I've heard, it's not that great a place.'

Wadi furrowed her brow. 'In a way, I think you're right. I should trust her. But I can't control this . . . desire, this *need*, to see Lazar. I *have* to go.'

They sat in silence for a while, Wadi's fingers running around the edge of her pendant. There were symbols carved into it and she traced these with her finger too. Then suddenly she stood up and pushed the pendant back beneath the fabric of her top. 'Thanks for the fight,' she said. 'I should get back to the rest of the tribe.'

Raim stared at her back as she left, at the muscles moving down between her shoulder blades, at the place where her shape nipped in at her waist. He desperately racked his brains for something to say but his mouth felt dry and his tongue tied in knots as hard to unravel as a promise. 'I could leech you!' he blurted eventually.

Wadi stopped and looked over her shoulder. 'What?'

'I mean *teach* – I could teach you – more about sword fighting, if you want. I know we don't have much time left but . . .'

To his surprise, she smiled back at him. 'I'd like that. But it will have to be a trade. I'm sure we can think of something . . .'

Raim watched her climb the dune out of the basin and disappear beyond his sight. When she was gone, he stood up himself, unable to control the huge grin on his face. He turned round to check on Draikh – and that's when he saw his spirit, curled up in a fit of laughter.

'*Leech* you? You are the worst with women.'

Raim threw the branch at Draikh's head.

23

When the mountains first appeared on the horizon, after they had left the second Eye, the mood in the tribe changed dramatically – a mixture of excitement and anticipation and, prevailing over all, dread.

'Lazar is . . . through . . . those cliffs,' Wadi told him between breaths of a deep meditation session.

'You're not . . . supposed to . . . talk while meditating,' Raim replied, opening one eyelid a crack to see what Wadi was up to. She had slumped back on the ground, out of the lotus position. Raim relaxed out of it as well.

'I don't think meditating is for me,' she said.

'My grandmother taught me it was as important as the rest of my training. Keeps the mind sharp,' he said, tapping his forehead.

'So about two seconds of meditation will do it for you then?' laughed Draikh in his ear.

Raim grimaced. Wadi saw the look but she was used to

it by now – to Raim responding to things she couldn't hear. In fact, she had even started to ask questions about Draikh and the rest of the haunts.

'Rude joke?' she asked, nodding in the direction of Draikh-as-shadow.

'Always,' Raim said. And then: 'Those mountains seem like pretty big markers for Lazar.'

'They are, but if you don't know the way to the city you will lose yourself in them. No one has ever found it without being led by someone who has been before.'

'Maybe no one has wanted to try hard enough to find it.'

'Good point.'

Raim pulled out the dagger from inside his boot and turned it over in his hands. The last remnant of his Yun life – of what could have been.

'Can I see?' Wadi asked.

Raim flipped the dagger over and handed it to her, hilt-first. 'Of course. Careful, though – it's sharp.'

She rolled her eyes. 'I know how to handle a blade just as well as you, Yun boy.' She considered the blade, testing the edge with her finger, quickly realizing just how sharp it really was. 'Very nice,' she said, before laying it down carefully in her lap. She gestured at the blade, then made the hand movements for the word 'knife', and Raim repeated them back to her. That had been their trade: sword skills for language. Raim was fascinated by the Alashan speech, which reminded him of Khareh and the secret sign language they had developed. The Alashan seemed to mostly use hand signals, with very few actual words. Those words were accompanied by a multitude of clicks and sounds Raim could hardly hope to replicate. Wadi laughed at his attempts until she admitted to him that the Alashan were born with an extra flap of skin in their throat – something she had inherited from her mother – to help keep the dust from their lungs, but which also helped make some of the stranger noises of their language. That hadn't stopped her from laughing at him as he attempted to replicate the sounds before finally revealing the truth.

Raim stood up and took a swig of water from his skin, which contained his tiny ration of water to last until Lazar.

Then, the faintest of rattles sounded from his left, a barely audible rat-a-tat-tat. The bottom of his stomach dropped. He dared to flick his eyes to Wadi, whose face confirmed his fear: it was drained of colour, her eyes wide as moons, hands deathly still.

He peered down at his left and there was a viper, its head and a quarter of its lithe body swaying a few inches from the ground. Its scales were mottled gold and copper, glowing in the dying dusk-light, its eyes tiny specks of onyx tipped with menacing horns, glaring at him, devoid of feeling. It flicked its tongue, a flash of pink, tasting the fear that emanated from Raim's body.

Then, before a moment passed to think, it lashed out at him, curved fangs bared.

Raim stumbled backward in panic.

'No sudden movements!' Wadi hissed, almost like she

was talking to the snake itself. In fact, while Raim had been paralysed with fear looking at the snake, Wadi had begun the agonizingly slow process of inching towards the reptile without attracting its attention.

Raim stilled his muscles, but his eyes kept moving, darting from the snake to Wadi. The snake lashed out again, but Raim realized it was probably just protecting its territory. For now.

He locked eyes with Wadi. Looking at her calmed him. He read the countdown in her eyes. *Three . . . two . . .*

One!

Wadi darted forwards and grabbed the snake just behind its head. Its body and tail squirmed in her grasp, a hideous hissing sounding from its throat, but Wadi's grip held firm, the dagger poised in her other hand just in case she miscalculated. She reached to the belt at her side, and from it pulled a small canvas bag she used to carry her food for the day. She dumped the food in the sand, and wrangled the snake inside instead.

Raim felt relief flood his muscles, but in that instant a stone shifted beneath his foot, turning his ankle. He re-balanced before he hit the floor, but not in time to save his skin of water, which flew out of his hand. The spout was open and the skin seemed to drift in slow motion to the ground. If the water spilled from the spout, Raim would be without anything to drink until they reached Lazar, which was still two days away at the very least. His heart felt caught beneath his tongue and all the muscles in his neck tightened. He tried to reach towards it but only the tips of his fingers brushed the bottle as it fell, tipping it in the air slightly so that water blossomed out of the spout. Raim felt a rush of air behind him and saw Draikh swoop down over the skin and catch it deftly in his hands.

None of the water touched the ground.

Raim was about to take the flask back from Draikh without thanks or thought, but a gasp from Wadi made him falter. She was gaping at the flask in Draikh's hand.

Raim stared from Wadi to Draikh and back again. He didn't understand what was making her look so surprised. He tried to see what she saw. Then it dawned on him. She couldn't see Draikh. But she could see the waterskin.

Raim held out his hand and locked eyes with Draikh. There was a glint of understanding in the spirit's eyes. He floated towards Raim, moving ever so slowly, until the skin slotted neatly into Raim's open palm.

Wadi was not someone who allowed shock to paralyse her for long. She quickly looked from side to side at the rest of the tribe, but no one seemed to be watching – except for Ryopi, who was sprinting over to the pair as fast as his legs could carry him.

'Why didn't you tell me you could do magic?' Wadi said, her voice barely rising over a fierce whisper.

'But ... I can't do magic,' Raim replied, still barely managing to retain a grip on the waterskin. His mind was whirling with consequences he didn't truly understand.

'You have the skills of a sage,' she stated.

A sage. Raim tried to remember what he had felt on that first day he had witnessed a magician, on the day of his brother's wedding. It seemed like so long ago, that sojourn up to the mountains. A different lifetime; a different Raim.

'So how did you do that?' she continued.

'I told you, I didn't do anything. I dropped my water bottle, Draikh caught it. That's it.'

'The shadows do this?'

'We can do more,' Draikh said, floating ominously behind Wadi. Raim's eyes flickered towards him, and Wadi spun round, searching the air for what Raim was seeing.

You can do more? But this time, Raim thought the words inside his head.

'Yes,' Draikh replied. 'Send the girl away, and I'll show you.'

But before Raim could answer him, Ryopi had reached them. 'Did Draikh just ... catch that...?' he asked, breathless. 'Do you think I could learn how to do that with him?' He shot a nervous look at his father.

'Over my dead body,' said his father. 'But that's right; I don't even have a body.' He released a gruesome cackle that made Ryopi shiver, yet instead of crawling back to the Chauk as he might have done before, Ryopi stared eagerly, hungrily, at Raim.

Suddenly, Raim felt overwhelmed. 'I don't know! I don't know what just happened. Leave me alone – both of you. I need to figure this out.'

Ryopi reluctantly withdrew, but Wadi looked hurt. Raim didn't know what to say to her . . . he had to find out from Draikh what was happening. Did it really just happen like that – one dropped water bottle and he was a sage? He gave her an apologetic shrug, but she threw her arms in the air and walked away.

When Wadi left, he wandered far enough from everybody not to worry about being overheard so he was free to speak out loud to Draikh.

'So . . . you can interact with our world, just the same as I can,' Raim said, and the words in his mouth seemed strange.

Draikh nodded. 'Not all the time. I have to choose it. And . . . it makes me feel weaker.'

'Does that mean,' Raim continued, 'that all these other spirits could make things move if they wanted to?'

'They could, but they won't. They won't do anything to help out an oathbreaker unless he or she had some powerful skills of persuasion. I will only do it if and when you ask me or need me to.'

Raim smiled. 'You would be that obedient?'

Draikh smiled back. 'You're right, maybe not always when you ask me to.'

Raim slumped down onto the ground cross-legged. 'What good am I to anyone as a sage? It just makes me more different from the Chauk again, when all I want to do is fit in and find some answers.'

'Why in Sola's name would you want to fit in?' Draikh

asked, though Raim's crumpled features clearly showed he needed more convincing. Draikh dropped down from his traditional perch floating in the sky and sat down in front of Raim. He leaned forward and spoke in a whisper, though none of the Chauk was close enough to hear them anyway. 'I can do other things too, you know.' He brought a knife out from beneath the folds of his clothing. It was the same knife all the spirits carried: long and curved, and black as night. 'This is the knife that makes the scars – like the one on your wrist, for example. Or your chest, although that is a slightly different kind.'

Raim sat up a little straighter, staring at the blade in awe and fear.

'But that's not what I can do for you.' As quick as lightning, he struck out with the blade and sliced open Raim's hand. Raim cried out in pain. The wound gaped like a mouth drawing breath before it released a torrent of blood. Carefully, Draikh took up Raim's hand and ran his own fingertips on top of it. Raim could feel nothing, not even Draikh's hand supporting his own. It was like he had encountered an isolated block of wind: it felt like air, but there was resistance as well. Then, in an instant, the wound was healed.

'You can heal?'

Draikh's face fell, as if suddenly he realized the magnitude of the revelation he had made. 'You cannot let anyone else know about this, especially none of the Chauk. It takes more effort too.'

Raim bit his lip. Then, he picked up the nearest rock and scraped the sharp stone violently against the back of his hand, until blood and skin coated its edges.

Heal this, he said, wordlessly. *Help me.* They stared at each other, for what seemed to Raim like an age. *Help me*, Raim pressured.

Then the pain in his hand was gone and his skin was once again unbroken.

'Thank you,' he said. Draikh nodded, and Raim was pleased to see he didn't look too upset at being made to heal. In fact, the wry smile told him something quite different.

'You're going to be quite the sensation in Lazar,' said Draikh. 'I can tell.'

24

Raim found Wadi sitting on the peak of a sand dune, her fingers stroking the smooth edge of her pendant. She had avoided him after the water skin incident. But now the day for the Chauk – and Raim – to enter Lazar had come, and he had searched for her to say goodbye. He asked Draikh to respect his privacy and stay below as he climbed up to reach her. For once, Draikh agreed.

He attempted to say her name in Alashan, but it came out a garbled mess. Luckily, she just laughed. He breathed a sigh of relief and took that as permission to sit down next to her.

'You could stay with us,' she said, not yet looking at him.

'No, I can't,' he said, and he began to trace a pattern in the sand with the tip of his finger. 'I may not have knotted it as an oath, but going to Lazar was the last thing Mhara asked of me. I owe that much to her.'

'But with the Alashan, you could be useful too – surely that is all that Mhara wanted?' She looked up at him now, her eyes not pleading, but full of determination. 'She just wanted you out of Darhan, where you would be punished for the scar you have no memory of. How do you know you will find answers in Lazar? Here, you could teach the young ones how to fight. With Draikh . . . you could practise more of your sage arts, away from the exiles. Look at Oyu. He belongs in the desert. You would keep him cooped up in the city, punished for no other reason than he sees you as his master?'

'Wadi . . .' He reached out to put his hand on her shoulder, but she angrily shrugged him off and turned away.

'Wadi?' he said again.

'What?' She ran the back of her hand across her cheek, wiping away a tear that had escaped her normally tough exterior.

'I want you to have this.' He took out his Yun training blade and laid it on the sand. 'You are more worthy of it than me. The owner of this blade should be a free person, not someone confined to a city of exiles.' He reached over and touched her shoulder again, and this time she didn't flinch. He ran his hand down her arm, over the smoothness of her dark skin, down to her palm, where he gently prised open her clenched fingers. Holding her hand in his own, with the other he pressed the hilt of the blade into her palm. He closed her fingers over it and held them there, letting her palm warm to the worn leather. 'This is yours now.' It suited her.

Her grip on the blade tightened beneath his fingers, and then she twisted round fully and kissed him.

The loose wisps of hair around her face tickled his cheek, the scent of her – of sand, of sweat, of a tear, of passion – filled his lungs and made colour rush to his cheeks. He reached up and clasped the back of her head, at the point where her thick, dark hair gathered into its braid, and pulled her even closer.

She whispered a word into his mouth. 'Stay.'

When the whistle sounded, her lips had almost convinced him. But her last embrace was rougher, harder than before, and he knew she understood he was leaving.

They walked together towards the Chauk, not holding hands or arm-in-arm, but close in a way Raim had never known before, every brush of the shoulder causing his heart to skip a beat, every swing of her hips filling him with the urge to stop the madness of his exile and stay with her.

When Wadi strode forward towards Old-maa, he immediately missed her presence. 'I am coming with you,' she said.

By this point, Raim could understand basic phrases of Alashan. Especially Old-maa's simple one word response: 'No.'

Old-maa then nodded towards Raim, who walked up to join the other Chauk, his wrists together. He knew that he had to be bound for this journey. The Alashan had to demonstrate their superiority. He watched the ongoing interaction between Wadi and Old-maa as Mesan stepped forward to wrap a hemp rope tightly around his wrists, attaching him to the line. After Mesan was done, he still had a link of rope left. He went and stood behind Wadi, and said another word that Raim understood: 'Sorry.'

Then, at a signal from Old-maa, he started to bind a screaming and struggling Wadi. Old-maa looked sad and relieved. 'This is for your own good, Wadi-child. You must not come with us to Lazar,' she said in Darhanian, pointedly for Raim's benefit. She pointed at a stake beaten down into the ground, just outside the boundaries of their camp, and Raim was instantly reminded of when he had first joined the Alashan. Now being bound to that stake would be Wadi's fate until Old-maa returned from Lazar. Raim was shocked that Old-maa would resort to such measures.

'Yes, but would you trust Wadi to stay behind otherwise?' whispered Draikh.

Raim knew Draikh was right. Old-maa had to restrain Wadi or else she could never expect her not to just try and make her way to Lazar of her own accord.

As if resigned to her fate, Wadi stopped struggling and nodded meekly. 'Yes, Old-maa.'

Raim felt a tug on the rope in front of him and was pulled into his first reluctant step towards the city of exiles. He craned his neck back for one final look at Wadi.

Mesan was leading her away by the arm towards the stake, her hands tied behind her back.

Just sticking out of her tunic at the back, only visible when Mesan's lantern dipped down low, a flash of red caught Raim's eye. It was the red jewel embedded in the leather of his Yun-apprentice blade hilt, and it was just within reach of Wadi's fingertips.

PART THREE

25

Raim couldn't decide which ached more: his wrist from the ropes that bound him to Ryopi in a single-file line, or his neck, from the strain of looking up at the mountains that contained Lazar. These mountains were nothing like the Amarapura range in the north of Darhan. From afar, the Amarapura mountains looked like the points of a thousand knives, their tops covered in snow or shrouded in cloud. These peaks, the Ailing mountains, were not as tall, but the rock thrust out of the ground in smooth vertical lines, and their tops appeared flattened out like tables. Old-maa paused briefly to allow the accompanying Alashan guards to light the lanterns; the cliffs at the mountains' base not only swallowed the heat but blocked the light almost completely too.

They walked only a few feet away from the cliffs, the lanterns' uneasy glow casting their hunched silhouettes onto the rocky surface. At first, the cliff faces appeared impassable, solid and buffed almost opal-smooth by the frequent sand storms. But every now and again he noticed tiny fissures in the rock, like slashes from a sword, barely wide enough to allow the passage of two people. Old-maa beckoned them into one of the gaps, no different from the hundreds they had already passed. He thought back to what Wadi had told him about the passage to Lazar: 'Only Old-maa knows the way. One day, she will pass that knowledge on, but for now . . .'

He wished he could see where they were going; all he could make out was the back of Ryopi's head, his black hair matted, full of sand, and thinning at the crown. The walls were so close, his shoulder snagged against stone if he slipped out of the line even by a step. Still, when he touched the walls he thought he could feel them vibrating. It was the sense of a city nearby, a hum of activity, of humanity, which he hadn't felt since Kharein. The path beneath his feet was well trodden. One of his footsteps placed him directly in the indent left by Ryopi. He was walking in the footsteps of a traitor, and of a million traitors before him. His stomach churned, and when he looked up to try and catch a glimpse of sky he could see nothing but the cliff walls, rising into darkness. On the wrist of the Alashan guard closest to him, held there by a thin piece of rope tied around his foot, Oyu shivered his feathers, clearly unsettled by this skyless passage.

When the cliff walls parted, Raim tumbled out into the light and bumped straight into the back of Ryopi. All the Chauk were standing and staring open-mouthed at a giant in the light. A giant made of red stone, his face twisted in agony.

They were in a circular courtyard. The gap they had come out of was the only place you could enter from, apart from a massive stone gate at the opposite side. At the centre of the circle was a large silver gong pocked with shallow dents and a mallet lying next to it on the ground. But the giant was unlike anything Raim had ever seen before. It was carved directly out of the rock, and so huge that if Raim stood at its base, he would have barely reached the height of the statue's ankle. The giant stood guard on one side of the gate. There was another giant on the other side, his features distorted with grief. Raim looked around, and their expressions matched those on the faces of all the Chauk as they entered Lazar.

Old-maa stepped forward, picked up the mallet and struck the gong. The sound echoed off the steep heights and made the cliff walls tremble. She rang it twice before an answer came.

'Who calls?' The voice came from high above them.

'Alashan! We bring nine cursed!'

'Gola? Is that you?' Then there was an abrupt silence, as if it hadn't meant to display such surprise. 'We thought your tribe had perished, it has been so long since you have journeyed to Lazar,' it said.

'No,' Old-maa replied, her lips pursed.

'And you bring nine to our ranks. How cursed we are

241

today. Do the rivers of Darhan run deep with deceit? Are the trees of Mauz rooted in betrayal?'

'Sola enabled,' Old-maa replied.

'How terribly unfortunate for these wretches, that the desert did not take them all. It will be assured that they will hate it here, exiles as they are. Let us begin the examination.'

There was a loud creak and the stone gate slid across the ground. But instead of seeing the city, as Raim expected, the doors opened into another courtyard – a small square surrounded by tall walls. There were two doors at the far end of the square, each with a burly guard standing in front of it. In the centre, there was a man, dressed in a simple white garment, bareheaded but with a long white beard that was tied into a knot at his waist. He had the same air of stillness as a Baril priest, but behind him was the proof that he was an exile – his haunt, floating in the air.

As they moved forward into the square, the hairs on the back of Raim's neck stood up. When he looked around for the source of such a chill, he saw eyes – hundreds, maybe even thousands of pairs of eyes, looking down on the group as they entered. The population of Lazar, peering out of holes in the rock. Raim thought back to all the stories he had heard of people being exiled, of those lost for ever. He had found them now. He was about to become one of them. His hands felt stone cold inside their bindings.

One by one, the Chauk were called forward. A young female Chauk was released from her bonds first, and she stumbled into the circle, her haunt hovering behind her. They stopped just before the old man.

All eyes in the place were fixed on the four figures. Two humans, two haunts.

The priest opened his hands, and addressed the haunt directly: 'What say you, spirit?'

The haunt raised her head to the sky. 'Forgiven,' she said.

'You are certain?' the priest said.

The spirit nodded.

'Then go forth, and return to be whole.'

Slowly, the haunt began to dissolve into the ether.

'Mother?' the Chauk cried out, her expression torn between horror and relief. When the haunt had disappeared completely, she outstretched her hand, stroking the air where the spirit of her mother had been.

The priest was gentle with her. 'Come, child. You have satisfied the consequences of breaking your oath by coming here to Lazar.'

The exiled woman collapsed to her knees. 'Is . . . is she gone for good?'

When the man nodded, tears began to stream down the woman's face. But they didn't look like tears of relief to Raim. The man directed her through the left-hand door.

The next six Chauk entered the square with the same results: the spirits stopped their tormenting and disappeared into the air.

But it wasn't until Ryopi stepped forward that Raim felt his stomach drop. *Wait.* He reached out to Draikh in his thoughts. *Are you leaving me?*

'No. I'm not. And if they try to make me—'

Raim's attention turned back to Ryopi, whose face broke into a grin as the old man went through the speech with the spirit of his father.

But his relief came too soon.

'NOT forgiven! Ha! Think I would let you off this easily? You are a pitiful fool and a coward and your punishment is not over. See these exiles? They are Chauk but you are worse than them because you still have me!' The spirit let out a stream of maniacal laughter.

Ryopi fell to the floor, and retched the contents of his stomach onto the ground.

This time the priest pointed to the right-hand door, but Ryopi didn't move. In fact, he stood up and started to bolt back the way they came. On cue, the Chauk guards who had been standing in front of the doors came rushing forward, catching Ryopi by the arm. They dragged him back and through the right-hand door, with his spirit following, still ranting and raving. The noise level had increased within the square too, all those pairs of eyes suddenly turning to their neighbours, clearly discussing what had just happened to Ryopi. Raim wondered if it was a rare occurrence.

That's what we have to do, thought Raim. *Pretend you hate me. And be convincing about it.*

'I don't think you have to worry about that,' chuckled Draikh.

The priest beckoned to him, the last and final Chauk to be evaluated.

As Raim stepped forward into the square, Draikh swooped in front of him, preparing to play the role of ultimate torturer to the most extravagant degree.

'You are the most awful human being alive!' said Draikh with a flourish. 'Traitor! Spawn of earthworm, lowly as a hyena's backside, blacker than a Chauk's soul . . .'

But he didn't get a chance to finish his sentence. From behind Draikh came a yell and the screech of swords being drawn. Two other Lazarite guards appeared in the doorway. Between them, kicking and struggling, was Wadi.

'We caught this one in the passage, trying to sneak in.'

Old-maa, who was still standing just inside the second gate, stood stock still. Raim surged towards Wadi, but the two guards who had taken Ryopi were back to grab him.

'Let her go!' he shouted. 'She's not Chauk!' But they weren't letting go – if anything, their grip was tightening.

'She is not Chauk, but she is a thief,' said the old man.

'I'm no thief!' Wadi said through laboured breaths, struggling against her guards' grip.

'Then explain how you have one of our pass-stones.'

Wadi's pendant was dangling freely around her neck, and Raim was shocked to see it looked as if it was glowing slightly. 'This is mine! My father gave it to me!' she protested.

One of the guards backhanded her across the head, and Wadi tumbled to her knees.

'That's it!' Raim shouted. In his head he said: *Draikh, let's do this.*

He twisted out of his guard's grasp, while Draikh slid round and grabbed the guard's dagger out of his belt. 'Catch!' he cried, and he launched the blade to Raim.

Raim snatched it out of mid-air and immediately flung it at the guard who had hit Wadi. His aim was true, and it struck the guard in his arm. The guard yelled out in pain – enough time for Wadi to wrench out of his grasp. She tore the knife out of her captor's blood-soaked bicep and slashed at the other.

Now Raim had caught the guards' attention, and a sharp command from the old man sent more of them pouring through the doors. They rounded on the trio, who were quickly becoming outnumbered.

But Draikh had been waiting for his opportunity, and when Wadi slashed at a guard and he dropped his sword, Draikh grabbed it and swung at the oncoming soldiers.

His blade bit into the man's hand and he dropped his weapon too – right into the waiting fingers of Raim. Raim pivoted round so that now he and Draikh were back-to-back and ready to fight. Wadi had her foot on the neck of one of the guards, and Raim's Yun dagger and the one she had wrenched from her captor's bicep in her hands, spinning menacingly.

The clang of metal filled the air. But neither Draikh nor Raim nor Wadi had moved. The guards were throwing their swords to the ground and edging back towards the doorway.

Raim stared, wide-eyed, his breathing shallow and tight. Even though the guards weren't fighting him any more, he kept a tight grip on his weapon.

A trap?

'I don't know.' Draikh sounded bemused.

The old man began to clap slowly. Wadi hesitated, then released the guard under her foot, who scrambled to his feet and raced through the left-hand doorway.

'So, two wonders return to us today, how fascinating.'

'I'm not returning anywhere,' said Wadi, breathless. She turned to look for Old-maa, who was shrinking back towards the gate they came through. Wadi held her hands together in apology. 'I only wanted to see the city for myself. Just once.'

'Now you will have plenty of time to explore it,' said the old man.

'No.' Wadi was shaking now.

'No,' echoed Raim. 'You can't make her stay in Lazar – Lazar is for the Chauk! Old-maa, you can't stand for this!'

But Old-maa was still moving away, her back towards the exit, her face blank of expression.

Wadi was showing enough distress for both of them,

tears streaming in rivers down her face. 'You told me never to come here. And now I think I know why.' The words came out as barely a whisper.

Before she disappeared through the cliffs back to the Alashan and the desert, Old-maa stopped and beckoned to Wadi. At the same time, the old man took a step back, as if giving Wadi permission to leave if she wanted to.

But Wadi didn't move.

Raim couldn't understand. 'Go, Wadi. You don't want to spend your life here.'

'I want to go with her.' Wadi's eyes glistened, but strangely Raim didn't see sadness there any more. 'But I feel calmer now. Calmer than I've ever felt.' She turned to the old man. 'This is where I'm meant to be.' There was a hint of a question in her voice, and the man just nodded.

Raim looked back at Old-maa, but she was gone. One of the Alashan guards who had accompanied them stood at the entrance to the tunnel. With a swift lift of his arm, he launched Oyu into the sky towards Raim. Oyu spread his wings and soared into the air, with a high-pitched shriek – a sound that Raim now found comforting. He held his arm outstretched, and Oyu swooped down to land on it, his great wings battering Raim on the head before being folded away.

'Well, that was quite the introduction,' said the old man. 'Come, you two, the time has come to show you your new home.'

26

Through the gate, Raim's jaw dropped. Lazar sprawled in front of them in undeniable beauty. Buildings exploded out of the mountainside, shadowy openings gaping like mouths out of the orange-red rock.

'My name is Puutra,' said the old man as the door closed behind them. The sound of the lock bolting across their only exit made Raim jump. 'I am the leader of the Shan, who govern this city.'

Puutra prattled on, but the man's voice faded in Raim's ears as the city came alive around them. The place was a hubbub of activity, so different from the miserable portrait painted by the elders in Darhan. Back home, they never told of a bustling city but of a slum, dirtier and more run-down than the poorest Darhan camp. Though it *was* dusty. Already, Raim's shoes were covered with a film of orange talc, finer than the sand on the dunes outside. But there was a sense of order to the way the city was designed, as if every inch had been carved and crafted with a specific purpose. It was supposed to be a place of deceit, treachery and repulsive shadow and none who lived in Lazar were supposed to live for very long. What it was not supposed to have was culture, activity and light.

And plants! These weren't the sparse shrubs of the desert but blooming greens that someone had obviously given precious water to help them thrive. It was an impossible thought after the strict rationing of water he had just experienced. He felt his mouth actually fill with water at the sight of all the green, and he had to restrain himself from taking a bite out of one of the more succulent looking leaves, purely for the desire for something fresh.

He could see the Chauk who had been led through before him being herded away like goats by some Lazarites. They shuffled their feet, looking dazed – bewildered. He started to move towards them.

Puutra threw his staff out in front of Raim's feet so he couldn't move any further. 'No, please follow me.'

'But . . . where are they taking them?'

'To their new homes,' he said, but didn't elaborate. Instead he led him in the opposite direction, and Ryopi and another Chauk, who introduced himself as Dumas, soon joined them.

Dumas seemed to embody all of Raim's immediate impressions of Lazar, both surprising and expected. He had a haunt, of course, a young woman with listless blonde hair whom he called Nava. He seemed in good health, but his clothes were worn and tattered. His sandals were made of quality leather, and yet in places they were patched up with careless stitching. This contrast – of new and old, of good and bad – was evident everywhere else in the city. There were elaborate stone carvings all over the walls and yet they were broken in many places. There were rugs of great intricacy thrown over balconies but they were full of holes.

Raim's jaw ached from being held wide open.

'Can you believe this?' he said aloud, more to himself than anyone else.

'No,' answered Draikh and Wadi, simultaneously.

It was just so different from what he had been told. It was overwhelmingly so, like everything that had ever been said to him about Lazar had been a lie. Wadi nudged him with her elbow. She seemed just as enraptured as him, her neck craned, looking in every direction. He followed her gaze over to a group of Chauk children, who had obviously been watching their arrival. Children, in Lazar – unadorned with scars. Of course there would be children, Raim scolded himself. They were exiled, not castrated. The children were staring at them with big, wide-open eyes. One little girl cocked her head and smiled shyly, holding the corner of a blanket to her mouth and letting the rest of the fabric trail on the ground. Raim's hand went to the scarf around his wrist and he felt a familiar pang in his heart for the sister he'd left behind.

They arrived in front of a building that was grander

than any Raim had seen in Kharein. It put the Rentai to shame. Four rounded columns stretched high into the mountainside, each carved with intricate figures that danced their way up in spirals. Red dust and grains of rock fell on Raim's head as they waited for the door to open. He looked up and saw men suspended by ropes, tapping at the intricate stonework.

'What are they doing?' asked Raim.

'They are making it right,' Puutra replied. But Raim couldn't understand. They were destroying it, eroding the details, obscuring the faces of the figurines and crumbling the stone.

'They're crazy,' said Draikh, shaking his head.

'We are Chauk, what do you expect?' said Dumas, spitting onto the ground. 'How can oathbreakers create anything of beauty and worth? That's why every time we manage to make something that could be called beautiful, we destroy a part of it. We're not worthy of it.'

The doors opened and they stepped into the heart of the mountain.

Raim's hood slipped down as he stretched his neck back to look up at the enormous hall. Arched beams like long, spindly fingers gripped the top of the ceiling. The beams disappeared into darkness as they rose and came together. Even the light from the torches mounted along the wall couldn't penetrate the upper reaches.

Puutra led them up curved stairs that wound up past the high, open balconies Raim had seen from the ground when he arrived. As they climbed higher and higher, they passed through a series of workrooms used by artists and dedicated craftsmen. Raim stopped at a man who was diligently adding the finishing touches to a magnificent statue.

They had statues in Darhan but they were nothing like this one – theirs were simply crude, unwieldy representations of animals, commissioned especially for the Khan. There were hardly any portraits of royalty, let alone statues. In their nomadic society, it was hard to find an artist willing to sit and work for months on a large piece of stone. In any case, it was difficult to travel with any piece of art that couldn't be rolled up and transported by camel.

This Lazarite carving depicted a beautiful woman, with long hair that curled down her shoulders almost to her navel. A loose dress folded in pleats down to the ground and pooled like frozen silver. But it was impossible to see the statue without being drawn in by the expression on her face. Her eyes were soft, round and intelligent, with highly arched brows that mirrored the outlines of caves in the Ailing mountains. Her nose was small and gently sloped, so different from the wide, flat noses he was used to seeing in Darhan. He was mesmerized.

'Who is that?' Wadi asked the artist, who was chipping the last bit of stone out of a lock of hair. Raim turned to see Wadi studying the statue with the same intensity that he was. But then again, in the desert she would have had even less exposure to art than he did in Darhan.

'That is Lady Chabi, a goddess,' the artist replied, bowing his head.

'A *living* goddess,' said Puutra. He reached out and put his index finger on her cold bottom lip, then pulled away. 'Her body passed through here, to continue its journey to Aqben. This statue will stand proudly in a place of honour. Come, we must keep moving.'

Just as Raim crossed the threshold into the next room, there came a sickening crack from behind him. He spun round and saw the sculptor, his hands grasping the handle of a pickaxe. The pick's head was buried deep within stone-Chabi's face. Her perfectly shaped nose lay like dirt upon the ground.

Wadi cried out in shock. 'What did he just do?'

'As Dumas explained before, he is making it right.' This time, Puutra didn't turn round or stop talking, so the group was forced to continue moving to keep up. 'The Lady Chabi will forgive us. She will understand that Chauk cannot be responsible for creating something so perfect.'

'Like I said before, he's crazy,' said Draikh.

The old man was sprightly and moved rapidly. Raim increased his pace to keep up with him as they started up yet another staircase. The building was much taller than Raim imagined. The stairs climbed endlessly, yet Puutra always remained a few steps ahead. Puutra finally left the staircase for a landing and Raim leaned up against the wall to catch his breath. Puutra disappeared behind a curtain hung over a low doorway.

'Beaten by an elder,' Draikh mocked.

'Talk to me when you stop floating.'

Wadi laughed at his muttering. 'Well, it doesn't bode well for your training,' she said, passing him by without so much as a laboured breath.

They bantered through the doorway, but were silenced upon entering. Puutra had led them into paradise.

Water, *everywhere*. Wadi reached back and grabbed Raim's wrist, and he could tell by the nail marks left by her grip just how shocked she was. Water flowed all around them, meandering in slow, rippling channels around a stepping-stone walkway. Lilies bloomed on the surface, delicate touches of pink and white, flirting amongst massive pads of deep, luscious green.

There was a peaked pagoda in the centre, where Puutra beckoned them forward. Raim and Wadi started across the stones, but Ryopi fell to his knees and started splashing water on his face. 'Water! Water! Water!' He repeated the word as if he believed it would all disappear if he stopped calling it by name.

His father stood by, repulsed, and then yelled at Ryopi so loudly he fell off balance into the pond. But for once Ryopi didn't care about his father's taunts. He was back in his element. He waded over to the pagoda and lifted himself out of the pond, dripping wet and shivering with glee.

When they were all together, Puutra turned to Wadi. 'Please, my dear. You must come with me.'

Raim bristled, as although Puutra had asked politely,

something in his tone set Raim on edge. Wadi eyed him nervously, then turned back to Puutra. 'Where are you taking me?'

'You have a special purpose, different from that of these two.'

'But—'

'It concerns that pendant around your neck. Are you not curious?'

Raim knew Wadi would go with the old man then. She turned to Raim. 'I will meet you back here, tonight.'

Raim nodded, but still couldn't shake the uneasy feeling in his stomach as Puutra led her away.

27

Without Puutra there to restrain him, Dumas drew himself up to full height and turned his steely-eyed gaze over Raim and Ryopi again. Although he barely looked older than Raim, his furrowed brow and grim-set jaw made Raim think that he took himself far too seriously. 'I've been told I must show you the Shan quarters, where you'll be living as apprentices. This pagoda indicates the beginning of the temple of the Shan. I hope you recognize what a privilege this is.'

Raim couldn't believe what he'd just heard. Apprentices? A temple? He wasn't sure if he was ready to be apprenticed to anyone ever again, not after Mhara.

Ryopi, however, asked Raim's question for him: 'I'm sorry . . . am I supposed to have heard of the Shan?'

Dumas rolled his eyes dramatically. 'Not only do the Shan govern Lazar, but we are also . . .' He paused for dramatic effect. '. . . sages.' Raim's eyes widened in disbelief and Ryopi let out a spluttering cough. Dumas laughed smugly. 'That's right. Just don't expect to become a sage yourself overnight. It takes most people years to accomplish even the slightest bit of sage magic.'

'Prove it,' said Draikh, challenging Dumas and his downcast-looking spirit. 'Prove you're a sage.' He pointed at a chair in the corner of the pagoda. 'Move that over here and take a seat.'

A red flush began creeping up Dumas's neck from beneath his tunic. It touched his cheeks as he spun round on his heels. 'I have nothing to prove to you.'

'Ask me out loud to move the chair,' Draikh murmured in Raim's mind.

'Move the chair,' ordered Raim. Draikh swooped over to the chair and pushed it into Dumas's path so he had to swerve round it to keep walking. Dumas said nothing, but Raim could see the flush on his face had not subsided.

You didn't have to do that.

'He's no sage,' Draikh said.

Neither am I! And I might need his help if I'm to figure anything out about my scar . . .

Draikh pouted. 'You're no fun any more.'

Dumas led them over another set of stepping stones, leading away from where Puutra took Wadi. They passed through another curtain, and into a long hallway. Raim was immediately struck by the statues that lined the walls.

'Who are they?' Raim couldn't help but stare at them.

They were so lifelike. He thought they were going to jump off the walls and join in the conversation.

'This room honours the sages of Lazar.'

'They were real? I thought they were just a story – a legend.'

'Just a legend in Darhan, maybe. But to us, they are gods. We strive to emulate them. It is the Shan's ultimate goal.'

'So these sages – they could levitate, and heal?'

'Oh, they could do so much more than that. And Lazar was once the centre of it all! Yes,' he said, in answer to Raim's sceptical look. 'Did you think this was always the city of unwanteds? No, some of the world's greatest men were taught and brought up within these walls. Khans and warlords from all of the world's corners competed to have the most powerful sage at their right hand. The difference between having a sage and not could mean life and death for a tribe. If only one tribe had a sage, it was virtually a guarantee of victory. But if there was a sage on each side . . . woe betide whoever had the weaker. It must have been so impressive. But that was many hundreds of years ago.'

None of the statues was in perfect condition, but the face of one in particular was completely obliterated.

'What happened to this statue?' asked Raim.

Dumas's face darkened. 'That is a sage we do not mention. The one who caused Lazar to be cut off from the rest of the world. The last seven saved us from him – but at the cost of their art, their knowledge. At the end of their battle, an enormous fire engulfed this city, destroying almost all the population and, most tragically, all the great books and journals. They say the fire was the work of the supernatural. That it was soul fire. No one has been able to leave since. It is only thanks to the Alashan that people arrive here at all.

'When the last of the sages died, Lazar became a place for the exiled. We are not bothered by the outside world, no one will touch us, no one will invade us, no one – except a very few Alashan – can even find us. If they knew of half the riches we possess, they would attempt to conquer us immediately. Instead, we are left alone to uncover the secrets of sage magic. Every new exile is tested as they enter the gates of Lazar. Those who pass the test, like you two, are apprenticed to the Shan.'

'Pass the test? It feels more like failure to me,' said Ryopi, eyeing the spirit of his father.

'If you had been forgiven, you could not be Shan. But if a haunt decides to stay . . . if the punishment of arriving in Lazar is not enough, then that person is blessed.'

'How in Sola's name can this be a blessing?'

'Have you not figured it out yet? The haunts are the secret behind a sage's power. Yes, of course, they hate you at first and will not cooperate with you. But if you can withstand their torment, slowly gain their trust, win them over . . . you could become a sage.'

A glimmer of hope, of possibility, sparked in Ryopi's eyes but behind them, his father started howling with laughter, a hollow noise that sounded like it would never cease. 'Tell him about the catch, the catch – there's always a catch, isn't there?'

Ryopi stuttered: 'Wh-what is the catch?'

'Most of the time, a Shan apprentice will never move past the first stage. For them, life is . . . difficult.' He eyed Ryopi's haunt nervously, and Raim could tell he thought Ryopi would be one of those. Dumas swiftly moved on. 'Puutra is our teacher and leader, and I am his youngest – but most advanced – disciple.' The pride in Dumas's voice was strong but it faltered as he trained his eye on Draikh. 'Anyway, our plan is to one day restore the art of the sages to the world.'

'But if everything was destroyed in the fire, how do you know this?'

'There is one book.' Dumas lifted his tunic, where he had a small but thick tome lashed onto his stomach. 'It was written by Hao, the last real sage to live – and die – in Lazar. He explains our history. Every Shan must have one, and study it well. You must keep it with you at all times. In fact, I have one for each of you.' He pulled out two other books from the bag at his side. Raim tentatively took it from Dumas's outstretched hand. He flipped through the pages with his thumb, then passed it back to Dumas. 'I don't want this.'

'What do you mean? It's essential for any Shan.'

'I can't read,' said Raim.

'Oh,' said Dumas, the smug look returning to his

face. 'Then this is going to take longer than we thought.'

Raim's room had nothing more than a mattress on the floor and an open window. He slumped down onto the makeshift bed and let the weariness seep out of his muscles. He hadn't realized how much tension he was holding between his shoulder blades. This place set him on edge. The weight of years of equating Lazar with the lowest of the low hung heavily around his neck. And yet, as he tried to push that weight away, it all seemed to converge around his wrist.

He sat up and rested the back of his head against the orange-stone wall. Steadily he unpicked the knot that tied Dharma's scarf around his scar, and let the shining fabric flutter onto the mattress beside him. Immediately, bile rose in his throat, but he forced himself to look. The ugly red scar throbbed beneath the skin of his arm, screaming at him, 'Traitor, traitor.' It hadn't changed since the night he had made his Absolute Vow to Khareh. Not even now that he was here, in Lazar.

'Could you look any more upset?' Draikh drifted into his line of sight.

'I thought . . . I don't know. I thought once I got to Lazar it would all become clear . . . like the spirit of the person who forced this promise on me would jump out of the stone or something.'

Draikh looked from side to side. 'No one here. Just me.'

'Right,' said Raim. He drummed on the wall with the

back of his head a couple of times, as if to shake the demons away. 'So we've come all this way, for what?'

'Well, no one knows more about oathbreaking than the Shan. They might be able to help. And if they can't . . .'

'If they can't . . .' Raim let that thought drift and hang in the room, filling the air with a heaviness that seemed to make it difficult to breathe.

He sat in that position until a squawk from the window snapped him out of his depressing meditation. Oyu was perched on the ledge, his black body contrasted against the red cliff face opposite.

Raim stood up and stroked his companion's oily feathers. Oyu clucked affectionately.

'Not much temptation for you here, hmm?' He looked out the window to see how far down Oyu's tail stretched. Vertigo hit him immediately; his head whirled and he forced himself back from the ledge. The drop careered down at least twenty storeys. It reminded him of the cliff he had almost fallen off just before Mhara had . . .

'Maybe she survived,' said Draikh, interrupting his private thoughts.

Raim gulped back the spark of hope Draikh's words ignited. 'I saw the height of those cliffs. No one could survive a fall like that.'

'She was strong, though. And you never found a body.'

Raim ignored him and concentrated hard on the view. He knew they were deep inside the mountain range he had seen on the approach with the Alashan, but he was so high up here that he could see beyond the cliffs and on to the desert, which stretched ahead, massive and all-consuming. The dunes that had appeared as mountains were now dwarfed by the immensity of the desert itself.

Oyu hopped inside and settled on Raim's shoulder.

Thinking of Mhara again set his resolve. 'I don't want to become Shan, or be a sage. If they can't help me figure out this scar and clear my name, then that's it. We get out of here and find someone who can.'

28

He watched the sun set from his window, the sensation of being indoors making him feel cooped up and uncomfortable. He knew Wadi must be feeling the same way, if not even worse. When the sun had disappeared completely, he found his way back to the water-pagoda to wait for her as they had agreed. Eventually, one of the Shan entered the pagoda and demanded he leave at once. He tried to protest, but the man grabbed his upper arm and started dragging him towards the door. Raim shrugged him off but understood the message. He stumbled back to his room. The book Dumas had given him lay abandoned on the bed. None of the characters were recognizable to him and at that point he was too tired and frustrated to feign any interest. Eventually, exhausted and hungry, he fell asleep.

The next morning, while Raim was still rubbing sleep out of his eyes, Dumas arrived at his doorway and thrust a lukewarm bowl of mushy rice into his hands. 'Eat this on the way,' he said.

Obediently, Raim followed Dumas, shovelling mounds of food into his mouth with chopsticks as they walked, and trying to shake the cobwebs from his mind. Dumas led him to a large room with a smooth stone floor, which he called the meditation room. There were four other disciples already there, along with Puutra, who was sitting in the lotus position in front of them all. Dumas's claim to be the most advanced of the apprentices turned out to be true. It also seemed that since the story of Raim and Draikh taking on a slew of Chauk guards had reached Dumas – making Raim the closest thing to a sage in Lazar – he was much less inclined to help Raim in any way.

Dumas went straight up to Puutra and bowed. 'Puutra, today I am nearing a breakthrough, I can feel it. I must train. I cannot waste my time showing some boy around.'

Raim felt his muscles tense at the word 'boy'. He took a closer look at Dumas's spirit: a woman, staring at her nails whilst floating behind Dumas. Slowly he was beginning to recognize all the other spirits. Remarkably, two of the Chauk seemed to have *the same spirit*. These haunts were so docile that it was hard to pick them out at once. Even Draikh – who wasn't a true haunt – was never that quiet and still. *But maybe that's just you.*

'Fine,' said Puutra. 'However, you will be training without me. I will be working with Raim today.' Dumas bowed stiffly and then stormed out of the room.

Raim shifted his weight from foot to foot as Puutra studied him with his small dark eyes. The pause went on for longer than Raim felt comfortable with. Then, Puutra clicked his fingers twice. The two Shan who had the same spirit stood up and introduced themselves as Vlad and Zu, husband and wife. They both had thick, dark hair, almost the same length. When Raim saw Zu, he almost stumbled into a bow on instinct. She looked almost identical to the Seer-Queen, Batar-Khan's wife.

She laughed at his confusion. 'I see you must have met my sister in Darhan? The more . . . privileged twin.' Standing at almost a foot shorter than her husband, Zu exuded intelligence, which was different from the Seer-Queen, who had only ever looked bored or sneering in Raim's presence. Together, Vlad and Zu made for an intimidating pair. Raim, by contrast, felt small, un-educated, and unworthy in their presence.

'So how do you do it?' The question gushed out of Vlad like water out of a torn flask.

Raim frowned. 'Do what?'

'Your haunt!' Vlad was staring at Draikh with wide eyes. 'We were in the square yesterday, watching the induction. We have to know, how did you fight together?'

Raim bit his lip. 'Um, well. I don't know really. I suppose it just seemed natural.'

Vlad was eyeing him, and he squirmed under his scrutiny. 'Perhaps, since it came to you instinctively, you are unable to tell us your process. When you have some education in the stages of becoming a sage, I'm sure you will tell us how you have managed to achieve so much in such little time.'

'Start at the beginning,' said Puutra. 'When did you break your vow to Khareh to cause his spirit to appear?'

'Never,' said Raim, practically spitting the word.

Puutra, Vlad and Zu were deathly still with shock.

Zu was first to break. 'What do you mean, *never?* You have a haunt; you must have broken your oath . . .'

'Look,' Raim said abruptly, holding up his hand to keep Zu from continuing. 'My vow to Khareh is still intact. I can prove it.' He showed the three Shan the ink-black mark of permanence on his chest.

'Scorching Sola be cursed,' said Puutra. Vlad began frantically flicking through his book, but his wife stopped him with a touch.

'You know there is nothing in there to explain this,' she said, still unable to take her eyes from Draikh.

'But Draikh is not my problem. My vow to Khareh – this mark – that's not the problem either,' Raim said, desperation creeping into his voice. '*This* is the problem.' He showed them his wrist, the blood-red scar there in all its terrible glory, which they all stared at in silence. He searched their faces but they were revealing nothing. 'This is why I came to Lazar. This is the scar without a shadow that sent me into exile – and I need to know its origins. Can you help me figure it out?'

The ensuing silence seemed to put a stop to Raim's

heart, and when Puutra stepped forward to put a hand on his shoulder, the breath he had been holding blew out of him in one swift sigh of relief. 'Of course we will help,' said Puutra, his eyes sparkling with warmth. He turned and looked at the couple. 'Vlad and Zu are former Baril priests,' Puutra explained. 'If anyone will be able to help you, they will. Now, if you will excuse me, I have some other matters to attend to . . .'

Raim's eyes widened involuntarily. Baril – just like his brother.

Vlad nodded, and smiled benevolently at Raim. 'Yes, I'm sure we can help you solve your mystery. But first, it would help us if we went over your relationship with your haunt.'

'It would?' asked Raim. He looked over at Draikh, who shrugged.

'Have you discussed with your haunt what he remembers when he first appeared?' pressed on Zu.

'My name is Draikh, not "haunt",' Draikh said, crossing his arms over his chest. 'And we've been over it many times. I remember seeing Raim writhing on the ground, being attacked by those pesky flies. I decided that I couldn't just let him die, so I helped him out a little.' Draikh shrugged. 'And then I thought I might as well stick around, since he always seems in need of my help. Then Raim let the bird – the garfalcon – swallow the knot so he chose to have me stick around here, for ever.'

Vlad narrowed his eyes slightly. 'There was nothing

else? No trigger – no inciting event – on the other end, when you were still as one with Khareh?'

Draikh hesitated, then said: 'No.'

Raim could feel Draikh's frustration mounting as Vlad continued to study him carefully, and so he tried to bring the focus back to his scar: 'My grandmother was a shaman, a healer. A few days before my Honour Age, she used memory tea on me to try to get me to remember the promise behind this scar. I saw a woman with me, in a tent near the desert . . . but the vision ended before I could find out what the vow was. I was told that I might be able to find answers here . . .'

Zu tapped a finger on her bottom lip. 'Well, we have no memory tea here.' She reached out towards his wrist. 'May I?'

Raim hesitated. It was the first time anyone had looked at the scar on his wrist without shying away in horror or staring at it in disgust. Finally, he nodded, and let her take his hand. She ran a finger over the scar. 'A promise made, unremembered . . . a vow so bold, it breaks even under the weight of an Absolute. You are a maze of mysteries, do you know that, young Raim? A puzzle to be solved. Luckily, we specialize in mysteries here . . .'

Tears pricked at the corners of his eyes, but he blinked them away. He wanted so badly to be normal and un-mysterious. Now he felt relieved and even – for the first time – glad that he had followed Mhara's advice. 'So tell me, why were you exiled?' Raim asked, changing the subject.

Vlad glanced sidelong at his wife, and she lowered her chin. 'Amongst the Baril our speciality was history.'

It was then he saw it. He wondered how he hadn't noticed immediately. The most noticeable characteristic of a Baril priest, a flat area about the size of a palm on the forehead. It was said to be formed by the many hours of intensive meditative prayer Baril undertook each day with their heads touching the ground. There were other rumours, though, that involved a harsher degree of self-mutilation where men and women would spend their days grinding their foreheads into rock or sleeping with huge weights balanced on their heads until the right shape was formed. He remembered asking Tarik what he had thought of a life like that. Tarik had, of course, gone on and on about how he would be honoured to have the opportunity to prove his piety . . . on that subject, you could never shut him up.

Raim stared up at the man's forehead, where the flat area was just visible now. It would have been plainer to see if the man had been bald, in Baril tradition. As if in answer to Raim's questioning gaze, Vlad asked him to bring over a light.

Raim plucked a candelabrum from the wall and brought it over to where Vlad was standing. Vlad then pulled back the tuft of dark brown hair that concealed the mark. It became much more visible. It was bigger than Raim's palm; it was more like his whole hand. Raim couldn't help but whistle in awe.

'My brother joined the Baril this past season,' Raim said.

'He will have to control his curiosity,' said Vlad.

Raim grimaced. 'He won't have any trouble doing that. You could never interest Tarik in anything but books.'

Vlad raised an eyebrow. 'But that is precisely the problem. Or it was our problem at least. We couldn't stop reading the books. Even the forbidden ones. Which is why we are here now, haunted by the same spirit of our Baril master.'

'There are forbidden books? Well, that does sound a bit more exciting than anything else I've heard about the Baril. What do forbidden books have to say that other books don't?'

'Magic. Sages. Spirits. Power. Secrets. All those lost things we're trying to discover here about spirit power, it has also been written down by Baril historians,' said Vlad, unable to disguise the excitement in his voice.

Zu was more temperate. 'Well, it is all written down, except no one can access it. Alas, curiosity almost killed us both. But here, we are closer to solving the mystery than ever before, even if we aren't in the Baril any more.'

'But . . . didn't you know that you would get caught?'

Zu's expression was pained, but Vlad's was blank, the excitement gone. It was Vlad who spoke. 'We made that choice. It wasn't easy. But the knowledge was worth breaking the vow for.' Vlad must have grasped a sense of how shocked Raim felt, because his next words were defensive. 'You're in Lazar, the city of oathbreakers, Raim! None of us here is perfect.'

And it was perfectly true. Every person here was a traitor.

Old Darhan prejudices pressed hard on Raim's soul. *If you didn't have your word, your honour, your knots, then what did you have?* He swallowed down his judgement. Nothing was so black and white any more.

'Tell me, Raim, which tribe were you with in Darhan?' There was a tremble in Zu's voice Raim did not know how to interpret.

He shrugged. 'Moloti. I was a Yun apprentice, but we travelled with the Khan, so we often met with other tribes.'

'We had only one treasure in Darhan – a daughter – wrenched from our grasp when we . . . were exiled.'

'Zu! Why must you always mention her . . . she could be anywhere now,' said Vlad, clenching his fists.

'But perhaps Raim will know!' Zu's voice was desperate now. 'Our daughter would have been given up for adoption in Darhan, away from the Baril so she wouldn't have to bear our shame. Our precious little girl, our darling Dharma.'

The candles Raim had been holding crashed to the floor. Snapping out of his shock, he stomped on the flames, singeing his sandals. When the smoke and momentary excitement died down, Zu spoke with quiet hope.

'You know her?'

Vlad was sceptical. 'It is a common name.'

Raim cleared his throat and tried to speak as calmly as possible. 'A girl named Dharma was brought to my grandfather two years ago. He refused to tell us why he had taken her in – an outsider – rather than someone from our tribe. But when he came back with her . . .' He curled his index fingers together, in recognition of the knot his grandfather had made. 'He never told us the meaning of the new knot, but we assumed it was to do with her. Perhaps her parents were Chauk and her own tribe rejected her . . . we had no idea. But I do know how I can tell if my Dharma-sister is the same as yours.' He turned to Zu. 'Dharma had something that belonged to her mother – the only memento she carried with her of her former life. Because of it we expected her to be of high blood or at least from a wealthy tribe, but I admit we would not have guessed Baril. Anyway . . .' He gulped.

'A scarf,' Zu whispered.

'Give me one second,' said Raim. He bolted out of the room and leaped two stairs at a time towards his chamber. He pounced on the bed, grabbing Dharma's scarf from underneath the pillow before rushing back down to Vlad and Zu.

'Was it this?' he said between deep breaths.

Zu was already in tears, but she beamed through them. 'May I . . . have it?'

Raim stared at the material in his hands; his only memory of his sister. He gripped it hard. Then he undid the knot, which was holding together the two halves made when Mhara had sliced it off his wrist. He passed one half to Zu. She pulled him into a big hug and he squirmed in her grasp. 'Your grandfather sounds like a good man. I am glad she was placed with your family.'

Her words were like a knife-wrench in his gut. 'Yes, he is a good man. And I love Dharma and my brother too. I hope they are all right. I wonder how much they know about what's happened to me . . . I hope she understands that I'm not an oathbreaker – it . . . it would break her heart. She believed in me so much.'

Vlad and Zu nodded in understanding, and didn't pester Raim with more questions.

But there was one person Raim cared about who was here in Lazar with him, and when Puutra returned to the doorway again, it was the perfect opportunity to ask: 'Where is Wadi? I tried to meet her last night in the water garden, but she never came. Is she living in a different part of Lazar?'

Puutra's face was dark. 'Wadi has her own path to follow, and she would do it best without distractions from you.'

'That's not fair! You pr—' Raim was going to say 'promised', but caught himself. 'Promise' felt like a dangerous word to use in Lazar. And Puutra was an oath-breaker. He would never want to make a promise again.

'You would do well to follow her lead, and concentrate on your own journey,' said Puutra. 'You have a long road ahead of you, if you are to become Shan.'

'I told you, I don't want to be Shan! I just want to go home.'

A fleeting smile crossed Puutra's face. 'That's a shame. If you don't train to be Shan . . . then you will never solve the mystery of your scar. You may have been young, but the memory is there, imprinted on your soul. All you have to do is learn how to access it. The Shan can teach you how.'

29

They started with meditation, and Raim had never realized it could be so exhausting. Puutra's sessions were more intense even than Yasmin's. For the first hour Puutra asked him to move constantly, from the lotus position, to balancing on one foot like a tree and even, for a minute, on his head with his feet resting up against the wall. Harder still was the next hour, when Puutra demanded he sit absolutely still without moving a single muscle. In fact, it was impossible. He managed five minutes before breaking, and then Puutra made him start all over again.

And Raim concentrated harder. He concentrated so hard that he felt it – felt a spark in his mind where he realized he could reach out to the spirit. But it wasn't Draikh he was reaching out to. It was the other person. The person who forced the unforgivable scar on him.

'I see you!' Raim leaped to his feet and spun round himself. All he caught was the hem of her white dress, before she swept away from his sight, disappearing to wherever it was she came from. 'Who are you? Show yourself! I command you.'

But she was gone.

'Damn!' Raim stomped his foot in frustration. 'Argh, I can't believe her! I know she is there, why doesn't she just show herself to me?'

Puutra's face was white, as if he had seen a ghost. He walked over to a desk that was set up in the corner and sat down to write.

'Why is she always running away from me?' Raim asked.

It took a while before Puutra replied. 'You have no idea who she is?'

Raim shook his head.

'More meditation will help unlock your memory, then,' Puutra said, with a half-hearted smile.

Somehow, Raim doubted it. He pressed on with a different question that had been bothering him. 'Puutra, are you a sage?'

Puutra shook his head. 'No. The five stages of becoming a sage are tolerance, separation, communication, cooperation and partnership. I reached communication and then . . . I have never managed to progress beyond that.'

'But what I don't understand is that I've seen a sage. Not . . . not a very good sage, I don't think, but he was arrested on the day of my brother's wedding.'

'Ah yes, that must have been Garus, that crazy fool. I wondered whether we would hear news of him. He would have been so intrigued by you if he had been here, that's certain. So he is performing tricks for the royals, is he?'

'Batar-Khan arrested him. I assume he has been executed by now.'

Puutra clucked in the back of his throat. 'His disappearance caused us a lot of pain. Before you arrived, he was the most powerful of all of us, the only one to breach cooperation. Even if he only had a small amount of control, it was something. The problem was, his vow was small, and his spirit was weak . . . she could only perform the simplest of tasks. Still, Garus grew tired of our isolated existence out here in the desert mountains and believed that he was ready to bring sages back to Darhan. He believed himself much more powerful than he was. He wanted to join the ranks of our ancestors, wanted to be worshipped as a hero . . . wanted to be the new sage at the right hand of the Khan. Obviously, much good that dream has done for him . . . although we tried to warn him. But he was old. Maybe he sensed his opportunity for greatness was running out.'

'He made a carpet fly.' That was one thing Raim could never forget.

Puutra grimaced. 'Yes . . . yes, cooperation. But they weren't true partners, not yet. Granted, it took him decades of study to accomplish even that, but it is nothing compared with the feats of the past.'

Raim shrugged. 'I think most people in the room were awed . . . I know my best friend was.'

Puutra released a long sigh. 'If he had stayed with us perhaps he could have been truly great. But he caused far more damage than good. The knowledge we've lost because he has gone, that is one thing. But it is not nearly so bad as *how* he chose to escape.'

'What do you mean?' asked Raim. 'Surely he would have had to join the Alashan . . .'

'No.' Puutra shook his head and cracked his knuckles. 'The Alashan never take Chauk back to Darhan. Never. But there is another way out of Lazar . . .'

Raim raised an eyebrow. 'I thought we were completely cut off here?'

'As far as most know, yes. But there are tunnels through the mountains that eventually lead to Darhan. They were once underground trade routes – the only real way through the desert to Aqben in the south. Lazar was a hub of activity. The Khans of Darhan, Mauz – even the southern kings – would send their heirs here to learn the ancient art of being a sage.'

Raim folded his arms across his chest. 'The Khans sent their children to be oathbreakers? Why in Sola's name would they do that?'

'Raim . . . I realize this is difficult for you. Most apprentices to the Shan discover this knowledge them-selves, from the book that you cannot read. That way they can come to these revelations slowly, unlocking the *real*

history of the past from the words inscribed on the page –
at their own pace. But you do not have that luxury. So I beg
of you to keep an open mind.'

Raim hesitated. *What would Khareh do?*

'He would listen,' said Draikh. 'He would try to learn.'

Raim knew Draikh was right. He nodded slowly.

Puutra walked over to a locked chest at the far end of
the room. From it, he pulled out a large scroll of paper.
Inscribed on the scroll in delicate inkwork was the most
detailed map Raim had ever seen in his life. Puutra spread
it out over the floor and pointed at Lazar. 'The sages
haven't always been oathbreakers.'

'Like me!' Raim exclaimed. 'You said I had to have
broken my oath for Draikh to appear, but that's not always
true, is it?'

'Like you, but not like you. The sages from the old
stories – the ones who sat at the right hand of the Khan –
were not oathbreakers. Lazar was where they came to learn
how to externalize *their own* spirits. They could perform
sage magic without breaking any oaths at all.'

'Then why don't you teach that? Surely that is much
better than having to become a traitor first!'

'We would, if we knew how. But that knowledge is even
more lost to the sands of time than our version of the art.
The sages could never become Khans of their own right,
because by externalizing yourself, you make yourself so
much weaker. You're losing part of your own spirit, after
all. One sage – whose name we do not speak – discovered

that he could become much stronger if he used someone else's spirit as his power. He dreamed of becoming both Khan and sage in one – he didn't want to be someone's second-in-command. He wanted to lead. There were seven other sages living in Lazar at the time, and when they realized what he had done, they were horrified. They chased him through the tunnels, battling him along the way, trying to prevent him from reaching Darhan. It was an epic battle, the seven against the one rogue. They defeated him, but at great cost. In the end, Hao – the strongest left – decided that the knowledge that oath-breaking could lead to becoming a sage was too dangerous. They sealed the tunnels into and out of Lazar, keeping one key – one pass-stone for each remaining sage – seven in total. Five of the sages left Lazar then, to travel back to Darhan and spread words of hatred and deceit against all oathbreakers. They encouraged their khans to exile oath-breakers into the desert to Lazar – the only way they could think of to keep oathbreakers from learning how to manipulate their spirits into becoming powerful sages.

'Only two of those keys remained in Lazar. And Garus stole one of them. That fool! We are lucky that another has returned to us very recently.'

'But why would you want to train sages again, if this Hao person and the others tried so hard to stop it?'

Puutra's face darkened. 'Because what else can we do . . . just wither away here and die? If I had been allowed to stay in Darhan, then perhaps I would have been able to earn my forgiveness from my lovely wife. But now, I have no choice but to live the last of my days here, with her as my haunt hating my every move, knowing that I will die a traitor. But if I dedicate myself to becoming a sage . . . well, then at least my betrayal will not be my only legacy.

'And you have brought hope back to us, Raim. Maybe you can prove that there is another way. Another path to becoming a sage – one that doesn't result in weakness or require treachery. One that will bring honour to the sages again . . . and to Darhan.' Puutra put his hand on Raim's arm, and then shuffled off, leaving Raim alone in the room.

Raim sat down on the very edge of the map, gazing out over his entire world. All Puutra had said about sages swirled in his head.

'See what I told you?' said Draikh, in Raim's mind. 'You could be great.'

Maybe.

'You will.'

Raim traced his finger to where Kharein was. He imagined all the people he knew there. Khareh, Erdene, Lars. What were they doing? Were they living out their lives as if nothing had happened? Would Lars take his empty place in the Yun? His finger migrated out onto the steppe, into the vast grasslands. Loni, Dharma, Yasmin. All out there somewhere. Did they worry about him? Did they presume him dead, or as good as, in the desert? Up into the mountains. Tarik. He wondered if word of his exile had reached the Baril. He wondered if Tarik would be surprised. Something they had both shared was a fierce sense of honour, and loyalty – with a jolt of pain, he knew Tarik would be ashamed of him.

He imagined going back there, scar gone for ever, not only reclaiming his honour, but taking his place alongside Khareh as his sage and Protector combined.

'You could do it,' said Draikh.

Yes, Raim thought, not daring to say it aloud. *We could. We could do it.*

All I have to do is clear my name.

30

As soon as night fell, Raim left his room. Puutra's words rang in his ears, cluttering his mind. But still one thing Puutra said stood out above the rest: 'Wadi has her own path to follow.'

Wadi might have her own path, but there was no way he was going to be able to follow his without her. If there was anyone who could help him make sense of what he had learned, it was her. And if she wanted to be alone – if she didn't want his help in return – then he could accept that. But only if he heard it from her mouth.

He had to find her.

He looked up and down the hallway. It was deserted. He crept towards the stairwell and followed the twisted staircase down, only once having to hide in the shadows as a strange noise caught his attention. He waited, holding his breath, until the sound disappeared. False alarm.

The curtain leading to the water garden billowed out

into the hallway, soft as a ghost. He kneeled down low beside it and drew it aside by the tiniest margin to give him a view into the garden. He peered through but had trouble seeing anything in the darkness beyond. It seemed empty.

Rules of surveillance. Excitement surged through him as memories of his Yun training flooded back. Even on this small scale, he loved the rush. *Look again*, Mhara would have said. *Is it really empty? Don't trust your first look.*

No rash decisions. He kept looking, his pupils adjusting to the lack of light. Then he saw a dip in the blackness – movement. Someone stood up from the centre of the pagoda, walked over the stepping stones, and exited through the curtain to the right of where Raim was looking. Raim caught a brief silhouette of the man in the light from the open door. A guard from the front gate. So they were still monitoring the pagoda.

So, what does it matter? he chided himself. It's not like he could get kicked out of Lazar – Puutra had made that clear.

Still, he didn't want to draw attention to himself and potentially get Wadi in trouble if she was waiting for him. But she wouldn't be waiting at the pagoda if it was under watch. It was now or never; he didn't know when the guard might return.

He slipped through the curtain, trying to move it as little as possible. The water reflected a tiny amount of light back, enough for him to pick out the opaque shapes of the stepping stones. He skipped lightly across to the pagoda, over the other side, and down the staircase they had climbed when they had first arrived. At every floor he paused, but there were no more signs of life.

At the ground floor, he stopped again. He had come to the huge, high-ceilinged room Puutra had led him through on his first day. There was more light here, from the dying embers of torches hung up against the walls. He pressed himself into the shadow against the wall. *What if there are more guards here?* Minutes passed, but still the silence dominated. He made his move.

He darted quickly across the stone floor, and headed straight for the door.

He pulled at the handle, but the door wouldn't budge. He felt around for a lock, but found nothing. He pulled again, using more force. Nothing. He was trapped inside the temple.

He resigned himself to going back to his room, defeated.

Then a noise sounded, like a pebble skittering across the ground. He rushed over to one of the pillars and crouched down behind it, his heart hammering in his ears.

Someone appeared at the far end of the room, but Raim couldn't move his head to look up without risking being seen. He pressed his body close to the heavy stone base of the pillar, so close he felt dust from the stone fly up his nose. He held his tongue to the roof of his mouth to stop from sneezing and after what felt like an eternity, the figure moved away.

When he was sure the person was gone, Raim trudged back upstairs, trying to avoid feeling dejected about not being able to find her.

He passed through the water pagoda again, and that's when he saw it: a round circle with a line through it, identical to the markings on Wadi's pendant, carved into one of the wooden benches in the pagoda.

She had been there.

31

He returned to the pagoda every night to wait for her, learning the cycles of the guards, slipping out to wait just round the corner as they did their rounds. The days passed insufferably slowly, with either Puutra or Vlad – whoever had decided to torture him that day – moving on from meditating to focus on him and Draikh.

They were in the middle of a very simple task, based on what Draikh had demonstrated on the first day. Puutra had asked Draikh to move a chair from one end of the room to the other end, where Raim would sit down on it. At first, Raim tried to imagine what it would be like if he couldn't see Draikh – how amazing it would look to see a chair fly across the room at his command. He could imagine Khareh's delight, and Raim felt the sudden desire to run all the way back to Darhan to show him. But as the task dragged on, and Puutra banged his cane and said, 'Again, again,' the novelty quickly wore off. His late night jaunts to the pagoda had made Raim feel more tired than usual. He felt his focus drift.

Where could they be keeping Wadi?

'No idea,' Druikh replied in his mind.

Also, I don't see how getting you to prove you can carry a chair is really helping me figure out anything to do with my scar.

Draikh picked up the chair, which was now on the far side of the room from Raim. 'It doesn't help you at all.'

Puutra banged his cane into the ground. 'Pay attention! You are not taking this seriously!'

Dumas stormed over now, anger in his voice. 'Please, Puutra, he clearly doesn't care about being a sage. But look, I have breached cooperation. Watch. Nava!' He turned to his spirit, who slowly raised her pointed face in his direction. 'Bring that scroll to me.'

She stared at him blankly.

Dumas's eyes filled with desperation. 'Nava, please, please, my sweet, my heart, the scrolls? Like you did before! I beg you.'

But the haunt remained motionless.

Draikh, with Khareh's mischievous look in his eye, picked up a pile of heavy books with ease from across the room and dropped them at Puutra's feet. He smiled benevolently at Dumas. Puutra looked pleased, and turned his attention to Raim.

Dumas turned a shade of red brighter than Lazar's walls after witnessing Draikh's display. Seeing he had lost

Puutra's attention, he turned abruptly on his heels and stormed out of the room. A few moments later, Nava got up from her perch and sauntered out behind him.

'You'd do better focusing your attention on him than me,' Raim told Puutra. 'He's right. I don't care.'

'You and Draikh think you are so strong, but you have so much to learn before you realize your true power together!'

'I don't *want* to "realize my true power". I just want to find out how to clear my name and then go home. For gods' sake let me at least go outside and get some air.'

'You haven't noticed that it has taken Draikh almost ten minutes to move the chair across the room this time.'

'That's because we've been talking.'

Puutra raised one eyebrow. 'Is it?'

Raim looked at Draikh and for a moment was taken aback. Draikh's form, normally so solid and clear, had taken on a translucent quality. Raim thought he could see through Draikh to the other side of the room.

Draikh, however, was defiant. 'I'm fine,' he said, and carried the chair the rest of the way towards Raim. Raim wasn't sure if it was his imagination, but he thought he saw the chair quiver in Draikh's hands. When he went to put it down behind Raim, it seemed like he dropped it instead of the bored, deliberate movement he had been using earlier. Raim sat down.

And Draikh whipped the chair from out under him. Raim tumbled onto the floor.

Raim rubbed his sore tailbone. 'See, Puutra? I think Draikh is fine.'

'You are a fool if you believe that. You must train. Or else you risk losing that part of your friend's soul for ever. Are you prepared for that responsibility?'

Raim suddenly looked horrified. 'My friend's *soul*?'

'Yes! What did you think he was? Just an apparition from nowhere? No, Draikh – as you call him – is part of Khareh. A big part, as it was an Absolute Vow. And if you wear him out with your magic, that's it. Gone. For ever.'

'He won't wear me out. I'm strong,' said Draikh.

Puutra's mouth set in a firm line, Draikh's form quivered, and suddenly Raim wasn't so sure.

By the time they were finished, Raim was weary to the bone and Draikh seemed even weaker, but he went again to the pagoda that night, over a week since the first night. The mark in the wooden bench was deeper than before; he had redrawn it with the sharpened end of a chopstick he had stolen from the Shan. He hoped if Wadi saw that, she would take it as a sign he was waiting.

He was almost ready to give up for the night, but a whisper reached him.

'Raim?'

'Wadi?'

'Oh, thank Sola, I've found you.'

Wadi stood in the doorway, her face and hair covered in a fine film of red dust, red-orange streaks of handprints all over her once-white tunic and trousers. She rushed over to him and buried herself in his embrace. He gripped her tightly in his arms, and they held each other in the centre of the pagoda.

'Where have you been?' he whispered into her hair. 'Puutra said something about some tunnels . . .'

'I'm so sorry.' She pulled away from him slightly, and he brushed the hair from her face. 'They caught me sneaking through here the first night, just after I made that mark. Tonight was the first night they left me alone – the person guarding me was called away. It sounded urgent, so I thought they might be a while. It was my only opportunity.'

'Now you're here, you're not going back to wherever it is they're keeping you. You're going to stay here, with me.'

She smiled. 'Raim, you don't understand. I won't let them keep us apart any more either, but for now I have to go back to what I'm doing for them. They need my help.'

'Your help?' His brow furrowed.

'Yes, it's all to do with my pendant.' She took it off from around her neck and placed it on the floor so it lay next to the mark she had drawn in the dust. 'It's a pass-stone.'

'You can use that to get out of Lazar . . .'

Wadi nodded. 'Not only that, but they think there's something special about the stone itself.'

It did look special. It was slightly luminous, more so than the small amount of light coming from the torches could account for. He touched it with his index finger, almost expecting a jolt, but it felt like cool stone.

Wadi leaned in closer as if someone could overhear them. 'They think it's able to hold a promise.'

Now Raim really was confused. 'What do you mean?'

'Like in Darhan. You knot your promises, but really what you are doing is sealing them inside the string. It doesn't matter what the material is, the knot carries it. What if the same was true for stone, or wood, or any other material for that matter? What if you could somehow use it to bind a promise?'

'Impossible,' said Raim, but actually, the possibilities were boggling his mind.

'Maybe,' she said. 'That's why I'm there to find out. Because I have an affinity for the stone. Or so Puutra says. He says that's why I wanted to come here so badly – the pendant itself contained a promise that its wearer had to come back to Lazar. They've been testing me down in the tunnels. They want to see if I can find the other six pendants, which means they can break the curse around Lazar.'

'Break the curse?'

'Yes – the tunnels lead back to Darhan. But no one can escape, unless they have a pass-stone. It was sealed by the seven sages of Darhan.'

'Don't you think it was sealed for a reason? I mean . . . why should we let oathbreakers back to Darhan?'

'Sola above, do your prejudices really run that deep? Look around you. Look at all those outside of the Shan, whose oaths have been forgiven, whose shadows have returned to their original masters. But still they are stuck in Lazar. They cannot return to Darhan, to their homes, to their families. Don't you think those they betrayed might forgive rather than sending them into exile? Not every betrayal runs so deep, yet all broken oaths are treated the same.'

Raim had never thought about it like that before.

Wadi's expression softened. 'You should *see* the tunnels, Raim. You would be amazed. The main cavern is the biggest room I've ever been in – so big, you can't see the other side of it when you enter. Tunnels lead out in every direction. It's like an enormous termite mound. And also, that's where the water is, and where the waterworms breed.'

Her excitement was infectious. 'You have to take me there!'

'I will.'

'I've missed you,' he said.

'Me too,' she said, her smile turning shy.

'You've been working in the tunnels, and all I've been doing is meditating and doing stupid exercises with Draikh. Puutra says he's going to help me unlock the memory of the promise that's buried deep up here.' He tapped his temple and shrugged. 'But I don't know. He might not be helping me at all, no more than Yasmin could. I think all he wants is another sage.'

'We'll make sure that he helps you.'

The sound of a gong sent a jolt through Raim's spine. Wadi jumped up and ran to the window.

The sound did not build steadily, like it had when Old-maa had struck it. Instead it was wild and erratic, as if someone was hitting it over and over again, the noise rebounding off the cliff walls and making them shiver with fear. Then there was a loud crack followed by a deep boom that reverberated through Raim's body. The gong had broken.

The pagoda suddenly filled with Shan, Vlad and Puutra at the back. Puutra immediately spotted Raim and Wadi but his mind was clearly on other things. As he swept past them, Vlad motioned for them to follow. Raim and Wadi exchanged worried looks, then hurried down the stairs toward the main entrance of the temple. Puutra pushed to the front, unlocking the door to the temple with a massive key. Then he ran out of the door, leading the crowd towards the main courtyard.

'Hai!' came a shout that seemed to echo off the walls in the stone city. 'Hai, let me in!'

'That is no Alashan.' Vlad's mouth was set in a firm line as they all tumbled outside after Puutra.

A flash of black momentarily blocked Raim's view. 'Oyu!' Raim exclaimed, as the bird swooped past him and perched on the open doorframe.

'Right after you'd left on your little nightly jaunt, I saw someone approaching and sent Oyu to investigate,' said Draikh. 'Raim. He's Yun.'

'What?' Raim sprinted after Puutra, dodging Shan and Chauk alike. 'How is that possible? Yun are never exiled.

Yun never break their oaths. Yun . . .' But then he arrived at the top of the gate, where he could look down on the entrance into Lazar. It was true.

Down in the courtyard, screaming like a feral beast, was a Yun, the gong smashed in two at his feet. Behind him was a haunt, the biggest and most fearsome haunt that Raim had ever seen, and he was holding a long sword over the Yun's head.

The Yun looked both terrifying and terrified, but Raim could only think of one thing. The Yun would have news of back home, and of Khareh.

He had to talk to him. And soon.

32

'Let me into those chambers. I need to see the Yun!' Raim said to Puutra. He was prepared to stand his ground. Puutra had barred him from approaching the Yun straight away, and had enlisted Dumas's help in restraining him – who was only too glad to help. Raim had sat down in protest outside Puutra's door, not willing to move until he was granted his wish. But to his surprise, Puutra nodded.

'Yes. It is time. But be careful. He has been through much these past few hours.'

Puutra led him to a part of the building he had never been before. It was reserved for those who were ill – physically and mentally – and was barricaded by heavy wooden planks and impenetrable-looking black metal locks.

Puutra stopped in front of one of the doors, took out a large set of keys and unlocked it. 'As I said before, be careful. He is still . . . sensitive.' He left Raim and Draikh to enter alone.

The Yun was crouched over a small brazier topped by a sizzling frying pan, sweat soaking through his thin white garment. His hair was long and matted with sand and dirt. The acrid stench of body odour mingled with cooking meat.

The man snapped his neck to the side so Raim caught a glimpse of the raw, blistering skin on his cheek. The man's eyes never rested on Raim but constantly scanned the wall in front of him.

'What do you want?' he said.

'Are you Yun?'

'My name is Silas.'

A spectre slid through the wall, causing Silas to jump up and knock the frying pan clattering to the floor. The haunt was tall and cloaked in black, a deeper black than any Raim had ever known. On his face was the polished mask of Malog. And he didn't carry a dagger as the other haunts did, but a sword. A Yun sword. It was pointed right at Silas's throat.

'What right do you have to call yourself that any more, wretch?'

Raim's ears rang with the sound of that terrible, deep voice. His hands trembled, although the reprimands weren't directed at him. Silas shook violently, as if an earth-quake was concentrated beneath his body. Raim repeated to himself, *He's just a haunt, he's just a haunt, talk to the Yun, talk to him!* But he couldn't work up the courage.

Draikh stepped forward, knowing what Raim wanted

to ask but couldn't. 'Tell us news of Darhan,' he said, as if nothing was happening.

'Khareh?' said Silas, and his shivering ceased. He stretched out along the floor like a cat, reaching as if to pick up the mess he had made. His fingers gripped the frying pan's handle. Then he flung it at Draikh.

'GET OUT!' he screamed.

The frying pan passed straight through Draikh's spectral form and thundered against the wall, but Draikh fled through the door anyway – Silas's snarling face was enough to frighten even the ethereal.

'Out, out, out!' Silas picked a red-hot stone up out of the fire and hurled it after Draikh. The smell of burned flesh filled the air as it seared Silas's palm. He didn't seem to care. The stone cracked the floor as it landed.

'What is the meaning of this?' Puutra rushed into the room. When he caught sight of the mess, he said, 'I told you to be careful!' and yanked Raim's arm to lead him away.

'No,' said Silas. 'Let him stay! I need to talk with him.'

Puutra stared from Raim to Silas and back. Raim nodded. 'Fine,' Puutra conceded, and he and his haunt left, the door snapping shut behind them.

Silas leaped up and began pacing in front of the now smouldering brazier, barely taking notice of his burned hand. He sneaked nervous glances in Raim's direction, as if he was afraid Raim was another apparition come to haunt him. Raim shuffled on the spot, feeling awkward. It didn't help that every five or ten seconds, the monstrous spirit behind Silas would slap his giant sword against the stone, making both of them jump.

'What do you want to know?'

'Everything!' said Raim breathlessly, then thought better of it. 'I want to know what's happening with . . . the Moloti tribe.' All he really wanted to know about was Khareh, but Silas's reaction to seeing Draikh was enough to frighten him off touching that subject directly.

Silas shrugged. 'Probably what is happening with all tribes. Forced into submission by the new Khan. Unable to continue their wanderings until all of Darhan is under his control.'

Raim was confused. New Khan? Unable to be nomadic? No Khan could enforce that upon his people. 'There's a new Khan?'

'I would not be surprised if he had declared himself Emperor by now. Dictator! Tyrant! Despot! Those would be more apt descriptions. Yes, and you should hope that your tribe submitted easily. It is those who opposed him that I cry for.'

'You should cry for no one but yourself,' snarled the haunt. 'How can you stand it, living with yourself after what you did, you stinking tyrfish, you treacherous leech, you disgrace of Sola . . .' The name-calling continued in an endless stream.

Silas ignored the haunt and cast a studious eye over Raim. 'I know who you are. How could any Yun forget?

You are the murderer of our leader and a traitor!' Raim was about to protest, but Silas continued to speak as if his thoughts were spilling out in one uncontrollable stream of babble. 'YOU should be haunted by him as well as me – but that's right, you never made the promise to the Yun, you coward. And why isn't that haunt of yours in here taunting you, torturing you, like mine does ceaselessly to me? In fact, why do you have Khareh as your spirit in the first place? He must have sworn you in as his Protector, didn't he?'

'You never answered my original question,' said Raim. 'Who is the new Khan? Did Batar-Khan die?'

'He was overthrown. By Khareh.'

A beat of silence, then Raim exploded. '*Khareh* is the new Khan? But how is that possible? The rules . . .'

Silas guffawed loudly, to the point where Raim thought he might be choking. 'Rules? Since when did Khareh care about those?'

But becoming a Khan was an immensely complex process in Darhan law, even for an heir. And Khareh was no longer the heir – or so Mhara had told him. 'How? Does he have a new Protector?'

'The girl Erdene is his Protector.' Raim's jaw dropped to the floor. He couldn't believe that Khareh would choose someone new. The thought hurt him most of all the things he had heard so far. Didn't Khareh believe in him enough to know that Raim was coming back? Silas continued, taking no notice of Raim's flabbergasted expression.

'It wasn't a shock to us, though, since she also . . .'

Raim finally found his voice and interjected: 'Erdene? She is Khareh's new Protector?' It felt so unreal. He tried to imagine it. Erdene – it seemed so long ago that he had worshipped the ground she walked on. But looking back on it, he hardly knew her at all. In fact, it sounded like she was getting everything she ever wanted.

One eyebrow crept up Silas's forehead. 'Not just Khareh's Protector, but his Seer-Queen too.'

'But she's no seer!' Raim protested.

The former Yun shrugged. 'She passed the test.'

Everything Raim knew was crumbling around him. He felt like the room was spinning, or maybe his brain was so confused it could no longer tell his eyes to see straight.

'I suppose you want to know why the entire population of Darhan allowed Khareh to overthrow his uncle . . . how a boy – barely sixteen – could become Khan with a young Yun Protector and no army to support him?'

Raim couldn't even bring himself to nod. It was unbelievable.

'He destroyed his uncle's family. You have never seen anything like it. The former Batar-Khan, now simply to be remembered as Batar, was brutally killed in front of his entire clan.'

Anger surged through Raim then. 'No!' he cried. 'You're lying. Khareh would never do that.'

'Khareh didn't do it. Not himself, anyway. He ordered Batar-Khan's own men to do the deed instead. Without a

Protector, Batar-Khan was too weak to defend himself. And with his death, all the promise-knots made by the warlords were undone. His entire tribe submitted to Khareh's rule. After that, one by one, the rest of the warlords capitulated. Including my tribe.'

A memory flashed before Raim's eyes, a recognition of Silas's countrymen. Silas hailed from the same territory as Ryopi, that contentious lot who scarcely strayed from the river. They would be the last to follow a plains-man; they followed currents and shoals. Raim wondered when Khareh-Khan had become Khareh-Tornado.

'Then why are you here?' asked Raim.

'Yes, tell him.' Silas's haunt slowly slid the blade through his spectral fingers, slicing the webby sinews had they been real. Raim's stomach turned.

A hacking cough escaped Silas. He doubled in half, convulsing in jarring gasps as if he expelled his life with every heave. By contrast, Raim's breath was caught in his throat. He waited for the man to calm and begin his story. In the moment before Silas began, Raim heard a flag flutter outside, the first time he had been able to hear any noise from beyond the room. Silas's haunt, for the first time since their conversation began, had ceased his spiteful mutterings.

'It all happened so quickly,' he said. He lowered himself onto the cot in the centre of the room and stared at the floor. His face contorted with conflicting emotions as the memories flooded back. 'The Yun held their council a few hours after the takeover was announced. The Rentai was chaos. Such turmoil!' There was a glint of excitement in his eye and he leaned in, his memory gaining momentum. 'This Erdene, this new Seer-Queen and Yun Leader, she would not accept the guidance of any elder Yun. It was obvious Khareh-Khan had coached her – but still you could see the look of sheer terror in her eyes.

'Some tried to be kind, saying she did not know how deep she was in Darhanian politics. The strongest and wisest Yun saw her fear and tried to calm her, to talk sense to her. But then, there was a group of us, all from the east that thought she would never see sense – and we were correct, I might add. We thought we could overcome her. When she demanded we pledge our lives to Khareh – imagine, not to the land, to Khareh, as if we were all his Protectors! – we threw off our masks in defiance. But our rebellion did not go as planned. As if a secret voice whispered in that childish ear and imbued her with strength, she banished us from the room, calmly telling us we would never know the secret behind the Khan's power, and that all the others present were forbidden to reveal it to us. The power became obvious before long. The girl had acted out of wisdom. To not know Khareh's secret . . . it was torturous. It is torturous.'

Raim could not hold his lips closed any longer. 'But what is his power?' If Khareh had possessed any power at all, beyond maybe a knack for inventing, he couldn't have kept it a secret from his best friend. Could he?

To his surprise, Silas burst out into laughter. 'His power? But which should I inform you of? How about the power to make objects move with his mind? No? Too easy, tricks with magnets, surely. Then try his ability to levitate, to fly. Still not wondrous enough to imagine the entire Yun along with every warlord in Darhan capitulating to his mastery? Then try this . . . he can heal his own wounds. He has become a sage, of the highest order.'

Raim felt Silas's hot breath on his ear as he spoke those last words. Then Silas leaned backward to allow the magnitude of his speech to sink in. When he spoke again, the voice was drained of its excited quality. Exhaustion laced his words. He rubbed the corners of his eyes with his fingertips.

'It wasn't enough that the four defiant Yun, including myself, were forced to fight Khareh – he defeated us with ease. I remember coming at him, his aristocratic muscles so weak compared to mine. I have been Yun for fifteen years and was passed through on my first attempt. Ceaseless training since birth! And I am cut down two feet from him, my tunic slashed and stained with my own blood. My sword is taken from me and I fall to the floor. My comrades fall with me – only they do not get up ever again. I look up as Khareh walks past . . . our swords, all four Yun blades floating in the air around him, and he is surrounded by light! I don't know what made me do it, perhaps the sight of my three dying warriors, perhaps the sting of my own wound . . . I reach into my boot, pull out

306

the dagger I had hidden there and slash at his bare calf. I felt such satisfaction, watching that string of blood-red pearls form where my dagger had performed its duty. I remember the clatter of two swords as they dropped from the air. I remember his anguished scream, taken by such surprise. I was distracted by my triumph, but when the pain on his face turned to pride, it was my turn to be shocked. The wound on his leg was gone, as if it had never been opened. But it happened. And Khareh-Khan never forgot it.'

'Enough of this babble!' screeched the grotesque haunt. Silas cowered. 'However much I take pleasure in the tragedy of your ignorance, it is not the story I permitted you to tell. You are so weak, so pathetic,' he snarled. 'Get on with what I told you to say, or I shall never permit you such freedom again.'

'Can't you shut up?' said Raim, agonizing to hear any story Silas had to tell. He cried out in pain as the flat of the haunt's blade landed squarely on the back of his hand. Blood pooled beneath his olive skin and he felt it begin to throb. He glared back at the haunt, but Silas began again.

'Such a terrible thing . . .'

'Nothing is as terrible as what you did, vow breaker,' growled the haunt.

Silas closed his eyes and shook his head as languidly as if he were under water. 'I drew his blood and in return he made me do the most awful deed. There were a number of . . . enemies that he had to be rid of. If you could even call them enemies.' He spat towards the ground.

The haunt caught the spit in mid-air. 'You are the enemy.' He wiped the spit on Silas's filthy tunic.

'He told me where Batar-Khan's Seer-Queen and her baby were, and made me promise . . . no, I can't say it, don't make me!' The haunt prodded him with the knife but it only made him more upset. 'What had happened . . . only opened my eyes to the true motivations of this boy's regime. I wouldn't carry out the task. He is a tyrant. I broke the vow instead. I shattered my Yun sword, breaking my vow to the Yun by not defending my warlord's tribe and cast myself out into the desert.'

'Traitor,' the voice said.

'I am not a murderer,' Raim said into the silence that followed, still reeling from Silas's words. But that accusation hurt the most. 'Mhara's death was an accident. She was . . . she was like a mother to me. And Draikh does not torment me because I never broke my promise to Khareh. I am still Khareh's Protector. And now I will be for life.' He pulled down the neck of his tunic to show Silas the ink-black mark. It couldn't be true what Silas was saying. It couldn't. 'He is my best friend.'

'You deserve everything that has come to you,' the voice continued over the top of Raim, taunting, ever taunting.

'He is your best friend, you say?' Silas leaped to his feet, as lightning fast as a cobra strike, and grabbed Raim by the tunic. With his other hand, he whipped a dagger out of his boot. Raim tried to fight back, but Silas was too quick, pressing the blade at his neck. 'This is not Yun workmanship,' he said. He angled the blade so light from the window bounced off its smooth surface. Raim felt the blade slice the skin on his neck, a trickle of blood winding its way down his throat. 'Which is a shame, because I had hoped to kill you in the proper way.'

The door slammed against the wall. Silas vomited a stream of curses as two people, a man and a woman, raced in, grabbed him by the shoulders and pinned him down. The dagger clattered to the floor.

'Are you all right?' It was Puutra. The anger from before was gone. 'What happened? You must relay every detail.'

'Let me see.' Draikh pushed his way into view of Raim. He ran his hand over the wound on his neck and healed it. Silas's mouth gaped open.

Puutra looked from Silas to Raim and his voice was edged with caution. 'Come, Raim.'

'You don't understand.' Raim was still desperate to talk to Silas, to learn more. 'When I left Darhan, Khareh wasn't the Khan, he didn't have powers. He was just . . . my friend. Tell me more, please, please.'

'Raim, this is not the time,' said Puutra.

To both their surprise, Silas sprung free from his captor's grasp. His charcoal eyes sparkled with purpose and, once again, sanity. 'You keep saying this. He was your friend, you say? Your best friend? Then explain to me this.

When I broke my vow to Khareh-Khan, it was as if a veil was lifted from my eyes and I could see all as it truly was. His shadow disappeared and transformed into something else. His haunt became as clear to me as my own haunt is now.' He stared at Raim, then laughed, then shed a tear, and then laughed and stared again.

'Who was it?' Raim's voice came out barely a whisper.

'Why, it was you, of course.'

33

'You knew.'

'Raim, I . . .'

Puutra had signalled the other Shan to drag Raim back to his room after Silas's devastating revelation. Vlad had pressed a cup of something steaming and hot into his hands, but Raim had smashed it against the wall. Still, not long after, he had fallen into a long and deep sleep. Drugged, probably, by the vapours of the tea. But when he woke up, he hadn't forgotten anything. The sight of Draikh floating there, an anxious look on his face, made him sick to his stomach.

Dharma.

Her face was all he could think about.

Dharma.

That was the promise Khareh had made to him. To keep Dharma safe. What did it mean if he had broken that? Only one person knew, and that person had hidden the truth from him.

'Don't you see?' Draikh's voice was quiet, his head hanging down low. 'That's why I had to break away from . . . me. Khareh was about to do something despicable. I couldn't bear it. That's why I decided to save you from those behrflies, so you would have a chance to avenge your sister. Otherwise—'

'Otherwise *nothing*. Why did you not save Dharma instead? She is the more worthy life.'

'It . . . doesn't work like that. You were the one carrying me. I hated Khareh for what he was doing, but I couldn't stop it either. He wanted to become a sage too much.'

'Oh, really? And how am I supposed to believe that? For all I know you're just here spying on me, on all of us. I wouldn't put it past Khareh.'

Draikh looked up, and Raim could see the hurt in his eyes. Raim wasn't moved. Khareh had been an actor too.

'Raim, I'm sorry – but now you can make it right. If we work together.'

'Shut up!' said Raim. 'I don't want to hear your pack of lies. Just go away!'

For once, Draikh did as he was told. As the spirit sadly floated away, Wadi opened the door. 'I didn't want to come in while you were talking with Draikh.'

Raim knew he must look a pathetic figure. He sat on the bed, his knees up against his chin. 'Dharma,' he said, as if the word were some kind of magic that could revive her.

Wadi placed an arm around him and he leaned into her shoulder.

'I came here hoping to find answers,' he said. 'But now – there is nothing for me. And, worst of all, I am tied to that monster for ever.'

'But . . . can't you just tell Draikh to go away permanently, like he's gone now?' she asked softly.

Raim put a hand on his chest, where the mark remained. 'The reminder will always be there. Nothing I do will change that.'

She brought her hand up to his and removed it gently. 'Think about that tomorrow. For now . . .'

He wept as she held him, until eventually he fell into a sleep that was dark and empty of dreams.

34

After Draikh's revelation, none of the Shan could persuade Raim to work on anything – no meditating, no sage practice, no reading and writing lessons, nothing. His saviour was, ironically, Silas.

Raim stayed in his room, refusing to move for all of Puutra and Wadi's attempts to rouse him. But a familiar noise outside piqued his interest for the first time in days. He slumped to the window and peered out over the side. Silas was down below, in the Shan courtyard, a dull, rusted sword in his hand. He was training Wadi; the familiar sound was the harsh clang of metal against metal. Raim watched them for a while, but at first, it only served to remind him of his former life.

The next morning, the clanging woke him up. This time, he decided to go down to the courtyard and watch them from the sidelines there. When he showed up on the edge of the dirt surface they were using as a duelling ground, Wadi was so surprised she almost lost her head to Silas in their practice. He unleashed a stream of curses, but Wadi just smiled.

'Why don't you join us?' Wadi asked.

Raim just shrugged. Wadi sighed.

Silas, by contrast, strode over to a large wooden box, which contained all the weapons in the Shan temple. He chose another sword and threw it down at Raim's feet. 'I thought you were a fighter?' Silas said. 'Train. Don't make me ask twice.'

Silas's haunt flew at him then, so violent and vengeful that even though Wadi couldn't see him or hear the words, she was so repulsed by the shadow that she had to flee.

Raim didn't pick up the sword.

But that night, as he lay in bed, he thought of Silas's words. He was a fighter. He needed to train. If he could train himself up to the Yun he might have been, he could go back to Darhan and avenge Dharma.

His vow meant he might not be able to bring any harm to Khareh directly, but he could make it easier for those who could. But he couldn't do anything if he could barely remember how to swing a sword. He had only ever been good at one thing his entire life, and that was fighting.

So at first light, before Silas arrived, he moved down to the courtyard and started warming up. When Silas did show, he did not seem surprised to see Raim there, and offered only a grunt of greeting. Then he picked up a sword, and ran at Raim.

Raim fought back. He used it as fuel. Every blow he struck, he thought of fighting Khareh – even if he knew he would never be able to do it in person. Silas was a surprisingly good teacher. A natural Yun leader. Raim did not blame Silas for being the bearer of the awful news.

When Wadi joined them, Raim worked with her on his hand-to-hand combat, while she worked on her swordplay. The swords were so old and rusted that one of them shattered as they were fighting and another's grip shed leather into Wadi's palm. Raim decided to look at their weapons store himself, and he yelled with delight when he found two ancient bows, complete with a quiver of arrows. He brought them down to Wadi and they spent the whole afternoon in the entrance courtyard, where Silas was unable to go, setting up targets as curious young Chauk children watched from their windows, some of them perched up on the window sills, their legs dangling precariously high against the cliffs.

Raim lined up a shot, relishing in the familiar ache that was warming up the space between his shoulder blades and the muscles of his fingers. He let the arrow loose and watched as it flew towards the piece of overly ripe fruit they had been using as a target, before yelling with glee as the fruit splattered against the wall, the arrow having demolished the centre of it.

'Yes!' He pumped a fist into the air and turned to Wadi. 'Still got it!'

She smiled at him and arched her back like a cat,

stretching out her own soreness. 'I think I've had enough archery practice for today.'

Raim nodded and jogged towards where his arrow landed to return it to the quiver. Then he turned back and caught up with Wadi, who was strolling back towards the Shan temple.

'I can't believe we found bows and arrows – I wonder what else Puutra has stored up in the temple.'

Wadi smiled again but it was smaller this time, and gone from her face in a heartbeat. Raim put his hand on her shoulder. 'Are you all right?'

She stopped abruptly and rounded on him. 'What are you doing here, Raim?'

Raim took a step back, in shock. 'What do you mean?'

'What are you doing here, now, in this place? You haven't said a word to Draikh. You haven't been meditating on your scar. The whole time I've known you, all you've ever cared about is finding out about this.' She reached over and grabbed his wrist, and he pulled it out of her grasp instinctively. She raised her eyebrows, but when she spoke again her tone was softer. 'All you've ever wanted was to be able to clear your name – that's why you came to Lazar in the first place.'

'And what good would it do me now?' Raim flung the bow down on the ground and shrugged the quiver off his back. He slumped down onto a low stone wall. 'The only answer I have is to get back to Darhan, and avenge Dharma. *That* is my life now.'

Wadi sat down next to him, shaking her head slowly. 'But you can't do it alone. Without Draikh, that plan is suicide . . .'

Raim stood up and stormed off, not daring to look back but knowing instinctively that Wadi wouldn't follow.

The next day, he felt like sticking to the basics – two swords, him, Silas and a deserted courtyard. Silas was the one person he could trust not to talk to him about Draikh or his other promise.

He arrived at the training ground. The ex-Yun was balancing on one leg, his hands clasped together over his head, his eyes closed. Without opening his eyes, he changed positions, lowering his leg, stretching one arm out in front of him and tilting his head back towards the sky. He must have sensed Raim's arrival, however, for he said, 'Just one more invocation to Naran, and I will be with you.'

Behind him, the dark shadow of a storm over a placid lake, the haunt boiled and seethed insults. There was no tolerance between this haunt and Chauk. But somehow, Silas had managed to become deaf to his insults. Now, he was much more the Yun Raim imagined he must have been in his Darhan days. He had strength and colour, and even a slight sparkle in the eye that hinted at his former prowess. He also now had much advice to give to Raim, who soaked it up eagerly.

'You must keep up your physical strength and maintain your Yun training in swordsmanship and archery, even as you are expanding your mental muscle,' Silas had said during one such session. 'War is on the horizon. You must be prepared.'

'War is on the horizon.' It was Silas's favourite phrase.

Raim was the only person, apart from Puutra and Wadi, who visited Silas. The others kept their distance, and that was how Raim liked it.

The other Shan had reason to be terrified by Silas. It was hardly a secret that the haunt was driving him insane. And who could blame him? Silas's haunt was the vilest and most insatiable of any Raim had ever seen. Silas had been insulted in ways Raim couldn't even imagine. There was nothing sacred from the haunt. Even 'haunt' seemed too kind a word for him, so they called him 'wraith'.

'Raim, I'm glad you are here. I remembered something important.' There were weapons lined up against the wall of the courtyard. Silas ran his fingers over the selection before finally resting on the scabbard of a broadsword. It was no ochir blade, but in the hands of a Yun it had become an extremely powerful weapon. 'Khareh was plotting something.'

'War?' Raim joked, but he sobered at Silas's expression.

'Yes, but also something else.' He flicked at the edge of the blade, testing its sharpness. 'I remember because the Yun who weren't in Khareh's personal guard were being sent away, to specific locations across Darhan. They were given tasks. Obviously, I don't know all the details since I was . . .'

'A traitor,' hissed the wraith, unhelpfully.

'. . . exiled before I could receive any assignment. But he was setting up small camps.'

'Watch stations?'

'Perhaps. But they seemed to have a deeper purpose than that. You wouldn't send your Yun to guard a watch-tower. You would use your army.'

Raim shrugged. 'Maybe he thinks the presence of Yun spread throughout Darhan will reduce rebellion.'

'I don't know. But I feel it is more sinister than that.'

'Of course you do,' said the wraith. 'Traitor once, a traitor for ever. Here you are, the two of you, plotting against your Khan. Oh, the things I would say to you too . . .' His eyes flashed at Raim. 'But you held no promise to me. You weren't able to pass the final test.'

'He almost did,' said Silas wryly.

They were interrupted by a light cough from the far end of the courtyard. Raim spun round in surprise, and saw Vlad and Zu shuffling awkwardly into the square.

'Ah.' Silas swung a couple of times in the air, then spoke to Raim. 'And here I was beginning to think there was no one else in Lazar apart from you, the girl and the old man.'

Raim waved them over. 'Silas, this is Vlad and Zu. They used to be Baril priests, you know.'

Vlad held his arm protectively around Zu. 'We are glad to finally meet you,' he said. Silas stared at Zu with an intensity that sent chills down Raim's back. 'How . . . the Seer-Queen . . . it's not possible . . .'

Then the wraith unsheathed his knife and began slicing at Silas's body, over and over again. 'Hated one! Traitor! Worthless scum.' The wounds did not bleed like flesh wounds, but immediately jumped into life as thick red scars. Promise scars. Broken promise scars. But Silas felt the pain as if it were a real blade. 'Take the punishment I give you as a man. One task to complete for your Khan. Just one. If you had obeyed, I wouldn't *slash* have *slash* to do *slash* this *slash* to *slash* you.'

'Do something!' yelled Raim to Vlad, but he was running Zu back inside, terrified for her safety. Raim turned to Silas. 'She's not the Seer-Queen. They are sisters, twins!'

Silas was beyond listening to Raim now. He moaned in agony. 'How could I do it? I couldn't do it. I would never have done it.'

'You made the vow, you broke the vow.'

'No, but it was too terrible. It was TOO TERRIBLE.' With an enormous push he sent his wraith reeling backward as if he was in contact with the real world. Then Silas locked eyes with Raim. 'War is on the horizon,' he said. He pushed the blade of his broadsword into his stomach and ripped upwards. He fell to his knees, and then onto his side, and jammed the sword in deeper.

'Noooo!' cried Raim and the wraith at the same time. With Silas dying, so was the wraith. But with his last burst of energy, the wraith turned to Raim and said: 'The Seer-Queen's baby. That's what he had to do to keep his vow and obey his khan. Kill the Seer-Queen and her baby. And he refused. That cowa—'

The wraith's word faded into the ether, his final insult never to be heard.

35

They buried him out in the sands. Raim tried to remember the details of a Yun funeral rite, to offer Silas some of the honour that Mhara had never been able to receive. He had been buried with a blade strapped to his right hand, so that he would still carry it with him in the afterlife. It wasn't his Yun blade – that had burned with his original promise knot. But it was something. It was more than Mhara had, anyway, and the realization of this sent a painful stab of guilt through Raim.

'I don't think I can do this any more,' Raim said to Puutra when they returned to the meditation room and to Wadi inside the temple.

Puutra managed a sad smile, full of pity. 'I know it has been difficult for you, Raim. First with the discovery about your sister, and now with Silas's suicide. But you know there is nowhere else for you to go.'

Draikh hung back in the shadows, looking despondent.

Puutra raised a hand to Draikh and gestured him over to where they were standing. Raim still found it impossible to look at him, no matter how many times he insisted it wasn't him who had hurt Dharma. Puutra looked up at Raim through bushy eyebrows. 'You must learn to work with your haunt . . . with your spirit again.'

'But—' Raim began to protest.

'But he has apologized, Raim, and you must forgive him. To think, you are in such a unique position here. You have a spirit in debt to *you*. Shan grovel and beg for forgiveness from our haunts, for them to grant us even the tiniest measure of power. And here you have a spirit willing and obedient . . .'

Raim looked up at Draikh and the pair locked eyes. Then Raim chuckled softly. 'Willing? Obedient? Are we talking about the same Draikh here? Never.'

'Maybe if you ask nicely,' Draikh said through a relieved smile.

Puutra clapped Raim on the back. 'Good. Good. We can make the pair of you great, you know.'

Raim was about to reply when Puutra silenced them with a sharp hiss. They all then seemed to hear it together. Footsteps. Hurried, urgent.

Indeed, as the person dashed round the corner, momentum threw him up against the stone wall. He bounced off again like a piece of rubber and came to a skidding halt in front of Puutra. It was Dumas.

'It's the Alashan,' Dumas managed to articulate

between deep gulps of breath. 'They're here, and they're dying.'

A young Chauk girl approached one pair of Alashan with a bowl of water in a crowd of hundreds. A woman cradling a man in her arms. The man's skin was drawn tight across his face; every bone was visible. The woman stared down into the mirror pool of water held by the girl and the thirst in her eyes was plain. They were both parched. But equal to the look of thirst in her eyes was the narrow glare of contempt. The little Chauk girl did not cower, however. She set down the bowl of water at the pair's feet and backed away, head bowed low to the ground.

The sight of such a large group of Alashan in a single place visibly shook Raim. They filled the open courtyard and spilled out of the gate. Raim wondered if there were some Alashan tribes that were much larger than others, or maybe there was some sort of annual gathering between Chauk and Alashan, something he had not had a chance to witness during his month at Lazar. Ordinarily, they only approached the walls to bring new Chauk. Puutra approached an isolated group of women to find out the cause of their unannounced arrival.

From just behind him, Wadi cried out and ran towards a group of her former tribe. Raim was shocked to see Old-maa, Mesan and the rest of the tribe. He hadn't expected them to come back to Lazar for a long time.

Raim followed Wadi, but couldn't help staring around at all the emaciated-looking people. He met first with Mesan. He was holding up another man that Raim had never seen before, and it was a visible effort. The man's lips were cracked and split like fissures in rock. Raim hurried over and took some of the weight from Mesan, so he could explain.

Mesan wheezed as he tried to talk, and Wadi hurried over to interpret.

'Wait,' said Raim. 'Let me give this man some water first.'

Mesan shook his head. And Raim felt the emaciated man's body shake even as he exerted the effort to also refuse. Wadi translated Mesan's words: 'This man cannot take water from you.'

'But I'm not Chauk, I'm a friend!'

'The water is not ours.' After more of Raim's vehement protestations, Mesan repeated the phrase: 'The water is not ours.' The man's legs gave out from under him then. Raim buckled under the sudden increase of weight, but managed to steady the man so he did not collide too violently with the floor. Wadi helped Raim steady him to the ground.

Raim stared at the group talking with Puutra. What was taking them so long? Was it not obvious that these people needed water, and quickly? He left Mesan with Wadi and strode over to Puutra, bracing himself for a confrontation. To his surprise, Puutra stepped aside to allow him to join the circle.

'What are you waiting for?' Raim said. 'We need to get these people water.'

'We must hear Old-maa's story, first.' Puutra spoke to Raim in a cool, deliberate monotone.

'When we left Wadi in Lazar' – Old-maa threw Raim a dirty look – 'we were free to bring Chauk here again. We sent anyone we could spare to the borders. But we found no one. We thought maybe we were losing exiles to the desert earlier – like the woman your bird found.' Raim nodded gravely. He remembered. 'Maybe the outcasts were giving up sooner. Mesan; he wandered the borders for an entire week without finding a single Chauk. He almost did not make it back to us alive. And then we came across another tribe. They had not found a single Chauk in over a month. The behrflies had been coming for them every night, which meant that even the flies weren't finding bodies to feast on in the desert. They lost their last water-worm a week before we found them. But they thought with no new Chauk to bring here . . .'

'. . . that we wouldn't give them water,' Puutra ended for her. Old-maa cast her eyes to the ground. 'Damn your Alashan pride. It has practically killed all of you. Let us help.' He snapped his fingers so that the girls who had been carrying water to the Alashan reappeared. The parched Alashan swayed in desperation towards the glistening bowls. But they did not reach out. Instead, they looked to Old-maa expectantly.

'No,' she said finally. Raim watched the collected

327

shoulders of the group slump. 'There must be a trade. This is the Alashan way. We cannot accept your water for nothing. We do not accept charity from the Chauk.'

Even Old-maa was faltering. They all were. But those lines of stubbornness were still etched across her face, as thick and unwavering as the desert dunes. She would let them all die rather than break with their code.

'I have an idea!' Dumas rushed forward. Vlad tried to hold him back, but he broke through. 'The Alashan can help us. If there are no more exiles coming to Lazar that means the new Khan has stopped exiling oathbreakers! We all know that the new Khan is different. Maybe he is wise enough to recognize that half his population is whiling away its time here when they could be useful to Darhan! We should return! This is his invitation! And the Alashan can come with us, to guide us on our journey back to Darhan. That will be our trade.'

'No,' said Raim, the word spitting out of him. 'Trust me, Khareh would never take kindly to oathbreakers. He won't see them as possible sages like himself. He will only see their weakness.'

But Dumas's words were spreading through Lazar like wildfire. Shouts of approval came from outside above the courtyard where the Alashan were being kept. 'Let's return to Darhan!'

Puutra stared from Dumas to Raim, and then at the rest of the Shan. 'Could Dumas be right?'

'I think he might be,' said Vlad.

'No!' said Raim, even louder this time. 'What are you thinking? Do you not remember all the things Silas said?'

'Silas was insane, and so are you if you believed anything he said.' Dumas's eyes shone with an excitement that could not be dulled. 'We return to Darhan.'

'I agree,' said Vlad. 'That's the only explanation.'

Raim exploded with rage. 'Vlad, I tried to protect you from the truth before because Puutra asked me to, but you can't go along with this. Silas said that *I* was Khareh's haunt. The only promise Khareh made to me was to *protect Dharma*. He broke that promise to become a sage. He is a monster now. Draikh?'

'Raim's right,' the spirit said. 'Khareh would never allow oathbreakers to return.'

Vlad tore at his cheeks in horror, Raim's words dawning on him slowly. All around them, Chauk were heading down towards the square, desperate to be among the first to leave the city.

Puutra angrily pushed Raim aside, and grabbed hold of Vlad. He shouted at Dumas, 'You're going to cause a stampede! We must think this through. Dumas, bar the gates and make sure no one attempts to leave the city via the desert. Get water to the Alashan now, then follow us. The rest of you' – he gestured to Raim, Wadi, Old-maa and Vlad – 'back to the temple, now.'

36

Dumas rummaged through a large trunk in the corner, haphazardly tossing aged vellum scrolls onto the floor. Puutra unrolled the scrolls, which turned out to be more maps, overlapping the edges until the surface of the floor in the circle between them was totally covered. Raim took in the vast breadth of landscape and couldn't help but release a long, deep breath of awe. It seemed so huge.

Puutra jammed his index finger down on the small brown smudge that represented Lazar. He slid a few finger lengths to the left. He looked into the eyes of everyone in the group in turn, and when he reached Dumas, he paused. 'Dumas, you let your excitement get the better of you out there. But I cannot deny that your idea is plausible.'

'No, it's not plausible. It's stupid; it's crazy,' shouted Raim. 'I've said, Khareh would nev—'

'Raim, you've done enough. I told you not to tell Vlad of what you knew about his daughter.'

'He had a right to know.'

'And you don't know for a fact that Khareh wouldn't change his mind about oathbreakers!' yelled Dumas.

'Neither do you know for certain that he has stopped exiling people!' retorted Raim.

'It's worth a try to find out!'

Old-maa raised a hand to speak, and both Dumas and Raim had the sense to fall silent. She spoke in Alashan, and Wadi translated in a low voice – although Puutra understood her, no one else would. 'Bring exiled back to Darhan? We could not.'

'You could not or you will not?' asked Puutra. 'You said yourself, it has been a long time without a single Chauk entering the desert. Your people are dying out there, Gola.'

'It will break every rule, every tradition our people know. We never bring Chauk back to Darhan,' Old-maa replied in Darhanian.

'It is only a tradition if oathbreakers are being exiled into the desert,' reasoned Puutra. 'What will you trade for new waterworms, if you don't have any Chauk? Trade this instead. Trade your knowledge of the desert for our water.'

If Old-maa was moved, she didn't show it, but her walking stick was tapping furiously on the ground. 'How many?'

'I want to go!' Dumas jumped in immediately.

Puutra nodded. 'Yes. A small group. Five, maybe.'

'Seven,' said Dumas. 'It should be seven.'

'Seven we can manage,' said Old-maa. 'It will take us a little over a week to reach Darhan, if we take the quickest path.'

'A week, is that all?' breathed Dumas.

Old-maa's eyes narrowed. 'Without the Alashan you wouldn't be able to find your way out of these mountains, let alone to Darhan.' She turned to Puutra. 'We will accept this trade.'

Puutra signalled to another Shan, who immediately fled the room to give the news to the Chauk, who could start reviving the Alashan with water.

Raim was almost shaking with fury. 'You can't be serious, Puutra? They'll be killed!'

Raim's fury was shattered by Dumas's own. Dumas launched at him, battering his arms against Raim's body. Raim staggered backward and all his muscles threatened to spring back and return the assault, but Wadi grabbed his arms before he could move. Vlad was similarly pinning down Dumas. He couldn't pin down Dumas's tongue, however: 'You say you have never broken a promise. That means you can NEVER know what we have gone through . . . what this opportunity could mean.'

Raim bit his own tongue back. It was true, he didn't know. And underneath Dumas's anger, he could recognize something else. Hope. Something he hadn't seen before in his entire time at Lazar. Nothing he could say was going to make a difference.

'Raim and Wadi, you should go back to the Shan quarters,' said Puutra. 'And Vlad . . .' His tone softened. 'You should go find your wife. Tell her what you know. Comfort yourselves. You won't be needed for this expedition.'

'You can't do that! You need us! You surely can't think this is a good idea . . .' Before Raim could continue more, Vlad grabbed him by the upper arm and hauled him to his feet. 'I'm going, I'm going.' He stumbled towards the door.

As soon as they started climbing the stairs towards the living quarters, Raim turned to Vlad. 'This is a mistake.'

'I know,' he said, his mouth a firm line. And instead of crossing the pagoda towards the rooms, Vlad turned down a different path.

'Where are you taking us?' demanded Raim.

'To the tunnels,' said Wadi, realization suddenly dawning.

'That's right,' said Vlad, his pace quickening as they started down another staircase. 'If he really did what you say he did . . . if he really harmed my daughter, then we can't let the Chauk go to Darhan and be killed by that monster.'

'We'll have to be quick, if we want to get there before Dumas.'

'The tunnels will be quick,' said Vlad. 'And the sooner we get to Darhan the better.' He cracked his knuckles together, and Raim saw a darkness in the man's eyes he had never seen before.

*   *   *

Wadi skipped a rock down into one of the side tunnels as they marched past. Large red Xs were plastered outside the entrance to each tunnel to mark dead ends. Here, so early in their journey, the rock was smooth and well worn. It looked almost natural. But then again, Wadi was telling him that the tunnels this close to Lazar had been built centuries ago. The rock felt cool to the touch as Raim leaned his hand up against it, pausing to take a breath.

They had taken nothing with them. The only thing of value was his half of Dharma's scarf, tied around his wrist like a talisman. A reminder.

The tunnel until now had been much wider than Raim had anticipated and supported by pillars carved from the rock. His only point of comparison was the mines that he had visited in the north of Darhan, close to the Amarapura mountains. There, the workers had used wooden beams to support the mines, and lumber was constantly being hauled down on wooden tracks to the site of the most recent excavation. There was no such timber framework in the Lazarite tunnels, but then again, Raim hadn't seen a tree since his exile. It was no wonder the people here were such amazing stone carvers. The sheer amount of rock and stone that needed to be excavated in order to construct such a complex labyrinth forced Raim to again admire the industriousness of these people who laboured towards an unknown – perhaps completely unattainable – goal. There was no real way of knowing whether the tunnels would ever be used again as a trade route back to

Darhan. But it hadn't prevented them from persevering.

Wadi grabbed his arm. 'We're getting near the river,' she said. 'If you haven't seen this before, then you must.'

Vlad shot Wadi a knowing look. 'We need to set up camp for the night anyhow,' he said.

'Will they come looking for us?' Raim asked.

Vlad shook his head. 'No. Did you see them? They looked so . . . excited. And no one will suspect I would leave without Zu.'

Wadi reached out and touched Vlad's arm gently. 'I think you're doing the right thing.'

Vlad's face darkened. 'If Zu knew what Khareh had done to our daughter, she would never have forgiven me for not going. Now, go and see.'

Wadi led Raim away from the main path through an offshoot of tunnels that were sometimes so narrow he had to turn sideways and the back of his head and the tip of his nose touched rock at the same time. The sensation of ascending was overwhelming. Every few side steps the ground would rise up in front of him, giant steps that reached up past his navel. He was forced to clamber over them, clumsily, his hands slipping against the cool stone.

It was pitch-black. Only the vague sense of Wadi's form moving a few paces ahead of him kept him from feeling utterly beyond the reaches of the world. That feeling of isolation, of going so far beneath the earth, sent a jolt of panic through his chest.

Wadi's laugh trickled down from above him. He

anticipated the step this time, and didn't bash his knees against the stone. 'There's only one way to go, you wouldn't be lost.'

They must have reached a landing, as the walls opened up substantially like a gaping mouth. Wadi struck a match against the rock and used the flame to light the torch in her hand.

Light flooded the cavern. They appeared to be in a narrow room, with a long window into darkness.

'It's a safe room,' said Wadi. 'It's Chauk policy to make sure the river is safe before we crowd in here. There are three river stations like this, each successively closer to Darhan. I've only ever reached the second station, another day's journey.'

At the next step forward, the ground beneath him began to shake and he was forced to shield his head with his arms from rock dust falling from the ceiling. He launched himself forward so he landed next to Wadi. He gripped the ledge to stabilize himself.

'Watch,' she whispered, excitement exhaled with every breath.

And Raim did. He couldn't see anything at first. His eyes felt distracted inside his skull, jumping from side to side, staring at the darkness, trying to search for some kind of light or movement. Eventually he shut his eyes and watched with all his senses. It took him a long while to focus them. The rush dominated all sound, as it had from when he first entered the tunnel with Wadi. It made it difficult to isolate sounds from each other. He tried to concentrate further, separating the rush from other noise. There was something coming from his left, the direction they had just come from, except further into the pitch-blackness. There was a low-pitched hum; it sounded like the wind as it rushed through the fissures in the cliffs that served as Lazar's walkways, but he guessed they were voices, and cracks and hisses from the rock as it was strained by enormous weight. He heard Wadi's deep and slow breathing behind him, and the beating of his own heart increase in anticipation.

Then, fire blazed momentarily before his eyelids, so bright he thought he had somehow opened his eyes without meaning to. When he did open his eyes, he watched as two flames leaped around the perimeter of the enormous circular cavern in opposite directions. The flame had passed directly underneath where he and Wadi were crouched against a window in the rock, racing to catch up with its partner at the other side of the cave.

The spots in front of his eyes swirled white and blue; he was focused, fascinated by the fire, for longer than was good for him. But as the spots cleared, Raim suddenly experienced true awe. He could hardly believe that the sight before him could have been obscured by darkness. It was as if the entire mountain had been hollowed out. The ceiling stretched for what seemed like miles above them.

And it wasn't as if they weren't high already: he spotted Vlad standing, torch in hand, at a small gap in the cavern's wall. From Raim's vantage point, it looked no larger than a mouse hole.

But the size wasn't even what shocked him the most. From the wall opposite him, water exploded from the rock in a magnificent waterfall. The river itself then ran through the centre of the cavern, dominating it with one meandering S-curve. The river ran directly beneath him. He leaned over the edge of the window and could now see the river as it hurtled into the rock, disappearing beneath his feet. The wind created by the force of the water lifted his hair and peeled back his eyelids.

'Wadi, do you see this!' He was unable to contain the grin that gripped at his cheeks. 'I knew what you meant when you said "underground river" but I could never have imagined . . .'

'Pretty amazing, right?'

'That's an understatement!'

He thought they had water a-plenty in the temple, but this was water in excess. This was what kept the Chauk alive.

As he watched the water, he gripped Wadi's hand in his own, interlocking their fingers. Then, a few figures started emerging out of other mouse holes around the cavern, converging on where Vlad was setting up camp. 'Who are they?' said Raim.

Wadi peered over the edge, squinting her eyes to get a better look. 'I think they're Chauk assigned to the mines. They must be . . . heading back to the main city.'

Raim's throat caught. 'Because of Dumas?'

Wadi squeezed his hand. 'Because they want to go home.'

37

Coming down was easier than going up. They raced down, and rejoined the main path towards the cavern. Streams of people flowed past them in the opposite direction. The snippets of conversation that he heard set his teeth on edge. 'Back to Darhan . . .' 'Khareh . . .' 'Seven chosen . . .'

Finally he could take it no longer, and he stopped one of the Lazarites as he passed by. 'Where are you going?' he said.

'To the temple, of course! Dumas is choosing his seven. I want to be one of the first back to Darhan. Back to my home! Can you believe it? Khareh was just a babe in arms when I was . . . when I left . . . and now look at him! I wonder if I can reach my tribe.'

'But Khareh is here, look!' *Draikh, come over here.* A still-meek Draikh floated over to stand in front of the Chauk. 'He will tell you that he would never allow Chauk back to Darhan.'

The man crossed his arms over his chest. 'I know you. Everyone does. You claim that the promise between you and Khareh is still intact, although his haunt is here, and that his haunt has no connection back to Khareh. If that's the case, then he doesn't know any more than we do. Maybe it was *him*' – he pointed to Draikh – 'that hates the Chauk, and not the rest of Khareh. Maybe the rest of his soul has seen the light.' The man shoved past Raim and Draikh, the conversation brusquely over.

They found Vlad seated next to a low flame on the other side of the river, having crossed a wide stone bridge made by the Chauk an age ago. 'So much water,' Raim muttered again.

'Yes,' said Vlad, and he went on to answer Raim's unasked question. 'But we dare not use too much, for if it dries up, that will be the end of Lazar. Can you imagine? That is why we trade water with the Alashan, not give of it freely. They have not toiled for years to dig these paths to this source.' An uncharacteristic flash of anger tinged Vlad's voice, but it soon settled. 'Ancient habits,' he mumbled, although Raim hadn't questioned him, or judged him for his bitterness. Raim had been in Lazar for too long to be bothered by the small gripes of ire that escaped the elders. They were at least less vehement than those that crowded the rhetoric of Dumas.

The fires projected Raim's flickering shadow up onto the wall, larger than life. While Wadi and Vlad sat, he paced, and his shadow paced with him. His other shadow,

Draikh, leaned up against a curve in the rock where the exit to the cave began.

At that moment, Draikh was in his head. 'You're nervous,' he said.

It's not like you to state the obvious, Raim replied.

Vlad spoke to Wadi. 'Do you know the fastest route north?'

'Not really, but I thought we would branch left after the second river station.'

Their conversation passed him by as Draikh continued. 'Glad you're speaking to me again.'

Raim bit his lip. *I could never forgive Khareh, but you . . . you're not him, are you?*

'I *am* him,' said Draikh, cocking his head to one side. 'But I am not the part that chose to hurt Dharma.'

Then that will be enough for me. Losing my best friend was . . . is . . .

'I'm still here.'

I know.

Raim felt soft. His legs felt soft and his arms felt soft and inside his chest his heart seemed turned to mush. They had been running. He, Vlad and Wadi had taken off after they had all had what they hoped was a night's rest.

But they couldn't run at a steady or normal pace. Knowing the Chauk were battling through the desert alongside them, moving as fast as they could, kept them motivated. They had to sprint as fast as they could, taking all the narrow shortcuts Wadi could remember until they raced across the second river and stopped to refill their canisters. It was here that Raim felt the exertion's toll on his body. He cursed the fact that, in spite of Silas's warnings, he had forfeited some of the fitness he had been so proud of as a Yun apprentice to focus on the meditation offered by Puutra and the temple.

He could read similar looks of pain on the faces of all his companions, except Draikh and Vlad's spirit. It offered him no consolation. Neither Vlad nor Wadi had trained like he had. He jumped up and down on the spot, knowing that if he let his heartrate slow, he would collapse onto the ground and need a longer rest.

Once the other two were ready, they started up again. Now they were beyond Wadi's previous experience of the tunnels. Draikh led the way, hovering faster than any of them could run and with a constant look of bemusement on his face that Raim saw whenever the spirit turned round to cheer them on.

Raim didn't know if anyone had ever met their spirit-self before, but soon both he and Khareh would. Spirits of the same person had met each other in Lazar – sometimes even disliked each other – but the experience would be different from the physical form meeting the spiritual. The difference was that Khareh didn't know he was about to meet Draikh. Raim debated whether to ask the spirit to stay back.

'No,' said Draikh inside Raim's head. He knew that any

effort requiring speech on Raim's part would drain his energy from running. 'The additional element of surprise could benefit us.'

Raim tried to concentrate but his breathing was laboured. He felt every rib against his lungs. Sharp pains shot through his sides and the soles of his feet. But he knew he just had to push on. As a result, it took him several minutes before he felt comfortable enough to reply coherently, even in thought.

It could benefit us, he said silently. *Or it could lead him to kill me on the spot. He will be convinced that I broke my promise to him – he knows of no other way that you could be visible. We didn't know that he could drive part of his own soul away.*

The conversation had, in fact, been more motivating than Raim realized. He had picked up his pace just thinking about Khareh and was soon several strides beyond Wadi and Vlad. He had been following the twisting tunnel path without much thought or difficulty, but now he found himself at a three-way junction, and he was forced to stop and allow his companions to catch up.

Wadi appeared first. Running had forced her into a kind of trance, so much so that Raim's stationary form shocked her and made her jump.

Raim put his hand on her shoulder as she gulped for breath. 'Any idea which way we should go?'

Vlad arrived by the time Raim finished his question, and doubled over with his hands on his knees.

Wadi abruptly shoved Raim's hand off her body and set to work examining the three separate entrances. She crawled up the rock, balancing on ledges until she reached the apex of one of the archways. Then she rubbed furiously at the stone. Dust plumed onto the ground. Eventually a small engraving became visible.

'Amazing!' said Raim. 'How'd you know that?'

'I knew we'd come to one of these eventually. Puutra told me about them, although I had never seen one before. These tunnels have not been used for a long time. Look – the markings are all covered in dust. But . . . I don't recognize this language,' said Wadi.

Vlad stepped forward to examine the marking more closely. 'Neither do I,' he admitted.

'But the Baril are supposed to be masters of language – of all language – so they claim,' protested Raim. 'My brother boasted he would even master the speech of birds and plants. How could a man-written hand be a mystery?'

Vlad grew quickly defensive. 'This mark could have been made five centuries ago or more! No Chauk comes north through the tunnels any more. Whatever language this is, must have been long lost. The Baril do not all deal in the lost languages. If you must know, my speciality was mammal language. When you learn to read a hoof print like I can, then you can mock me. If you ever learned to read at all, that is – ignorant soldier-boy.'

'Enough, you two.' Wadi jumped down from the rock after uncovering the symbols from above the other two doors. 'Instead of bickering, you could have helped me uncover the writing, and then we wouldn't still be standing around. And, as a matter of fact, I *have* seen this script before.'

'Really?' said Raim. He was glad to see that Vlad flushed with shame as well.

'Yes.' Wadi loosened the leather thong around her neck and pulled out the large stone pendant from beneath her tunic. She brushed it off with her hand, although there was no need – it was absolutely spotless.

Wadi chewed on her lower lip thoughtfully. 'Two paths will lead back to Lazar,' she said. 'So we mustn't choose incorrectly. But if I can just find where to . . .'

'Where to what?' Raim asked. Vlad quieted him, but his expression clearly showed he was wondering as much as Raim.

Vlad stared over Wadi's shoulder. 'Look! The symbol on your pendant is the same as the symbol over the left door! That must be the right way.'

Without looking at him, Wadi rotated the pendant in her hand. Vlad's open mouth snapped shut. The symbol was now the same as the sign in the middle. A third rotation had the symbol predictably looking like the symbol over the right door.

Wadi's eyes searched the cavern. Then she began to randomly kick at the ground, trying to uncover a symbol in the ground. Raim followed suit. But there was nothing. Finally she said, 'Search the walls for anywhere that looks more distressed than other areas in the cave – or like it could be moved . . . a hairline fracture in the rock, or something.' They set to work. Raim's fingers groped at the dust. His torch flickered, obscuring the detail on the stone and making lines and shadows appear where there were none.

Draikh didn't help to look. Instead, he stood at the front of the central doorway and sniffed at the air.

'There's something at work here,' he said aloud. 'These doorways aren't right. I believe that one will lead us in the right direction but . . .'

His open musing was interrupted by Raim's excited cry. The rock had shifted beneath his fingertips and Raim was prising open a piece of the wall. It came apart in one large, distractingly light and almost paper-thin square of stone. It revealed a small round indent, almost the size of Raim's palm.

Wadi rushed over to him. 'You found it!' She took the pendant and set it into the indentation.

Nothing happened. 'Maybe we have the wrong pendant?' said Vlad.

'Or maybe it's turned the wrong way,' said Raim, trying to sound a little more optimistic. He looked from the pendant to Wadi's face, and saw that tears were streaming down her face.

'Damn you,' she said. Then in her next breath she spoke words that were too quiet for them to hear.

A bright beacon of light emanated from the left

347

doorway. In contrast, the other two doorways were engulfed by shadow. Raim felt immediately repulsed by the shadowed doorways. The repulsion took over his entire body; he couldn't even look at the darkness and was instead drawn into the light. He hadn't felt that kind of visceral reaction to a shadow since . . .

'That's promise light!' Vlad cried. 'And promise shadow! Impossible!'

'Come on,' said Wadi, yanking the pendant out of the wall and back over her neck. 'There should be a supply room just beyond this doorway where we can take a rest and I can explain . . . as long as that old sage Garus didn't use it all. Just don't go turning your nose up at two-hundred-year-old meat.'

'Shouldn't we try to remember which doorway we came through?' said Raim.

'It wouldn't do us – or anyone in the future – any good.'

'The doors change!' exclaimed Draikh. 'That was what was so strange about them . . . like there was someone or something there that would mislead you – if you didn't know how to choose properly.'

Wadi smiled wanly. 'That's right. You can't guess. You are either granted passage or you're not.'

They found themselves in a small supply room, so small it barely allowed them all in comfortably. It was also near-empty. Where there had once been shelves of food and water, here there were only the bare essentials – a bit of food and a few bags of what looked to be Alashan camping supplies. The foods were supposed to be non-perishable, but the slabs of dried meat were rock-hard and inedible. They were also thick with dust.

'You don't really expect us to eat this, do you?' Raim asked. He ran his finger across one of the pieces of meat and the tip turned black. He had eaten many strange things in his life, but this was pushing it even for him.

Wadi rolled her eyes. 'Of course not. But around here there should be . . . ugh, will you look at this?' Wadi kneeled down and gently stroked the roughly cut stalk of a jarumba plant. 'Garus couldn't even be bothered to ensure the plant would grow again!' She got to work, attempting to salvage what she could from the plant that was close to death. Raim noted the care she took in slicing only the most mature parts of the root, so that the rest would continue to grow. 'We must subsist on jarumba root from now on,' she said. 'Hope you haven't lost your taste for it.' She grinned at Raim.

Raim shook his head. 'Jarumba? My favourite.' He took the root from her hand, and then paused. 'What happened back there?' he asked. 'The pass-stone just has to be returned to Lazar and then others can use it, right?'

Wadi's face darkened. She looked on the verge of tears again. 'Yes. That is true. But how many people who leave bring their stones back? Zero. For who would want to go back to Lazar after leaving it? No one.'

Vlad had his hand to his forehead and was rubbing the

flat part of his skull. 'Forgive me, I still don't understand. That was promise light we saw back there. And promise shadow from the other doorways. What does that mean?'

Draikh roared with sudden understanding. 'Of course! That was it all along – there were spirits in the doorway. They are the guides! But what was the promise made?'

Wadi lowered her head. 'It is the same promise anyone who uses a stone must make – and I knew it the moment I placed the stone in the wall. I had to promise to return with the stone to Lazar.'

Raim remembered her whispered curse. 'Did you know you would have to make that promise?'

Wadi shook her head miserably. 'No . . . but it's the only way to get you back to Darhan.'

'But why can't you act like the other people who have fled Lazar? Just never come back, despite the vow?'

'Because the stone will eventually destroy me, same as all those others who used it. Same as it must have destroyed my mother, and then my father. And then the curse will be passed down to whoever I leave it to – or if I leave it to no one, then whoever finds the stone accidentally. And unless I bequeath the stone to someone, they will never know what the task is that they have to achieve. And they will subsequently die.'

'I thought that a promise died with the person who guards it,' said Raim. 'Which is why oathbreakers aren't killed, they're sent away.'

Vlad broke the awkward silence. 'There are promises

that are even more important than Absolute Vows, Raim.'
He sighed and rubbed his temples. 'And you have one of
them. We've known it since you arrived. I'm sorry we didn't
tell you before, but Puutra was so determined to make you
the greatest sage in Chauk history . . . The scar around your
wrist – the fact that you don't remember what it is about, the
fact it was made before your Honour Age – is an indication
of a generational promise.' He expelled a deep breath after
that, as if he couldn't believe the words he had just said.

'I'm sorry . . . what? A generational promise? You mean
. . . all this is because I'm being punished for something
my parents did? Or my grandparents? How is that fair?'
Raim's face burned with anger, both at finding out about
the generational promise and that the Shan had kept the
knowledge from him this whole time. Raim looked up and
shouted at the ceiling. 'Why don't you show yourself to me
then, huh? Ancestor? Are you out there? Tell me how to
break this curse!'

Of course, there was no reply.

Raim turned on Vlad. 'What else do you know, that
you haven't told me?'

Vlad held his palms up to the sky. 'As Baril, we read
about these things in the ancient books. Generational
promises are a legend . . . no one was ever thought to have
made one, the consequences are too dire. You are
essentially damning yourself and your descendants for
eternity! The risk that the meaning behind the promise
could be lost is too great.'

'I guess I'm the perfect example of that,' said Raim, his face crossed with frown lines. He was fed up with things having to be explained to him.

'We should get moving,' said Wadi.

Raim wasted no time in getting ready: he could dwell on the generational promise later. For now, he had a more pressing concern, and that was getting to Darhan as quickly as possible. Wadi looked inside all the camping packs, selected a couple and gave one to Vlad to carry. They all pushed the jarumba root to the space behind their back teeth, where it would continue to provide nourishment as they ran. Raim took off first, not waiting for the others. When Wadi and Vlad caught up, Wadi was doing her planning aloud: 'The spirits in the doorways should guide us to Darhan using the quickest route possible. Then if we keep to the highest ground, we can try to spot Khareh's camp.'

'So tonight,' Raim said, barely as a whisper because he didn't dare believe it to be true, 'we will sleep in Darhan.'

They passed through five more portals in much the same way, but when they reached the seventh, they knew it would be the final one before Darhan. Even before the pass-stone showed Wadi the way, Raim felt confident he could've chosen the right path no matter how the spirits decided to guide him. There was a freshness to the way the air smelled and a cleanness of taste – totally devoid of the sand particles Raim had been ingesting with every breath in the desert.

He felt currents of energy nipping at his toes and fingertips, making him jumpy.

'Would you stop that?' Draikh said, turning a critical eye on Raim's feet, which were incessantly hopping backward and forward.

'I can taste it!' Raim said with glee that could not be dampened by Draikh, try as he might.

Even Vlad's energy had changed, grown younger and more lively.

The first blast of true fresh air was like coming up from being trapped underwater.

Raim gulped in the air and almost choked on the freshness. Outside it was dusk. The tunnel exited onto a rocky ledge. There was a good thirty feet between the ledge and the ground. Raim peered out over the edge. There was a cluster of fireflies hovering just below and beyond was an enormous plain of grass, which stretched out before him like a welcome mat.

Vlad reached out and put his hand on Raim's shoulder, as if he had to stop the young boy from launching himself off the ledge and into the grass. But when Raim looked in the man's eyes, he saw that they shared the same sense of longing. Looking out into the vast expanse of open land, the clear sky and the unexpected breath of moisture in the air, Raim suddenly had a pang for Oyu – the garfalcon would have loved this.

'He will find his way here,' said Draikh.

Are you sure? thought Raim.

'He wouldn't miss this for the world.'

Wadi was the last through the tunnel and onto the ledge. When she was out in the fresh air, there was a deep rumble behind them. Raim spun round in time to see the ceiling of the tunnel collapse a few feet away from where they had exited. He gripped Wadi's wrist beside him, both of them tense. When the rumble stopped, it was clear that there was no way back through the tunnel to Lazar.

'I'm sorry . . .' Wadi said. 'I guess I should've been nicer to the spirits when asking them to get us to Darhan as quickly as possible.'

'It's not so bad,' said Draikh. 'Look at these vines hanging down from the top of the mountain. They will probably hold your weight and you can lower yourself down.'

'Easy for you to say, you can float,' said Raim, staring at the vines uncertainly. The source of the vines wasn't even visible. The thick green strands disappeared into the low-lying clouds above them.

Vlad clasped one of them and shook it brusquely. Leaves and dirt tumbled past them, but the vine held. He shrugged and passed the vine to Raim first.

Raim grabbed the vine from Vlad's hands and was surprised at how solid it seemed. He took a deep breath and without a second thought he launched himself off the cliff. The descent was relatively easy as the vine was smooth and thankfully free of thorns. He slid down, occasionally pushing himself off the cliff face, and in minutes he touched the ground.

'I've landed!' he called up to the others. 'Send Wadi now!'

But the next figure to launch off the cliff was not Wadi, but Vlad.

'Good to see you haven't lost any of your Baril arrogance,' said Raim as Vlad's boots touched the ground. 'You send me down first so you know it's safe and then you go yourself, before the only woman.' Raim's expression hovered between disapproval and worry. Vlad ignored him, brushed the dirt off his knees and walked onto the plain, breathing in the thick, green air.

'Just because I'm a woman, doesn't mean I need any special treatment!' said Wadi as she yanked the vine. But halfway through her descent, a sickening crack shuddered through the air and the vine slackened in Wadi's hands. For a moment, she seemed suspended in the air and then she shrieked and began to plummet.

'Wadi!' Raim cried. He leaped forward.

But then a curtain of white descended on his vision and he collided with it, solid as a brick wall.

Raim's face stretched into a horrified, anguished scream. By the time he could see again, it was too late. Wadi landed with a thud that resonated through Raim's heart. He could have been there. He could have saved her.

Raim dropped to his knees at her side, not daring to touch her in case he hurt her more. Her lip was split and gushing blood; bits of rock and dirt were embedded into her cheek. Her leg and arm on her right side – the side she fell on – were clearly broken and jutting out at horrible, unnatural angles.

Vlad was there now too, placing two fingers against her neck. 'Her heart is beating,' he said, but there was no relief in his voice. Wadi's body had shut down in shock, and she lay motionless.

Raim staggered to his feet. 'How dare you!' he screamed at the invisible force that had blocked him, unable to control the sheer flood of anger and terror and shock that was bombarding his system. He fell to the ground. Grass brushed his cheek, for the first time since he had been exiled. How long had he yearned for this? But now he knew what was more important to him than his homeland.

'I can heal her,' said Draikh.

Raim looked back over his shoulder. Draikh was already standing over Wadi, as if assessing her injuries. He scrambled over to them, his despondency fading just a little. Draikh was steeling himself for the sheer amount of power it was going to take to heal Wadi's wounds.

He started with her right leg, his ghostly hands gripping her knee and slowly righting the bone beneath the skin. Raim could see the swelling compress; and after a few moments the leg's shape was more normal, though the bruising was just coming to the surface now. Draikh's face was the picture of concentration. He moved on to her arm. Although he had to penetrate less muscle to get to the bone in her arm than the one in her leg, it took him longer this time. Healing the fractures required so much power. Raim wasn't sure if it was his imagination, but Draikh seemed less solid, more transparent. The arm bone eventually set, and the moment it did, Draikh slumped in the air. It seemed to be using all his force just to stay floating.

Wadi still looked terrible. Draikh didn't have the strength to tackle her facial injuries, nor the bruising beneath the skin, which was beginning to show now that her body didn't have to worry about healing the broken bones. Raim couldn't find the words to thank Draikh. He tried, many times, but there was just no way to articulate it.

Draikh whispered inside his head, so meek and soft compared to normal. 'I know,' he said. 'So you forgive me now? Sorry I couldn't do the rest.'

'Of course I forgive you,' said Raim, his voice choking with emotion. He turned to Vlad. 'We have to take her back to Lazar – she needs a healer.'

'Raim . . .'

'Wadi!'

Her face was still etched with pain but Draikh's healing had allowed her to recover the strength to speak. 'You've come so far. You can't go back now. I'll be all right.'

Raim paused for a moment, then nodded.

Vlad hushed Wadi, and picked her up in his arms. 'We

must find somewhere to rest for the night. We will move away from the entrance to the tunnel – just in case – but we cannot go looking for Khareh tonight. Both Draikh and Wadi need to recover some of their strength. And you need to calm yourself.' His eyes were filled with worry as he addressed Raim. 'Do you think you are strong enough for this? To face Khareh?'

Raim bit his lower lip. 'I thought so, but Draikh . . . he's going to need time to recover. Maybe if we had trained more. I should have listened to you and Puutra, no matter what your intentions were.'

'The past is past,' said Vlad.

They walked in silence until the sun had completely set and the mountain drifted into the distance. Raim and Vlad took turns in carrying Wadi, her body resolving to heal itself through deep slumber. They walked in hopes of finding some shelter – a forest, a grove, a cave, anything – but the grassy plain stretched all around them with no end in sight. It got to the point where Vlad could no longer bear his share of the weight, and they were forced to camp out in the open. The best they could do was to settle on a place where the grass was high enough to tickle their knees.

They set up camp in the Alashan fashion, unrolling the sturdy woven bundle of sticks Vlad carried on his back and planting it into the ground as a semicircle. Wadi had a large blanket clipped to her waist pack, which Raim threw on top of the semicircle to create a rough shelter.

Raim took the first watch, and let Wadi and Vlad inside to sleep. He wanted to see the stars anyway. He knew all the constellations intimately, but they almost seemed foreign to him now. These were the stars he had been exiled from. Were they friendly to him now?

After he judged by the moon's steady track across the sky that two hours had passed, he gently shook Vlad awake. Vlad blinked the sleep out of his eyes and took his post without complaint. Raim curled up in the shelter and felt his body drift into a deep, much-needed sleep . . .

He was jolted awake by thick arms wrapped around his neck. He heard Vlad's muffled warning and an anguished cry of pain from Wadi. Raim tried to yell but couldn't, as a rattan sack was forced over his head and pinned his arms to his sides. Then he realized. This was the Yun way – the Yun abduction. Only one person in the world would know to give Raim that message.

'It's Khareh!' he yelled through the sack, trying to reach the ears of Wadi and Vlad. 'He's found us!'

38

The movement and the darkness and the voices had been terrifying, even though he knew what was happening. The blindfold now wrapped tightly over his eyes was coarse and scratched at his eyelids as he tried to open them. His wrists were bound too. He tugged at the knots but he knew they were solid. As he struggled, the knots only drew tighter, so he let his muscles relax and focused his attention on his other senses.

He could hear others in the room, smell them. The breaths to his left were quick and shallow, making him think they belonged to Wadi. The freshness of the outdoors had been replaced by the thick scent of dirt-stiffened carpets. They were inside a yurt. The smell of blood and sweat dominated over even that, but Raim was certain it emanated from his own body, his skin burning where it had been scraped as he was dragged brutally over the terrain. He must have blacked out after their initial capture, for he had no sense of time passing. Only the strange sense of déjà vu: the opaque rattan sack pulled over his head, the strong hands throwing him onto the back of a broad-shouldered and soon-to-be-swiftly-moving horse, the ropes lashing him in place. His head pounded with pain. A groan penetrated the barrier of agony, and it took a moment for Raim to realize it hadn't come from his own mouth. Hesitantly, he whispered Wadi's name.

Another groan replied. There was a slump next to him, as if Wadi had launched herself towards his voice. He even thought he felt strands of her hair tickle against his fingertips and he groped to stroke them, to let her know he was there, but strong footsteps shook the ground beneath him and lifted Wadi back upright.

The darkness momentarily brightened in front of his eyes and Raim assumed someone was entering the tent, pulling the curtain door aside. He was about to protest the treatment they were receiving, when the new arrival did it for him.

'What is this?' cried the voice. Raim felt his heart simultaneously leap and harden at the sound. He had found his best friend at last – both the worst and best feeling in the world. 'Untie them! Such brutality is uncalled for – these are my friends, or at least, I think they are.'

The cold blade against his forearm made Raim jump. The moment he felt the bonds release, he tugged the blindfold down off his eyes.

And for a brief moment, he hardly recognized the

person standing in front of him. Khareh loomed enormous, a thick cloak of luxurious black velvet broadening his muscular frame by several inches. Layers of jewels hung off his neck, so many of them that Raim couldn't even see the shirt on Khareh's chest, although that too was surely blazoned in gold. The next items that caught Raim's eye were the two giant blades that protruded from Khareh's cloak like elephant tusks; impractical position for battling, sure, but Khareh had enough bodyguards not to have to worry about the functionality of his blades. Even more shocking to Raim was that the blades were translucent, like those supposedly reserved for the members of the Yun.

It took him so long to process Khareh's new clothing that he had hardly looked at his friend's face. When he did, he physically recoiled in shock. Khareh's features were refreshingly familiar; the smug look on his face the same as when he had left it and the same look that he had encountered so often with Draikh. But Khareh's turban was monstrous. It was not in the traditional purple that represented the Khanate of his uncle and his ancestors, but fashioned in a new, bright, jade green. Wrapped in the middle of the green fabric and sitting directly on top of Khareh's head was the terrifying skull of a Darhan jaguar, two immense fangs curving down past its bone jaw until they reached Khareh's eyebrows. Khareh was wearing the traditional headgear of the sages.

Raim knew he was staring, but he couldn't tear his eyes from his former friend. Then it struck him. Khareh had taken over the Khanate in every way, surpassed his uncle in all measure. He was more a Khan than his uncle had ever been. Raim felt the nakedness of his own head more acutely then, realizing the magnitude of Khareh's new position. Here he was, at the feet of the Khan of Darhan. Hatred boiled over.

'You sicken me,' he said, staring straight into Khareh's eyes.

'Oh, that's some way to treat your best friend when you see them for the first time in months.'

'My best friend?' The term strangled his throat. 'You expect me to be your friend after what you did?'

'After what *I* did?' Khareh said. Raim bristled as the hands of Khareh's bodyguards moved deliberately to the handles of their swords, and Khareh continued to speak: 'You are the one who betrayed your sacred vow to me, and I stood by you. They all said – those Yun leaders that you admired so much – that you were a traitor and I should hope for your death. I believed with all my heart that you must have had good reason for not meeting me in Pennar, and that when you returned, you would have rid yourself of that disgrace.'

'I did not betray you,' said Raim.

'Don't lie to me, Raimanan!' Khareh's voice shook the tent posts; but Raim did not let himself be moved by his former friend's rage. Khareh stomped his foot and two of his guards leaped to action. Raim braced himself, but the guards simply pushed past him, although one with an outstretched elbow clipped him hard round the head, toppling him, his feet still bound, to the ground. The guards disappeared into the folds of cloth that hung behind him. Then, a few moments later, they came in dragging Draikh, and threw him onto the tent floor beside Raim. It was then that Raim, and Vlad, judging by his audible gasp, realized that Khareh's guards were themselves spirits.

'Look!' Khareh was seething. Even the jaguar on his head seemed to hiss and boil, grow angrier by the moment. 'You did break your vow to me. How dare you?'

'No!' cried Raim.

'Yes! There is the proof!'

'No, look!' Raim ripped the fabric down from around his neck and showed Khareh his chest. There was the tattoo on his skin, the mark of permanence. Raim looked up into Khareh's face and saw the angry spark in his eyes begin to flicker, begin to go out. Raim pushed onward. 'I was given the choice to make my promise absolutely permanent to you, unbreakable in every way. Have you ever seen a mark like this?'

'Never,' breathed Khareh.

'A garfalcon caused this.'

'But those are legend!'

'I assure you, they are not.'

'But then explain this!' Khareh gestured violently in Draikh's direction, trying to make his voice sound angry now, but Raim knew that wonderment had taken over. He wasn't safe yet, though; he had to be careful. Khareh was more unstable than Raim had ever known him.

'Explain it? It is a mistake! If I had known who you were . . . what you were capable of . . . I would never have made the vow to you. I would have rather broken it, crushed it, destroyed my promise to you, been truly exiled, but now I can't even do that. Tell me Khareh, where am I? Where is your haunt?'

Slowly, calm returned to Khareh's face. 'I will have to consult Garus about this.' He rubbed his chin slowly. He continued, completely ignoring Raim's question, 'Still, I don't understand why you didn't come to Pennar. I could have helped you, and then none of this would've happened. You would be here beside me, instead of . . .' He waved a dismissive hand at the others in the room.

'It was Mhara—'

There was a swift, simultaneous drawing of swords from all the guards around, this time directed at Raim. He put his hands up in shock and felt the tips of the swords graze his palms.

'No, no, put your weapons away.' Khareh turned back to Raim and rested his chin on one of his enormous ruby-inlaid rings. 'To say her name or the name of my uncle is treason, but you don't know that, do you? What did . . .' Khareh's mouth twisted in disgust as he tried, and failed, to say her name. '. . . she tell you?'

'That you had informed the Yun I was heading to Pennar.'

'She lied!' hissed Khareh.

'I know – she was smart, she guessed the truth – but I thought she was being treasonous against you, and that's why I fought against her . . .'

'That's why you had to protect me. I always believed in you!' Khareh stomped his foot again, this time with a smile on his face, and he missed the end of Raim's sentence: '. . . to my everlasting shame.'

'Undo his ankle bindings,' said Khareh. 'And the bindings of his companions too.'

When the bonds were finally loosened from around his ankles, Raim stood up abruptly.

'Come with me,' said Khareh.

'Wait.' It was the first time Vlad had spoken since Raim had woken up. It was then that Raim realized Vlad had been forced to wear a mouth gag the entire time. Wadi too, was unhinging the thick wad of fabric from behind her teeth and massaging the corners of her mouth.

Vlad kept his eyes on the ground, not even daring to look up at Khareh. 'You will answer for your crime.'

Raim had never seen Vlad move so fast. He had heard rumours – of a specialized Baril fighting skill – but he had never seen it in action. What it amounted to was a whirl of kicks, punches and dizzying acrobatics.

The screech of swords being loosed from their sheaths filled the room, but too slow. Vlad had already leaped half the distance between him and the Khan – another two steps and he would be there.

'Raim!' It was Draikh's voice.

Raim threw himself in front of Khareh, taking a sharp chop to the shoulder from Vlad's hand. But Raim had been working up his hand-to-hand skills with Wadi and with Silas. If Vlad had once been a Baril martial master, he had not exercised the moves in a long time. All his energy had been focused on getting to Khareh and killing him that first time. Only Raim could have come between them. And Raim had.

'What are you doing? Get out of my way!' Vlad screamed. But by then it was too late. Khareh's guards were all over him, throwing him to the floor and binding his arms and legs again. 'Dharma! He killed my daughter!'

Raim stared wide-eyed at Vlad, sweat pouring off his brow. 'I . . . I'm sorry. I just . . .'

'How can you protect that monster? How could y—' the gag was thrust firmly back in his mouth and Vlad's sharp words became muffled cries as he was dragged from the room.

What did I do that for? I hate Khareh. He deserved whatever Vlad had planned for him.

'But you are still under oath to protect him,' said Draikh inside his head.

The thought made Raim fall to his knees, bile rising in his throat. His gaze met Wadi's, who stared at him as if she didn't know him. He wasn't sure he knew himself.

It was even worse when Khareh started clapping, a slow, drawn out clap that made Raim wince with every sound.

'My apologies, Raimanan. I thought you were my

betrayer. But I see you really are my true Protector. I knew you would understand. Now, it's on to business. I have great plans you need to get up-to-date with, Raim. You are going to be so excited when you see what I have in store.' And just like that, Khareh seemed almost back to his normal self – full of infectious energy and enthusiasm.

With a smile, he beckoned Raim to follow him. But when Raim didn't budge, Khareh seemed to notice Wadi in the room for the first time. 'Who are you?' he asked, but he didn't wait for her to respond. In fact, he leaned forward slightly and squinted. 'Is that . . . what I think it is?'

Raim followed Khareh's line of sight. An edge of the pass-stone caught the light, the pearlescent stone shimmering gently. Wadi looked down in alarm and tried to tuck it away quickly, but Khareh had already seen it.

'So this is how you got here . . . But Garus said there was only supposed to be one left. Why did they give it to you?' Khareh paused, furrowing his brow, his eyes lowered and seemingly tracing the fringe of the rug. Raim wondered whether Khareh had revealed more than he meant to. Then the Khan looked up, his eyes sparkling with purpose. 'Maybe I will bring him here. Wait a moment,' he said, as if Raim and Wadi had anywhere else to go.

'I don't trust him,' said Wadi, setting her mouth in a grim line.

Raim slumped down next to her. 'Neither do I. You have to warn the Chauk.'

Wadi hissed at him and widened her eyes, gesturing

over to the guards. Then she started speaking much quieter, using a few words of Alashan sign language that Raim had learned. 'Don't talk out loud. Spies everywhere.'

Raim whispered back, 'I think I can get him to let you go.'

'Don't fall for his lies,' she said, her eyes pleading with him. 'I can see you still care for your friend. But while you have been entranced by Khareh, I have noticed other things. This yurt, it's not secured to the ground; it's a temporary settlement. He is on the move. And do you not hear that steady hum in the background? And the smell that lingers in the air? My blindfold was not as secure as they believed when they dragged us in here. I glimpsed what is going on out there. There are people all around us. Thousands of them, perhaps. This is an army on the march.'

There was rustling at the entrance of the tent that broke the stiff tension developing in the room. Raim gaped when he saw it was Lars, the boy he had defeated in battle so long ago. But now Lars was equipped in the traditional Yun uniform, with thick leather boots laced up to the knee and a long, dark cloak edged with Khareh's jade green slung around his shoulders. Lars seemed equally surprised to see Raim, but smiled smugly, clearly comparing his elegant garb to Raim's tattered and dirt-infused clothing.

Khareh followed a moment later. 'Let's go then! Come on . . . I can't stop all day because you have arrived.'

'Khareh . . .'

'Yes?' Khareh drummed his fingers against the sheath of his sword.

'I know I am hardly in a position to ask you anything, but please let Wadi go. Her aim was to get me to you. She's accomplished that. She should go back home now.'

'And where is home for her?'

Raim glanced at her sidelong. 'With the Alashan.'

Khareh murmured approval. 'Yes, I can see. Such beautiful, rich skin you have, my lady.'

Wadi simply stared at the ground, not bringing her eyes up to meet his.

'And demure! Yes, I like her! Not your type though, Raim, you like them feisty.' He winked. 'She can go, if that's what you wish. Think of it as my thanks for saving my life – that scary old man you brought with you looked like he really was going to kill me! My men will take her away by blindfold, and then she is free to go wherever she wants.'

Raim glanced at Wadi. Her face was grey but set with determination. She stood perfectly still as the guards came over and refitted the blindfold around her eyes. Then, as she was led away through the curtained door of the yurt, she held her hands behind her back and spoke one final sign to Raim.

'Protect us.' The words formed in her hands, the traditional Alashan signing prayer to Sola. Then she dropped one of her fingers and changed the meaning of the sign completely, a message just to Raim, before disappearing behind the folds of the curtain.

'Protect me.'

39

'Raimanan, I have so many things to tell you about!'

Raim had been blindfolded again and bombarded by sound when he had first been moved from the tent. Metal clashing together, the sound of shields being tossed on top of carts, the hawing and spitting of camels, the trumpet of a great elephant close by. Then his knees bashed up against the rungs of a ladder, and as he stabilized himself his hands collided against the hardened leather hide of another elephant. Coarse hairs tickled his knuckles. He clambered up the rungs, blindly reaching up to feel the next step, until he dived headfirst into the caravan, aided by a shove from behind by whoever was his guide. When he reached the top they released his blindfold. He fell down immediately onto a sea of soft, silk cushions.

They started moving immediately, and the swaying motion of the carriage made Raim's stomach turn. The walls of the howdah were made of a delicate, sheer fabric, but there were so many layers that Raim couldn't see out-side, and much of the sound was blocked out, too.

Khareh stood up and lifted the turban off his head, skull and all. His legs bent and swayed with the movement of the great elephant below them, so steady it was as if the beast were an extension of his person. There was no way Raim would be as steady as Khareh if he stood up. His fingers gripped the edge of a pillow tightly, trying to keep his stomach out of his throat.

Now that he was stripped of his costume, Khareh seemed and sounded more like the friend Raim had left behind and less like the Khan of Darhan. He stretched out on a pile of pillows woven in the same velvety fabric as his cloak, and helped himself to a handful of what looked like Rago berries. 'Want some?' he mumbled, his mouth full. 'You know, they finally figured out a way to preserve these things for more than a day? Of course, I have them deliv-ered fresh anyway, that way they're most succulent.' But Raim could only think of his first day in the desert and the disgusting taste of the rotten Rago berries. He shook his head. 'Suit yourself.' Khareh shrugged and popped a few more in his mouth.

Khareh stretched back and cradled his head in his hands. 'Relax, Raimanan, we'll be here for a while.'

Raim realized then how stiffly he had been sitting, but he couldn't get his muscles to relax. Just being around Khareh felt wrong. Looking at Draikh next to him, the two side by side, made his head hurt. He longed for his friend to be Draikh – not the power-mad Khan who was willing to hurt his best friend's sister to get what he wanted.

Luckily, or maybe unluckily, Khareh didn't seem to need him to provide much conversation. 'I'm supposed to be over by the Erudine River today to ensure the final takeover of their lands goes smoothly, but there's a small errand we have to complete along the way. It shouldn't take long.'

'The Erudine?' The homeland of Ryopi and Silas. 'You're taking over by force?'

'Oh, don't be so naive. I'm the youngest Khan there's been in years; there were bound to be issues in certain places. Some people are just too stupid to realize how futile their resistance is.'

'Do you know how strange it is to see yourself in spirit form?' Khareh was staring at Draikh now. Raim turned to the sullen face of Draikh and compared it to the unbridled grin that seemed permanently plastered on Khareh's face. One was real, the other a dream.

'I am more real than that monster,' spoke Draikh into Raim's mind, so that Khareh could not hear. 'My words are more real. My truth is. The things that matter.'

Raim kept his eyes trained nervously on Draikh, but the spirit made no indication of the fact that he was communicating with Raim. Raim tried to keep his own features neutral. Khareh was looking at him expectantly.

'I'm sure I will learn what it's like soon enough.'

Khareh's proud exterior cracked. He put his hands on his temples and rubbed, scrunching his eyes tightly shut. 'I don't know what you expected me to do, Raimanan. That day, I thought you had betrayed me. I thought you had abandoned me! And Garus, that old sage, had just told me the first step: I had to break an oath. Something I thought I would never do! I was *so angry* with you. And there, right in front of me, was a chance to make all my dreams come true. I took it, all right? I took it, and I know you won't understand, not for a while, but it had to be done. To get to where I am today . . . it had to be done.'

Raim raised his eyes, cold and hard. 'Keep telling yourself that, Khareh.'

Then the proud, power-hungry Khan came back. 'Don't ever forget who you are speaking to, Raimanan. I will send you somewhere worse than Lazar if you're not careful. I thought we could get over this, but if you're going to insist on being difficult, then so be it. I have come this far without you, I can keep going.' Khareh stood up, his back to Raim. He moved to walk away, but then he spun on his heels and faced him. 'You know, I shouldn't be so surprised. When I broke my oath to you, and your spirit came, I have never seen your face show so much anger. Oh, how you fought me, Raim. Oh, you railed against me. Raged. Cursed. You were full of fury, and I was scared.

'But Garus reminded me to be strong. He knew our bond, and he knew our potential – he told me to remember that deep down, all parts of your spirit belonged to me.

That you were loyal to a fault, and that would shine through in the end.

'I told your spirit my plans. I told him everything. And now, look – a part of you is on my side. You might not understand it now, but you are my greatest asset. Through you, through your strength, I have been able to control a spirit army, with you at its head!'

'I would never allow such a thing!'

'One part of you has allowed it. It would be better for you if the rest of you followed.'

'Never!'

Khareh stormed through to the back of the elephant-drawn carriage, and Raim realized it was much larger than he had assumed. Khareh disappeared behind a set of curtains Raim had believed to be the back of the howdah. It wasn't the case. In fact, as Khareh brushed the curtains aside, Raim caught a glimpse of the next room behind. There were people – servants, beyond doubt – lined up against the far wall of the room. Their heads were bent down so low Raim couldn't see their faces. Khareh snapped his fingers and the first servant leaped to his feet, and then the curtain closed on Raim's view of the action.

Deep lines crossed Draikh's forehead as he frowned in concentration. He lifted one arm in the air straight out in front of him and then the other. He clenched and relaxed his wrists. They were simple movements but his face belied the exertion. He cringed even as he attempted to lift his arms over his head.

Dread welled into Raim's stomach and sat there like lead.

Draikh finally turned to Raim. Under the steely black stare of the spirit, Raim felt his insides disintegrate into mush.

'I won't be able to fight.'

'But we're going to need to.'

'Yes.'

'But . . . Draikh, you made me stop Vlad when he attacked Khareh. You're not going to allow me to fight him one-on-one. If that's not breaking the vow of protection, I don't know what is.'

The howdah lurched forward; the elephant was sitting down. Raim's limbs couldn't muster a reaction in time. He tumbled across the floor, with just enough sense to grab hold of the pole in the centre of the room before he slid right through the curtained walls. His feet shot out under the sheer material. He scrambled to get back inside but the howdah lurched again and did the work for him, pivoting him round the post.

Draikh laughed. He floated through the entire debacle.

'Oh,' said Raim, throwing him a dark look as he rubbed his sore hipbones, 'so at least your sense of humour is back in full force.'

Light flooded the room. Raim shielded his eyes with his arm. Squinting into the sunlight, he could just make out the outline of Khareh's body. Raim craned his neck to catch a glimpse of the outside world, but Khareh blocked his view. He caught sight of greenery. Inside, he kicked himself. He had been back in Darhan for how many days now? He hadn't even seen enough sunlight to tell. They had arrived in Darhan in darkness and he hadn't been able to enjoy their first night outside, their first night in the grass, not the sand, their first night under the constellations over Darhan. He had been too worried about Wadi to appreciate it. And after that, every moment had been spent in Khareh's clutches.

'We've arrived!' said Khareh, brimming with enthusiasm. 'I just took a walk outside to stretch my legs. Everything is going according to plan, Raimanan, you should see it!'

'Where are we?'

But Khareh didn't budge from the doorway. In fact, Raim didn't think he had heard him at all. 'I wish you had been a part of this. From the beginning.'

'Where are we?' Raim pressed.

'We had to take a little detour. But first, there is something I must know. Who told you about . . . my power?'

'You mean, who told me you hurt a little girl so you could feed your sick ambition? Silas, the last person you exiled.'

'Silas was a coward.'

Raim felt the blood rush to his face. Silas had been his mentor and confidante, his saviour through his time in Lazar. He was not going to let even Khareh the Khan take that away from him. 'You have no idea what he went through. His haunt was the most terrible man you've ever seen . . . he was more like a demon. That haunting would have driven any man mad, even you.'

'He should have controlled it,' said Khareh.

'What, the spirit?' Raim let out a bitter laugh. 'Impossible. You didn't know this haunt . . . he was crazy.'

'On the contrary, I knew him very well. And but for the illiterate, uncultured society promoted by my uncle, you – the best Yun apprentice in a century – should also have known him. We cannot even recognize the heroes of our past . . . you cannot even recognize the founder of the community you hold so dear. He was haunted by Malog.'

Raim gasped. 'No!'

'Oh yes, so you do know the name? Malog, the original Yun founder, with that messed up face. All the Yun make their vow to him. If you'd manage to pass your test, you would have known that. And if Silas had managed to control him, can you imagine the power he would have had? Of course, Silas did not have the mental strength.'

'Controlling a spirit like that . . . that's impossible! It takes decades of intense training just to get to the point where the spirit isn't a haunt any more!'

'Then how do you explain me? How do you explain you? It doesn't take decades of training, it simply takes the right mind. Funnily enough, in both our cases, that mind is mine . . . but you only have a small, useless part of me. Look at him over there. As if I ever needed that? And now I will extend my power, and create a whole army of spirit-warriors, soon to be enhanced by an entire flock of subjugated people who will be only too happy to submit to my will. Oh yes. I'm so glad the Chauk are coming. I will lay out a special welcome greeting for them.'

Raim was on his feet now. His hands were clenched tightly against his sides. 'What did you say?'

'You think I stopped the Chauk from leaving Darhan because they deserve forgiveness? The Chauk are the scum of the earth. That hasn't changed. They don't have the mental strength to be sages, like me.'

'You are exactly like them. You are an oathbreaker like any other. Worse, because you had to harm an innocent child to do it!'

'I am nothing like them! I am all-powerful! I will make Darhan great again, not the pitiful country it is now. I will make us greater than Mauz! Greater than the south! Greater than any place on earth. You cannot deny my strength, my genius! And the Chauk only serve to complete that.'

'I don't understand.' Raim was out of his mind now. It had been a trap. He had been right. Would Wadi get to Dumas and the Chauk on time? Could she warn them?

'Of course you don't! Your strength was always solely in your muscles, Raimanan. I'm going to use them, use them all and then they can die for all I care. Starting with that girl you brought here. She would make a strong spirit, don't you think?'

Raim hurled himself at Khareh then, even as Draikh

flashed to intervene. He felt savage, betrayed a thousand times over, raw with worry and ire. But attacking Khareh directly wasn't Raim's intention; instead he hurtled into the side of the carriage, splintering the fragile frame. He came flying out the other side, bouncing off the tough grey hide of the elephant and hitting the ground hard. Khareh screamed, 'Raim!' as the carriage lurched sideways, the force of Raim's collision sending it sliding down the elephant's side. Khareh's giant turban threw him off balance and he toppled through the curtain door, breaking the ladder as he punched through it, rung by rung. Raim rolled away, winded by the fall. Pain stabbed at his sides. Then, fingers gripped his throat and lifted him clear off the ground. Raim's eyes were clenched shut and he struggled against his attacker, kicking out his legs and trying to pry his fingers off his Adam's apple. When the worst of the shock and the initial pain passed, he opened his eyes. He found himself staring at his own face, frowning with concentration.

Khareh struggled up to his feet. He brushed the dust off his clothing and waved aside the guards who had rushed to his aid. Raim's eyes flickered between Khareh and the spirit form of himself. His brain was unable to comprehend, unable to work fast enough. It alternated between trying to free his throat from the suffocating grasp and trying to understand how he could be killing himself.

'Raimanan,' Khareh said, his voice hard. 'Meet Raim.'

The spirit-Raim threw him to the ground. Raim lay in

a crumpled heap, his hands around his own throat, massaging it back to life. He coughed and spluttered, tasting his own blood. He spat it into the dirt. With every breath he drew in clumps of dust. Other smells filled his nostrils as he wrenched himself to his feet. Ashes. Smoke. Fire.

Khareh's eyes narrowed. 'The power I wield is greater than anyone could ever imagine! And I have you to thank for that, Raimanan. Why not turn round and take a look?'

'I will do nothing you ask of me.'

'Of course you will,' he snarled. He strode over and grabbed Raim by the hair. He forced him round and jerked his head backward. 'Because you must follow orders, mustn't you, Raimanan? You couldn't be a leader if you tried. You can't even control your own spirit – because you made that promise to me permanent.' He threw Raim to the ground. 'You see?'

And Raim couldn't help but see. Khareh had parked them right on the edge of a cliff. The cliff was a vertical rock face that speared straight down into the valley beneath. There was nothing to block the view of the turmoil below and, with Khareh's foot firmly planted on the back of Raim's neck, there was nowhere to look but down.

'Your little girlfriend led us here, to these seven Chauk and their savage companions.'

There was swarming chaos below. It wasn't hard to see

what had gone on. The Alashan and the group of seven Chauk were clashing with the Yun at the entrance of an enormous cave – a tunnel entrance, like the one Raim, Vlad and Wadi had exited from only a day before. They were surrounded. Further into the valley, Raim could see the scattered remains of the Alashan tents: flimsy, temporary wooden frames. Frames that were now consumed by fire. The cloth that had once wrapped around them rose, billowed and flapped in the smoke from the flames, looking for all the world like tortured birds, great wings trying to fly, to escape. But there was no way free.

It was the screaming that was the worst. Raim could barely make out the Chauk and the Alashan for all the smoke but gods, he could hear the screams. Dumas hadn't picked warriors – he had picked the younger ones, the ones he thought would most appeal to Khareh's sensitivity.

Every now and then, a glint of light would pierce his vision. It was the bright glint of a Yun sword. Letting Wadi go had all been part of one big trap. One that he, Raim, had led the Chauk directly into.

He scanned the scene, desperate for a glimpse of Wadi. Was she amongst all the destruction below?

Khareh leaned down and whispered in Raim's ear, 'I'm invincible. There's only one anomaly in my plan, Raimanan. You. You and him.' He pointed at Draikh. 'You just don't fit in.' Khareh's bodyguards rushed forward with their weapons and Raim cringed, but the Khan put out his hand to stop them. 'No,' he said. 'I want him to die with the blade that gave me this.' He lifted his palm and Raim saw the scar his spirit-self had given Khareh the day he broke his vow. It curved cruelly across his lifeline, festering and red, and Raim had no doubt of the deed Khareh had committed in order for it to have attained that crimson colour.

The haunt-Raim drew his sword slowly. It was a spirit-blade, black as night and viciously curved. Raim had no weapon and behind him, the drop of the cliff.

His eyes met those of his haunt-self. 'Why are you going to do this to me?' he said to the haunt. 'Why are you following his orders?'

Instead of replying, the haunt-Raim quickened his pace, his sword readied in front of him. Khareh's other bodyguards fenced him in. But Raim was resolved not to go down without a fight. He steadied his feet on the ground and slowed his breathing. He tensed his muscles. How would Mhara get out of this? She would fight the haunt. *It's not you*, he told himself.

The haunt-Raim was upon him now. Raim felt all his muscles tense in anticipation. But it was Draikh who intercepted the blow for Raim and the two spirits were locked in battle. 'I'll take the haunt,' Draikh said inside Raim's mind. 'You just concentrate on the flesh and blood.'

The other bodyguards jumped into action and began attacking Raim. He ducked and dived out of the way, and it quickly became clear they weren't Yun. Khareh had grown cocky, and felt his haunt was enough protection. All the Yun were battling the Chauk down below. These men were regular soldiers. Raim could tell as soon as they drew their blades. Just ordinary steel.

Still, when Raim had nothing, ordinary steel came out on top. 'Draikh!' Raim shouted. He could only avoid for so long, and he could feel the drop yawn behind him. Terror filled his throat, made him stumble, made him slow. A sword blow slashed down the side of his arm, and his sleeve instantly turned red. He was going down.

'On three, do you trust me?' Draikh said into his mind.

On three? On three what?

'Kill him!' Khareh shrieked. 'I want him to die!'

'On three and over the cliff! Ready? Three!'

Raim abruptly stopped moving, sending his enemies reeling forward. He spun round, took a step forward and without allowing another moment for thought, leaped off the cliff and into the chaos below.

They were falling. Draikh grabbed the shoulder of Raim's tunic and it caught under his chin. But they were still falling. Plummeting, in fact.

'Draikh?' Raim screamed.

Draikh readjusted his position and grabbed Raim under his arm. Their descent slowed but the ground – and the Yun army – loomed closer by the moment. 'I'm not strong enough!' he said.

'You told me to trust you!'

'Sorry!' Draikh's grip slackened.

Raim thought his stomach dropped out of his body.

He kicked out his legs, imagining he was going to hit the ground running. Who was he kidding? His leg bones would shatter on impact. But then he felt an enormous tug on his other shoulder. He looked up and saw the woman in the white dress again, stabilizing him in the air, but from that angle he could not see her face. 'I will not let you die,' her voice said, firmly.

The Yun on the ground below pointed up at him and shouted. One of the Yun sent a bird, a huge hawk with razor-sharp claws, soaring up to intercept them. Raim could hear the beating of its enormous wings in the air.

The Yun's orders whistled up to the bird, and although Raim couldn't understand the sounds he soon realized what they meant. *Attack him.* He was the weakest link of the three, as the Yun were still unsure what the bird's talons would do to the haunts. But they knew exactly what they would do to Raim.

The hawk dive-bombed into Raim's back and beat his wings so that Raim was being pulled in two directions. He cried out in anguish. The sound echoed against the tall cliffs and his own screams filled the air. He could feel the curved talons wrenching at his skin. The wind surrounded him, buffeting the four beings as they struggled in mid-air, cooling the blood that was spilling down his back in thick streams. He shivered violently and darkness crept at the edge of his eyes.

A screech, this time not from his own throat, sounded from above him and something crashed into the bird on his back. The talons released. The collision shook them all and Raim lurched from Draikh's grasp. Raim's head flipped back and he caught sight of Oyu battling with the hawk above him. But then the birds were drawing further away from him, and the ground neared.

The cries from the ground got louder, the action halting as faces turned to look up at him. Then one voice cried out, clearer than the rest.

'RAIM!' It was Wadi.

With a final surge of energy, Draikh shot down and slowed Raim's descent enough for him to hit the ground and roll, protecting his bones from breaking on impact.

Wadi was running towards him, two swords in hand. She threw one at Raim's feet, and he snatched it up right away and scrambled to his feet. Now that his feet were on the ground, the Yun wasted no more time. 'I can't fight them all, Wadi!' Raim said.

'The tunnel. If we get back to the tunnel, I can seal it!'

There was another familiar wail. It was Dumas. His face was caked with blood and the sword in his hand was trembling. 'I'm so sorry. I should have believed you.'

'Dumas, pull yourself together.' They had a few moments to spare. *Khareh doesn't want a massacre*, Raim reminded himself. *He wants them alive.*

He looked at the terrified Chauk. There were only three, apart from Dumas. The tunnel entrance wasn't that far. 'Run!' he screamed, and Wadi's voice joined with his own. 'Run to the tunnel!'

They fled, but some were faster than others. Raim saw one woman go down, a soldier at her back. Raim got his sword between them, battling back against the soldier, giving the woman time to get up again and run.

'Wadi!' he cried, as his sword clashed with the soldier's again and again. 'You have to do something.'

He disarmed the soldier, throwing all his energy into the blow, ignoring the pain shooting up and down his arm but didn't wait to find out who was next.

He turned and ran as fast as his legs could carry him to the tunnel entrance.

Wadi was already there. Her fingers were gripped white around her pendant, and she was screaming at it – at the spirits who guarded the tunnel. 'Protect us!' she screamed. 'Protect Lazar!'

There was a rumble beneath their feet and a chunk of rock slammed to the ground inches from Raim's feet. There was a sharp cry from the soldiers behind him as more rock and dirt tumbled from the cliff face onto their heads. 'Look out!' cried Wadi, and Raim leaped to one side just as a massive boulder came down in front of the tunnel's entrance. The tunnel was protecting itself. They were going to get away with this.

Wind rushed by Raim's head and he looked up to see Khareh – turban gone, decorative swords abandoned – flying down into the melee with the help of his spirit-Raim.

He landed between Raim and the tunnel entrance, stumbling as he hit the floor, hard. 'See, you're not the only one who can fly, Raim!' Spirit-Raim looked exhausted, transparent, like Draikh.

'Khareh, let me pass! Let me go back to Lazar!'

'Tut tut, Raim. You forget, you're so easy to manipulate.' The rocks were falling faster now, filling up the entrance to the tunnel. But around Khareh there was a stillness that Raim couldn't describe, an aura of invincibility that only true confidence, true power can provide.

That was when Raim saw Wadi creeping up behind Khareh, Raim's old dagger raised in her hand. At the last moment, Khareh pivoted round, blocking Wadi's strike with his arm, twisting her round and bringing her down so she was forced to her knees, the dagger tumbling out of her hand.

Khareh's own blade now was at her throat.

'Khareh, no!' Raim screamed. He launched himself towards them but stumbled, weak from blood loss in his arm and his back.

Still pressing the blade at her neck, Khareh reached down and grabbed the pass-stone from around Wadi's neck. 'I have what I want, now.' He snatched the blade away and pushed her forward.

But Wadi had been waiting for that moment. She sprung round, her hands aiming for Khareh's neck. Khareh raised his arms in defence, and the knife in his hand jammed deep into Wadi's chest.

'Nooooo!' Raim screamed, his world collapsing around him.

He felt strong arms lift him from beneath his armpits, pulling him out of the way as another boulder slammed into the place he had been standing. He couldn't tear his eyes away from Khareh and Wadi, the red blossoming across her front like a lotus bloom, her eyes wide-open and full of pain.

Wadi! He couldn't believe she was dead. He wanted to go down there to her, to join her. *Why hadn't Khareh killed him instead?*

Another boulder fell dangerously close and his brain snapped out of its shock. Dumas had dragged him that far, but Raim suddenly tried to surge forward to where he could still see Khareh through the wall of falling rock.

'You can't go back that way,' shrieked Dumas.

'But—'

Dumas gave him one final haul towards the tunnels, but then looked up at the caving ceiling and decided to run for it.

Then suddenly, it was quiet. Dust pooled about Raim's legs and if he'd had the energy to cough, he would have. The cave mouth was shut out completely.

He turned and stumbled. Back down the tunnel. It was the only way he could go.

40

He had followed the light until it had led him to another exit. Here there was no sense of the battle he had just left, but he didn't know where 'here' was. He felt weak from blood loss, the wound in his arm still dripping, leaving a trail of red drops to follow if the Yun had broken through the rock wall.

Raim didn't care. He tripped and fell onto the rocky ground, and didn't have the energy to move.

His cheek felt glued to the floor. He reeked of blood and his back stung like it was being attacked by behrflies. High above him, an ear-piercing cry caught his attention and Raim turned his eye up towards the sky. Oyu's silhouette was black against the grey and orange sky, and he circled the valley twice before swooping down towards Raim. He landed on Raim's upturned elbow and hopped along his upper arm to his shoulder. Then he dropped a still-steaming chunk of hawk wing in front of Raim's face.

Raim coughed and spluttered. He had to sit up and cover his mouth with his sleeve. Oyu fluttered his wings, expecting praise.

Raim couldn't speak, couldn't move. He felt vibrations in the ground beneath him, and knew that horses were approaching. Khareh's soldiers. *That was quick,* Raim thought. *You should have left me there, to die with Wadi. Now the soldiers will just kill me here.*

And he would let them. He looked over at Draikh, who seemed barely there at all. He wouldn't be able to prevent his death this time. There was no sign of the woman in white at all.

Wadi's face swam in front of his eyes. She had died fighting to protect the Chauk, the Alashan and him. She had fought until the bitter end.

Rage filled him. Now Khareh was coming to capture him again – to kill him.

But why should he go down without a fight? He tested his muscles by rotating his shoulders and cocking his head from side to side. The pain was intense but he would bear it for these last moments. He picked up his sword and got up.

He wouldn't speak, in case making that effort drained what little energy he had and prevented him from dying with valour.

Horses careered round the corner, their hooves pounding the earth. Raim charged towards them. He let out a ferocious roar, forgetting his desire for silence, releasing all the pent-up pain and anguish in one blazing moment. The dust washed over him like a wave, but as he charged towards them the horses slowed to a stop. Raim kept running, the dust burning his eyes. But he kept them wide open. The lead horseman dismounted.

The sword fell out of Raim's hands. He dropped to his knees.

The horseman wrapped his arms around Raim's shoulders. It was his grandfather. It was Loni.

'Come on, boy, let's take you home.'

41

The pungent aroma of bitterbark tea thickened the air in the tiny yurt. Raim sipped slowly. He tried to concentrate on the taste and he let the warm water swirl in his mouth. Anything to avoid thinking about the past day.

No such luck. He could think of nothing else. And his wounds burned despite the poultice Loni had applied. He wanted to rub his back up against the post in the centre of the room just to relieve the terrible itch. But he sat motionless on his cushion, apart from the intermittent moments when he brought the cup to his lips and lowered it again down into his lap.

He was following Loni's orders: 'Sit here and wait for me. Drink your tea.'

They had travelled most of the night to get to this place. Loni hadn't named it, but it was clear what it was: a Cheren community, a settlement for old people who had lost their usefulness to society.

Raim was a shell of himself. There was nothing left inside him. Seeing his grandfather cooped up in a Cheren, when he had so much vigour and youth left, shattered whatever pieces were left of Raim's heart.

Loni reappeared in the yurt. He carried with him a small bowl of rice with a smattering of boiled meat. He placed the bowl in front of Raim, along with some coarsely cut wooden chopsticks. Raim couldn't even look at it. Instead, he stared straight into Loni's limitless black eyes.

'How did you find me?' It was the question that kept on bubbling to the surface of the boiling cauldron of questions in his mind.

Loni put a finger to his lips. 'I will show you. We must be quick. We must go while the night is still long.'

Raim followed Loni outside. His yurt was one of many, too many for Raim to count in one glance. It was a tent city like Kharein during festival – but unlike Kharein, this was a city of decay. Even in the dark of night, Raim could see just how permanent the settlement was. Cobwebs hung from the guy ropes that anchored the tents to the ground. Rust stained the few metal joints and spread like orange dye onto the canvas fabric. There were scatterings of fire pits, the dark amber glow of dying embers still visible in most of them. Loni was moving away from the settlement and Raim dragged his feet as he followed.

Draikh floated behind. He hadn't said a word since the battle the night before. Before they exited the perimeter of the Cheren completely, Loni turned round and circled the air in front of Draikh with an open palm.

'The spirit can go no further.'

'You can see him?' said Raim.

'No. But the white glow of his presence will disturb where we are going. It is necessary that we learn to manoeuvre in blindness,' said Loni cryptically.

They moved round a corner and out of sight of the Cheren. Every step they took increased the darkness. At first, the stars made visible at least the outline of Loni's form. Then, even that tiny illumination disappeared. When Raim tilted his head, he could see the pinpoints of light, but their light didn't reach their surroundings. In front of him, he could see nothing. He spread his arms to the side to try to touch something – a wall, a tree, anything – to try to guide himself, but there was nothing. He reached forward and groped for Loni. He felt foolish, desperately searching for his grandfather to hold onto, but he couldn't find him.

Then he couldn't trust his sense of direction. It was black now – he couldn't even describe it as darkness – just everywhere black.

'Use your feet and follow the ground,' said Loni. 'Just keep moving. We are almost there.'

Hearing his grandfather's voice stilled Raim. He tried to use the sound to guide him, but it threw him even more off balance. It was suffocating – not knowing where to turn or which direction to move.

Concentrate on the ground! Raim lifted his foot, although it felt as if his shoes were made of lead. He placed his heel directly in front of his toe, almost on top of it so at least he felt the pressure of his own body, then repeated the process so he moved forward at a slow, laborious pace.

When the first flicker of light flashed Loni's silhouette into view, Raim sprinted forward.

'What was that?'

'The blinding path.'

Raim shook off his shivers and turned back to look where they had just stumbled from the cave. The opening gaped like the mouth of a sleeping beast. 'And we have to return through this path?'

'Yes. And if you ever want to reach this place again, then you will have to learn to cross it without fear. Here.' Loni passed him an unlit torch and held it against his own flickering one. It caught immediately and a flame leaped to life. The light threw their shadows onto the trees behind. They were deep inside a forest.

'I hope I never have to come here ag—' Something caught his eye just above Loni's head. The old man moved out of his way but Raim barely noticed. He was drawn to what he saw. It was a carpet, the corners nailed roughly between the trunks of two enormous trees. The colouring was so unusual. The rugs of Darhan were filled with greens and browns and reds – colours taken from the earth – vibrant, deep colours that could only be made from natural dyes. But the entire face of this enormous piece was made up of different yellows. The yellows rose and dipped in waves, so intricately woven that it looked like it was moving. Up this close, Raim could see the details of every knot. He moved down the carpet slowly, his entire vision filled with yellows and golds. There was only one tiny blemish on the golden sea. A little figurine, made up of a few threads of deep brown colour. Raim reached up and touched the figure with his fingertips.

The figure was down on his knees. The figure was all alone on the yellow landscape. The figure was . . .

'Ach! Do you want to set the entire forest alight?' Loni yanked his arm back from the carpet. Raim hadn't even realized how close he had been holding the torch to the carpet, but he had only wanted to try to catch more of the detail.

'That's me!' Raim said, pointing back at the figure.

'They are all of you.'

'All?' And then Raim looked beyond the yellow carpet and saw another one nailed between the next two trees. And then another draped across a large branch just behind. The entire forest was filled with the woven master-pieces, blanketing the trees and the ground.

Loni took his arm and walked him through the make-shift gallery. Some of the images of him were up close, so that his expression filled an entire canvas. Others were more like the first one he saw; mostly of the landscape, always with his tiny figure featuring somewhere in the picture. He saw Lazar again, in all its subdued and degen-erated glory. Oyu was pictured, with his great wingspan and the promise-knot dripping from his mouth. They didn't seem to be in any particular order, just pieces of his life tossed over the trees like laundry hanging out to dry.

And then they came across the panel where the behrflies attacked him. Raim cringed just looking at it, knowing the immense pain those flies had brought. And standing over him was Draikh's form, swatting at the flies with his sword, blocking them from Raim's face.

'This was one of the first ones. What were we to make of this?' Loni spoke almost apologetically. 'I thought somehow the carpets were showing us what you were doing, where you were, but when this came up, how could it be? After all, it shows Khareh in the desert. And Khareh could not have been in the desert when he was just taking power in Kharein. It had to be a dream and then, your grandmother and I, we despaired, because we did not know where you were. We had only the rumours to go by – that you murdered Mhara and instigated the whole chain of events that led to Khareh becoming Khan. We thought maybe it was your way of helping him. But the more of these that were made, the more we realized they were about you. And then this one is the most recent.' He gestured to the carpet they were standing on.

The curvature of the hill, the rough, haphazard placement of the rocks, all indicated that this was the valley where he had crawled out of the tunnel and been found by Loni. He took a moment to study the expressions on Draikh's face. They both looked exhausted, as it was expected. What he didn't expect were the looks of absolute defeat. If there was anything about his spirit companion that could be counted on, it was his enthusiasm. He was a resolute optimist. But depicted here, he just looked downcast.

Maybe it was because Draikh knew Raim had no future now. Was it his destiny to peter out with the elders? He could not stay in Darhan – everywhere he went he would be hunted down by Khareh's soldiers – and he could not go back to Lazar – he had no idea how to find it again without going back to the Alashan. And after he'd led several of their people to certain death, he didn't know if he could face it.

The dark thoughts turned his stomach even as he turned his attention back to the rug beneath his feet. 'I still don't understand how you found me from this. There must be hundreds of valleys and rocks that look like this in Darhan.'

'I might be a useless old man now, but in my day I was a tracker in the Khan's army. You know, not all of us can be Yun, but that doesn't mean we don't have our talents. I've found rebel locations from rougher descriptions of terrain.' Loni's voice brimmed with such ageless pride that Raim almost smiled. 'And this is almost as good as seeing it with your own eyes. The journey was long, though. If I had delayed even for a moment, you could've been gone from there.'

'I almost attacked you,' Raim admitted. 'How long ago was this . . .'

'Almost five days ago now, this vision came. She knew what it meant and acted on it much faster than she ever had before.'

'She? Yasmin?'

Loni did not answer him but continued the long walk through the forest. Raim found himself immobilized by the woven stills from his life. These were private moments – moments he was afraid to relive – like when had first found out about Dharma.

At gentle pressing from Loni, Raim kept moving.

The gentle purring of the forest had seemed foreign to him at first; the dense brush thick and claustrophobic. But as fast as he had grown used to the desert's massive expanses, the forest had faded into the background for him, the carpets stealing all of his attention. Even now, as they walked further, the number of the carpets did not dwindle. Raim wondered aloud, unable to contain his curiosity about how these carpets had been made, and in such a short time.

But then Raim was struck with a thought: what if these had been here all along? Had his destiny been planned right from the start? He had never heard of such a thing happening, not in the ancient texts in Lazar or from the mouths of Vlad or Puutra.

Loni revealed the truth to him as they moved deeper into the forest. He brought him to a clearing, and suddenly Raim knew how the carpets had been made.

There were looms everywhere. Men and women, shrivelled and bent with age, recruited from the Cheren community, crowded around masses of threads, weaving, endlessly weaving. There were vats of dye bubbling away in one corner, with one man dipping a stick wrapped with wool into the liquid while another tossed more leaves or berries to increase the intensity of the colour. It was a weaving community more bustling than Una. No wonder there were so many rugs.

'But . . . how?'

'The weaving has instilled new life in the Cheren community. Everyone is involved. We work from these.' He led Raim over to a loom, and picked up a piece of paper covered in black scrawling symbols. 'These symbols represent the pattern that they weave.'

'Where does the pattern come from? How is it my life is being woven like this?'

Instead of answering, Loni gestured towards a flickering light at the far end of the weavers.

The light was filtered through a soft canvas yurt erected at the end of a small pathway that had been meticulously brushed free of leaves and other foliage. There was an other-worldliness to the lodging.

He was drawn to the light like a moth to a flame, and just as tentatively – almost leaping forward at certain points then lingering, turning back to stare at his grand-father who had stopped at the edge of the pathway.

When he was close enough to touch the fabric, the air thickened around his hand until he felt like he was push-ing through honey.

But the curtain lifted before his hand reached it and three women, their faces covered with a mesh-like cloth, exited the tent. They moved fast but barely lifted their feet from the ground. The first woman carried a tall broom, which she swept along the pathway before they walked. The steady sweep-sweep of her broom on the ground guided their movements like an army drum, and they disappeared around the back of the yurt as Raim watched.

They appeared more like mystics than weavers. Raim debated whether to follow them. But the light compelled him forward.

He stepped through the curtain.

'Dharma?'

The name tumbled out of his mouth, his eyes knowing her before his brain had a moment to process. Her back was to him, but the moment he spoke her name she turned her ear towards him. The fingers of her right hand twitched across the loom that lay in her lap, as if reading the threads that lay on the carpet in front of her. Wrapped around all her slim fingers were hundreds of tiny threads.

'Raim!' The loom clattered to the ground and she bounded towards him. He fell to his knees and she collided against his chest, burrowing her nose into his neck.

'Dharma, you're safe! I thought . . . but Khareh . . . I thought I had lost you for ever. Thank Sola!' They held each other tightly for a long moment, before he loosened his embrace. She still kept her cheek against his shoulder, and would not move for all his gentle pressing. He reached up and stroked her head, and he felt a knot of coarse linen in amongst the soft curls of her hair. 'What is this?' He traced the linen until it came to the edge of her temple. He took her chin between his fingers and turned her head towards him.

A blindfold. The rough knot held a crimson blindfold tightly around her eyes. He tried to touch it but she shrank away from him. He cupped her face in his hands. 'Don't worry,' he said, 'it's only me.'

His fingertips barely touched the bottom edge of the material but with the tiniest of friction he slid the fold down her nose and cheekbone.

'No!' he cried aloud. Fear shook him. 'No!' He could barely contain his shock, his eyes darting across her face, unable to see anything but the two dark spaces where the skin was puckered and wrinkled with age where the rest of her was young and innocent. But he knew they were not wrinkles. They were Khareh's revenge. This was how Khareh had won his spirit servant: at the price of Dharma's sight. 'And it is all my fault,' he said, shaking now. 'Dharma, what pain and torment have I caused you? Blind. You are blind.' *Because of me.*

This time, it was Dharma who reached out to him. She stroked his cheek. 'But I can see!' she said. The absence of fear in her voice calmed his beating heart.

'What do you mean?'

'You! I have been seeing you! Every day, every night, I see visions of where you are, brother. I have lived your journey with you! And I always weave an image of what I see.'

'And you can see me?'

'I can see many things now. But I choose only to see

you, my dearest Raim.' She threw her arms around his neck and kissed him on the cheek.

He hugged her tightly to him. Then he took the luminous silver scarf from around his wrist and tied it around her eyes, instead of the rotten piece of cloth she had been wearing before. She gasped with delight and couldn't stop touching the fabric. 'My parents!'

Raim kissed her fingertips in reply. His eyes lingered on her joyful face. Her hopeful face. He hadn't seen hope in a very long time.

She reached up to his face. 'Raim, why are you crying?'

He clutched Dharma tighter again, breathing in her hair and feeling her pulse against his skin. Alive, she was alive. His heart filled with joy and sadness.

'Don't cry, Raim. Look at this.' She lifted up the loom from where she had set it down on the floor beside her. Raim stared at it, and he blinked in recognition, but he thought his tears must be obscuring his vision. He wiped them away brusquely and looked again.

Dharma had woven a scene. Two figures were in the centre. One was tall, dominant, with a crown upon his head. Khareh. The other was tied up to a stake, her clothes blood-soaked, but alive, her eyes open and full of fierce anger. He reached out and placed his index finger on her woven cheek. 'Wadi,' he whispered. 'Dharma . . . these weavings. You have seen this?'

Dharma nodded.

'Then Wadi is alive.'

404

Suddenly his body was flooded with purpose, his heart pumping harder than it had in any battle. 'Wadi is alive,' he repeated, barely willing to believe it. But if it was true, he had to go back.

He had to find her.

EPILOGUE

Wadi spat in Khareh's face. She struggled against the ropes that bound her wrists. 'You think this is the end, Khareh? Raim is much more powerful than you. He always has been.'

He walked over to her, his strut like an over proud peacock. He drew the pass-stone out from under her shirt. She shivered with disgust as his fingertips touched her neck. He reached down and kissed the pass-stone with his lips, then spun round and left the room, leaving Wadi alone in the darkness.

Acknowledgements

Just before I was due to send the final manuscript of this book off to my editor, I had a nostalgic moment and looked back over an old Livejournal I kept during the initial stages of writing *The Oathbreaker's Shadow*. I found this entry from 21 July 2006:

I don't know if anyone but the writers out there will under-stand this, but I've reached the point where I realize just how much this novel means to me. Way beyond worrying about literary agents or publishing. Way beyond the initial excitement of planning a new novel and writing the first 100 pages. Way beyond plotting and writer's block and outlining and character development. I'm at the point now where this novel has changed my life. And whether this book goes nowhere or everywhere, I'm pretty sure this is all that matters.

I don't think at that point in my life – seven years before

this book would see the light of day – I could have imagined getting to where I am. And I would never have reached this point without an incredible amount of support from a huge team of people, all of whom I feel so lucky to be able to thank right now.

First mention of all is to Juliet Mushens, the literary agent who is so much more than an agent. All I can say is that I am so glad to have been the first to hitch my wagon to your rising star. You've made this often-agonizing process more fun than I could ever have believed. Not going to lie – best decision I ever made. To Nelle Andrews, Rachel Mills and the team at PFD Literary, thank you so much for your support.

To the entire team at Random House Children's Publishers, thank you for making this process feel so seamless – especially Lauren Buckland, editor extraordinaire. You've been amazing to work with, and you have my endless gratitude. Also, to Amy Black, Janice Weaver, Kristin Cochrane and the team at Doubleday Canada, thank you for making me feel so welcome on my home turf.

My first reader – Adam Parks – you've been watching this novel grow since its inception at a Starbucks on Bloor Street in Toronto. Emma Coode, Jane Johnson and Natasha Tanczos – you know this stuff better than anyone; thanks for bearing with me as I realize life on the other side of the curtain. To Sarah Mumford, who travelled with me to the biggest sand dunes in the world (and then slid down them with me at high speeds). To Maria Felix Miller, whose huge heart and brilliant mind motivates me to be better even from the other side of the planet. And to David Alward, who has borne witness to the highest highs and the lowest lows a writer (and a person) can experience, and who still loves me throughout. You mean more to me than you will ever know.

But the final words of thanks have to go to whom this book is dedicated: Sophie McCulloch, you are my biggest inspiration. To match your work ethic, your creativity, your dedication, and your passion are all things I aspire to. To Mum and Dad: the life you've built for us has always been based on adventure and on love. You taught me that risk is to be embraced, not feared; that following your passion – no matter where that leads – is the most important aspect of life; and that hard work will one day breed success. Your unwavering belief in me is the sole reason this book exists, and there are no words to describe my gratitude.

THE SHADOW'S CURSE

Available in June 2014 from
Doubleday Canada